Susan Howatch was born in Surrey in 1940. After taking a
degree in law, she emigrated to America, where she married,
had a daughter and embarked on her career as a novelist.
Her first six books, all mysteries written in the 1960s, were
*The Dark Shore*, *The Waiting Sands*, *Call in the Night*, *The
Shrouded Walls*, *April's Grave* and *The Devil on Lammas Night*.
But in between writing these stories she worked on the long
novel which was to become her first international bestseller:
*Penmarric*, published in 1971, was followed by the equally
successful *Cashelmara*, *The Rich are Different*, *Sins of the
Fathers* and *The Wheel of Fortune*. In 1976 she left America and
spent four years in the Republic of Ireland before returning to
live in Britain. She is now at work on a series of novels about
the Church of England in the twentieth century.

Also by Susan Howatch in Pan Books

The Susan Howatch Collection Volume II:

The Shrouded Walls
April's Grave
The Devil on Lammas Night

Cashelmara
Sins of the Fathers
The Wheel of Fortune
The Rich are Different

# The Susan Howatch Collection
## Volume I

# The Dark Shore
# The Waiting Sands
# Call in the Night

Pan Books
London, Sydney and Auckland

*The Dark Shore* first published in Great Britain 1972 by Hamish Hamilton Ltd
© Susan Howatch 1965

*The Waiting Sands* first published in Great Britain 1972 by Hamish Hamilton Ltd
© Susan Howatch 1966

*Call in the Night* first published in Great Britain 1972 by Hamish Hamilton Ltd
© Susan Howatch 1967

This collection published 1989 by Pan Books Ltd, Cavaye Place, London sw10 9pg

9 8 7 6 5 4 3

© Susan Howatch 1989

ISBN 0 330 31153 0

Typeset by Selectmove Ltd, London
Printed in England by Clays Ltd, St Ives plc

# contents

The Dark Shore         7

The Waiting Sands         193

Call in the Night         367

*for my mother*

# The Dark
# Shore

*prologue*

Jon was alone. Outside in the night the city teemed and throbbed and roared but in the room there was only the quiet impersonal silence of the hotel room, softly lit and thick-carpeted. He went over to the window. Six floors below him to the left a bus crawled along Berkeley Street, a noiseless fleck of red against the dark surface of the road, while immediately below him the swarms of taxis cruised past the hotel entrance before turning south towards Piccadilly. The sense of isolation was accentuated by the stillness in the room. The polish on the furniture gleamed; the white pillowcases on the bed were spotlessly smooth; the suitcases stood marshalled along the wall in faultless formation. He was alone in a vast city, a stranger returning to a forgotten land, and it seemed to him as he stood by the window and stared out at the world beyond that he had been foolish to hope that he could establish any contact with the past by coming back to the city where he had been born.

He spent ten minutes unpacking the basic items from his luggage and then paused to light a cigarette. Below him on the bed lay the evening paper, his own photograph still smiling up at him from the gossip column, and as he picked up the paper again in contempt he was conscious of a stab of unreality, as if the photograph was of someone else and the lines beneath described a man he did not know. They called him a Canadian, of course, and said he was a millionaire. There was a line mentioning his mother too and her connection with pre-war London society, a final sentence adding that he was to remarry shortly and that his fiancée was English. And then the columnist passed on to other topics, confident that he had fully exploited the snob value of this particular visitor to London.

Jon tore the newspaper to shreds and thought of his mother. She would have read it an hour, perhaps two hours ago, when the evening paper was delivered to the spacious house off Halkin Street. So she would know. He wondered if she had any desire to see him, any shred of interest in meeting him again after ten years. He had never written to her. When he had told Sarah that he and his mother no longer kept in touch with each other she had been so shocked that he had felt embarrassed, but justification had been easy and he had thought no more about it. Sarah simply did not understand. She had grown up in a happy sheltered home, and any deviation from the pattern of life which she had always known only emphasized how vulnerable she was when separated from that narrow comfortable little backwater her parents had created for her. One of the reasons why he wanted to marry Sarah was because she was untouched and unspoiled by the world he lived and worked in every day. When they were married, he thought, he would work all day in an atmosphere of boardrooms and balance sheets, and then at last he would be home away from it all and Sarah would be waiting for him . . . He could see it all so clearly. Sarah would talk of the things he loved and after dinner he would play the piano, and there would be a still cool peace as night fell. And afterwards when they were in bed he would let her know how grateful he was to her for that wonderful peace, and Sarah would love him because he was her shield from the harshest flares of life and she needed him even more than he needed her.

It would all be so different from the past.

He thought of Sophia then, the memory flashing through his brain in the split second before he shut his mind against it. He mustn't think of Sophia. He would not, could not think of her . . . But he was. While he was in London he would meet Justin and as soon as he saw Justin he would think of Sophia . . . Nonsense. Justin was a young Englishman nineteen years old with the conventional English background of public school and perhaps a first job in the city. He would think of sports cars and parties and pretty girls and cricket in summer. Justin would be as utterly remote from Sophia as London was from Toronto, and on meeting him again there would be no cruel memories of the past, no dreadful searing pain.

The telephone rang.

The jangling bell was obscene, blasting aside the still silence of the room and making Jon start. Slumping on to the bed he reached for the receiver and leaned back against the pillows.

'Yes?'

'Call for you, Mr Towers.'

'Thank you.'

There was a click, and then a silence except for the humming of the wire.

'Hullo?' He was tense suddenly, taut with nervousness.

Another pause. Someone far away at the other end of the wire took a small breath.

'Hullo?' Jon said again. 'Who's this?' There was ice suddenly, ice on his forehead, at the nape of his neck, at the base of his spine, although he didn't know why he was afraid.

And then very softly the anonymous voice from the past whispered into the receiver, 'Welcome home, Mr Towers. Does your fiancée know you killed your first wife ten years ago?'

# Part 1

# chapter 1

1

Justin Towers very nearly didn't buy an evening paper. When he left the office at half past five his eyes were tired after hours spent poring over figures and the prospect of his return journey on the underground filled him with a violent revulsion. He hated the rush-hour tubes, hated being crammed into the long sweating corridors, hated the endless stream of faceless people who jostled past in the subterranean nightmare. He thought for a long aching moment of his childhood, of the days beneath blue skies by a swaying sea, of the yellow walls and white shutters of Buryan, and then the moment was past and he was standing irresolutely by one of the innumerable entrances to the underground at Bank while the diesel fumes choked his lungs and the traffic roared in his ears. Across the road a number nine bus crawled on its way to Ludgate Circus. Justin made up his mind quickly: as the traffic lights changed he crossed Poultry and Queen Victoria Street and boarded the bus as it wedged itself deep in a line of stationary cars.

By the time the bus reached Green Park he was so sick of the constant waiting and the frustration of the traffic jams that he got out and walked towards the tube without hesitation. He felt desperately tired, and in an attempt to stave off the tedium of the last stretch of the journey he stopped by the newsvendor's stall and bought an evening paper.

He opened it on the platform, glanced at the stock exchange prices and then folded it up again as a train drew in. On finding a small corner at one end of the compartment he glanced at the front page, but he was conscious of his hatred of the crowded train once more and he started thinking not of the paper in his hand but of Buryan on those bright summer afternoons long ago. The scene etched itself clearly in his mind. Flip would be lying on his back, his long tail waving gracefully and the lawn would be soft and green and smooth. From the open windows of the house would come the sound of a piano being touched softly on light keys, and on the wrought-iron white swing-seat across the lawn a woman would be lying relaxed with a bowl of cherries on the wrought-iron table nearby. If he were to venture towards her and ask for a cherry the woman would yawn a wide, rich yawn and smile a warm, luxurious smile and say indulgently in her strange English, 'But you'll get so fat, Justin!' And then she would pull him closer to her so that she could kiss him and afterwards she would let him have as many cherries as he wanted.

The hunger of those days was one of the things he remembered best. He had always been hungry, and the days had been full of Cornish cream and Cornish pasties until one evening the man, who would spend so many hours of a beautiful day indoors with a piano, said to him that it was time they both had some exercise before Justin became too fat to move. After that they had fallen into the habit of walking down to the cove together after tea. Farther along the cliff path that curled away from the cove were the Flat Rocks by the water's edge, and they would go down there together, the man helping the child over the steeper parts of the cliff. It was a stiff climb. The shore was scored with vast boulders and gigantic slabs of granite, and after the scramble to the water's edge they would lie in the sun for a while and watch the endless motion of the sea as it sucked and spat at the rocky shelves beneath them. Sometimes the man would talk. Justin loved it when he talked. The man would paint pictures in words for him, and suddenly the world would be rich and exciting and full of bright colours. Sometimes the man wouldn't talk at all, which was disappointing, but the excitement was still there because the man was exciting in himself and whenever Justin was with him it seemed that even a walk to the cove and the Flat Rocks could be transformed into a taut racing adventure pounding with life and danger and anticipation. The man seemed to enjoy the walks too. Even when they had people staying at Buryan there would come times when he would want to get away from them all and then Justin had been his only companion, the chosen confidant to share the hours of seclusion.

Justin, immensely proud of his position, would have followed him to the ends of the earth.

And then had come that other weekend, creeping stealthily out of a cloudless future and suddenly the world was grey amd streaked with pain and bewilderment and grief . . .

Afterwards, all he could remember was his grandmother, looking very smart and elegant in a light-blue suit. 'You're going to come and live with me now, darling – won't that be nice? So much nicer for you to live in London instead of some dreary little place at the back of beyond . . . What? But didn't your father explain it to you? No, of course you can't go abroad with him! He wants you to grow up in England and have a proper education, and anyway he doesn't want a nine-year-old child with him wherever he goes. Surely you can see that . . . Why hasn't he written? Well, darling, because he simply never writes a letter – gracious me, I should know that better than anyone! But he'll send you something at Christmas and on your birthday, I expect. Unless he forgets. That's more than likely, of course. He was always forgetting my birthday when he was away at school . . .'

And he had forgotten. That was the terrible thing. He had forgotten and Justin had never heard from him again.

The train thundered along the dark tunnel and suddenly he was in the present again with his collar damp against the back of his neck and the newspaper crumpling in his hot hands. Useless to think back. The past was over, closed, forgotten, and he had long ago schooled himself not to waste time feeling bitter. He would never see his father again and now he had no wish to. Any attachment that had ever existed between them had been severed long ago.

The train careered into Hyde Park station, and as several passengers moved out on to the platform, Justin folded the paper down the centre and started to turn each half-page mechanically. The photograph caught his eye less than five seconds later.

'Jon Towers, the Canadian property millionaire . . .'

The shock was like a white light exploding behind his eyes.

When he got out of the train at Knightsbridge he felt sick and ill as if he had just vomited and he had to sit down for a moment at one of the benches on the platform before fighting his way to the surface. Someone stopped to ask him if he was all right. Outside in the open air he paused for a moment among the swirling crowds on the pavement and then very slowly he threw the evening paper in a litter bin and started the walk home to his grandmother's house in Consett Mews.


2


In the house in Consett Mews, Camilla opened the top drawer of her dressing table, took out a small bottle and tipped two white pills into the palm of her hand. It was wrong to take two, of course, but it wouldn't matter once in a while. Doctors were always over-cautious. After she had taken the tablets she returned to the dressing table and reapplied her make-up carefully, taking special care with the eyes and with the lines about the mouth, but it seemed to her as she stared into the mirror that the shock still showed in her expression in spite of all the pains she had taken with the cosmetics.

She started to think of Jon again.

If only it were possible to keep it from Justin . . . Jon was obviously only in England on account of his English fiancée or possibly because of some business reason, and did not intend to see any of his family. It would only hurt Justin to know that his father was in London and would be making no attempt to contact him.

17

The anger was suddenly a constriction in her throat, an ache behind her eyes. It was monstrous of Jon, she thought, to disown his family casually to the extent of returning to England after ten years without even letting his own mother know he was in the country. 'It's not that I want to see him,' she said aloud, 'I don't give a damn whether he comes to see me or not while he's in London. It's merely the principle of the thing.'

The tears were scorching her cheeks again, scarring the new make-up irrevocably, and in an involuntary movement she stood up and moved blindly over to the window.

Supposing Justin heard his father was in London. Supposing he went to see Jon and was drawn inevitably towards him until he was completely under his father's influence . . . It was all very well to say that Justin was grown up, a level-headed sensible young man of nineteen who would hardly be easily influenced by anyone, let alone by a father who had treated him so disgracefully, but Jon was so accustomed to influencing everyone within his reach . . . If he should want to take Justin away from her – but he wouldn't, of course. What had Jon ever done for Justin? It was she who had brought Justin up. Jon couldn't have cared less. Justin belonged to her, not to Jon, and Jon would realize that as clearly as she did.

She thought of Jon again for one long moment, the memory a hot pain behind her eyes.

He was always the same, she thought. Always. Right from the beginning. All those nursemaids – and none of them could do anything with him. He would never listen to me. He was always struggling to impose his will on everyone else's and do exactly as he liked when he liked how he liked.

She thought of the time when she had sent him to boarding school a year early because she had felt unable to cope with him any longer. He hadn't missed her, she remembered sardonically, but had revelled instead in his independence; there had been new fields to conquer, other boys of his own age to sway or bully, masters to impress or mock as the mood suited him. And then had come the piano.

'My God!' she said aloud to the silent room. 'That dreadful piano!' He had seen one when he was five years old, tried to play it and failed. That had been enough. He had never rested after that until he had mastered the instrument completely, and even now she could remember his ceaseless practice and the noise which had constantly set her nerves on edge. And then after the piano, later on in his life, there had been the girls. Every girl had been a challenge; a whole new world of conquest had suddenly materialized before his eyes as he had grown old enough to see it around him. She remembered worrying in case he entangled himself in some impossible scrape, remembered threatening that he would have to go to his father for help if he got into trouble, remembered how much it had hurt when he had laughed, mocking her anger. She could still hear his laugh even now. He hadn't cared! And then when he had only been nineteen there had come the episode with the little Greek bitch in a backstreet restaurant in Soho, the foolhardy marriage, the casual abandonment of all his prospects in the City . . . Looking back, she wondered bitterly who had been the angrier, her first husband or herself. Not that Jon had cared how angry they had been. He had merely laughed and turned his back as if his parents had meant even less to him than the future he had so casually discarded, and after that she had hardly ever seen him.

The memories flickered restlessly through her brain: her refusal to accept his wife, Jon's retaliation by moving to the other end of England; after his marriage he had only contacted his mother when it suited him.

When Sophia was dead, for example. He had contacted her then soon enough. 'I'm going abroad,' he had said. 'You'll look after Justin, won't you?'

Just like that. You'll look after Justin, won't you? As if she were some domestic servant being given a casual order.

She had often asked herself why she had said yes. She

hadn't intended to. She had wanted to say 'Find someone else to do your dirty work for you!' but had instead merely agreed to do as he wished, and then all at once Justin was with her and Jon was in Canada . . . And he had never once written to her.

She hadn't believed it would be possible for Jon to ignore her so completely. She had not expected to hear from him regularly, but since she had taken charge of his son for him she had expected him to keep in touch with her. And he had never written her a single letter. She had refused to believe it at first. She had thought, there'll be a letter by the next post; he must surely write this week. But he had never written.

The tears were scalding her cheeks, and she turned swiftly back to the dressing table again in irritation to repair the make-up.

'It's because I'm so angry,' she said to herself as if it were necessary to vindicate herself from any accusation of weakness. 'It's because it makes me so angry.' It wasn't because she was upset or hurt or anything foolish. It merely made her so angry to think that after all she had done to help him he had never even bothered to write to thank her.

She glanced at her watch. Justin would be home soon. With unsteady, impatient movements she obliterated the tears with a paper tissue and reached for the jar of powder. Speed was very important now. Justin must never see her like this . . .

As she concentrated once more upon the task of make-up she found herself wondering if anyone had ever heard from Jon once he had gone to Canada. Perhaps he had written to Marijohn. She had heard nothing more of Marijohn since the divorce with Michael. She had not even seen Michael himself since the previous Christmas when they had met unexpectedly at one of the drearier cocktail parties someone had given at that time . . . She had always been so fond of Michael. Jon had never cared for him, of course, always preferring that dreadful man – what had his name been? She frowned, annoyed at the failure of memory. She could remember so well seeing his name mentioned in the gossip columns of the lower type of daily paper . . . Alexander, she thought suddenly. That was it. Max Alexander.

From somewhere far away, the latch of the front door clicked and someone stepped into the hall.

He was back.

She put the finishing touches to her make-up, stood up and went out on to the landing.

'Justin?'

'Hullo,' he said from the living room. He sounded calm and untroubled. 'Where are you?'

'Just coming.' He doesn't know, she thought. He hasn't seen the paper. It's going to be all right.

She reached the hall and moved into the living room. There was a cool draught of air, and over by the long windows the curtains swayed softly in the mellow light.

'Ah, there you are,' said Justin.

'How are you, darling? Nice day?'

'Hm-hm.'

She gave him a kiss and stood looking at him for a moment. 'You don't sound too certain!'

He glanced away, moving over to the fireplace, and picked up a packet of cigarettes for a moment before putting them down again and moving towards the long windows.

'Your plants are doing well, aren't they?' he said absently, looking out into the patio, and then suddenly he was swinging round, catching her unawares when she was off her guard, and the tension was in every line of her face and body.

'Justin?—'

'Yes,' he said placidly. 'I've seen the paper.' He strolled over to the sofa, sat down and picked up *The Times*. 'The photograph didn't look much like him, did it? I wonder why he's in London.' When no reply was forthcoming, he started to glance down the personal column but soon abandoned it for the centre pages. The room was filled with the rustle of the newspaper being turned inside out, and then he added, 'What's for dinner, G? Is it steak tonight?'

'Justin darling—' Camilla was moving swiftly over to the sofa, her hands agitated, her voice strained and high. 'I know just how you must be feeling—'

'I don't see how you can, G, because to be perfectly honest, I don't feel anything. It means nothing to me at all.'

She stared at him. He stared back tranquilly and then glanced back at *The Times*.

'I see,' said Camilla, turning away abruptly. 'Of course you won't be contacting him.'

'Of course not. Will you?' He carefully turned the paper back again and stood up. 'I'll be going out after dinner, G,' he said presently, going over to the door. 'Back about eleven, I expect. I'll try not to make too much noise when I come in.'

'I see,' she said slowly. 'Yes. Yes, that's all right, Justin.'

The door closed gently and she was alone in the silent room. She felt relieved that he seemed to have taken such a sensible view of the situation, but she could not rid herself of her anxiety, and amidst all her confused worries she found herself comparing her grandson's total self-sufficiency with Jon's constant assertion of his independence . . .


3


Eve never bought an evening paper because there was usually never any time to read it. The journey from her office in Piccadilly to her flat in Davies Street was too brief to allow time for reading and as soon as she was home, there was nearly always the usual rush to have a bath, change and go out. Or if she wasn't going out, there was even more of a rush to have a bath, change and start cooking for a dinner-party. Newspapers played a very small, insignificant part in her life, and none more so than the ones which came on sale in the evening.

On that particular evening, she had just finished changing and was embarking on the intricate task of make-up when an unexpected caller drifted into the flat and upset all her carefully planned schedules.

'Just thought I'd drop in and see you . . . Hope you don't mind. I say, I'm not in the way, am I?'

It had taken at least ten minutes to get rid of him, and even then he had wandered off leaving his tatty unwanted rag of an evening paper behind as if he had deliberately intended to leave his hallmark on the room where he had wasted so much of her valuable time. Eve shoved the paper under the nearest cushion, whipped the empty glasses into the kitchen out of sight and sped back to add the final touches to her appearance.

And after all that, the man had to be late. All that panic and rush for nothing.

In the end she had time to spare; she took the evening paper from under the cushion and went into the kitchen absently to put it in the rubbish bin, but presently she hesitated. The paper would be useful to wrap up the bacon which had been slowly going bad since last weekend. Better do it now while she had a moment to spare or otherwise by the time next weekend came . . .

She opened the paper carelessly on the table and turned away towards the refrigerator.

A second later, the bacon forgotten, she turned back towards the table.

'Jon Towers, the Canadian property millionaire . . .'

Towers. Like . . . No, it couldn't be. It was impossible. She scrabbled to pick up the page, allowing the rest of the paper to slide on to the floor, not caring that her carefully painted nails should graze against the surface of the table and scratch the varnish.

Jon without an H. Jon Towers. It was the same man.

A Canadian property millionaire . . . No, it couldn't be the same. But Jon had gone abroad following the aftermath of that weekend at Buryan . . . Buryan! How funny that she should still remember the name. She could see it so clearly, too, the yellow house with white shutters which faced the sea, the green lawn of the garden, the hillside sloping down to the cove on either side of the house. The back of beyond, she had thought when she had first seen it, four miles from the nearest town, two miles from the main road, at the end of a track which led to nowhere. But at least she had never had to go there again. She had been there only once and that once had certainly been enough to last her a lifetime.

'. . . staying in London . . . English fiancée . . .'

Staying in London. One of the more well-known hotels, probably. It would be very simple to find out which one . . .

If she wanted to find out. Which, of course, she didn't.

Or did she?

Jon Towers, she was thinking, as she stood there motionless, staring down at the blurred uncertain photograph. Jon Towers. Those eyes. You looked at those eyes and suddenly you forgot the pain in your back or the draught from the open door or a thousand and one other tiresome things which might be bothering you at that particular moment. You might loathe the piano and find all music tedious but as soon as he touched those piano keys you had to listen. He moved or laughed or made some trivial gesture with his hands and you had to watch him. A womanizer, she had decided when she had first met him, but then afterwards in their room that evening Max had said with that casual amused laugh, 'Jon? Good God, didn't you notice? My dear girl, he's in love with his wife. Quaint, isn't it?'

His wife.

Eve put down the paper, and stooped to pick up the discarded pages. Her limbs were stiff and aching as if she had taken part in some violent exercise, and she felt cold for no apparent reason. After putting the paper automatically in the rubbish bin, she moved out of the kitchen and found herself re-entering the still, silent living room again.

So Jon Towers was back in London. He must have the hell of a nerve.

Perhaps, she thought idly, fingering the edge of the curtain as she stared out of the window, perhaps it would have been rather amusing to have met Jon again. Too bad he had probably forgotten she had ever existed and was now about to marry some girl she had never met. But it would have been interesting to see if those eyes and that powerful body could still infect her with that strange unnerving excitement even now after ten years, or whether this time she would have been able to look upon him with detachment. If the attraction were wholly sexual, it was possible she would not have been so impressed a second time . . . but there had been something else besides. She could remember trying to explain to Max and yet not being sure what she was trying to explain. 'It's not just sex, Max. It's something else. It's not just sex.'

And Max had smiled his favourite, tired cynical smile and said, 'No? Are you quite sure?'

Max Alexander.

Turning away from the window she went over to the telephone and after a moment's hesitation knelt down to take out a volume of the London telephone directory.


4

Max Alexander was in bed. There was only one other place which he preferred to bed and that was behind the wheel of his racing car, but his doctors had advised him against racing that season and so he had more time to spend in bed. On that particular evening he had just awakened from a brief doze and was reaching out for a cigarette when the telephone bell rang far away on the other side of the mattress.

He picked up the receiver out of idle curiosity.

'Max Alexander speaking.'

'Hullo Max,' said an unfamiliar woman's voice at the other end of the wire. 'How are you?'

He hesitated, aware of a shaft of annoyance. Hell to these women with their ridiculous air of mystery and cool would-be call-girl voices which wouldn't even fool a two-year-old child . . .

'This is Flaxman nine-eight-double-one,' he said drily. 'I think you have the wrong number.'

'You've got a short memory, Max,' said the voice at the other end of the line. 'It wasn't really so long ago since Buryan, was it?'

After a long moment he managed to say politely into the ivory receiver, 'Since *when*?'

'Buryan, Max, Buryan. You surely haven't forgotten your friend Jon Towers, have you?'

The absurd thing was that he simply couldn't remember her name. He had a feeling it was biblical. Ruth, perhaps? Or Esther? Hell, there must be more female names in the Scriptures than that, but for the life of him he couldn't think of any more. It was nearly a quarter of a century since he had last opened a copy of the Bible.

'Oh, it's you,' he said for lack of anything better to say. 'How's the world treating you these days?'

What the devil was she telephoning for? After the affair at Buryan he had seen no more of her and they had gone their separate ways. Anyway, that was ten years ago. Ten years was an extremely long time.

'. . . I've been living in a flat in Davies Street for the past two years,' she was saying. 'I'm working for a Piccadilly firm now. Diamond merchants. I work for the managing director.'

As if he cared.

'You've seen the news about Jon, of course,' she said carelessly before he could speak. 'Today's evening paper.'

'Jon?'

'You haven't seen the paper? He's back in London.'

There was a silence. The world was suddenly reduced

to an ivory telephone receiver and a sickness below his heart which hurt his lungs.

'He's staying here for a few days, I gather he's here on some kind of business trip. I just wondered if you knew. Didn't he write and tell you he was coming?'

'We lost touch with each other when he went abroad,' said Alexander abruptly and replaced the receiver without waiting for her next comment.

He was sweating, he noticed with surprise, and his heart was still pumping the blood around his lungs in a way which would have worried his doctors. Lying back on the pillows he tried to breathe more evenly and concentrate on the ceiling above him.

Really, women were quite extraordinary, always falling over themselves to be the first bearers of unexpected news. He supposed it gave them some peculiar thrill, some spurious touch of pleasure. This woman had obviously been revelling in her role of self-appointed newscaster.

'Jon Towers,' he said aloud. 'Jon Towers.' It helped him to recall the past little by little, he decided. It was soothing and restful and helped him to view the situation from a disinterested, dispassionate point of view. He hadn't thought of Jon for a long time. How had he got on in Canada? And why should he have come back now after all these years? It had always seemed so obvious that he would never under any circumstances come back after his wife died . . .

Alexander stiffened as he thought of Sophia's death. That had been a terrible business; even now he could remember the inquest, the doctors, the talks with the police, as if it were yesterday. The jury had returned a verdict of accident in the end, although the possibility of suicide had also been discussed, and Jon had left the house after that, sold his business in Penzance and had been in Canada within two months.

Alexander shook a cigarette out of the packet by his bed and lit it slowly, watching the tip burn and smoulder as he pushed it into the orange flame. But his thoughts were quickening, gathering speed and clarity as the memories slipped back into his mind. Jon and he had been at school together. To begin with they hadn't had much in common, but then Jon had become interested in motor-racing and they had started seeing each other in the holidays and staying at one another's houses. Jon had had an odd sort of home life. His mother had been an ex-débutante type, very snobbish, and he had spent most of his time quarrelling with her. His parents had been divorced when he was seven. His father, who had apparently been very rich and extremely eccentric, had lived abroad after that and had spent most of his life making expeditions to remote islands in search of botanical phenomena, so that Jon had never seen him at all. There had been various other relations on the mother's side, but the only relation of his that Alexander had ever met had come from old Towers' side of the family. She had been a year younger than Jon and Alexander himself, and her name had been Marijohn.

He wasn't in the room at all now. He was far away in another world and there was sun sparkling on blue waters from a cloudless sky. Marijohn, he thought, and remembered how they had even called her that too. It had never been shortened to Mary. It had always been Marijohn, the first and last syllable both stressed exactly the same. Marijohn Towers.

When he had been older he had tried taking her out for a while as she was rather good looking, but he might just as well have saved his energy because he had never got anywhere. There had been too many other men all with the same aim in view, and anyway she had seemed to prefer men much older than herself. Not that Alexander had minded; he had never even begun to understand what she was thinking, and although he could tolerate mysterious women in small doses he always became irritated if the air of mystery was completely impenetrable . . . She had married a solicitor in the end. Nobody had known why. He had been a very ordinary sort of fellow, rather dull and desperately conventional. Michael, he had been called. Michael something-or-other. But they were divorced now anyway and Alexander didn't know what had happened to either of them since then.

But before Marijohn had married Michael, Jon had married Sophia . . .

The cigarette smoke was hurting his lungs and suddenly he didn't want to think about the past any more. Sophia, astonishingly enough, had been a Greek waitress in a Soho café. Jon had been nineteen when he had met her and they had married soon afterwards – much to the disgust of his mother, naturally, and to the fury of his father who had immediately abandoned his latest expedition to fly back to England. There had been appalling rows on all sides and in the end the old man had cut Jon out of his will and returned to rejoin his expedition. Alexander gave a wry smile. Jon hadn't given a damn! He had borrowed a few thousand pounds from his mother, gone to the opposite end of England and had started up an estate agent's business down in Penzance, Cornwall. He had paid her back, of course. He had made a practice of buying up cottages in favourable parts of Cornwall, converting them and selling them at a profit. Cornwall had been at its height of popularity then, and it was easy enough for a man like Jon who had had capital and a head for money to earn enough to pay his way in the world. Anyway he hadn't been interested in big money at that particular time – all he had wanted had been his wife, a beautiful home in peaceful surroundings and his grand piano. He had got all three, of course. Jon had always got what he wanted.

The memories darkened suddenly, twisting and turning in his mind like revolving knives. Yes, he thought, Jon had always got what he wanted. He wanted a woman and he had only to crook his little finger; he wanted money and it flowed gently into his bank account; he wanted you to be a friend for some reason and you became a friend . . . Or did you? When he was no longer there, it was as if a spell had been lifted and you started to wonder why you had ever been friends with him . . .

He thought of Jon's marriage again. There had only

been one child, and he had been fat and rather plain and hadn't looked much like either of his parents. Alexander felt the memories quicken in his mind again; he was recalling the weekend parties at Buryan throughout the summer when the Towers' friends would drive down on Friday, sometimes doing the journey in a day, sometimes stopping Friday night *en route* and arriving on Saturday for lunch. It had been a long drive, but Jon and Sophia had entertained well and anyway the place had been a perfect retreat for any long weekend . . . In a way it had been too much of a retreat, especially for Sophia who had lived all her life in busy crowded cities. There was no doubt that she had soon tired of that beautiful secluded house by the sea that Jon had loved so much, and towards the end of her life she had become very restless.

He thought of Sophia then, the voluptuous indolence, the languid movements, the dreadful stifled boredom never far below the lush surface. Poor Sophia. It would have been better by far if she had stayed in her cosmopolitan restaurant instead of exchanging the teeming life of Soho for the remote serenity of that house by the sea.

He went on thinking, watching his cigarette burn, remembering the rocks beneath the cove where she had fallen. It would have been easy enough to fall, he had thought at the time. There had been a path, steps cut out of the cliff, but it had been sandy and insecure after rain and although the cliff hadn't been very steep or very big the rocks below had been like a lot of jagged teeth before they had flattened out in terraces to the water's edge.

He stubbed out his cigarette, grinding the butt to ashes. It had been a beautiful spot below those cliffs. Jon had often walked out there with the child.

He could see it all so clearly now, that weekend he had been at Buryan for one of the parties which Sophia had loved so much. He had come down with Eve, and Michael had come down with Marijohn. There had been no one else, just the four of them with Jon, Sophia and the child. John had invited another couple as well but they hadn't been able to come at the last minute so there had only been four visitors at Buryan that weekend.

He saw Buryan then in his mind's eye, the old farmhouse that Jon had converted, a couple of hundred yards from the sea. There had been yellow walls and white shutters. It had been an unusual, striking place. Afterwards when it was all over, he had thought Jon would sell his home, but he had not. Jon had sold his business in Penzance, but he had never sold Buryan. He had given it all to Marijohn.


5


As soon as Michael Rivers reached his home that evening he took his car from the garage and started on the long journey south from his flat in Westminster to the remote house forty miles away in Surrey. At Guildford he paused to eat a snack supper at one of the pubs, and then he set off again towards Hindhead and the Devil's Punchbowl. It was just after seven o'clock when he reached Anselm's Cross, and the July sun was flaming in the sky beyond the pine trees of the surrounding hills.

He was received with surprise, doubt and more than a hint of disapproval. Visitors were not allowed on Tuesday as a general rule; the Mother Superior was very particular about it. However, if it was urgent, it was always possible for an exception to be made.

'You are expected, of course?'

'No,' said Rivers, 'but I think she'll see me.'

'One moment, please,' said the woman abruptly and left the room in a swirl of black skirts and black veil.

He waited about a quarter of an hour in that bare little room until he thought his patience must surely snap and then at last the woman returned, her lips thin with disapproval. 'This way, please.'

He followed her down long corridors, the familiar silence suffocating him. For a moment he tried to imagine what it would be like to live in such a place, cut off from the world, imprisoned with one's thoughts for hours on end, but his mind only recoiled from the thought and the sweat of horror started to prickle beneath his skin. To counteract the nightmarish twists of his imagination he forced himself to think of his life as it was at that moment, the weekdays crammed with his work at the office, his evenings spent at his club playing bridge or perhaps entertaining clients, the weekends filled with golf and the long hours in the open air. There was never any time to sit and think. It was better that way. Once long ago he had enjoyed solitude from time to time, but now he longed only for his mind to be absorbed with other people and activities which would keep any possibility of solitude far beyond his reach.

The nun opened a door. When he passed the threshold, she closed the door again behind him and he heard the soft purposeful tread of her shoes as she walked briskly away again down the corridor.

'Michael!' said Marijohn with a smile. 'What a lovely surprise!'

She stood up, moving across the floor towards him, and as she reached him the sun slanted through the window on to her beautiful hair. There was a tightness in his throat suddenly, an ache behind the eyes, and he stood helplessly before her, unable to speak, unable to move, almost unable to see.

'Dear Michael,' he heard her say gently. 'Come and sit down and tell me what it's all about. Is it bad news? You would hardly have driven all the way down here after a hard day's work otherwise.'

She had sensed his distress, but not the reason for it. He managed to tighten his self-control as she turned to lead the way over to the two chairs, one on either side of the table, and the next moment he was sitting down opposite her and fumbling for his cigarette case.

'Mind if I smoke?' he mumbled, his eyes on the table.

'Not a bit. Can you spare one for me?'

He looked up in surprise, and she smiled at his expression. 'I'm not a nun,' she reminded him. 'I'm not even a novice. I'm merely "in retreat".'

'Of course,' he said clumsily. 'I always seem to forget that.' He offered her a cigarette. She still wore the wedding ring, he noticed, and her fingers as she accepted the cigarette were long and slim, just as he remembered.

'Your hair's greyer, Michael,' she said. 'I suppose you're still working too hard at that office.' And then, as she inhaled from the cigarette a moment later: 'How strange it tastes! Most odd. Like some rare poison bringing a slow soporific death . . . How long is it since you last came, Michael? Six months?'

'Seven. I came last Christmas.'

'Of course! I remember now. Have you still got the same flat? Westminster, wasn't it? It's funny but I simply can't picture you in Westminster at all. You ought to marry again, Michael, and live in some splendid suburb like – like Richmond or Roehampton or somewhere.' She blew smoke reflectively at the ceiling. 'How are all your friends? Have you seen Camilla again? I remember you said you'd met her at some party last Christmas.'

His self-possession was returning at last. He felt a shaft of gratitude towards her for talking until he felt better and then for giving him the precise opening he needed. It was almost as if she had known. . . But no, that was impossible. She couldn't possibly have known.

'No,' he said. 'I haven't seen Camilla again.'

'Or Justin?'

She must know. His scalp started to prickle because the knowledge was so uncanny.

'No, you wouldn't have seen Justin,' she said, answering her own question before he could reply. She spoke more slowly, he noticed, and her eyes were turned towards the window, focused on some remote object which he could not see. 'I think I understand,' she said at last. 'You must have come to talk to me about Jon.'

The still silence was all around them now, a huge tide of noiselessness which engulfed them completely. He tried to imagine that he was in his office and she was merely another client with whom he had to discuss business, but although he tried to speak, the words refused to come.

'He's come back.'

She was looking at him directly for the first time, and her eyes were very steady, willing him to speak.

'Yes?'

Another long motionless silence. She was looking at her hands now, and the long lashes seemed to shadow her face and give it the strange veiled look he had come to dread once long ago.

'Where is he?'

'In London.'

'With Camilla?'

'No, at the May Fair Hotel.' The simple routine of question and answer reminded him of countless interviews with clients and suddenly it seemed easier to talk. 'It was in the evening paper,' he said. 'They called him a Canadian property millionaire, which seemed rather unlikely, but it was definitely Jon because there was a photograph and of course, being the society page, the writer had to mention Camilla. The name of the hotel wasn't stated but I rang up the major hotels until I found the right one – it didn't take long, less than ten minutes. I didn't think he would be staying with Camilla because when I last met her she said she had completely lost touch with him and didn't even know his Canadian address.'

'I see.' A pause. 'Did the paper say anything else?'

'Yes,' he said, 'it did. It said he was engaged to an English girl and planned to marry shortly.'

She looked out of the window at the evening light and, the clear blue sky far away. Presently she smiled. 'I'm glad,' she said, glancing back at him so that she was smiling straight into his eyes. 'That's wonderful news. I hope he'll be very happy.'

He was the first to look away, and as he stared down at the hard, plain, wooden surface of the table he had a sudden longing to escape from this appalling silence and race back through the twilight to the garish noise of London. 'Would you like me to—' he heard himself mumbling but she interrupted him.

'No,' she said, 'there's no need for you to see him on my behalf. It was kind of you to come all this way to see me tonight, but there's nothing more you can do now.'

'If – if ever you need anything – want any help . . .'

'I know,' she said. 'I'm very grateful, Michael.'

He made his escape soon after that. She held out her hand to him as he said goodbye but that would have made the parting too formal and remote so he pretended not to see it. And then, minutes later, he was switching on the engine of his car and turning the knob of the little radio up to the maximum volume before setting off on his return journey to London.

6

After he had gone, Marijohn sat for a long while at the wooden table and watched the night fall. When it was quite dark, she knelt down by the bed and prayed.

At eleven o'clock she undressed to go to bed, but an hour later she was still awake and the moonlight was beginning to slant through the little window and cast long, elegant shadows on the bare walls.

She sat up, listening. Her mind was opening again, a trick she thought she had forgotten long ago, and after a while she went over to the window and opened it as if the cool night air would help her struggle to interpret and understand. Outside was the quiet closed courtyard, even more quiet and closed than her room, but now instead of soothing her with its peace the effect reversed itself stealthily so that she felt her head seem to expand and the breath choke in her throat, making her want to scream. She ran to the door and opened it, her lungs gasping, the sweat breaking out all over her body, but outside was merely the quiet, closed corridor, suffocating her with its peace. She started to run, her bare feet making no sound on the stone floor, and suddenly she was running along the cliffs by the blue sparkling Cornish sea, running and running towards a house with yellow walls and white shutters, and the open air was all round her and she was free.

The scene blurred in her mind. She was in the garden of the old house in Surrey and there was a rose growing in a bed nearby. She plucked it out, tearing the petals to shreds, and then suddenly her mind was opening again and she was frightened. Nobody, she thought, nobody who hasn't this other sense can ever understand how frightening it is. They could never conceive what it means. They can imagine their bodies being scarred or hurt by some ordinary physical force but they can never imagine the pain in the mind, the dark struggles to understand, the knowledge that your mind doesn't belong to yourself alone . . .

She knelt down, trying to pray, but her prayer was lost in the storm and she could only kneel and listen to her mind.

And when the dawn came at last she went to the Mother Superior to tell her that she would be leaving the house that day and did not know when she would ever return.

## chapter 2

1

The hotel staff at the reception desk were unable to trace the anonymous call.

'But you must,' said Jon. 'It's very important. You must.'

The man behind the desk said courteously that he regretted that it was quite impossible. It was a local call made from a public telephone booth but the automatic dialling system precluded any possibility of finding out any further information.

'Was it a man or a woman?'

'I'm afraid I don't remember, sir.'

'But you must!' said Jon. 'Surely you remember. The call only came through a minute ago.'

'But sir—' The man felt himself stammering. 'You see—'

'What did he say? Was it a deep voice? Did he have any accent?'

'No, sir. At least it was difficult to tell because—'

'Why?'

'Well, it was little more than a whisper, sir. Very faint. He just asked for you. "Mr Towers, please," he said, and I said, "Mr Jon Towers?" and when he didn't answer I said, "One moment, please" and connected the lines.' He stopped.

Jon said nothing. Then after a moment, he shrugged his shoulders abruptly and turned aside, crossing the hall and reception lounge to the bar, while the man behind the desk wiped his forehead, muttered something to his companion and sat down automatically on the nearest available chair.

In the bar Jon ordered a double Scotch on the rocks. There was a sprinkling of people in the room but it was easy enough to find a seat at a comfortable distance from the nearest group, and when he sat down he lit a cigarette before starting his drink. After a while he became conscious of one definite need dominating the mass of confused thoughts in his mind, and on finishing his drink he stubbed out his cigarette and returned to his room to make a phone call.

A stranger's voice answered.

Hell, thought Jon in a blaze of frustration, she's moved or remarried or both and I'll have to waste time being a bloody private detective trying to discover where she is.

'Mrs Rivington, please,' he said abruptly to the unknown voice at the other end of the wire.

'I think you have the wrong number. This is—'

'Is that forty-one Halkin Street?'

'Yes, but—'

'Then she's moved,' said Jon wearily and added, 'Thank you' before slamming down the receiver.

He sat and thought for a moment. Lawrence, the family lawyer, would probably know where she was. Lawrence wouldn't have moved in ten years either; he would be seventy-five now, firmly embedded in his little Georgian house at Richmond with his crusty housekeeper who probably still wore starched collars and cuffs.

Ten minutes later he was speaking to a deep mellifluous voice which pronounced each syllable with meticulous care.

'Lawrence, I'm trying to get in touch with my mother. Can you give me her address? I've just rung Halkin Street but I gather she's moved from there and it occurred to me that you would probably be able to tell me what's been happening while I've been abroad.'

Lawrence talked for thirty seconds until Jon could stand it no longer.

'You mean she moved about five years ago after her second husband died and is now living at five Consett Mews?'

'Precisely. In fact—'

'I see. Now Lawrence, there's just one other thing. I'm extremely anxious to trace my cousin Marijohn – I was planning to phone my mother and ask her, but I suppose I may as well ask you now I'm speaking to you. Have you any idea where she is?'

The old man pondered over the question.

'You mean,' said Jon after ten seconds, 'you don't know.'

'Well, in actual fact, to be completely honest, no I don't. Couldn't say. Rivers could tell you, of course. Nice chap, young Rivers. Sorry their marriage wasn't a success . . . You knew about the divorce, I suppose?'

There was a silence in the softly lit room. Beyond the window far-away traffic crawled up Berkeley Street, clockwork toys moving slowly through a model town.

'The divorce was – let me see . . . six years ago? Five?

My memory's not so accurate as it used to be . . . Rivers was awfully cut up about it – met him at the Law Society just about the time the divorce was coming up for hearing and he looked damn ill, poor fellow. No trouble with the divorce, though. Simple undefended desertion – took about ten minutes and the judge was pretty decent about it. Marijohn wasn't in court, of course. No need for her to be there when she wasn't defending the petition . . . Are you still there, Jon?'

'Yes,' said Jon, 'I'm still here.' And in his mind his voice was saying Marijohn, Marijohn, Marijohn, over and over again, and the room was suddenly dark with grief.

Lawrence wandered on inconsequentially, reviewing the past ten years with the reminiscing nostalgia of the very old. He seemed surprised when Jon suddenly terminated the conversation, but managed to collect himself sufficiently to invite Jon to his home for dinner that week.

'I'm sorry, Lawrence, but I'm afraid that won't be possible at the moment. I'll phone you later, if I may, and perhaps we can arrange something then.'

After he had replaced the receiver he slumped on to the bed and buried his face in the pillow for a moment. The white linen was cool against his cheek, and he remembered how he had loved the touch of linen years ago when they had first used sheets and pillowcases which had been given to them as wedding presents. In a sudden twist of memory he could see the double bed in their room at Buryan, the white sheets crisp and inviting, Sophia's dark hair tumbling over the pillows, her naked body full and rich and warm . . .

He sat up, moved into the bathroom and then walked back into the bedroom to the window in a restless fever of movement. Find Marijohn, said the voice at the back of his brain. You have to find Marijohn. You can't go to Michael Rivers so you must go to your mother instead. Best to call at Consett Mews, and then maybe you can see Justin at the same time and arrange to have a talk with him. You must see Justin.

But that phone call. I have to find out who made that phone call. And most important of all, I must find Marijohn . . .

He went out, hailing a taxi at the kerb, and giving his mother's address to the driver before slumping on to the back seat. The journey didn't take long. Jon sat and watched the dark trees of the park flash into the brilliant vortex of Knightsbridge, and then the cab turned off beyond Harrods before twisting into Consett Mews two minutes later. He got out, gave the man a ten-shilling note and decided not to bother to wait for change. It was dark in the mews; the only light came from an old-fashioned lamp set on a corner some yards away, and there was no light on over the door marked five. Very slowly he crossed the cobbles and pushed the bell hard and long with the index finger of his right hand.

Perhaps Justin will come to the door, he thought. For the hundredth time he tried to imagine what Justin would look like, but he could only see the little boy with the short fat legs and plump body, and suddenly he was back in the past again with the small trusting hand tightly clasping his own throughout the walks along the cliff path to Buryan . . .

The door opened. Facing him on the threshold was a woman in a maid's uniform whose face he did not know.

'Good evening,' said Jon. 'Is Mrs Rivington in?'

The maid hesitated uncertainly. And then a woman's voice said, 'Who is it?' and the next moment as Jon stepped across the threshold, Camilla came out into the hall.

There was a tightness in Jon's chest suddenly, an ache of love in his throat, but the past rose up in a great smothering mist and he was left only with his familiar detachment. She had never cared. She had always been too occupied in finding lovers and husbands, too busy trekking the weary social rounds of cocktail parties and grand occasions, too intent on hiring nursemaids to do her work for her or making arrangements to send him off to boarding school a year early so that he would no longer be in the way. He accepted her attitude and had adjusted himself to it. There was no longer any pain now, least of all after ten years far away from her.

'Hullo,' he said, hoping she wouldn't cry or make some emotional scene to demonstrate a depth of love which did not exist. 'I thought I'd just call in and see you. No doubt you saw in the paper that I was in London.'

'Jon . . .' She took him in her arms, and as he kissed her on the cheek he knew she was crying.

So there was to be the familiar emotional scene after all. It would be like the time she had sent him to boarding school at the age of seven and had then cried when the time had come for him to go. He had never forgiven her for crying, for the hypocrisy of assuming a grief which she could not possibly have felt in the circumstances, and now it seemed that the hypocrisy was about to begin all over again.

He stepped backwards away from her and smiled into her eyes. 'Why,' he said slowly, 'I don't believe you've changed at all . . . Where's Justin? Is he here?'

Her expression changed almost imperceptibly; she turned to lead the way back into the drawing room. 'No, he's not. He went out after dinner and said he wouldn't be in until about eleven . . . Why didn't you phone and let us know you intended to see us? I didn't expect a letter, of course – that would have been too much to hope for – but if you'd phoned—'

'I didn't know whether I was going to have time to come tonight.'

They were in the drawing room. He recognized the familiar pictures, the oak cabinet, the pale yellow-pattern china.

'How long are you here for?' she said quickly. 'Is it a business trip?'

'In a way,' said Jon abruptly. 'I'm also here to get married. My fiancée is travelling over from Toronto in ten days' time and we're getting married quietly as soon as possible.'

'Oh?' she said, and he heard the hard edge to her voice

and knew the expression in her eyes would be hard too. 'Am I invited to the wedding? Or is it to be such a quiet affair that not even the bridegroom's mother is invited?'

'You may come if you wish.' He took a cigarette from the box on the table and lit it with his own lighter. 'But we want it to be quiet. Sarah's parents had the idea of throwing a big society wedding in Canada, but that was more than I could stand and certainly the last thing Sarah wanted, so we decided to have the wedding in London. Her parents will fly over from Canada and there'll be one or two of her friends there as well, but no one else.'

'I see,' said his mother. 'How interesting. And have you told her all about your marriage to Sophia?'

There was a pause. He looked at her hard and had the satisfaction of seeing the colour suffuse her neck and creep upwards into her face. After a moment he said to her carefully, 'Did you phone the May Fair Hotel this evening?'

'Did I—' She was puzzled. He saw her eyes cloud in bewilderment. 'No, I didn't know you were staying at the May Fair,' she said at last. 'I made no attempt to phone you . . . Why do you ask?'

'Nothing.' He inhaled from his cigarette, and glanced at a new china figurine on the dresser. 'How are Michael and Marijohn these days?' he asked casually after a moment.

'They're divorced.'

'Really?' His voice was vaguely surprised. 'Why was that?'

'She wouldn't live with him any more. I've no doubt there were various affairs too. He divorced her for desertion in the end.'

He gave a slight shrug of the shoulders as if in comment, and knew, without looking at her, that she wanted to say something spiteful. Before she could speak he asked, 'Where's Marijohn now?'

A pause.

'Why?'

He looked at her directly. 'Why not? I want to see her.'

'I see,' she said. 'That was why you came to England I suppose. And why you called here tonight. I'm sure you wouldn't have bothered otherwise.'

Oh God, thought Jon wearily. More histrionic scenes.

'Well, you've wasted your time coming here in that case,' she said tightly. 'I've no idea where she is, and I don't give a damn either. Michael's the only one who keeps in touch with her.'

'Where does he live now?'

'Westminster,' said Camilla, her voice clear and hard. 'Sixteen, Grays Court. You surely don't want to go and see Michael, do you, darling?'

Jon leant forward, flicked ash into a tray and stood up with the cigarette still burning between his fingers.

'You're not going, are you, for heaven's sake? You've only just arrived!'

'I'll come again some time. I'm very rushed at the moment.' He was already moving out into the hall, but as she followed him he paused with one hand on the front door latch and turned to face her.

She stopped.

He smiled.

'Jon,' she said suddenly, all anger gone. 'Jon darling—'

'Ask Justin to phone me when he comes in, would you?' he said, kissing her goodbye and holding her close to him for a moment. 'Don't forget. I want to have a word with him tonight.'

She moved away from him and he withdrew his arms and opened the front door.

'You don't want to see him, do you?' he heard her say, and he mistook the fear in her voice for sarcasm. 'I didn't think you would be sufficiently interested.'

He turned abruptly and stepped out into the dark street. 'Of course I want to see him,' he said over his shoulder. 'Didn't you guess? Justin was the main reason why I decided to come back.'

Michael Rivers was out. Jon rang the bell of the flat three times and then rattled the door handle in frustration, but as he turned to walk away down the stairs he was conscious of a feeling of relief. He had not wanted to see Rivers again.

He turned the corner of the stairs and began to walk slowly down the last flight into the main entrance hall, but just as he reached the last step the front door swung open. The next moment a man had crossed the threshold and was pausing to close the door behind him.

It was dark in the hall. Jon was in shadow, motionless, almost holding his breath, and then as the man turned, one hand still on the latch, he knew that the man was Michael Rivers.

'Who's that?' said the man sharply.

'Jon Towers.' He had decided on the journey to Westminster that it would be futile to waste time making polite conversation or pretending that ten years had made any difference to the situation. 'Forgive me for calling on you like this,' he said directly, moving out of the shadows into the dim evening dusk. 'But I wanted your help. I have to trace Marijohn urgently and no one except you seems to know where she is.'

He was nearer Rivers now, but he still could not see him properly. The man had not moved at all, and the odd half-light was such that Jon could not see the expression in his eyes. He was aware of a sharp pang of uneasiness, a violent twist of memory which was so vivid that it hurt, and then an inexplicable wave of compassion.

'I'm sorry things didn't work out,' he said suddenly. 'It must have been hard.'

The fingers on the latch slowly loosened their grip; Rivers turned away from the door and paused by the table to examine the second post which lay waiting there for the occupants of the house.

'I'm afraid I can't tell you where she is.'

'But you must,' said Jon. 'I have to see her. You must.'

The man's back was to him, his figure still and implacable.

'Please,' said Jon, who loathed having to beg from anyone. 'It's very important. Please tell me.'

The man picked up an envelope and started to open it.

'Is she in London?'

It was a bill. He put it back neatly in the envelope and turned towards the stairs.

'Look, Michael—'

'Go to hell.'

'Where is she?'

'Get out of my—'

'You've got to tell me. Don't be so bloody stupid! This is urgent. You must tell me.'

The man wrenched himself free of Jon's grip and started up the stairs. When Jon moved swiftly after him he swung round and for the first time Jon saw the expression in his eyes.

'You've caused too much trouble in your life, Jon Towers, and you've caused more than enough trouble for Marijohn. If you think I'm fool enough to tell you where she is, you're crazy. You've come to the very last person on earth who would ever tell you, and it so happens – fortunately for Marijohn – that I'm the only person who knows where she is. Now get the hell out of here before I lose my temper and call the police.'

The words were still and soft, the voice almost a whisper in the silent hall. Jon stepped back and paused.

'So it was you who called me this evening?'

Rivers stared at him. 'Called you?'

'Called me on the phone. I had an anonymous phone call welcoming me back to England and the welcome wasn't particularly warm. I thought it might be you.'

Rivers still stared. Then he turned away as if in disgust. 'I don't know what you're talking about,' Jon heard him say as he started to mount the stairs again. 'I'm a solicitor, not a crank who makes anonymous phone calls.'

The stairs creaked; he turned the corner and Jon was alone suddenly with his thoughts in the dim silent hall.

He went out, finding his way to Parliament Square and walking past Big Ben to the Embankment. Traffic roared in his ears, lights blazed, diesel oil choked his lungs. He walked rapidly, trying to expel all the fury and frustration and fear from his body by a burst of physical energy, and then suddenly he knew no physical movement was going to soothe the turmoil in his mind and he stopped in exhaustion, leaning against the parapet to stare down into the dark waters of the Thames.

Marijohn, said his brain over and over again, each thought pattern harsh with anxiety and jagged with distress. Marijohn, Marijohn, Marijohn . . .

If only he could find out who had made the phone call. Even though he had for a moment suspected his mother he was certain she wasn't responsible. The person who had made that call must have been at Buryan during that last terrible weekend, and although his mother might have guessed what had happened, with the help of her own special knowledge, she would never think that he . . .

Better not to put it into words. Words were irrevocable forms of expression, terrible in their finality.

So it wasn't his mother. And he was almost certain it wasn't Michael Rivers. Almost . . . And of course it wasn't Marijohn. So that left Max and the girl Max had brought down from London that weekend, the tall, rather disdainful blonde called Eve. Poor Max, getting himself in such a muddle, trying to fool himself that he knew everything there was to know about women, constantly striving to be a second-rate Don Juan, when the only person he ever fooled was himself . . . It was painfully obvious that the only reason why women found him attractive was because he led the social life of the motor-racing set and had enough money to lead it in lavish style.

Jon went into Charing Cross underground station and shut himself in a phone booth.

It would be Eve, of course. Women often made anonymous phone calls. But what did she know and how much? Perhaps it was her idea of a practical joke and she knew nothing at all. Perhaps it was merely the first step in some plan to blackmail him, and in that case . . .

His thoughts spun round dizzily as he found the number in the book and picked up the receiver to dial.

He glanced at his watch as the line began to purr. It was getting late. Whatever happened he mustn't forget to phone Sarah at midnight . . . Midnight in London, six o'clock in Toronto. Sarah would be playing the piano when the call came through and when the bell rang she would push the lock of dark hair from her forehead and run from the music room to the telephone . . .

The line clicked. 'Flaxman nine-eight-double-one,' said a man's voice abruptly at the other end.

The picture of Sarah died.

'Max?'

A pause. Then: 'Speaking.'

He suddenly found it difficult to go on. In the end he merely said, 'This is Jon, Max. Thanks for the welcoming phone call this evening – how did you know I was in town?'

The silence that followed was embarrassingly long. Then: 'I'm sorry,' said Max Alexander. 'I hope I don't sound too dense but I'm completely at sea. John—'

'Towers.'

'Jon Towers! Good God, what a sensation! I thought it must be you but as I know about two dozen people called John I thought I'd better make quite sure who I was talking to . . . What's all this about a welcoming phone call?'

'Didn't you ring me up at the hotel earlier this evening and welcome me home?'

'My dear chap, I didn't even know you were in London until somebody rang up and told me you'd been mentioned in the evening paper—'

'Who?'

'What?'

'Who rang you up?'

'Well, curiously enough it was that girl I brought down to Buryan with me the weekend when—'

'Eve?'

'Eve! Why of course! Eve Robertson. I'd forgotten her name for a moment, but you're quite right. It was Eve.'

'Where does she live now?'

'Well, as a matter of fact, I think she said she was living in Davies Street. She said she worked in Piccadilly for a firm of diamond merchants. Why on earth do you want to know? I lost touch with her years ago, almost immediately after that weekend at Buryan.'

'Then why the hell did she phone you this evening?'

'God knows . . . Look, Jon, what's all this about? What are you trying to—'

'It's nothing,' said Jon. 'Never mind, Max – forget it; it doesn't matter. Look, perhaps I can see you sometime within the next few days? It's a long while since we last met and ten years is time enough to be able to bury whatever happened between us. Have dinner with me tomorrow night at the Hawaii at nine and tell me all you've been doing with yourself during the last ten years . . . Are you married, by the way? Or are you still fighting for your independence?'

'No,' said Alexander slowly. 'I've never married.'

'Then let's have dinner by ourselves tomorrow. No women. My days of being a widower are numbered and I'm beginning to appreciate stag parties again. Did you see my engagement mentioned in the paper tonight, by the way? I met an English girl in Toronto earlier this year and decided I was sick of housekeepers, paid and unpaid, and tired of all American and Canadian women . . . You must see Sarah when she comes to England.'

'Yes,' said Alexander. 'I should like to.' And then his voice added idly without warning: 'Is she like Sophia?'

The telephone booth was a tight constricting cell clouded with a white mist of rage. 'Yes,' said Jon rapidly. 'Physically she's very like her indeed. If you want to alter the dinner arrangements for tomorrow night, Max, phone me at the hotel tomorrow and if I'm not there you can leave a message.'

When he put the receiver back into the cradle he leant against the door for a moment and pressed his cheek against the glass pane. He felt drained of energy suddenly, emotionally exhausted.

And still he was no nearer finding Marijohn . . .

But at least it seemed probable that Eve was responsible for the anonymous phone call. And at least he now knew where she lived and what her surname was.

Wrenching the receiver from the hook again he started dialling to contact the operator in charge of Directory Enquiries.


3


Eve was furious. It was a long time since she had been let down by someone who had promised to give her an entertaining evening, and an even longer time since she had made a date with a man who had simply failed to turn up as he had promised. To add to her feeling of frustration and anger, the phone call to Max Alexander, which should have been so amusing, had been a failure, and after Alexander had slammed down the receiver in the middle of their conversation she had been left only with a great sense of anticlimax and depression.

Hell to Max Alexander. Hell to all men everywhere. Hell to everyone and everything.

The phone call came just as she was toying with her third drink and wondering whom she could ring up next in order to stave off the boredom of the long, empty evening ahead of her.

She picked up the receiver quickly, almost spilling the liquid from her glass.

'Hullo?'

'Eve?'

A man's voice, hard and taut. She sat up a little, the glass forgotten.

'Speaking,' she said with interest. 'Who's this?'

There was a pause. And then after a moment the hard voice said abruptly, 'Eve, this is Jon Towers.'

The glass tipped, jerked off balance by the reflex of her wrist and hand. It toppled on to the carpet, the liquid splashing in a dark pool upon the floor, and all she could do was sit on the edge of the chair and watch the stain as it widened and deepened before her eyes.

'Why, hullo, Jon,' she heard herself say, her voice absurdly cool and even. 'I saw you were back in London. How did you know where I was?'

'I've just been talking to Max Alexander.'

Thoughts were flickering back and forth across her mind in confused uncertain patterns. As she waited, baffled and intrigued, for him to make the next move, she was again aware of the old memory of his personal magnetism and was conscious that his voice made the memory unexpectedly vivid.

'Are you busy?' he said suddenly. 'Can I see you?'

'That would be nice,' she said as soon as she was capable of speech. 'Thank you very much.'

'Tonight?'

'Yes . . . Yes, I could manage tonight.'

'Could you meet me at the May Fair Hotel in quarter of an hour?'

'Easily. It's just round the corner from where I live.'

'I'll meet you in the lobby,' he said. 'Don't bother to ask for me at the reception desk.' And then the next moment he was gone and the dead line was merely a dull expressionless murmur in her ear.


4


After he had replaced the receiver, Jon left the station, walked up to Trafalgar Square and on towards Piccadilly. As he walked he started to worry about Sarah. Perhaps he could clear up this trouble with Eve during the ten days before Sarah arrived, but if not he would seriously have to consider inventing some reason for asking Sarah to delay her arrival. Whatever happened, Sarah must never discover the events which had taken place at Buryan ten years ago. He thought of Sarah for a moment, remembering her clear unsophisticated view of life and the naïve trust which he loved so much. She would never, never be able to understand, and in failing to understand she would be destroyed; the knowledge would tear away the foundations of her secure, stable world and once her world had collapsed she would be exposed to the great flaming beacon of reality with nothing to shield her from the flames.

He walked down Piccadilly to Berkeley Street, and still the traffic roared in his ears and pedestrians thronged the pavements. He was conscious of loneliness again, and the bleakness of the emotion was at once accentuated by his worries. It would have been different in Canada. There he could have absorbed himself in his work or played the piano until the mood passed, but here there was nothing except the conventional ways of finding comfort in a foreign city. And he hated the adolescent futility of getting drunk and would have despised himself for having a woman within days of his coming marriage. It would have meant nothing, of course, but he would still have felt ashamed afterwards, full of guilt because he had done something which would hurt Sarah if she knew. Sarah wouldn't understand that the act with an unknown woman meant nothing and less than nothing, and if she ever found out, her eyes would be full of grief and bewilderment and pain . . .

He couldn't bear the thought of hurting Sarah.

But the loneliness was hard to bear too.

If only he could find Marijohn. There must be some way of finding her. He would advertise. Surely someone knew where she was . . .

His thoughts swam and veered in steep sharp patterns, and then he had reached the Ritz and was turning off into Berkeley Street. Ten yards down the road he paused, listening, but there was nothing, only a sense of unrest and distress which was too vague to be identified. He walked on slowly, and two minutes later was entering the lobby of the hotel.

As he crossed the floor to the desk to ask for his key, he was conscious of someone watching him. With the key in his hand a moment later he swung round to look at the occupants of the open lounge directly behind him, and as he moved, the tall blonde with the faintly disdainful expression stubbed out her cigarette and looked across at him with a slight, cool smile.

He recognized her at once. He had never had any difficulty in remembering faces, and suddenly he was back at Buryan long ago and listening to Sophia saying languidly, 'I wonder who on earth Max will turn up with this time?'

And Max had arrived an hour later in a hot-rod open Bentley with this elegant, fastidious blonde on the front seat beside him.

Jon slipped the key of his room into his pocket and crossed the lobby towards her.

'Well, well,' she said wryly when he was near enough. 'It's been a long time.'

'A very long time.' He stood before her casually, his hands in his pockets, the fingers of his right hand playing with the key to his room. Presently he said, 'After I'd spoken to Max on the phone this evening, I realized I should get in touch with you.'

She raised her eyebrows a fraction, almost as if she didn't understand him. It was cleverly done, he thought. 'Just because I phone Max out of interest and tell him you're back in town,' she said, 'and just because Max later tells you that I phoned him, why does it automatically follow that you should get in touch with me?'

The lobby was sprinkled with people; there was one group only a few feet away from them seated on the leather chairs of the open lounge.

'If we're going to talk,' he said, 'you'd better come upstairs. There's not enough privacy here.'

She still looked slightly bewildered, but now the

bewilderment was mingled with a cautious tinge of pleasure, as if events had taken an unexpected but not unwelcome turn. 'Fine,' she said, her smile still wary but slightly less cool as she rose to her feet to stand beside him. 'Lead the way.'

They crossed the wide lobby to the lift, the girl walking with a quick smooth grace which she had acquired since he had last seen her. Her mouth was slim beneath pale lipstick, the lashes of her beautiful eyes too long and dark to be entirely natural, her fair hair swept upwards simply in a soft, full curve.

On entering the lift he was able to look at her more closely, but as he glanced across towards her he knew she was aware of his scrutiny and he turned aside abruptly.

'Six,' he said to the lift operator.

'Yes, sir.'

The lift drifted upwards lazily. Canned music was playing softly from some small, insidious loudspeaker concealed beneath the control panel. Jon was reminded of Canada suddenly; ceaseless background music was one of the transatlantic traits which he had found most difficult to endure when he had arrived from England long ago, and even now after ten years he still noticed it with a sense of irritation.

'Six, sir,' said the man as the doors opened.

Jon led the way down the corridor to his room, unlocked the door and walked in.

The girl shrugged off her coat.

'Cigarette?' said Jon shortly, turning away to take a fresh packet of cigarettes from a drawer by the bed.

'Thanks.' He could feel her watching him. While he was giving her the cigarette and offering her a light he tried to analyse her expression, but it was difficult. There was a hint of curiosity in her eyes, a glimpse of ironic amusement in the slight curve of her smile, a trace of tension in her stillness as if her composure were not as effortless as it appeared to be. Some element in her manner puzzled him, and in an instinctive attempt to prolong the opening conversation and give himself more time to decide upon the best method of handling the situation, he said idly, 'You don't seem to have changed much since that weekend at Buryan.'

'No?' she said wryly. 'I hope I have. I was very young when I went to Buryan, and very stupid.'

'I don't see what was so young and stupid about wanting to marry Max. Most women would prefer to marry rich men, and there's always a certain amount of glamour attached to anyone in the motor-racing set.'

'I was young and stupid not to realize that Max – and a hell of a lot of other men – just aren't the marrying kind.'

'Why go to the altar when you can get exactly what you want by a lie in a hotel register?' He flung himself into a chair opposite her and gestured to her to sit down. 'Some women have so little to offer on a long-term basis.'

'And most men aren't interested in long-term planning.'

He smiled suddenly, standing up in a quick, lithe movement and moving over to the window, his hands deep in his pockets. 'Marriage is on a long-term basis,' he said. 'Until the parties decide to get divorced.' He flung himself down in the chair again with a laugh, and as he felt her eyes watching him in fascination he wondered for the hundredth time in his life why women found his restlessness attractive.

'I should like to meet your new fiancée,' she said unexpectedly, 'just out of interest.'

'You wouldn't like her.'

'Why? Is she like Sophia?'

'Utterly different.' He started to caress the arm of the chair idly, smoothing the material with strong movements of his fingers. 'You must have hated Sophia that weekend,' he said at last, not looking at her. 'If I hadn't been so involved in my own troubles I might have found the time to feel sorry for you.' He paused. Then: 'Max did you a bad turn by taking you down to Buryan.'

She shrugged. 'It's all in the past now.'

'Is it?'

A silence. 'What do you mean?'

'When you called me on the phone this evening it seemed you wanted to revive the past.'

She stared at him.

'Didn't you call me this evening?'

She still stared. He leaned forward, stubbed out his cigarette and was beside her on the bed before she had time to draw breath.

'Give me your cigarette.'

She handed it to him without a word and he crushed the butt to ashes.

'Now,' he said, not touching her but close enough to show her he would and could if she were obstinate. 'Just what the hell do you think you're playing at?'

She smiled uncertainly, a faint fleeting smile, and pushed back a strand of hair from her forehead as if she were trying to decide what to say and finding it difficult. He felt his irritation grow, his patience fade, and he had to hold himself tightly in control to stem the rising tide of anger within him.

Something in his eyes must have given him away; she stopped, her fingers still touching her hair, her body motionless, and as she looked at him he was suddenly seized with a violent longing to shake her by the shoulders and wrench the truth from behind the cool, composed expression.

'Damn you,' he said quietly to the woman. 'Damn you.'

There was a noise. He stopped. The noise was a bell, hideous and insistent, a jet of ice across the fire of his anger. Pushing the woman aside, he leant across and reached for the cold black receiver of the telephone.

'Jon—' she said.

'It's my son.' He picked up the receiver. 'Jon Towers speaking.'

'Call for you, Mr Towers. Personal from Toronto from a Miss Sarah—'

'Just a minute.' He thrust the receiver into the pillow, muffling it. 'Go into the bathroom,' he said to the woman.

'It's a private call for me. Wait in the bathroom till I've finished.'

'But—'

'Get out!'

She went without a word. The bathroom door closed softly behind her and he was alone.

'Thank you,' he said into the receiver. 'I'll take the call now.'

The line clicked and hummed. A voice said, 'I have Mr Towers for you,' and then Sarah's voice, very clear and gentle, said, 'Jon?' rather doubtfully as if she found it hard to believe she could really be talking to him across the entire length of the Atlantic Ocean.

'Sarah,' he said, and suddenly there were hot tears pricking his eyes and an ache in his throat. 'I was going to phone you.'

'Yes, I know,' she said happily, 'but I simply couldn't wait to tell you so I thought I'd ring first. Jonny, Aunt Mildred has come back to London a week early from her cruise – she got off at Tangier or something stupid because she didn't like the food – and so I've now got a fully qualified chaperone earlier than I expected! Is it all right if I fly over to London the day after tomorrow?'

## chapter 3

1

After Jon had replaced the receiver he sat motionless on the edge of the bed for a long moment. Presently the woman came out of the bathroom and paused by the door, leaning her back against the panels as she waited for him to look up and notice her.

'You'd better go,' he said at last, not looking at her. 'I'm sorry.'

She hesitated, and then picked up her coat and slipped

it quietly over her dress without replying straight away. But after a moment she said, 'How long will you be in London?'

'I'm not sure.'

She hesitated again, toying with the clasp of her handbag as if she could not make up her mind what to say. 'Maybe I'll see you again if there's time,' she said suddenly. 'You've got my phone number, haven't you?'

He stood up then, looking her straight in the eyes, and she knew instinctively she had said the wrong thing. She felt her cheeks burn, a trick she thought she had outgrown years ago, and suddenly she was furious with him, furious at his casual invitation to his hotel, furious at the casual way he was dismissing her, furious because his casual manner was an enigma which she found as fascinating as it was infuriating.

'Have a lovely wedding, won't you,' she said acidly in her softest, sweetest voice as she swept over to the door. 'I hope your fiancée realizes the kind of man she's marrying.'

She had the satisfaction of seeing the colour drain from his face, and then the next moment she was gone, slamming the door behind her, and Jon was again alone with his thoughts in his room on the sixth floor.


2


After a long while it occurred to him to glance at his watch. It was late, well after midnight, and Justin should have phoned an hour ago. Jon sat still for a moment, his thoughts swiftly recalling the evening's events. Perhaps Camilla had forgotten to ask Justin to phone the hotel. Or maybe she hadn't forgotten but had deliberately withheld the message out of malice. Perhaps she also knew where Marijohn was and had lied when she had told him otherwise . . . But no, Rivers had said he was the only one who had any form of contact with Marijohn, so Camilla had been telling the truth.

Michael Rivers.

Jon leaned over on the bed, propping himself up on one elbow, and picked up the telephone receiver.

'Yes, sir?' said a helpful voice a moment later.

'I want to call number five, Consett Mews, SW1. I don't know the number.'

'Thank you, sir. If you would like to replace the receiver we'll ring you when we've put through your call.'

The minutes passed noiselessly. The room was still and peaceful. After a while Jon idly began to tidy the bed, straightening the counterpane and smoothing the pillows in an attempt to smother his impatience by physical movement, and then the bell rang and he picked up the receiver again.

'Your number is ringing for you, Mr Towers.'

'Thank you.'

The line purred steadily. No one answered. They're in bed, thought Jon, half-asleep and cursing the noise of the bell.

He waited, listening to the relentless ring at the other end of the wire. Ten . . . Eleven . . . Twelve . . .

'Knightsbridge five-seven-eight-one.'

This was an unknown voice. It was quiet, very distinct, and even self-possessed.

'I want,' said Jon, 'to speak to Justin Towers.'

'Speaking.'

There was a silence. God Almighty, thought Jon suddenly. To his astonishment he noticed that his free hand was a clenched fist, and felt his heart hurting his lungs as he drew a deep breath to speak. And then the words wouldn't come and he could only sit and listen to the silence at the other end of the wire and the stillness in the room around him.

He tried to pull himself together. 'Justin.'

'Yes, I'm still here.'

'Did your grandmother tell you I'd called at the Mews this evening?'

'Yes, she did.'

'Then why didn't you phone when you arrived back? Didn't she tell you that I wanted you to phone me?'

'Yes, she did.'

Silence. There was something very uncommunicative about the quiet voice and the lack of hesitation. Perhaps he was shy.

'Look, Justin, I want to see you very much – there's a lot I have to discuss with you. Can you come round to the hotel, as soon as possible tomorrow morning? What time can you manage?'

'I'm afraid I can't manage tomorrow,' said the quiet voice. 'I'm going out for the day.'

Jon felt as though someone had just thrown an ice-cold flannel in his face. He gripped the receiver tightly and sat forward a little farther on the edge of the bed.

'Justin, do you know why I've come to Europe?'

'My grandmother said you were here to get married.'

'I could have married in Toronto. I came to England especially to see you.'

No reply. Perhaps the nightmare was a reality and he simply wasn't interested.

'I have a business proposition to make you,' said Jon, fumbling for an approach which would appeal to this impersonal voice a mile away from him in Knightsbridge. 'I'm very anxious to discuss it with you as soon as possible. Can't you put off your engagement tomorrow?'

'All right,' said the voice indifferently after a pause. 'I suppose so.'

'Can you have breakfast with me?'

'I'm afraid I'm very bad at getting up on Saturday mornings.'

'Lunch?'

'I'm – not sure.'

'Well, come as soon after breakfast as you can and then we can talk for a while and maybe you can have lunch with me afterwards.'

'All right.'

'Fine,' said Jon. 'Don't forget to come, will you? I'll see you tomorrow.'

After he had replaced the receiver he sat for ten seconds on the edge of the bed and stared at the silent telephone. Presently when he went into the bathroom, he saw that there was sweat on his forehead and his hands as he raised them to flick the sweat away were trembling with tension. This is my mother's fault, he thought; she's turned the boy against me just as she tried to turn me against my father. When I meet Justin tomorrow he'll be a stranger and the fault will be hers.

He felt desolated suddenly, as if he had taken years of accumulated savings to the bank only to have them stolen from him as he approached the counter to hand over the money. He had a shower and undressed, but the desolation was with him even as he slid into bed, and he knew he would never be able to sleep. He switched out the light. It was after one o'clock, but the night yawned effortlessly ahead of him, hours of restless worry and anxiety, a steady deepening of the pain behind his eyes and the ache of tension in his body. The thoughts whirled and throbbed in his brain, sometimes mere patterns of consciousness, sometimes forming themselves into definite words and sentences.

Sarah would be coming to London in two days' time. Supposing Eve made trouble . . . He could pay her off for a time, but in the end something would have to be done. If only he could find Marijohn . . . but no one knew where she was, no one at all except Michael Rivers. Hell to Michael Rivers. How could one make a man like Michael talk? No good offering him money. No good urging or pleading or cajoling. Nothing was any good with a man like that . . . But something would have to be done. Why did no one know where Marijohn was? The statement seemed to imply she was completely withdrawn from circulation. Perhaps she was abroad. Perhaps there was some man. She wouldn't live with Michael any more, Camilla had said; no doubt there were affairs too.

But that was all wrong. There would have been no real affairs. No real affairs.

But no one knew where Marijohn was and something would have to be done. Perhaps Justin would know. Justin . . .

The desolation nagged at him again, stabbing his consciousness with pain. Better not to think of Justin. And then without warning he was thinking of Buryan, aching for the soft breeze from the sea, pining for the white shutters and yellow walls and the warm mellow sense of peace . . . Yet that was all gone, destroyed with Sophia's death. The sadness of it made him twist over in bed and bury his face deep in the pillow. He had forgotten until that moment how much he had loved his house in Cornwall.

He sat up in bed, throwing back the bedclothes and going over to the window. 'I want to talk about Buryan,' he thought to himself, staring out into the night. 'I want to talk about Sophia and why our marriage went so wrong when I loved her so much I could hardly bear to spend a single night away from her. I want to talk about Max and why our friendship was so completely destroyed that we were relieved to go our separate ways and walk out of each other's lives without a backward glance. I want to talk about Michael who never liked me because I conformed to no rules and was like no other man he had ever had to deal with in his narrow little legal world in London. I want to talk about Justin whom I loved because he was always cheerful and happy and comfortable in his plumpness, and because like me he enjoyed being alive and found all life exciting. And most of all I want to talk to Marijohn because I can discuss Buryan with no one except her . . .'

He went back to bed, his longing sharp and jagged in his mind, and tossed and turned restlessly for another hour. And then just before dawn there was suddenly a great inexplicable peace soothing his brain and he knew that at last he would be able to sleep.

After he had breakfasted the next morning, he went into the open lounge in the hotel lobby and sat down with a newspaper to wait for Justin to arrive. There was a constant stream of people crossing the lobby and entering or leaving the hotel, and at length he put the paper aside and concentrated on watching each person who walked through the swing-doors a few feet away from him.

Ten o'clock came. Then half past. Perhaps he had changed his mind and decided not to come. If he wasn't going to come he should have phoned. But of course he would come. Why shouldn't he? He had agreed to it. He wouldn't back out now . . .

A family of Americans arrived with a formidable collection of white suitcases. A young man who might easily have been Justin drifted in and then walked up to a girl who was sitting reading near Jon in the lounge. There was an affectionate reunion and they left together. A couple of foreign businessmen came in speaking a language that was either Danish or Swedish, and just behind them was another foreigner, dark and not very tall, who looked as though he came from Southern Europe. Italy, perhaps, or Spain. The two Scandinavian businessmen moved slowly over towards one of the other lounges, their heads bent in earnest conversation, their hands behind their backs like a couple of naval officers. The young Italian made no attempt to follow them. He walked slowly over to the reception desk instead, and asked for Mr Jon Towers.

'I think, sir,' said the uniformed attendant to him, 'that Mr Towers is sitting in one of the armchairs behind you to your left.'

The young man turned.

His dark eyes were serious and watchful, his features impassive. His face was plain but unusual. Jon recognized the small snub nose with the high cheekbones but not the gravity in the wide mouth nor the leanness about his jaw.

He walked across, very unhurried and calm. Jon stood

up, knocking the ashtray off the table and showering ash all over the carpet.

'Hullo,' said Justin, holding out his hand politely. 'How are you?'

Jon took the hand in his, not knowing what to do with it, and then let it go. If only it had been ten years ago, he thought. There would have been no awkwardness, no constraint, no polite empty phrases and courteous gestures.

He smiled uncertainly at the young man beside him. 'But you're so thin, Justin!' was all he could manage to say. 'You're so slim and streamlined!'

The young man smiled faintly, gave a shrug of the shoulders which reminded Jon instantly and sickeningly of Sophia, and glanced down at the spilt ash on the floor.

There was silence.

'Let's sit down,' said Jon. 'No point in standing. Do you smoke?'

'No, thank you.'

They both sat down. Jon lit a cigarette.

'What are you doing now? Are you working?'

'Yes. Insurance in the city.'

'Do you like it?'

'Yes.'

'How did you get on at school? Where were you sent in the end?'

Justin told him.

'Did you like it?'

'Yes.'

There seemed suddenly so little to say. Jon felt sick and ill and lost. 'I expect you'd like me to come to the point,' he said abruptly. 'I came over here to ask you if you'd be interested in working in Canada with a view eventually to controlling a branch of my business based in London. I haven't opened this branch yet, but I intend to do so within the next three years. Ultimately, of course, if you made a success of the opportunity I would transfer the entire business to you when I retire.

My business is property. It's a multi-million-dollar concern.'

He stopped. The lounge hummed with other people's steady conversation. People were still coming back and forth through the swing-doors into the hotel.

'I don't think,' said Justin, 'I should like to work in Canada.'

A man and woman near them got up laughing. The woman had on a ridiculous yellow hat with a purple feather in it. The stupid things one noticed.

'Any particular reason?'

'Well . . .' Another vague shrug of the shoulders. 'I'm quite happy in England. My grandmother's very good to me and I've got plenty of friends and so on. I like working in London and I've got a good opening in the City.'

He was reddening slowly as he spoke, Jon noticed. His eyes were still watching the spilt ash on the floor.

Jon said nothing.

'There's another reason too,' said the boy, as if he sensed his other reasons hadn't been good enough. 'There's a girl – someone I know . . . I don't want to go away and leave her just yet.'

'Marry her and come to to Canada together.'

Justin looked up startled, and Jon knew then that he had been lying. 'But I can't—'

'Why not? I married when I was your age. You're old enough to know your own mind.'

'It's not a question of marriage. We're not even engaged.'

'Then she can't be so important to you that you would ignore a million-dollar opening in Canada to be with her. OK, so you've got friends in England – you'd find plenty more in Canada. OK, so your grandmother's been good to you – fine, but what if she has? You're not going to remain shackled to her all your life, are you? And what if you have a good opening in the City? So have dozens of young men. I'm offering you the opportunity of a lifetime, something unique and dynamic and exciting. Don't you want to be your own master of your own business? Haven't you got the drive and ambition to want to take up a challenge and emerge the winner? What do you want of life? The nine-till-five stagnation of the City and years of comfortable boredom or the twenty-four-hour excitement of juggling with millions of dollars? All right, so you're fond of London! I'm offering you the opportunity to come back here in three years' time, and when you come back you'll be twenty times richer than any of the friends you said goodbye to when you left for Canada. Hasn't the prospect any real appeal to you at all? I felt so sure from all my memories of you that you wouldn't say no to an opportunity like this.'

But the dark eyes were still expressionless, his face immobile. 'I don't think property is really my line at all.'

'Do you know anything about it?'

Justin was silent.

'Look, Justin—'

'I don't want to,' said the boy rapidly. 'I expect you could find someone else. I don't see why it has to be me.'

'For Christ's sake!' Jon was almost beside himself with anger and despair. 'What is it, Justin? What's happened? Don't you understand what I'm trying to say? I've been away from you for ten whole years and now I want to give you all I can to try and make amends. I want you to come into business with me so we'll never be separated again for long and so that I can get to know you and try to catch up on all the lost years. Don't you understand? Don't you see?'

'Yes,' said Justin woodenly, 'but I'm afraid I can't help you.'

'Has your grandmother been talking to you? Has she? Has she been trying to turn you against me? What has she said?'

'She's never mentioned you.'

'She must have!'

The boy shook his head and glanced down at his watch. 'I'm afraid—'

'No,' said Jon. 'No, you're not going yet. Not till I've got to the bottom of all this.'

'I'm sorry, but—'

'Sit down.' He grasped the boy's arm and pulled him back into his chair. Justin wrenched himself away. 'There's one question I'm going to ask you whether you like it or not, and you're not leaving till you've given me a proper answer.'

He paused. The boy made no move but merely stared sullenly into his eyes.

'Justin, why did you never answer my letters?'

The boy still stared but his eyes were different. The sullenness had been replaced by a flash of bewilderment and suspicion which Jon did not understand.

'Letters?'

'You remember when I said goodbye to you after I took you away from Buryan?'

The suspicion was gone. Only the bewilderment remained. 'Yes.'

'You remember how I explained that I couldn't take you with me, as I would have no home and no one to help look after you, and you had to go to an English school? You remember how I promised to write, and how I made you promise you would answer my letters and tell me all you'd been doing?'

The boy didn't speak this time. He merely nodded.

'Then why didn't you write? You promised you would. I wrote you six letters including a birthday present, but I never had a word from you. Why was it, Justin? Was it because you resented me not taking you to Canada? I only did it for your own good. I would have come back to see you, but I got caught up in my business interests, so involved that it was hard even to get away for the odd weekend. But I wanted to see you and hear from you all the time, yet nothing ever came. In the end I stopped writing because I thought that in some strange way the letters must be hurting you, and at Christmas and on your birthday I merely sent over money to be paid into your trust fund at your grandmother's bank . . . What happened, Justin? Was it something to do with that last time at Buryan when—'

'I have to go,' said the boy, and he was stammering, his composure shattered. 'I – I'm sorry, but I must go. Please.' He was standing up, stumbling towards the swing-doors, neither seeing nor caring where he went.

The doors opened and swung in a flash of bright metal, and then Jon was alone once more in his hotel room and the failure was a throbbing, aching pain across his heart.


4

It was eleven o'clock when Justin arrived back at Consett Mews. His grandmother, who was writing letters in the drawing room, looked up, startled by his abrupt entrance.

'Justin—' He saw her expression change almost imperceptibly as she saw his face. 'Darling, what's happened? What did he say? Did he—'

He stood still, looking at her. She stopped.

'What happened,' he said, 'to the letters my father sent me from Canada ten years ago?'

He saw her blush, an ugly red stain beneath the careful make-up, and in a sudden moment he thought, It's true. He did write. She lied to me all the time.

'Letters?' she said. 'From Canada?'

'He wrote me six letters. And sent a birthday present.'

'Is that what he said?' But it was only a half-hearted attempt at defence. She took a step towards him, making an impulsive gesture with her hands. 'I only did it for your own good, darling. I thought it would only upset you to read letters from him when he had left you behind and gone to Canada without you.'

'Did you read the letters?'

'No,' she said at once. 'No, I—'

'You let six letters come to me from my father and you

destroyed them to make me think he had forgotten me entirely?'

'Justin, no, Justin, you don't understand—'

'You never had any letters from him so you didn't want me to have letters from him either!'

'No,' she said, 'no, it wasn't like that—'

'You lied and deceived and cheated me year after year, day after day—'

'It was for your own good, Justin, your own good . . .'

She sat down again as if he had exhausted all her strength, and suddenly she was old to him, a woman with a lined, tear-stained face and bent shoulders and trembling hands. 'Your father cares nothing for anyone except himself,' he heard her whisper at last. 'He takes people and uses them for his own ends, so that although you care for him your love is wasted because he never cares for you. I've been useful to him at various times, providing him with a home when he was young, looking after you when he was older – but he's never cared. You'll be useful to him now to help him with his business in Canada. Oh, don't think I can't guess why he wanted to see you! But he'll never care for you yourself, only for your usefulness to him—'

'You're wrong,' said Justin. 'He does care. You don't understand.'

'Understand! I understand all too well!'

'I don't believe you understood him any better than you understood me.'

'Justin—'

'I'm going to Canada with him.'

There was a moment of utter silence.

'You can't,' she said at last. 'Please, Justin. Be sensible. You're talking of altering your whole career, damaging all your prospects in London, just because of a ten-minute meeting this morning with a man you hardly know. Please, please be sensible and don't talk like this.'

'I've made up my mind.'

Camilla looked at him, the years blurring before her eyes, and suddenly the boy before her was Jon saying in that same level, obstinate voice which she had come to dread so much: 'I've made up my mind, I'm going to marry her.'

'You're a fool, Justin,' she said, her voice suddenly harsh and not clear. 'You've no idea what you're doing. You know nothing about your father at all.'

He turned aside and moved towards the door. 'I'm not listening to this.'

'Of course,' said Camilla, 'you're too young to remember what happened at Buryan.'

'Shut up!' he shouted, whirling to face her. 'Shut up, shut up!'

'I wasn't there, but I can guess what happened. He drove your mother to death, you do realize that, don't you? The jury said the death was accidental, but I always knew it was suicide. The marriage was finished, and once that was gone there was nothing else left for her. Of course anyone could have foreseen the marriage wouldn't last! Her attraction for him was entirely sexual and after several years of marriage it was only natural that he should become bored with her. It was the same old story – she cared for him, but basically he never cared for her, only of the pleasure she could give him in bed. And once the pleasure had been replaced by boredom she meant nothing to him at all. So he started to look round for some other woman. It had to be some woman who was quite different, preferably someone rather aloof and unobtainable, because that made the task of conquest so much more interesting and exciting. And during the weekend that your mother died just such a woman happened to be staying at Buryan. Of course you never knew that he and Marijohn—'

Justin's hands were over his ears, shutting her voice from his mind as he stumbled into the hall and banged the door shut behind him. Then, after running up the stairs two at a time, he reached his room, found a suitcase and started to pack his belongings.

# 5

It was noon. On the sixth floor of the May Fair Hotel, Jon was sitting in his room working out an advertisement for the personal column of *The Times* and wondering whether there would be any point in trying to see Michael Rivers again. Before him on the table lay his pencilled note of Eve's telephone number, and as he worried over the problem he picked up the slip of paper idly and bent it between his fingers. He would have to get in touch with the woman to get to the bottom of this business of the anonymous phone call, but if only he could find Marijohn first it would be easier to know which line to adopt . . . He was just tossing the scrap of paper aside and concentrating on his message for *The Times* when the phone rang.

He picked up the receiver. 'Yes?'

'There's a lady here to see you, Mr Towers.'

'Did she give her name?'

'No, sir.'

It would be Eve ready to lay her cards on the table. 'All right. I'll come down.'

He replaced the receiver, checked the money in his wallet and went out. Canned music was still playing in the lift. On the ground floor he walked out into the lobby and crossed over to the leather chairs of the open lounge below the reception desk.

His mind saw her the instant before his eyes did. He had a moment of searing relief mingled with a burst of blazing joy, and then he was moving forward again towards her and Marijohn was smiling into his eyes.

# Part 2

## chapter 1

1

Sarah spent the journey across the Atlantic alternating between a volume of John Clare's poetry and the latest mystery by a well-known crime writer. Occasionally it occurred to her that she hadn't understood a word she was reading and that it would be much more sensible to put both books away, but still she kept them on her lap and watched the written page from time to time. And then at last, the lights of London lay beneath the plane, stretching as far as the eye could see, and she felt the old familiar feeling of nervousness tighten beneath her heart as she thought of Jon.

She loved Jon and knew perfectly well that she wanted to marry him, but he remained an enigma to her at times and it was this strange unknown quality which made her nervous. She called it the Distant Mood. She could understand Jon when he was gay, excited, nervous, musical, sad, disappointed or merely obstinate, but Jon in the Distant Mood was something which frightened her because she knew neither the cause of the mood nor the correct response to it. Her nervousness usually reduced her to silence, and her silence led to a sense of failure, hard to explain. Perhaps, she had thought, it would be different in England; he would be far from the worries and troubles of his work, and perhaps when he was in an easier, less complex frame of mind she would be able to say to him: 'Jon, why is it that sometimes you're so far away that I don't know how to reach out to communicate with you? Why is it that sometimes you're so abrupt I feel I mustn't talk for fear of making you lose your temper and quarrel? Is the fault mine? Is it that I don't understand something in you or that I do something to displease you? If it's my fault, tell me what I'm doing wrong so that I can put it right, because I can't bear it when you're so far away and remote and indifferent to the world.'

He had been in the Distant Mood when she had telephoned him in London two nights ago. She had recognized it at once, and although she had done her best to sound gay and cheerful, she had cried when she had replaced the receiver. That had led to the inevitable scene with her parents.

'Sarah dear, if there's any doubt in your mind, don't . . .'

'Far better to be sorry now than be sorry after you're married.'

'I mean, darling, I know you're very lucky to be marrying Jon. In many ways your father and I both like him very much, but all the same, he's many years older than you and of course, it *is* difficult when you marry out of your generation . . .'

And Sarah had very stupidly lost her temper in the face of these platitudes and had locked herself in her room to face a sleepless night on her own.

The next day had been spent in packing and preparing for the journey to London on the following day. He would phone that night, she had thought. He would be certain to phone that night, and when he talked he would sound quite different and everything would be all right again.

But the phone call never came.

Her mother had decided Sarah's distress was due to premarital nerves and had talked embarrassingly for five whole minutes littered with awkward pauses on the intimate side of marriage. In the end, Sarah had gone out to the nearest cinema to escape and had seen an incredibly bad epic film on a wide screen which had given her a headache. It had been almost a relief to board the plane for London the following day and take a definite course of action at last after so much restless waiting and anxiety.

The plane drifted lower and lower over the mass of lights until Sarah could see the pilot lights of the runway rising from the ground to meet them, and then there were the soft thumps of landing and the long cruise to a halt on English soil. Outside the plane, the air was damp and cool. The trek through customs came next, her nerves tightening steadily as the minutes passed, until at last she was moving into the great central lobby and straining her eyes for a glimpse of Jon.

Something had gone wrong. He wasn't there. He was going to break off the engagement. He had had an accident, was injured, dying, dead . . .

'God Almighty,' said Jon's voice just behind her. 'I thought you were a white sheet at first! Who's been frightening the life out of you?'

The relief was a great cascading warmth making her limbs relax and the tears spring to her eyes.

'Oh Jon, Jon.'

There was no Distant Mood this time. He was smiling, his eyes brilliantly alive, his arms very strong, and when he kissed her it seemed ridiculous that she should ever have had any worries at all.

'You look,' he said, 'quite frighteningly sophisticated. What's all this green eye-shadow and mud on your eyelashes?'

'Oh Jon, I spent hours—' She laughed suddenly in a surge of happiness and he laughed too, kissing her again and then sliding his arm round her waist.

'Am I covered in Canada's most soigné lipstick?'

He was. She produced a handkerchief and carefully wiped it off.

'Right,' he said briskly, when she had finished. 'Let's go. There's dinner waiting for us at the Hilton and endless things to be discussed before I take you to your Aunt Mildred's, so we've no time to waste . . . Is this all your luggage or has Cleopatra got another gold barge full of suitcases sailing up the customs' conveyor belt?'

There was a taxi waiting and then came the journey into the heart of London, through the Middlesex suburbs to Kensington, Knightsbridge and the Park. The warmth of London hummed around them, the roar of engines revved in their ears, and Sarah, her hand clasped tightly in Jon's, thought how exciting it was to come home at last to her favourite city and to travel through the brightly lit streets to the resplendent glamour of a lush, expensive world.

'How's Cleopatra feeling now?'

'Thinking how much nicer than Mark Antony you are and how much better than Alexandria London is.'

He laughed. She was happy. When they reached the Hilton she had a moment's thrill as she crossed the threshold into the luxury which was still new to her, and then they were in the dining room and she was trying hard to pretend she was quite accustomed to dining in the world's most famous restaurants.

Jon ordered the meal, chose the wines and tossed both menu and wine list on one side.

'Sarah, there are a lot of things I have to discuss with you.'

Of course, she thought. The wedding and honeymoon. Exciting, breath-taking plans.

'First of all, I want to apologize for not phoning you last night. I became very involved with my family and there were various difficulties. I hope you'll forgive me and understand.'

She smiled thankfully, eager to forgive. 'Of course, Jonny. I thought something like that must have happened.'

'Secondly I have to apologize for my manner on the phone the other night. I'm afraid I must have sounded very odd indeed but again I was heavily involved with other things and I wasn't expecting you to call. I hope you didn't think I wasn't pleased that you were going to come over to England earlier than expected. It was a wonderful surprise.'

'You – did sound a little strange.'

'I know.' He picked up the wine list and put it down again restlessly. 'Let me try and explain what's been happening. I arrived here to find my mother had left her house in Halkin Street, so naturally I had to spend time tracing her before I could go and see her. That all took time, and then I managed to meet Justin and have a talk with him—'

'You did?' She had heard all about Justin, and Jon's plans to invite him to Canada. 'Is it all right? What did he say?'

'He's coming to Canada. He hesitated at first, but now he's made up his mind, so that's all settled, thank God.' He unfolded the table napkin absentmindedly and fingered the soft linen. 'Then there were various other people I had to see – Max Alexander, an old friend of mine, for instance . . . and various others. I haven't had much time to spare since I arrived.'

'No, you must have been very busy.' She watched his restless fingers. 'What about the wedding, Jonny, and the honeymoon? Or haven't you had much chance to make any more definite arrangements yet?'

'That,' said Jon, 'is what I want to talk to you about.'

The first course arrived with the first wine. Waiters flitted around the table and then withdrew in a whirl of white coats.

'What do you mean, darling?'

He took a mouthful of hors-d'oeuvres and she had to wait a moment for his reply. Then: 'I want to get married right away,' he said suddenly, looking straight into her eyes. 'I can get a special licence and we can be married just as soon as possible. Then maybe a honeymoon in Spain, Italy, Paris – wherever you like, and a few days in England before we fly back to Canada with Justin.'

She stared at him, the thoughts whirling dizzily in her brain. 'But Jon, Mummy and Daddy aren't here. I – I haven't bought all the trousseau . . . I was waiting till Mummy was here before I bought the last few things—'

'Hell to the trousseau. I don't care if you come away with me dressed in a sack. And why can't you go shopping without your mother? I'm sure your taste is just as good if not better than hers.'

'But Jon—'

'Do you really feel you can't get married without your parents being here?'

She swallowed, feeling as if she was on a tightrope struggling to keep her balance. 'I – I just want to be fair to them, and – and I know . . . Yes, I do want them to be here, Jon, I really do . . . But if – I just don't understand. Why are you in such a hurry to get married all of a sudden?'

He looked at her. She felt herself blush without knowing why, and suddenly she was afraid, afraid of the Distant Mood, afraid of hurting her parents, afraid of the wedding and the first night of the honeymoon.

'Jon, I—'

'I'm sorry,' he said, his hand closing on hers across the table. 'That was wrong of me. Of course you shall have your parents here. I was just being selfish and impatient.'

'Perhaps I'm the one who's being selfish,' she said ashamed. 'I did say I wanted a quiet wedding—'

'But not as quiet as the one I've suggested.' He wasn't angry. 'It's all right – I understand. We'll keep it the way you want it. After all, the actual wedding will be much more important to you than to me. That's only natural.'

'I suppose so,' she said, struggling to understand. 'The wedding's the bride's day, isn't it? And then of course you've been married before so—'

'So I'm blasé about it!' he teased, and she smiled.

They concentrated on the hors-d'oeuvres for a few minutes.

'Sarah.'

Something else was coming. She could sense her nerves tightening and her heart thudding a shade quicker as she waited.

'No matter when we get married, I would like to talk to you a little about Sophia.'

She took a sip of wine steadily, trying to ignore the growing tension in her limbs. 'You needn't talk about her if you don't want to, Jon. I understand.'

'I don't want you to get one of these dreadful first-wife complexes,' he said, laying down his knife and fork and slumping back in his chair. 'Don't, for God's sake, start imagining Sophia to be something so exotic that you can hardly bear to tiptoe in her footsteps. She was a very ordinary girl with a lot of sex appeal. I married her because I was young enough to confuse lust with love. It's quite a common mistake, I believe.' He drained his glass and toyed idly with the stem as his eyes glanced round the room. 'For a while we were very happy, and then she became bored and I found I could no longer love her or confide in her as I had when I married her. We quarrelled a lot. And then, just as I was thinking of the idea of divorce, she had the accident and died. It was complete and utter hell for me and for everyone who was staying at Buryan at the time, especially as the inquest had a lot of publicity in the local papers and all sorts of rumours started to circulate. One rumour even said that I'd killed her. No doubt some vicious-minded crank had heard we weren't on the best of terms and had drawn his own melodramatic conclusions when he heard that Sophia had fallen down the cliff path and broken her neck on the rocks below . . . But it was an accident. The jury said it could have been suicide because she wasn't happy at Buryan, but that was ridiculous. They didn't know Sophia and how much she loved life – even if life merely consisted of living at Buryan far from the glamour of London. Her death was an accident. There's no other explanation.'

She nodded. Waiters came and went. Another course was laid before her.

'And anyway,' said Jon, 'why would I have wanted to kill her? Divorce is the civilized method of discarding an unwanted spouse, and I had no reason to prefer murder to divorce.' He started to eat. 'However, I'm wandering from the point. I just wanted to tell you that you needn't ever worry that you're inadequate compared to Sophia, because there simply is no comparison. I love you in many different ways and Sophia I only loved in one way – and even that way turned sour in the end . . . You understand, don't you? You follow what I'm saying?'

'Yes, Jon,' she said. 'I understand.' But her thoughts,

the most private of her thoughts which she would never have disclosed to anyone, whispered: she must have been very good in bed. Supposing . . . And then, even her private thoughts subsided into a mass of blurred fears and worries which she automatically pushed to the furthest reaches of her mind.

Jon was smiling at her across the table, the special message of laughter and love in his eyes. 'You still want to marry me?'

She smiled back, and suddenly she loved him so much that nothing mattered in all the world except her desire to be with him and make him happy. 'Yes,' she said impulsively. 'I do. But don't let's wait for my parents, Jonny – I've changed my mind. Let's get married right away after all . . .'

2

At half-past eleven that night, Jon dialled a London telephone number.

'Everything's fine,' he said into the receiver presently. 'We're marrying this week, honeymoon in Paris for ten days, a pause for a day or two in London to collect Justin, and then we all go back to Canada – and well away from the anonymous phone caller and any danger of Sarah finding out anything. It's best for her not to know.'

A pause.

'Yes, I did. No trouble at all. She didn't even ask any questions about Sophia. I concentrated on the angle you suggested.'

Another pause. The night deepened. Then: 'How will I explain to her? It'll look pretty damned odd if I go back there, especially in view of my conversation with her tonight about Sophia . . . Why yes, of course! Yes, that's reasonable enough . . . All right, I'll see you in about a fortnight's time, then. Goodbye, darling . . . and think of me.'

The hotel in Paris was very large and grand and comfortable, and Sarah beneath her gay smile and excited eyes felt very small and lost and nervous. Later in the evening at the famous restaurant she tried to do justice to the food that was placed before her, but the nervousness and tension only increased until she could not eat any more. And then at last they returned to the hotel, said goodnight to the team on duty at the reception desk and travelled up in the lift to their suite on the first floor.

Jon wandered into the bathroom. As Sarah undressed slowly she heard the hiss of the shower, and knew that she would have a few minutes to herself. She tried not to think of Sophia. What would Sophia have done on her wedding night? She wouldn't have sat trembling through an exotic dinner or spent precious minutes fumbling to undress herself with leaden fingers . . . Perhaps Jon had lived with Sophia before he had married her. He had never asked Sarah to do such a thing, but then of course she was different, and Sophia had been so very attractive – and foreign . . . Being foreign probably made a difference. Or did it?

She sat down at the dressing table in her nightdress and fidgeted uncertainly with her hair. I wonder what Sophia looked like, she thought. I've never asked Jon. But she must have been dark like Justin, and probably slim and supple. Darker and slimmer than I am, I expect. And more attractive, of course. Oh God, how angry Jon would be if he could hear me! I must stop thinking of Sophia.

Jon came back from the bathroom and threw his clothes carelessly into an armchair. He was naked.

'Perhaps I'll have a bath,' said Sarah to her fingernails. 'Would it matter, do you think?'

'Not in the least,' said Jon, 'except that we'll both be rather hot in bed.'

The bathroom was a reassuring prison of steam and warmth. The bath took a long time to run, almost as long as it took her to wash. She lingered, drying herself and then paused to sit on the stool as the tears started to prick her eyes. She tried to fight them back, and then suddenly she was caught in a violent wave of homesickness and the tears refused to be checked. The room swam, the sobs twisted and hurt her throat as she fought against them, and she was just wondering how she would ever have the strength to return to the bedroom when Jon tried the handle of the locked door.

'Sarah?'

She wept soundlessly, not answering.

'Can you let me in?'

She tried to speak but could not.

'Please.'

Dashing away her tears she stumbled to the door and unlocked it. As she returned blindly to the stool and the mirror she heard Jon come in. She waited, dreading his mood, praying he wouldn't be too angry.

'Sarah,' she heard him say. 'Darling Sarah.' And suddenly he had taken her gently in his arms as if she had been very small, and was pressing her tightly to him in a clumsy comforting gesture which she found unexpectedly moving. She had never before thought him capable of great tenderness. 'You're thinking of Sophia,' he whispered in her ear. 'I wish you wouldn't. Please, Sarah, don't think of Sophia any more.'

The fears ebbed from her mind; when he stooped his head to kiss her on the mouth at last she was conscious first and foremost of the peace in her heart before her world quickened and whirled into the fire.


4


When they arrived back in London ten days later, Jon spent two hours making involved transatlantic telephone calls and dealing with various urgent business commitments; his right-hand man, whom Sarah had met in Canada, had flown to Europe for some reason connected with the business, and the first night in town was spent in dining with him at a well-known restaurant.

On the following day they had lunch with Camilla in Knightsbridge. When they were travelling back to their hotel afterwards, Sarah turned to Jon with a puzzled expression in her eyes.

'Where was Justin? He was never mentioned, so I didn't like to ask.'

'There was a slight awkwardness when he decided he was going to Canada to work for me. After he had given in his notice and finished his work in the City I gave him some money and told him to go on holiday until I was ready to go back to Canada, and in fact he's gone down to Cornwall to stay with a cousin of mine.'

'Oh, I see.'

The taxi cruised gently out of the Hyde Park underpass and accelerated into Piccadilly. On the right lay the green trees of the park and the warmth of the summer sun on the short grass. It was hot.

'As a matter of fact,' said Jon idly, glancing out of the window, 'I'd rather like you to meet this cousin of mine. I thought maybe we might hire a car and drive down to Cornwall this weekend and spend a few days in the country before flying straight back to Canada.'

Sarah glanced up at the cloudless sky and thought longingly of golden sands and waves breaking and curling towards the shore. 'That sounds lovely, Jonny. I'd like to stay just a little longer in England, especially as the weather's so good now.'

'You'd like to go?'

'Very much. Whereabouts does your cousin live?'

'Well . . .' He paused. The taxi approached the Ritz and had to wait at the traffic lights. 'As it happens,' he said at last, 'she's now living at Buryan.'

The lights flashed red and amber; a dozen engines throbbed in anticipation.

'When I left ten years ago,' Jon said, 'I never wanted to see the place again. I nearly sold it so that I could wash my hands of it once and for all, but at the last minute I changed my mind and gave it to my cousin instead. It was such a beautiful place, and so unique. I loved it better than any other place in the world at one time, and I suppose even after everything that had happened I was still too fond of the house to sell it to a stranger. My cousin goes back there once or twice a year and lets it for periods during the summer. I saw her briefly in London before you arrived, and when she talked of Buryan and how peaceful it was I found I had a sudden longing to go back just to see if I could ever find it peaceful again. I think perhaps I could now after ten years. I know I could never live there permanently again, but when my cousin suggested we go down to stay with her for a few days I felt so tempted to go back for a visit . . . Can you understand? Or perhaps you would rather not go.'

'No,' she said automatically, 'I don't mind at all. It won't have any memories for me. If you're willing to go back, Jon, then that's all that matters.' But simultaneously she thought: how could he even think of going back? And her mind was confused and bewildered as she struggled to understand.

'It's mainly because of my cousin,' he said, as if sensing her difficulties. 'I'd love to have the chance to see her again and I know she's anxious to meet you.'

'You've never mentioned her to me before,' was all she could say. 'Or is she one of the cousins on your mother's side of the family, the ones you said you wouldn't trouble to invite to the wedding?'

'No, Marijohn is my only relation on my father's side of the family. We spent a lot of time together until I was seven, and then after my parents' divorce my father took her away from the house where I lived with my mother and sent her to a convent. He was her guardian. I didn't see much of her after that until I was about fifteen, and my father returned to England for good to live in London and removed Marijohn from the convent. I saw a great deal of her then until I married and went down to Cornwall to live. I was very fond of her.'

'Why didn't you invite her to the wedding?'

'I did mention it to her, but she couldn't come.'

'Oh.'

'I don't know why I didn't mention her to you before,' he said vaguely as the taxi drew up outside the hotel. 'I lost touch with her when I went to Canada and I didn't honestly expect to see her again when I returned. However, she heard I was in London and we had a brief meeting . . . So much happened in those two days before you arrived, and then, of course, when you did arrive I forgot everything except the plans for the wedding and the honeymoon. But when I woke this morning and saw the sunshine and the blue sky I remembered her invitation to Buryan and started wondering about a visit to Cornwall . . . You're sure you'd like to come? If you'd rather stay in London don't be afraid to say so.'

'No, Jon,' she said. 'I'd like to spend a few days by the sea.' And as she spoke she thought: there's still so much about Jon that I don't understand and yet he understands me through and through. Or does he? Perhaps if he really understood me he'd know I don't want to go to the house where he lived with his first wife . . . But maybe I'm being unnecessarily sensitive. If he had an ancestral home I would go back there to live with him no matter how many times he'd been previously married, and wouldn't think it in the least strange. And Jon has no intention of living at Buryan anyway; he's merely suggesting a short visit to see his cousin. I'm being absurd, working up a Sophia-complex again. I must pull myself together.

'Tell me more about your cousin, Jon,' she said as they got out of the taxi. 'What did you say her name was?'

But when they went into the hall Jon's Canadian business associate crossed the lobby to meet them, and Marijohn wasn't mentioned again till late in the afternoon when Jon went up to their room to make two telephone calls, one to his cousin in Cornwall and the other to enquire about hiring a car to take them to St Just. When he came back he was smiling and her uneasiness faded as she saw he was happy.

'We can have a car tomorrow,' he said. 'If we leave early we can easily do the journey in a day. We'll be a long way ahead of the weekend holiday traffic, and the roads shouldn't be too bad.'

'And your cousin? Is she pleased?'

'Yes,' said Jon, pushing back his hair in a luxurious, joyous gesture of comfort. 'Very pleased indeed.'


5


The sun was a burst of red above the sea by the time they reached the airport at St Just, and as Jon swung the car off on to the road that led to Buryan, his frame seemed to vibrate with some fierce excitement which Sarah sensed but could not share. She glanced back over her shoulder at the soothing security of the little airport with its small plane waiting motionless on the runway, and then stared at the arid, sterile beauty of the Cornish moors.

'Isn't it wonderful?' said Jon to her, his hands gripping the wheel, his eyes blazing with joy. 'Isn't it beautiful?'

And suddenly she was infected by his excitement so that the landscape no longer seemed repellent in its bleakness but fascinating in its austerity.

The car began to purr downhill; after a moment Sarah could no longer see the small huddle of the airport buildings with their hint of contact with the civilized world far away, and soon the car was travelling into a green valley dotted with isolated farms and squares of pasture bordered by grey stone walls. The road was single-track only now; the gradient was becoming steeper, and the sea was temporarily hidden from them by sloping hills. Soon they were passing the gates of a farm, and the next moment the car was grating from the smooth tarmac on to the rough uneven stones of a cart-track. As they passed the wall by the farm gate, Sarah was just able to catch a glimpse of a notice with an arrow pointing down the track, and above the arrow someone had painted the words 'To Buryan'.

The car crawled on, trickling downhill stealthily over the rough track. On either side the long grass waved gracefully in the soft breeze from the sea, and above them the sky was blue and cloudless.

'There's the water-wheel,' said Jon, and his voice was scarcely louder than an unspoken thought, his hands tightening again on the wheel in his excitement. 'And there's Buryan.'

The car drifted on to smoother ground and then turned into a small driveway. As the engine died Sarah heard for the first time the rushing water of the stream as it passed the disused water-wheel on the other side of the track and tumbled down towards the sea.

'How quiet it is,' she said automatically. 'How peaceful after London.'

Jon was already out of the car and walking towards the house. Opening her own door she stepped on to the gravel of the drive and stood still for a moment, glancing around her. There was a green lawn, not very big, with a white swing-seat at one end. The small garden was surrounded by clumps of rhododendrons and other shrubs and there were trees, bent backwards into strange contorted shapes by the prevailing wind from the sea. She was standing at one side of the house but slightly in front of it so that from her angle she could glimpse the yellow walls and white shutters as they basked in the summer sun. A bird sang, a cricket chirped and then there was silence, except for the rushing stream and, far away, the distant murmur of the tide on the pebbled beach.

'Sarah!' called Jon.

'Coming!' She stepped forward, still feeling mesmerized by the sense of peace, and as she moved she saw that he was in the shade of the porch waiting for her.

She drew closer, feeling absurdly vulnerable as she crossed the sunlit drive while he watched her from the shadows, and then she saw that he was not alone and the odd feeling of defencelessness increased. It must be a form of self-consciousness, she thought. She felt exactly as if she were some show exhibit being scrutinized and examined by a row of very critical judges. Ridiculous.

And then she saw the woman. There was the dull

gleam of golden hair, the wide slant of remote eyes, the slight curve of a beautiful mouth, and as Sarah paused uncertainly, waiting for Jon to make the introductions, she became aware of an extreme stillness as if the landscape around them was tensed and waiting for something beyond her understanding.

Jon smiled at the woman. He made no effort to speak, but for some odd reason his silence didn't matter, and it suddenly occurred to Sarah that she had not heard one word exchanged between the two of them even though she had been well within earshot when they had met. She was just wondering if Jon had kissed his cousin, and was on the point of thinking that it was most unlikely that they would have embraced without some form of greeting, when the woman stepped from the shadows into the sunlight.

'Hullo, Sarah,' she said. 'I'm so glad you could come. Welcome to Buryan, my dear, and I hope you'll be very happy here.'

## chapter 2

1

Their bedroom was filled with the afternoon sun, and as Sarah crossed to the window she saw the sea shimmering before her in the cove, framed by the twin hillsides on either side of the house. She caught her breath, just as she always did when she saw something very beautiful, and suddenly she was glad they had come and ashamed of all her misgivings.

'Have you got everything you want here?' said Marijohn, glancing round the room with the eye of a careful hostess. 'Let me know if I've forgotten anything. Dinner will be in about half an hour, and the water's hot if you should want a bath.'

'Thank you,' said Sarah, turning to face her with a smile. 'Thank you very much.'

Jon was walking along the corridor just as Marijohn left the room. Sarah heard his footsteps pause.

'When's dinner? In about half an hour?'

Marijohn must have made some gesture of assent which she didn't say aloud. 'I'll be in the kitchen for a while.'

'We'll come down when we're ready, and have a drink.' He walked into the room, closed the door behind him and yawned, luxuriously stretching every muscle with slow precision. 'Well?' he inquired presently.

'Well?' She smiled at him.

'Do you like it?'

'Yes,' she said. 'It's very beautiful, Jon.'

He kicked off his shoes, pulled off his shirt and waded out of his trousers. Before she turned back uneasily towards the window to watch the sun sparkling on the sea she saw him pull back the covers from the bed and then fling himself down on the smooth white linen.

'What shall I wear for dinner?' she said hesitantly. 'Will Marijohn change?'

He didn't reply.

'Jon?'

'Yes?'

She repeated the question.

'I don't know,' he said. 'Does it matter?' His fingers were smoothing the linen restlessly, and his eyes were watching his fingers.

She said nothing, every nerve in her body slowly tightening as the silence became prolonged. She had almost forgotten how frightened she was of his Distant Mood.

'Come here a moment,' he said abruptly, and then, as she gave a nervous start of surprise: 'Good God, you nearly jumped out of your skin! What's the matter with you?'

'Nothing Jon,' she said, moving towards him. 'Nothing at all.'

He pulled her down on to the sheets beside him and

kissed her several times on the mouth, throat and breasts. His hands started to hurt her. She was just wondering how she could escape from making love while he was in his present mood, when he rolled away from her and stood up lazily in one long fluent movement of his body. He still didn't speak. She watched him open a suitcase, empty the entire contents on to the floor and then survey the muddle without interest.

'What are you looking for, darling?'

He shrugged. Presently he found a shirt and there was a silence while he put it on. Then: 'You must be tired after the long journey,' he said at last.

'A little.' She felt ashamed, inadequate, tongue-tied.

For a moment she thought he wasn't going to say anything else but she was mistaken.

'Sex still doesn't interest you much, does it?'

'Yes, it does,' she said in a low voice, the unwanted tears pricking at the back of her eyes. 'It's just that it's still rather new to me and I'm not much good when you're rough and start to hurt.'

He didn't answer. She saw him step into another pair of trousers and then, as he moved over to the basin to wash, everything became blurred and she could no longer see. Presently she found a dress amongst the luggage and started to change from her blouse and skirt, her movements automatic, her fingers stiff and clumsy as she fumbled with zip fasteners and buttonholes.

'Are you ready?' he said at last.

'Yes, almost.' She didn't dare stop to re-apply her lipstick. There was just time to brush her hair lightly into position and then they were going out into the corridor and moving downstairs to the drawing room, the silence a thick invisible wall between them.

Marijohn was already there but Justin had apparently disappeared to his room. Sarah sat down, her limbs aching with tension, the lump of misery still hurting her throat.

'What would you like to drink, Sarah?' said Marijohn.

'I – I don't mind . . . Sherry or – or a martini—'

'I've some dry sherry. Would that do? What about you, Jon?'

Jon shrugged his shoulders again, not bothering to reply. Oh God, thought Sarah, how will she cope? Should I try to cover up for him? Oh Jon, Jon . . .

But Marijohn was pouring out a whisky and soda without waiting for him to answer. 'I've enjoyed having Justin here,' she said tranquilly, handing him his glass. 'It's been fascinating getting to know him again. You remember how we used to puzzle over him, trying to decide who he resembled? It seems so strange now that there could ever have been any doubt.'

Jon turned suddenly to face her. 'Why?'

'He's like you, Jon. There's such a strong resemblance. It's quite uncanny sometimes.'

'He doesn't look like me.'

'What on earth have looks got to do with it? Sarah, have a cocktail biscuit. Justin went specially to Penzance to buy some, so I suppose we'd better try and eat a few of them . . . Jon, darling, do sit down and stop being so restless – you make me feel quite exhausted, just sitting watching you . . . That's better. Isn't the light unusual this evening? I have a feeling Justin has sneaked off somewhere to paint one of his secret watercolours . . . You must persuade him to show you some of them, Jon, because they're very good – or at least, they seem good to me, but then I know nothing about painting . . . You paint, don't you, Sarah?'

'Yes,' said Jon, before Sarah could reply, and suddenly his hand was on hers again and she knew in a hot rush of relief that the mood had passed. 'She also happens to be an authority on the Impressionists and the Renaissance painters and the—'

'Jon, don't exaggerate!'

And the golden light of the evening seemed to deepen as they laughed and relaxed.

After dinner Jon took Sarah down to the cove to watch the sunset. The cove was small and rocky, its beach strewn with huge boulders and smooth pebbles, and as

Jon found a suitable vantage point Sarah saw the fins of the Atlantic sharks coasting offshore and moving slowly towards Cape Cornwall.

'I'm sorry,' said Jon suddenly from beside her.

She nodded, trying to tell him without words that she understood, and then they sat down together and he put his arm round her shoulders, drawing her closer to him.

'What do you think of Marijohn?'

She thought for a moment, her eyes watching the light change on the sea, her ears full of the roar of the surf and the cry of the gulls. 'She's very—' The word eluded her. Then: '—unusual,' she said lamely at last, for lack of anything better to say.

'Yes,' he said. 'She is.' He sounded tranquil and happy, and they sat for a while in silence as the sun began to sink into the sea.

'Jon.'

'Yes?'

'Where—' She hesitated and then plunged on, re-assured by his complete change of mood. 'Where did Sophia—'

'Not here,' he said at once. 'It was farther along the cliff going south to Sennen. The cliff is shallow and sandy in parts and during the last war they cut steps to link the path with the flat rocks below for some reason. I won't take you out there, don't worry.'

The sun disappeared beyond the rim of the world and the twilight began to gather beneath the red afterglow of the sky. They lingered for a while, both reluctant to leave the restless fascination of the sea, but in the end Jon led the way up the path back to the house. As they entered the driveway Marijohn came out to meet them, and Sarah wondered if she had been watching them from some vantage point upstairs as they walked up from the beach.

'Max phoned, Jon. He said you'd mentioned something about inviting him to Buryan for a day or two.'

'God, so I did! When I dined with him in London he said he would have to go down to Cornwall to visit a maiden aunt at Bude or Newquay or one of those huge tourist towns up the coast, and I told him there was a remote possibility that I might be revisiting Buryan at about this time . . . What a bloody nuisance! I don't want Max breezing up in his latest sports car with some goddamned woman on the seat beside him. Did he leave his phone number?'

'Yes, he was speaking from Bude.'

'Hell . . . I'd better invite him to dinner or something. No, that's not really very sociable – I suppose he'll have to stay the night . . . No, damn it, why should he turn up here and use Buryan as a base for fornication? I had enough of that in the past.'

'He may be alone.'

'What, Max? Alone? Don't be ridiculous! Max wouldn't know what to do with himself unless he had some woman with him all the time!'

'He didn't mention a woman.'

Jon stared. 'Do you want him here?'

'You made the gesture of having dinner with him in London and renewing the friendship. He's obviously content to forget. If you made a semi-invitation to him to visit Buryan, then I don't see how you can turn round now and tell him to go to hell.'

'I can do what I damn well like,' said Jon. He turned to Sarah. 'I've told you about Max, haven't I? Would you be cross if he came to dinner tomorrow and spent the night?'

'No, darling, of course not. I'd like to meet him.'

'All right, then. So be it.' He turned aside and then glanced at her. 'You go up to bed if you're tired. I won't be long. I'd better phone Max now while I still feel in a hospitable mood.'

'All right,' he said, glad of the excuse to go to bed, for she was by now feeling sleepy after the long journey followed by the long hours of sea air. 'I'll go on up. Goodnight, Marijohn.'

'Goodnight.' The mouth smiled faintly. When Sarah paused at the top of the stairs to glance back into the hall, she saw that the woman was still watching her, but even as she stopped abruptly on the landing, Marijohn merely smiled again and moved into the living room to join Jon.

The door closed softly behind her.

Sarah still stood motionless at the top of the stairs. Two minutes elapsed, then a third. Suddenly, without knowing the reason but moving through instinct, she padded softly back downstairs and tiptoed across the hall until she was standing outside the door of the drawing room.

Jon wasn't on the phone.

'There's only one thing that puzzles me,' she heard him say, and her cheeks were hot with shame as she stood eavesdropping on their conversation. 'And that's the anonymous phone call I had on my arrival in London, the call saying I'd killed Sophia. I still don't understand who it could have been. It must have been either Michael or Max or Eve, but why didn't they follow it up with something definite such as blackmail? It doesn't make sense.'

There was a long pause. And then Jon said sharply: 'What do you mean?'

'I tried to tell you before dinner when we were all having drinks.'

Another silence. Then: 'No,' said Jon. 'I don't believe it. It couldn't have been. You don't mean—'

'Yes,' said Marijohn quietly from far away. 'It was Justin.'


2


The sound of the piano drifted from the house and floated up the cliff path which led north to Cape Cornwall and Zennor Head. Justin's knowledge of classical music was adequate but not exceptional; he could not name the title of the Mozart composition.

He was just gathering his painting gear together and stowing it neatly in his canvas bag when below him he heard the music stop and then far away the distant click of a latch as the french windows into the garden opened. He paused, straining his eyes in the gathering dusk, and saw a figure leave the shadow of the rhododendrons and stop to scan the hillside.

Automatically, without hesitation, Justin stepped behind a rock.

Footsteps sounded faintly, growing louder with every second. Justin scowled at his painting gear, shoved it behind a boulder and sat down waiting, his eyes watching the night darken the sea. He didn't have to wait very long.

'Ah, there you are,' said Jon easily, stepping out of the darkness. 'I thought you might be up here. Have you been painting?'

'No, I went for a walk.' He stared out to sea, as his father sat down beside him on the long rock and took out a cigarette case.

'Justin, if I ask you an honest question will you try and give me an honest answer?'

The sea was a dark motionless pool, the surf distant flecks of grey. 'Of course,' said Justin politely, and felt the sweat begin to moisten his palms.

'Does this place remind you too much of your mother?'

'My mother?' His voice was untroubled, vaguely surprised, but his eyes didn't see the view before him any more, only the bowl of cherries long ago and the woman's voice saying indulgently, 'But you'll get so *fat*, Justin!' He cleared his throat. 'Yes, it does remind me of her from time to time. But not enough to matter. I'm glad I came back because it was like coming home after a long time abroad.'

'You were very fond of your mother, weren't you?'

Justin said nothing.

'I didn't realize,' said Jon, 'that you blamed me for her death.'

Horror ebbed through Justin in dark suffocating waves. Putting his hands palm downwards on either side of his thighs, he clasped the ridge of rock and stared blindly down at the dusty path beneath his feet.

'What happened, Justin?' said his father's voice gently. 'Why did you think I'd murdered her? Did you overhear something? Did you see us quarrel once when we didn't know you were there?'

He managed to shake his head.

'Then why?'

'I—' He shrugged his shoulders, glad of the darkness which hid his tears. 'I – I don't know.'

'But there must be some reason. You wouldn't have made the phone call unless there was some reason.'

'I hated you because I thought you hadn't written and because I thought you were going to pass through London without bothering to contact me. It – it doesn't matter now.' He took a deep breath, filling his lungs with the sea air. 'I'm sorry,' he whispered, the apology little more than a sigh. 'I didn't mean it.'

The man was silent, thinking.

'How did you know about the call?' said Justin suddenly. 'How did you know it was me?'

'Marijohn guessed.'

'But how did she know?'

'She says you are very like me and so she finds it easy to understand you.'

'I don't see how she can possibly understand.' He clasped the ridge of rock a little tighter. 'And I'm not like you at all.'

There was a silence.

'When I was ten,' said Jon, 'my father paid one of his rare visits to London. The news of his arrival was in the evening paper because the expedition had received a certain amount of publicity, and my mother spent the entire evening saying she was quite sure he wouldn't bother to come and see me. So, just out of interest, I sent a telegram to his hotel saying I was dead, and sat back to watch the results. I expect you can imagine what happened – complete chaos. My mother wept all over the house saying she couldn't think who could have been so cruel as to play such a dreadful practical joke, and my father without hesitation took me by the scruff of the neck and nearly belted the life out of me. I never forgave him for that beating; if he hadn't neglected me for years at a time I wouldn't have sent the telegram, so in effect he was punishing me for his own sins.'

Justin swallowed unevenly. 'But you didn't neglect me.'

'I did when you didn't answer my letters.' He leaned back, slumping against another rock and drew heavily on his cigarette so that the glowing tip wavered in the darkness. 'Justin, I have to know. Why did you think I'd killed your mother?'

'I – I knew she wasn't faithful to you.' He leaned forward, closing his eyes for a moment in a supreme effort to explain his emotions of ten years ago. 'I knew you quarrelled, and it gradually became impossible for me to love you both any more. It was like a war in which one was forced to choose sides. And I chose your side because you always had time for me and you were strong and kind and I admired you more than anyone else in the world. So when she died, I – I didn't blame you, I only knew it was just and right, and so I never said a word to anyone, not even to you because I thought it was the best way of showing my – my loyalty – that I was on your side. And then when you went away to Canada and I never heard from you again, I began to think I'd made the wrong judgement and gradually I grew to hate you enough to make that phone call when you came back to London.' He stopped. Far away below them the surf thudded dully on the shingle and the waves burst against the black cliffs.

'But Justin,' said Jon, 'I didn't kill your mother. It was an accident. You must believe that, because it's the truth.'

Justin turned his head slowly to face him. There was a long silence.

'Why did you think I'd killed her, Justin?'

The night was still, the two men motionless beneath the dark skies. For a moment Justin had a long searing desire to tell the truth, and then the ingrained convictions of ten years made him cautious and he shrugged his shoulders vaguely before turning away to stare out to sea.

'I suppose,' he said vaguely, 'because I knew you were always quarrelling and I felt you hated her enough to have pushed her to her death. I was only a child, muddled and confused. I didn't really know anything at all.'

Was it Justin's imagination or did his father seem to relax almost imperceptibly in relief? Justin's senses sharpened, his mind torn by doubts. In the midst of all his uncertainties he was aware of his brain saying very clearly: I must know. I can't let it rest now. I must find out the truth before I go away to Canada. Aloud he said: 'Shall we go back to the house? I'm getting rather cold as I forgot to bring a sweater and Marijohn and Sarah will be wondering where we are . . .'

3

It was late when Jon came to the bedroom, and Sarah, opening her eyes in the darkness, saw that the luminous hands of her clock pointed to half-past eleven. She waited, pretending to be asleep, and presently he slid into bed beside her and she felt his body brush lightly against her own. He sighed, sounding unexpectedly weary, and she longed to take him in her arms and say, 'Jonny, why didn't you tell me about the anonymous phone call? You told me about the dreadful rumours which circulated after Sophia's death, so why not tell me about the call? And after Marijohn had said the caller was Justin, why did you go through to the other room to the piano and start playing that empty stilted rondo of Mozart's which I know perfectly well you dislike? And why did you say nothing else to Marijohn and she say nothing to you? The conversation should have begun then, not ended. It was all so strange and so puzzling, and I want so much to understand and help . . .'

But she said nothing, not liking to confess that she had eavesdropped on their conversation by creeping back downstairs and listening at the closed door, and presently Jon was breathing evenly beside her and the chance to talk to him was gone.

When she awoke the piano was playing again far away downstairs and the sun was slanting sideways through the curtains into the room. She sat up. It was after nine. As she went down the corridor she heard the sound of the piano more clearly and she realized with a shaft of uneasiness that he was again playing Mozart. After a quick bath she dressed in a pair of slacks and a shirt and went tentatively downstairs to the music room.

He was playing the minuet from the thirty-ninth symphony, lingering over the full pompous chords and the mincing quavers so that the arrangement bore the faint air of a burlesque.

'Hullo,' she said lightly, moving into the room. 'I thought you didn't like Mozart? You never played his music at home.' She stooped to kiss the top of his head. 'Why have you suddenly gone Mozart-mad?' And then she suddenly glanced over her shoulder and saw that Marijohn was watching them from the window-seat.

Jon yawned, decided to abandon classical music altogether and began to play the Floyd Cramer arrangement of Hank Williams' *You Win Again*. 'Breakfast is ready and waiting for you, darling,' he said leisurely. 'Justin's in the dining room and he'll show you where everything is.'

'I see.' She went out of the room slowly and made her way towards the dining room; she felt baffled and ill-at-ease for a reason she could not define, and her uneasiness seemed to cast a shadow over the morning so that she started to feel depressed. She opened the dining-room door and decided that she didn't want much breakfast.

'Good morning,' said Justin. 'Did you sleep well?'

'Yes,' she lied. 'Very well.'

'Cereal?'

'No, thank you. Just toast.' She sat down, watching him pour out her coffee, and suddenly she remembered the conversation she had overheard the previous night and recalled that for some unknown reason Justin had anonymously accused Jon of murdering Sophia.

'Are you sure you wouldn't like a cooked breakfast?' he asked politely. 'There are sausages and eggs on the hot plate.'

'No, thank you.'

The piano started to play again in the distance, abandoning the American country music and reverting to classical territory with a Chopin prelude.

'Are you going painting this morning, Justin?' she asked, her voice drowning the noise of the piano.

'Perhaps. I'm not sure.' He glanced at her warily over *The Times* and then stirred his coffee with nonchalance. 'Why?'

'I thought I might try some painting myself,' she said, helping herself to marmalade. 'I was going to consult you about the best views for a landscape watercolour.'

'Oh, I see.' He hesitated, uncertain. 'What about my father?'

'It rather sounds as if he's going to have a musical morning.'

'Yes,' he said. 'I suppose it does.'

'Does Marijohn play the piano?'

'No, I don't think so.'

'Oh . . . the piano seems very well-tuned.'

'Yes,' said Justin. 'But then she knew he was coming.'

'She didn't know for certain till yesterday afternoon!'

He stared at her. 'Oh no, she knew a long while before that. She had a man up from Penzance to tune the piano last week.'

The shaft of uneasiness was so intense that it hurt. Sarah took a large sip of her coffee to steady her nerves and then started to spread the marmalade over the buttered toast.

From somewhere far away the piano stopped. Footsteps echoed in the corridor and the next moment Jon was walking into the room.

'How are you this morning, darling?' he said, kissing

her with a smile and then moving over to the window to glance out into the garden. 'You hardly gave me a chance to ask just now . . . What do you want to do today? Anything special?'

'Well, I thought I might paint this morning, but—'

'Fine,' he said. 'Get Justin to take you somewhere nice. Marijohn has shopping to do in Penzance and I've promised to drive her over in the car. You don't want to come to Penzance, do you? It'll be crammed with tourists at this time of year and much too noisy. You stay here and do just what you like.' He swung round to face her again, still smiling. 'All right?'

'Yes . . . all right, Jon.'

'Good! Look after her, Justin, and be on your best behaviour.' He moved to the door. 'Marijohn?'

There was an answering call from the kitchen and he closed the door noisily behind him before moving off down the corridor to the back of the house.

Justin cleared his throat. 'More coffee, Sarah?'

'No,' she said. 'No, thank you.'

He stood up, easing back his chair delicately across the floor. 'If you'll excuse me, I'll just go and assemble my painting gear. I won't be long. What time would you like to leave?'

'Oh . . . any time. Whenever you like.'

'I'll let you know when I'm ready, then,' he said and padded out of the room towards the hall.

She lingered a long time over the breakfast table before going upstairs to extract her paintbox and board from one of her suitcases. Jon called her from the hall just as she was pausing to tidy her hair.

'We're just off now, darling – sure you'll be all right?'

'Yes, I'm almost ready myself.'

'Have a good time!'

She sat listening to the closing doors, the quick roar of the engine bursting into life, the crunch of the tyres on the gravel, and then the sound of the car faded in the distance and she was alone. She went downstairs. In the drawing room she found Justin waiting, studiously reading *The*

*Times*, scrupulously dressed in the best English tailored casual clothes, but still managing to look like a foreigner.

'I don't know which way you'd like to go,' he said. 'We could take Marijohn's car and drive south to Sennen and Land's End, or north to Kenidjack Castle and Cape Cornwall. The views from the cliff out over the ruined mines of Kenidjack are good to paint.' He paused, waiting for her comment, and when she nodded he said politely, 'Would you care to go that way?'

'Yes, that sounds fine.'

They set off, not speaking much, and drove north along the main road to the crossroads beyond St Just where the left fork took them towards the sea to the mine workings of Kenidjack. At the end of the road high up on the cliffs they parked the car and started walking and scrambling over the hillside to the best view of the surrounding scenery. Below them the sea was a rich blue, shot with green patches near the offshore rocks, and there was no horizon. As the cliff path wound steeply above the rocks the great cliffs of Kenidjack and the withered stones of the old mine workings rose ahead of them, and Sarah saw that the light was perfect. When she sat down at last, gasping after the climb, she felt the excitement quicken within her as she gazed over the shimmering view before her eyes.

'I've brought some lemonade and some biscuits,' said Justin, modestly demonstrating his presence of mind. 'It's hot walking.'

They sat down and drank some lemonade in silence.

'It would be nice for a dog up here,' said Sarah after a while. 'All the space in the world to run and chase rabbits.'

'We used to have a dog. It was a sheepdog called Flip, short for Philip, after the Duke of Edinburgh. My mother, like many foreigners, loved all the royal family.'

'Oh.' She broke off a semi-circle of biscuit and looked at it with unseeing eyes. 'And what happened to Flip?'

'My mother had him put to sleep because he tore one of her best cocktail dresses to shreds. I cried all night. There was a row, I think, when my father came home.' He reached for his canvas bag and took out his painting book absentmindedly. 'I don't feel much like doing watercolours this morning. Perhaps I'll do a charcoal sketch and then work up a picture in oils later when I get home.'

'Can I see some of your paintings?'

He paused, staring at a blank page. 'You won't like them.'

'Why not?'

'They're rather peculiar. I've never dared show them to anyone except Marijohn, and of course she's quite different.'

'Why?' said Sarah. 'I mean, why is Marijohn different?'

'Well, she is, isn't she? She's not like other people . . . This is a watercolour of the cove – you probably won't recognize it. And this—'

Sarah drew in her breath sharply. He stopped, his face suddenly scarlet, and stared down at his toes.

The painting was a mass of greens and greys, the sky torn by storm clouds, the rocks dark and jagged, like some monstrous animal in a nightmare. The composition was jumbled and unskilled, but the savage power and sense of beauty were unmistakable. Sarah thought of Jon playing Rachmaninov. If Jon could paint, she thought, this is the type of picture he would produce.

'It's very good, Justin,' she said honestly. 'I'm not sure that I like it, but it's unusual and striking. Can you show me some more?'

He showed her three more, talking in a low hesitant voice, the tips of his ears pink with pleasure.

'When did you first start painting?'

'Oh, long ago . . . when I went to public school, I suppose. But it's just a hobby. Figures are my real interest.'

'Figures?'

'Maths – calculations – odds. Anything involving figures. That's why I started with an insurance firm in the City, but it was pretty boring and I hated the routine of nine till five.'

'I see,' she said, and thought of Jon talking of his own

first job in the City, Jon saying, 'God, it was boring! Christ, the routine!'

Justin was fidgeting with a stick of charcoal, edging a black square on the cover of his paint book. Even his restlessness reminded her of Jon.

'You're not a bit as I imagined you would be,' he said unexpectedly without looking up. 'You're very different from the sort of people who used to come down here to Buryan.'

'And very different from your mother too, I expect,' she said levelly, watching him.

'Oh yes,' he said, completely matter-of-fact. 'Of course.' He found a clean page in his book and drew a line with his stick of charcoal. 'My mother had no interests or hobbies, like painting or music. She used to get so bored, and the weekend parties were her main interest in life. My father didn't really want them. Sometimes he and I used to walk down to the Flat Rocks just to get away from all the people – but she used to revel in entertaining guests, drawing up exotic menus and planning midnight swimming parties in the cove.'

'There were guests staying here when she died, weren't there?'

'Yes, that's right.' He drew another charcoal line. 'But no one special. Uncle Max drove down from London and arrived on Friday evening. He had a new car which he enjoyed showing off and boasting about as soon as he arrived, but it really was a lovely thing. He took me for a ride in it, I remember . . . Have you met Uncle Max yet?'

'No, not yet.'

'He was fun,' said Justin. 'He and my father used to laugh a lot together. But my mother thought he was rather boring. She was never interested in any man unless he was good looking and was always bitchy to any woman who didn't look like the back end of a bus . . . Uncle Max was very ugly. Not that it mattered. He always had plenty of girlfriends. My parents used to play a game whenever they knew he was coming down – it was

103

called the Who-Will-Max-Produce-This-Time, and they used to try to guess what she would look like. The girl was always different each time, of course . . . During that last weekend they played the game on the morning before Max arrived and bet each other he would turn up with a petite redhead with limpid blue eyes. They were so cross when he turned up with a statuesque blonde, very slim and tall and elegant. She was called Eve. I didn't like her at all because she never took any notice of me the entire weekend.'

He closed the paintbook, produced a pair of sunglasses and leaned back against the grassy turf to watch the blue sky far above. 'Then Uncle Michael came down with Marijohn. They'd been in Cornwall on business, I think, and they arrived together at Buryan just in time for dinner. Uncle Michael was Marijohn's husband. I always called him Uncle, although I never called her Aunt . . . I don't know why. He was nice, too, but utterly different from Uncle Max. He was the sort of person you see on suburban trains in the rush-hour reading the law report in *The Times*. Sometimes he used to play French cricket with me on the lawn after tea . . . And then there was Marijohn.' He paused. 'To be honest, I never liked her much when I was small, probably because I always felt she was never very interested in me. It's different now, of course – she's been so kind to me during the past fortnight, and I've become very fond of her. But ten years ago . . . I think she was really only interested in my father at the time. Nobody else liked her except him, you see. Uncle Max always seemed to want to avoid being alone with her. Eve, the statuesque blonde, never seemed to find a word to say to her, and my mother naturally resented her because Marijohn was much more beautiful than she was. And Uncle Michael . . . no, I'd forgotten Uncle Michael. It was obvious he loved her. He kissed her in public and gave her special smiles – oh God, you know! The sort of thing you notice and squirm at when you're a small boy . . . So there they all were at Buryan on Friday evening, and twenty-four hours later my mother was dead.'

The sea murmured far away; gulls soared, borne aloft by the warm breeze.

'Was it a successful party?' Sarah heard herself say tentatively at last.

'Successful?' said Justin, propping himself up on one elbow to stare at her. 'Successful? It was dreadful! Everything went wrong from start to finish. Uncle Max quarrelled with the statuesque blonde – they had an awful row after breakfast on Saturday and she went and locked herself in her room. I've no idea what the row was about. Then when Uncle Max went to his car to work off his anger by driving, my mother wanted him to take her to St Ives to get some fresh shellfish for dinner; but my father didn't want her to go so there was another row. In the end my father went off to the Flat Rocks and took me with him. It was terrible. He didn't speak a word the entire time. After a while Marijohn came and my father sent me back to the house to find out when lunch would be ready. We had a maid help at Buryan in those days to do the midday cooking when there were guests. When I got back to the house I found Uncle Michael looking for Marijohn so I told him to go down to the Flat Rocks. After I'd found out about the lunch and stopped for elevenses I started off back again, but I met my father on his own coming back from the cliff path and he took me back to the house and started to play the piano. He played for a long time. In the end I got bored and slipped back to the kitchen to enquire about lunch again. I was always hungry in those days . . . And then Uncle Michael and Marijohn came back and shut themselves in the drawing room. I tried listening at the keyhole but I couldn't hear anything, and anyway my father found me listening and was cross enough to slap me very hard across the seat of my trousers so I scuttled down to the cove out of the way after that. My mother and Uncle Max didn't come back for lunch and Eve stayed in her room. I had to take a tray up to her and leave it outside the door, but when I came to collect it an hour later it hadn't been touched so I sat down at the top of the stairs and ate it myself. I didn't think anyone would mind . . .

'My mother and Uncle Max came back in time for tea. I was rather frightened, I think, because for some reason I expected my father to have the most almighty row with her, but—' He stopped, pulling up grass with his fingers, his eyes staring out to sea.

'But what?'

'But nothing happened,' said Justin slowly. 'It was most odd. I can't quite describe how odd it was. My father was playing the piano and Marijohn was with him, I remember. Uncle Michael had gone fishing. And absolutely nothing happened . . . After tea Uncle Max and my mother went down to the cove for a bathe, and still nothing happened. I followed them down to the beach but my mother told me to go away, so I walked along the shore till I found Uncle Michael fishing. We talked for a while. Then I went back and snatched some supper from the larder as I wasn't sure whether I'd be dining with the grown-ups or not. As it happened I was, but I didn't want to be hungry. Then Eve came downstairs, asking for Uncle Max and when I told her he'd gone swimming with my mother she walked off towards the cove.

'Dinner was at eight. It was delicious, one of my mother's best fish dishes, fillet of sole garnished with lobster and crab and shrimps . . . I had three helpings. I particularly remember because no one else ate at all. Eve had gone back to her room again, I believe, so that just left Max, Michael, Marijohn and my parents. My mother made most of the conversation but after a while she seemed bewildered and didn't talk so much. And then—' He stopped again, quite motionless, the palms of his hands flat against the springy turf.

'Yes?'

'And then Marijohn and my father started to talk. They talked about music mostly. I didn't understand a word of what they were saying and I don't think anyone else did either. At last my mother told me to go to bed and

I said I'd help with the washing-up – my usual dodge for avoiding bed, as I used to walk into the kitchen and straight out of the back door – but she wouldn't hear of it. In the end it was Uncle Michael who took me upstairs, and when we stood up from the dinner table, everyone else rose as well and began to filter away. The last thing I remember as I climbed the stairs and looked back into the hall was my father putting on a red sweater as if he was going out. Uncle Michael said to me: "What are you looking at?" and I couldn't tell him that I was wondering if my father was going out for a walk to the Flat Rocks and whether I could slip out and join him when everyone thought I was in bed . . . But Uncle Michael was with me too long, and I never had the chance. He read me a chapter of *Treasure Island* which I thought was rather nice of him. However, when I was alone, I lay awake for a long time, wondering what was going on, and listening to the gramophone in the music room below. It was an orchestral record, a symphony, I think. After a while it stopped. I thought: maybe he's going down now to the Flat Rocks. So I got out of bed and pulled on a pair of shorts and a pullover and my sand shoes. When I glanced out of the window, I saw it was late because the moon was high in the sky, and then I saw a shadow move out of the driveway and so I slipped out to follow him.

'It was rather spooky in the moonlight. I remember being frightened, especially when I saw someone coming up the path from the beach towards me and I had to hide behind a rock. It was Eve. She was breathing hard as if she'd been running and her face was streaked with tears. She didn't see me.'

He was silent, fingering the short grass, and after a while he took off his sunglasses and she saw his dark eyes had a remote, withdrawn expression.

'I went up the cliff path a long way, but he was always too far ahead for me to catch him up and the sea would have drowned my voice if I'd called out. In the end I had to pause to get my breath, and when I looked back I saw someone was following me. I was really scared then. I dived into a sea of bracken and buried myself as deep as I could. Presently the other person went by.'

A pause. Around them lay the tranquillity of the summer morning, the calm sea, the still sky, the quiet cliffs.

'Who was it?' said Sarah at last.

Another pause. The scene was effortlessly beautiful. Then: 'My mother,' said Justin. 'I never saw her again.'

## chapter 3

1

When they arrived back at Buryan they found the car standing in the drive but the house was empty and still. In the kitchen something was cooking in the oven and two saucepans simmered gently on the stove; on the table was a square of paper covered with clear printed writing.

'Justin!' called Sarah.

He was upstairs putting his painting gear away. 'Hullo?'

'Marijohn wants you to go up to the farm to get some milk.' She replaced the note absently beneath the rolling pin and wandered out into the hall just as he came downstairs to join her. 'I wonder where they are,' she said to him as he stopped to check how much money he had in his pockets. 'Do you think they've gone down to the beach for a stroll before lunch?'

'Probably.' He apparently decided he had enough money to buy the milk, and moved over to the front door. 'Do you want to come up to the farm?'

'No, I'll go down to the beach to meet them and tell them we're back.'

He nodded and stepped out into the sunshine of the drive. The gravel crunched beneath his feet as he walked away out of the gate and up the track to the farm.

After he had gone, Sarah followed him to the gate and

took the path which led down to the cove, but presently she stopped to listen. It was very still. Far away behind her she could still hear the faint rush of the stream as it tumbled past the disused water-wheel. But apart from that there was nothing, only the calm of a summer morning and the bare rock-strewn hills on either side of her. London seemed a thousand miles away.

Presently the path forked, one turning leading up on to the cliffs, the other descending into the cove. She walked on slowly downhill, and suddenly the sound of the sea was in her ears and a solitary gull was swooping overhead with a desolate empty cry, and the loneliness seemed to increase for no apparent reason. At the head of the beach she paused to scan the rocks but there was no sign of either Jon or his cousin and presently she started to climb uphill to meet the cliff path in order to gain a better view of the cove.

The tide was out; the rocks stretched far into the sea. She moved farther along the path round the side of the hill until presently, almost before she had realized it, the cove was hidden from her and the path was threading its way through the heather along the shallow cliff.

And below were the rocks. Hundreds of thousands of rocks. Vast boulders, gigantic slabs, small blocks of stone all tumbled at the base of the cliff and frozen in a jagged pattern as if halted by some invisible hand on their race into the sea.

The path forked again, one branch leading straight on along the same level, the other sloping downhill to the cliff's edge.

Sarah stopped.

Below her the rocks formed a different pattern. They were larger, smoother, flatter, descending in a series of levels to the waves far below. There were little inlets, all reflecting the blue sky, and the waves of the outgoing tide were gentle and calm as they washed effortlessly over the rocky shelves and through the seaweed lagoons.

It was then that she saw Jon's red shirt. It lay stretched out on a rock to dry beneath the hot sunshine, and as she strained her eyes to make sure she was not mistaken, she could see the pebbles weighting the sleeves to prevent the soft breeze from blowing it back into the water.

She moved on down the path to the cliff's edge. The cliff was neither very steep nor very high but she had to pause all the same to consider how she was going to scramble down. She saw the rough steps, but one was missing and another seemed to be loose; the sand around them bore no trace of footmarks to indicate that the others had come that way, and she guessed that it would be easy enough to find another way down. She stood among the heather, her glance searching the cliff's edge, and suddenly she realized she was frightened and angry and puzzled. This was where Sophia had died. The steps were the ones leading down the cliff and the rocks below were the Flat Rocks. And Jon had come back. He had come back deliberately to the very spot where his wife had been killed. Marijohn had taken him. It was her fault. If he had not wanted to see her again he wouldn't have dreamed of returning to Buryan. He had talked of how fond he was of the place and how much he wanted to see it again in spite of all that had happened, but it had been a lie. He had come back to see Marijohn, not for any other reason.

She sat down suddenly in the heather, her cheeks burning, the scene blurring before her eyes. But why, her brain kept saying, trying to be sensible and reasonable. Why? Why am I crying? Why do I feel sick and miserable? Why am I suddenly so convinced that Jon came back here not because he loved Buryan but solely because of his cousin? And why should it matter even if he did? Why shouldn't he be fond of his cousin? Am I jealous? Why am I so upset? Why, why, why?

Because Jon lied to me. He had planned this trip before he ever mentioned it to me – and Marijohn had the piano tuned because she knew he was coming.

Because he talks to Marijohn of things which he has never mentioned to me.

Because this morning he preferred Marijohn's company to mine . . .

She dashed away her tears, pressing her lips together in a determined effort to pull herself together. She was being absurd, worse than an adolescent. Trust was a basic element of marriage, and she trusted Jon. Everything was perfectly all right and she was imagining all kinds of dreadful possibilities without a grain of proof. She would go down to the rocks to meet them because there was no reason why she should be afraid of what she might find and because it was utterly ridiculous to sit on top of a cliff weeping. She would go right away.

She found a way down to the first shelf after a few minutes and started to scramble over towards the red shirt. In spite of herself she found she was thinking about Marijohn again. Marijohn wasn't like other people, Justin had said. Marijohn could talk to Jon when he was in the Distant Mood. She could cope with him when Sarah did not even begin to know how to deal with the situation. Marijohn . . .

The scramble over the rocks was more difficult than it had appeared from the cliff path above. She found herself making wide detours and after a time she had lost sight of the red shirt and realized she had been forced to move too far over to the left.

It was then that she heard Jon laugh.

She stopped, her heart thumping from the exertion of the scramble and from something else which she refused to acknowledge. Then, very slowly, despising herself for the subterfuge, she moved forward quietly, taking great care that she should see them before they should see her.

She suddenly realized she was very frightened indeed.

There was a large white rock ahead, its surface worn smooth by centuries of wind and rain. It was cold beneath her hot hands. She moved forward, still gripping the rock, and edged herself sideways until she could see round it to the rocks beyond.

Relief rushed through her in great warm overwhelming waves.

Beyond her was a small lagoon, similar to the ones she had seen from the cliff-path, and a flat ledge of rock sloped gently to the water's edge. Marijohn was lying on her back on the rocks enjoying the sunshine. She wore a white bathing costume and dark glasses which were tilted to the edge of her nose and as she gazed up at the blue sky far above her, her arms were behind her head, the palms of her hands pillowing her hair.

Jon, in black bathing trunks, was sitting by the water's edge some distance away from her and was paddling his feet idly in the still water of the lagoon.

Sarah was just about to call out to him and move out from behind the rock when Jon laughed again and splashed one foot lazily in the water.

Marijohn sat up slowly, propping herself on one elbow, and took off her sunglasses. Sarah couldn't see her face, only the back of her shining hair and the smooth tanned skin above the edge of her bathing costume.

'Why?' she said. She said nothing else at all, only the one monosyllable, and Sarah wondered what she meant and what she was querying.

Jon swivelled round, and Sarah instinctively withdrew behind the white boulder so that he would not see her.

'I don't know,' she heard him say uneasily. 'There's no reason why I should feel so happy.'

'I know.'

There was a silence. When Sarah had the courage to look at them again she saw that Jon was standing up, looking out to sea and that although Marijohn was also standing up she was still several paces away from him.

They were motionless.

The sea lapped insistently at the rocks beyond the lagoon; a wave broke into the pool and the spray began to fly as the tide turned. Nothing else happened. There was no reason at all why suddenly Sarah should feel aware of panic. And as she stood rigid with fear, hardly able to breathe, she heard Jon say quietly to his cousin, 'Why don't you come to Canada?'

There was a pause. Everything seemed to cease except the sea. Then: 'My dear Jon, what on earth would be the point of that?'

'I don't know,' he said, and he sounded strangely lost and baffled. 'I don't know.'

'We've been into all this before, Jon.'

'Yes,' he said emptily. 'We've been into all this before.'

'After your wife was dead and my marriage was in ruins we went into it in detail right here at Buryan.'

'For God's sake!' he shouted suddenly. 'For God's sake don't talk of that scene with Sophia again! Christ Almighty—'

'Jon, darling.'

And still they stood apart from one another, he slumped against a rock, his hands tight, white fists at his sides, she motionless by the water's edge, the sun shining full on her hair.

'Marijohn,' he said, 'I know we've never, never mentioned this in words either now after I met you again or ten years after it all happened, but—'

'There's no need to mention it,' she said swiftly. 'I understand. There's no need to talk about it.'

'But . . . oh God, why? Why, Marijohn? Why, why, why?'

She stared at him, still motionless, but somehow that strange stillness was lost as if a spell had been broken and the mystery of the quiet scene was shattered.

She doesn't understand him, thought Sarah suddenly. She's going to have to ask him what he means.

And somehow the knowledge was a victory which she could neither understand nor explain.

'Yes,' said Jon. 'Why? Why did you have to kill Sophia?'

A wave thudded against the rocks and exploded in a cloud of spray so that the lagoon was no longer still and peaceful but a turmoil of boiling surf. And after the roar of the undertow had receded came a faint shout from the cliff high above them, and Sarah saw Justin standing on the top of the cliffs waving to attract their attention.

She drew farther out of sight at once so that he wouldn't see her, and began to scramble back over the rocks to find a hiding place before the others started to retrace their steps to the cliff path. When she eventually sank down to rest behind a pile of boulders her breath was coming in gasps which hurt her lungs, and her whole body was trembling with the shock. She sat there numbly for a while, and then the tide began to surge across the rocks towards her as it ate its way greedily inland to the cliffs, and she knew she would have to go back.

Moving very slowly, she stood up and began to stumble blindly back towards the cliff path to Buryan.


2


When Justin returned from the farm with the milk he met the postman pushing his bicycle up the track from Buryan and they paused for a moment to talk to one another.

'Only two letters today,' said the Cornishman placidly, extracting a large handkerchief to mop his forehead. 'One for Mrs Rivers, t'other for yourself. Lor', it's hot today, ain't it! Makes a change, I say. Too much rain lately.'

Justin agreed politely.

Presently when he reached the house he put the milk down on the hall table and stopped to examine the mail. The letter to Marijohn was postmarked London, the address typewritten. Perhaps it was from Michael Rivers' office. Rivers, Justin knew, still handled Marijohn's legal affairs.

The other envelope was white and square and covered by a large level handwriting which he did not recognize. *J. Towers, Esq*, the writer had scrawled, *Buryan, St Just, Penzance, Cornwall*. The postmark was also London.

Justin fumbled with the flap of the envelope, wondering who could be writing to him. The sensation of puzzled interest was pleasant and when he pulled the single sheet of white paper from the close-fitting envelope he sat down on the stairs before opening the folded slip of paper to see the signature.

The signature was very short. Only three letters. Someone had merely written *Eve* in that same large level handwriting, but even as he realized with a jolt that the letter wasn't meant for him his glance travelled to the top of the paper automatically.

*Dear Jon*, Eve had written. *Had dinner with Max in London last week. He wanted to know why you had asked him where I lived and why you had sounded so interested in me. We ended up by having a long talk about that time ten years ago, and in the end he told me you were back at Buryan and that he had decided to come down and see you. Just thought I'd drop you a line to warn you to be pretty damn careful, as he knows more than you think. If you're interested in hearing more about this, why don't you come and see me any time from Saturday onwards – address and phone number above. I'm staying in St Ives for a few days and won't be going back to town till Tuesday. Eve.*

Justin read the letter three times. Then, very carefully, he replaced the sheet of notepaper in its neat white envelope and tucked the letter deep into the privacy of his wallet.


3


When Sarah reached the house at last there was a silver-grey Rolls-Royce in the driveway and the sound of laughter floated from the open windows of the drawing room towards her on the still air. She slipped into the house by the side door and managed to creep up to her room without being seen. Sitting down in front of the dressing table she stared into the mirror for one long moment before fumbling with the jars of make-up, and then she stood up blindly and moved into the bathroom to wash the tear stains from her face. When she came back to the dressing table Jon was on the lawn below and calling something over his shoulder.

'. . . imagine what can have happened to her,' she heard him say. 'Are you sure she said she was going down to the cove, Justin?'

She could not hear Justin's reply. She stood by the

window shielded by the curtain and watched Jon as he began to move forward again across the lawn.

'. . . better go and find her in case she's got lost . . .' His voice tailed away and presently she found her view of him was blurring before her eyes until she could scarcely see.

She sat down again at the dressing table.

'Of course she's not lost,' Marijohn's voice said clearly from the lawn below, sounding surprisingly close at hand. 'She's probably gone for a walk before lunch.'

'Another walk?' said a man's unfamiliar drawl, sounding amused. 'God, she must be an Amazon! No normal woman would spend the morning toiling up the cliffs at Kenidjack and then toiling over some more cliffs around Buryan for a preprandial stroll! Jon never told me he'd married one of those keen outdoor types.'

'He hasn't,' said Marijohn briefly. 'She's not.'

'Thank God for that! I had a sudden hideous vision of a hearty female with muscular shoulders and tombstone teeth . . . What's she like? Is she pretty? Jon said that physically she was just like Sophia.'

'Justin,' said Marijohn to the room behind her. 'Would you—'

'He's gone. He slipped out a second ago when I was making my anti-Amazon speech. Well, tell me about Sarah, Marijohn. Is she—'

'You'll meet her soon enough.'

'Is Jon very much in love with her?'

'He married her.'

'Yes, I know. I was very surprised. She must be damn good.'

'Good?'

'In bed. Can I have another drink?'

'Of course.'

There was a pause, the stillness of a hot summer morning.

'And you,' said Max Alexander. 'You, I'm surprised you never married again. What happened after the divorce? Did you go abroad? I never saw you in London.'

'I worked in Paris for a while.'

'God, that sounds glamorous!'

'It was extremely boring. I could only endure it for a year.'

'And then?'

'I came back. Do you want some ice in your drink?'

'No, no, I can't bear this American fetish of loading every drink with ice . . . Thanks . . . I see. And what did you do when you returned?'

'Nothing special.'

'Did you come back here?'

'Not straight away.'

'Lord, it's strange coming back! Didn't it seem strange to you?'

'No, why should it?'

'Why should it?'

'Yes, why should it? Buryan has many happy memories for me.'

'You're not serious, of course.'

'Perfectly. Why shouldn't I be?'

'Oh.'

Another pause. A gull drifted overhead, its wings outstretched, its neck craning towards the sun.

'I must say,' said Max Alexander, 'I never thought Jon would come back here, least of all with his new wife. Does he ever speak of Sophia?'

'Never.'

'He's closed the door, as it were, on that part of his past?'

'Why do you suppose he asked you down here?'

'I was hoping,' said Alexander, 'that you could tell me.'

'I'm not sure I quite understand you.'

'No? Hell, Jon was crazy about Sophia, wasn't he? Any husband would have been. With a woman like that—'

'Sophia no longer exists. Jon's made a new life for himself and Sophia's memory is nothing to him now. Nothing at all.'

'Yet he's married someone who's physically and sexually—'

'Men often prefer one type of looks in a woman. It means nothing at all. Besides there's more to love than merely a sexual relationship or a physical attraction.'

'That *is* the common delusion, I believe.'

'You think any relationship between a man and a woman is basically sexual?'

'Of course it is! It's impossible for a man and a woman to have an intimate relationship with no sex in it whatsoever!'

'I think,' said Marijohn, 'we've somehow succeeded in wandering from the point.'

'But don't you agree with me?'

'Agree with you? What am I supposed to be agreeing with?'

'That it's impossible for a man and a woman to have an intimate relationship with no sex in it whatsoever.'

'That would depend upon the man and woman.'

'On the contrary I'd say it depended entirely on their sexual capacity! Take Jon for instance. He's married twice and had a lot of women but no woman's going to interest him unless she attracts him physically.'

'Why shouldn't Jon have his share of sex? Most men need it and get it so why shouldn't he? And why should his "sexual capacity", as you call it, affect any other relationship he might have? And what's so special about sex anyway? It often has nothing whatsoever to do with real intimacy. Why talk of it as if it were the beginning and end of everything? Sex is so often nothing but point-less futility.'

Alexander hesitated slightly before he laughed. The hesitation made the laughter sound a little uncertain.

'For pointless futility it certainly seems to be doing very well!' And when she didn't answer he said easily, 'That sounds very much a woman's point of view, Marijohn.'

'Perhaps,' she said flatly, not arguing, her footsteps moving into the house. 'I must go and see how burnt the lunch is getting. Excuse me.'

'Of course.'

There was silence. Sarah found she was still clutching the edge of the dressing table stool. She glanced into the mirror. Her dark eyes stared back at her, her dark hair straggling untidily from its position, her mouth unsmiling, devoid of make-up. She reached automatically for her lipstick.

I want to go, she thought; please, Jon, let's go – let's go anywhere so long as it's somewhere far from this place. Let's go now. If only I could go . . .

She started to re-apply her powder.

I don't want to meet Max. I don't care if he was your friend once, Jon; I don't want to meet him because I can't bear men who talk of women and sex in bored amused voices as if they've seen all there is to see and know all there is to know. I want to go, Jon, now, this minute. If only we could go . . .

She undid her hair and let it fall to her shoulders before brushing it upwards again and picking up her comb.

And most of all, Jon, I want to go away from your cousin because she doesn't like me, Jon. I know she doesn't, and I hate her, no matter how hard I try to pretend I don't . . . I hate her and I'm afraid of her although I don't know why, and Jon, can't we go soon, Jon, because I want to escape . . . It's not just because she dislikes me – in fact 'dislike' is the wrong word. She despises me. You won't believe she despises me, Jon, because she's always been so kind to me ever since we set foot in this house, but she does, I know she does, because I can feel it. She despises me just as she despised Sophia.

She put down her comb and examined the little jar of liquid eye-shadow.

Better not to think of Sophia.

But all those lies, Jon, all those lies. And you swore to me her death was an accident. You lied and lied and lied for Marijohn . . .

Oh, God, I want to go, I want to get away. Please Jon, take me away from this place because I'm frightened and I want to escape . . .

She went out into the corridor. It was cool there, and the banister was smooth against her hot palm. She walked downstairs, crossed the hall and entered the drawing room.

The man turned as she came in. He turned to face her and she saw all she had not seen when she had listened to his conversation earlier – the humorous mouth, the wide blue eyes that for some reason seemed very honest and trusting, the broken nose, the traces of plastic surgery which stretched from his left temple to the jawbone. There were lines about his mouth. They were deep lines which would get deeper with time, but apart from this there was no other indication that he had suffered and known pain. He looked older than Jon, but not much older. The suffering hadn't aged him, as it would have aged some men, nor had it given him the worn, tired appearance of exhaustion.

She stood staring, suddenly at a loss for words. It was some seconds before she realized that he too was experiencing difficulty in choosing his opening remarks.

'Good Lord!' he said at last, and his blue eyes were wide with honest surprise. 'But you're young! I thought you were Jon's age. No one ever told me you were young.'

She smiled awkwardly. 'Not as young as all that!'

He smiled too, not saying anything, his eyes still faintly astonished, and she wondered what he was thinking and whether she was as like Sophia as he had imagined she would be. 'Where's Jon?' she said, for lack of anything else to say.

'He went out to look for you, as a matter of fact.'

'Did he? I must have just missed him.' She helped herself to a cigarette and he gave her a light. 'When did you arrive?'

'About half an hour ago. Justin was the only one at home so he went down to to the cove to tell everyone I'd arrived. Apparently I wasn't expected to lunch . . . Jon tells me you're both going over to see some old friends of his in Penzance this afternoon?'

'Are we? I mean—' She blushed and laughed. 'I haven't

seen Jon since breakfast. He and Marijohn went into Penzance this morning to do some shopping—'

'Ah, he must have arranged something when he was over there . . . I was just wondering what I could do with myself while you're out. Marijohn says uncompromisingly that she has "things to do" and Justin is taking her car to go over to St Ives for some reason, so I'll be on my own. Maybe I'll have a swim or a paddle, depending on how Spartan I feel. I never usually bathe except in the Mediterranean . . . Ah, here's Jon! He must have decided you hadn't lost yourself after all . . . Jon!' He moved out through the open french windows on to the lawn beyond, his arm raised in greeting, and when he next spoke she heard the hard careless edge return to his voice. 'Jon, why didn't you tell me how young and pretty your new wife is?'


4

'I don't want to go,' she said to Jon. 'Would it matter awfully if I didn't come? I feel so tired.'

The bedroom was quiet, shadowed by the Venetian blinds.

'Just as you like,' said Jon. 'I happened to meet this fellow when I was in Penzance this morning – I used to do a certain amount of business with him in the old days. When he invited us over this afternoon for a spin in his motor-boat, I thought it would be the sort of invitation you'd enjoy.'

'I – I'm sorry, Jon.'

'Of course you must rest if you're tired. Don't worry.' He stooped to kiss her on the forehead. 'Perhaps Marijohn will come,' he said presently. 'I'll ask her.'

'She told Max she was going to be very busy this afternoon.'

'That was probably merely a polite way of excusing herself from entertaining him. I'll see what she says.' He turned to go.

'Jon, if you don't want to go alone, I'll—'

'No, no,' he said. 'You lie down and rest. That's much the most important thing. But I'll have to go over and see this fellow and his new motor-boat – I've committed myself. If Marijohn doesn't want to come I'll go alone.'

She waited upstairs in misery as he went down to talk with Marijohn, but when he came back she heard that Marijohn had decided against going with him.

'I'll be back around six,' he said, kissing her again before he left the room. 'Sleep well.'

But she did not sleep. Presently she dressed, putting on slacks and a shirt, and went downstairs. Justin had gone off to St Ives and Marijohn was relaxing on the swing-seat in the garden with some unanswered correspondence and a pen. Alexander was nowhere to be seen.

In order that Marijohn should not see her, Sarah left the house by the back door and moved through the back gate on to the hillside behind the house. Five minutes later she was by the beach of the cove.

Alexander wasn't paddling. He had taken off his shirt to bask in the heat and eased off his shoes but he was sitting on one of the rocks facing the sea, a book in his hands, a pair of sunglasses perched insecurely on the bridge of his nose. As she moved forward and began to scramble towards him he caught sight of her and waved.

'Hullo,' he said when she was in earshot. 'I thought you were resting.'

'I decided I didn't want to waste such a lovely afternoon.' She ignored his outstretched hand and climbed up on to the rock beside him. The tide was still rising and before them the surf thundered among the boulders and reefs in great white clouds of spray.

'I see,' said Alexander. His skin was already tanned, she noticed. He had probably been abroad that summer. His chest and shoulders were muscular but were beginning to run to fat. She thought of Jon's body suddenly, remembered the powerful lines and hard flesh and strong muscles, and suddenly she wondered how often Max Alexander had been compared with his friend in the past and how often the comparison had been unfavourable.

'Tell me about yourself,' Alexander said sociably, closing the book and fumbling for a cigarette. 'How on earth did you come to be in a god-forsaken country like Canada?'

She started to talk. It was difficult at first for she was shy but gradually she began to relax and speech came more easily. He helped her by being relaxed himself.

'I've been mixed up in motor racing most of my adult life,' he said casually when she asked him a question about his hobbies. 'It's a hell of a thing to get mixed up in. It's all right if you want to play chess with death and have half your face burnt off and get kicks out of a fast car and the smell of scorched rubber, but otherwise it's not much fun. I've more or less had enough.'

'What are you going to do now, then?'

'Depends on how long I live,' he said laconically. 'I have heart trouble. I'll probably go on doing damn all and paying my taxes until I drop dead, I should think.'

She wasn't sure how she should reply. Perhaps she was beginning to sense that he wasn't nearly as relaxed and casual as he appeared to be.

'It must be strange for you to come back here,' she said suddenly after a pause. 'Are you glad you came?'

He swivelled his body slightly to face her, and the sun shone straight into the lenses of his dark glasses so that she could not see his expression.

'It's nice to see Jon again,' he said at last. 'We'd drifted right apart. I was rather surprised when he rang up and said he wanted to bury the hatchet . . . There was a hatchet, you know. Or did you?'

'Yes,' she said, lying without hesitation. 'Jon told me.'

'Did he? Yes, I suppose he would have.' He fidgeted idly with the corner of his book. 'When I knew he was going back to Buryan, I – well, quite frankly I was astonished. So astonished that I couldn't resist coming down here when the opportunity arose to find out why he'd come back.' There was a little tear in the dust jacket of his book, and he tore the paper off at right angles so that he had a small yellow triangle of paper in his hand. 'I didn't know Marijohn was living here.'

'Jon was very anxious to see her before he returned to Canada.'

'Yes,' said Alexander. 'I dare say he was.'

'Jon told me all about it.'

He looked at her sharply again. 'About what?'

'About himself and Marijohn.'

'I didn't know,' said Alexander, 'that there was anything to tell.'

'Well . . .' She was nonplussed suddenly, at a loss for words. 'He said how fond of her he was as they'd spent some of their childhood together.'

'Oh, I see.' He sat up a little and yawned unconcernedly. 'Yes, they're very fond of each other.' For a moment she thought he wasn't going to say any more and then without warning he said abruptly: 'What do you think of Marijohn?'

'I—'

'Sophia hated her; did Jon tell you that as well? To begin with, of course, it didn't matter because Jon worshipped the ground Sophia walked on and for Sophia the world was her oyster. She could say, do, want anything she wished. A pleasant position for a woman to be in, wouldn't you think? Unfortunately Sophia didn't know how lucky she was – she had to abuse her position until one day she discovered she hadn't any position left and her worshipping husband was a complete stranger to her.' He drew on his cigarette for a moment and watched the surf pound upon the rocks a few yards away before being sucked back into the ocean with the roar of the undertow. 'But of course – I was forgetting. Jon's told you all about that.'

The waves were eating greedily across the shingle again, swirling round the rocks.

'I felt sorry for Sophia,' said Alexander after a while. 'I think I was the only person who did. Marijohn despised her; Jon became totally indifferent to her; Michael – well,

God, a conventional pillar of society such as Michael would always look down his nose at a sexy little foreign girl like Sophia who had no more moral sense than a kitten! But I felt sorry for her. It was terrible at the end, you know. She couldn't understand it – she didn't know what to do, I mean, Christ, what was there to do? There was nothing there, you see, nothing at all. It wasn't as if she'd caught Jon in bed with someone else. It wasn't as if he'd thrashed her with a horsewhip twice a day. There was nothing tangible, nothing you could pinpoint, nothing you could grasp and say, "Look, this is what's wrong! Stop it at once!" She discovered quite suddenly that her loving husband didn't give a damn about her, and she didn't even know how it had happened.'

'Maybe she deserved it. If she was constantly unfaithful to Jon—'

'Oh God, it wasn't like that! She behaved like a spoiled child and grumbled and sulked and complained, but she wasn't unfaithful. She flirted at her weekend parties and made Jon go through hell, time and again with her tantrums and whims, but she wasn't unfaithful. What chance did she have to be unfaithful stuck down here at the back of beyond? And anyway underneath her complaints and sulks she probably found Jon attractive enough and it was pleasant to be adored and worshipped all the time. It was only when she realized that she'd lost him that she was unfaithful in an attempt to win him back.'

Sarah stared at him.

'And he didn't give a damn. She flaunted her infidelity and he was indifferent. She was sexy as hell in an attempt to seduce him back to her bed and he was still indifferent. It was a terrible thing for a woman like Sophia whose only weapons were her sex and her femininity. When she found both were worthless she had nothing – she'd reached the end of the road. And still he didn't care.'

'He—' The words stuck in Sarah's throat. 'He must have cared a little. If he'd loved her so much—'

'He didn't give a damn.' He threw away his cigarette and the glowing tip hissed as it touched the seaweed pool below. 'I'll tell you exactly what happened so that you can see for yourself.

'I came down to Buryan that weekend with a friend called Eve. We were having an affair, as I'm sure Jon has told you, but at that particular stage the affair was wearing rather thin. We arrived on Friday evening, spent an unsatisfactory night together and quarrelled violently after breakfast the next morning. Not a very bright start to a long weekend by the sea! After the quarrel she locked herself in her room or something equally dramatic, and I went out to my car with the idea of going for a spin along the coast road to St Ives or over the hills to Penzance. I find driving soothing after unpleasant scenes.

'I was just getting into the car when Sophia came out. God, I can see her now! She wore skin-tight black slacks and what Americans would call a "halter" – some kind of flimsy arrangement which left her midriff bare, and exposed an indecent amount of cleavage. Her hair was loose, waving round her face and falling over her shoulders in the style which Brigitte Bardot made famous. "Ah Max!" she said, smiling brilliantly. "Are you going into St Ives? Take me with you!" She made it sound so exactly like an invitation to bed that I just stood and gaped, and then as I started to stammer "Of course" or something mundane, Jon came out of the front door and called out to her, but she took no notice, merely sliding into the passenger seat and wriggling into a comfortable position.

'"Sophia," he said again, coming over to the car. "I want to talk to you."

'She just shrugged idly and said she was going into St Ives with me to buy shellfish for dinner that night. Then Jon turned on me. "Did you invite her," he said furiously, "or did she invite herself?"

'"Jon darling," said Sophia before I could reply, "you're making *su-uch* an exhibition of yourself." She had the habit of drawing out some syllables and thickening her foreign accent sometimes when she was annoyed.

'Jon was shaking with rage. I could only stand and

watch him helplessly. "*You're* the one who's making an exhibition of yourself!" he shouted at her. "Do you think I didn't notice how you did your damnedest to flirt with Max last night? Do you think Eve didn't notice? Why do you think she and Max quarrelled this morning? I'll not have my wife behaving like a whore whenever we have guests down here. Either you get out of that car and stop acting the part of a prostitute or I'll put a stop to your weekend parties once and for all."

"'Look, Jon—" I tried to say, but he wouldn't listen to me. I did my best to pour oil on troubled waters, but I was wasting my breath.

"'That's ridiculous!" cried Sophia, and she was as furious as hell too. "Your stupid jealousy! I want to get some shellfish for dinner and Max is going to St Ives – why shouldn't he give me a lift there? Why shouldn't he?"

'Well, of course, put like that it did make it seem as if Jon was making a fuss about nothing. But there she sat in the front seat of my car, her hair tumbling over her shoulders, her breasts all but spilling out of that scanty halter, her mouth sulky – Christ, any husband would have had the excuse for thinking or suspecting or fearing all kinds of things! "You'd better stay, Sophia," I said. "I'll get your shellfish for you. Tell me what you want."

"'No," she said. "I'm coming with you."

'It was extremely embarrassing. I didn't know what to do. She was looking at Jon and he was looking at her, and I was just trying to work out how I could tactfully make my escape when there was the sneeze from the porch. Jon and I swung round. It was the child. He'd been standing listening, I suppose, poor little bastard, and wondering what the hell was going on. After he sneezed, he turned to sidle indoors again but Jon called out to him and he came sheepishly out into the sunlight.

"'Come on, Justin," Jon said, taking him by the hand. "We're going down to the Flat Rocks."

'He didn't say anything else. He took the child's hand in his and the child looked up at him trustingly, and the next moment they were walking across the lawn away from us and we were alone.

'So we went to St Ives. It was a hot day, rather like this one, and after we'd bought the shellfish we paused at one of the coves down the coast to bathe. I've forgotten what the cove was called. It was very small and you could only reach it when the tide was out a certain distance. No one else was there.

'I don't make excuses for what happened. I made love with my best friend's wife, and there can be no excuse for that – no valid excuse. Of course it was Sophia who suggested the swim, and Sophia who knew the cove, and Sophia who took off her clothes first and Sophia who made the first physical contact with her hands, but what if it was? I suppose if I'd had half an ounce of decency I could have said no all along the line, but I didn't. I suppose I'm not really a particularly decent person. And there were other reasons . . . Jon had often taken things of mine, you see. I'd had girls and then as soon as they saw Jon they weren't interested in me any more. He was interested in motor racing for a while, and when I introduced him to the right contacts it turned out that he could drive better than I could and the contacts became more interested in him than in me. Oh, there were other situations too, other memories . . . It wasn't Jon's fault. It was just the way he was made. But I built up quite a store of resentment all the same, a long list of grudges which I barely acknowledged even to myself. When his wife was mine for the taking, I never even hesitated.

'We arrived back at Buryan at about four o'clock in the afternoon. Everything was very still. At first we thought everyone must be out, and then we heard the piano.

'"He's crazy," said Sophia indolently. "Imagine playing the piano indoors on a beautiful afternoon like this!" And she walked down the corridor and opened the door of the music room. "Jon—" she began and then stopped. I walked down to see why she had stopped, and then I saw that Jon wasn't alone in the music room. Marijohn was with him.

'I can't describe how strange it was. There was no reason why it should be strange at all. Marijohn was sitting on the window-seat, very relaxed and happy, and Jon was on the piano stool, casual and at ease. They weren't even within six feet of each other.

'"Hullo," said Marijohn to Sophia, and her eyes were very blue and clear and steady. "Did you manage to get the shellfish in St Ives?" I'll always remember the way she said that because I saw then for the first time how much she despised Sophia. "Did you manage to get the shellfish in St Ives?"

'And Sophia said, "Where's Michael?"

'Marijohn said she had no idea. And Jon said, "Didn't he go fishing?" And they laughed together and Jon started to play again.

'We might as well not have existed.

'"I'm going down to the cove with Max," said Sophia suddenly.

'"Oh yes?" Jon said, turning a page of music with one hand.

'"Don't get too sunburnt," said Marijohn. "The sun's hot today, isn't it, Jon?"

'"Very," said Jon, and went on playing without looking up.

'So we went out. Sophia was furious although she said nothing. And then when we arrived at the beach we found the child was following us, and she vented her temper on him, telling him to go away. Poor little bastard! He looked so lost and worried. He wandered off along the shore and was soon lost from sight amongst the rocks.

'We had a swim and after that Sophia started to talk. She talked about Marijohn, and in the end she started to cry. "I hate it when she comes here," she said. "I hate it. Nothing ever goes right when she comes." And when I asked what Marijohn did, she couldn't explain and only cried all the more. There was nothing, you see, that was what was so baffling. There was nothing there to explain . . .

'I was just trying to console her and take her in my arms

when the worst thing possible happened – Eve had heard I was back from St Ives and had come down from her room to look for me. Of course she found me in what I believe is generally termed a "compromising" position, so there was another row and she went back to the house. She didn't come down to dinner that evening.

'Dinner was very unnerving. Sophia had been supervising the cooking in the kitchen so we didn't come into the dining room together, but it was obvious she had decided to act the part of the good hostess and be bright and talkative, pretending nothing had happened at all. I responded as best I could and Michael joined in from time to time, I remember. But Marijohn and Jon never said a word. Gradually, after a while, their silence became oppressive. It's very difficult to describe. One was so conscious somehow of their joint silence. If one had been silent and the other talkative it wouldn't have mattered, but it was their joint silence which was so uncanny. In the end Sophia fell silent too, and I could think of nothing more to say, and Michael was quiet. And it was then, when the whole room was silent, that Marijohn started to speak.

'She talked exclusively to Jon. They discussed music, I remember, a topic which was open to no one but themselves because no one else knew much about it. They talked to one another for ten minutes, and then suddenly they were silent again and I was so taut with uneasiness I could scarcely move my knife and fork. Presently Sophia told the child to go to bed. He made rather a fuss, I remember, and didn't want to go, but in the end Michael took him upstairs. I remember having the strong impression that Michael wanted to escape . . . We all stood up from the table then and Jon went out into the hall. He put on a red sweater and Sophia said: "You're not going out, are you?" and he said, "Marijohn and I are going for a stroll down to the cove."

'So they went out. They weren't gone too long, only ten minutes or so and then they came back and went to the music room. Presently Michael came downstairs and went into the music room to join them. I was in the kitchen with Sophia helping her wash up, but when they came back she went to the door to listen. The gramophone was playing. She said, "I'm going in to see what's happening," and I said, "Leave them alone – come out with me for a while. Michael's with them anyway." And she said, "Yes, I want to hear what he says." I told her there was no reason why he should say anything at all, but she said she still wanted to see what was happening.

'We were in the hall by then. She said she would meet me later in the evening – "somewhere where we can be alone," she said, "somewhere where we can talk and not be overheard. I'll meet you down by the Flat Rocks at ten o'clock." When I agreed, she went into the music room and I was alone in the hall. I can remember the scene so clearly. The gramophone stopped a moment later. There was no light in the hall, just the dusk from the twilight outside, and Jon's discarded red sweater lay across the oak chest by the door like a pool of blood.

'I went out soon after that. I walked down to the cove and watched the sea for a while, and then I walked back to the house to get a sweater as it was rather colder than I'd anticipated. After that I went out again, taking the cliff path which led out to the Flat Rocks, and about quarter of an hour later I was waiting by the water's edge.'

He stopped. The tide roared over the shingle.

'I waited some time,' he said, 'but of course Sophia never came. I heard the scream just as I was wondering what could have happened to her, but although I moved as fast as I could she was dead when I reached her.'

He stopped again. Presently he took off his sunglasses and she saw the expression in his eyes for the first time.

'Poor Sophia,' he said slowly; 'it was a terrible thing to happen. I always felt so sorry for Sophia . . .'

## chapter 4

1

Justin was in St Ives by the time the church clock near the harbour was tolling three that afternoon. Holiday-makers thronged the streets, spilling over the pavements to make driving hazardous. The pedestrians ruled St Ives, dictating to the cars that crawled through the narrow streets, and Justin was relieved when he reached the freedom of the car park at last and was able to switch off the engine. He got out of the car. The air was salt and fresh, the sun deliciously warm. As he walked up the steps along the town wall the gulls wheeled around the fishing boats in the harbour and the houses clustered on the rising ground of the peninsula were white-walled and strangely foreign beneath that hot southern sky.

Justin reached the harbour, turned up Fish Street and then turned again. There was an alley consisting of stone steps leading to a higher level, and at the top was another narrow cobbled lane slanting uphill. The door marked Five was pale blue, and a climbing plant trailed from the corner of the windows to meet above the porch.

He rang the bell.

A woman answered the door. She had a London accent and London clothes and a paint smear across the back of her left hand.

'Is Eve in?' said Justin hesitantly, suddenly nervous.

'Ah yes, you're expected, aren't you? Come on in. She's upstairs – second door on the right.'

'Thank you.' The hall was a mass of brass and copper ornaments. His hand gripped the hand rail of the stairs tightly and then he was walking quietly up the steps, neither pausing nor looking back. The woman was watching him. He could feel her eyes looking him up and down, wondering who he was and what connexion he could possibly have with the woman waiting upstairs, but he didn't stop and the next moment he was on the landing and pausing to regain his breath. It suddenly seemed very hot.

The second door on the right was facing him. Presently he took a pace forward and raised his hand to knock.

'Come in,' called the woman's voice from beyond as his knuckles touched the wood, and suddenly he was back in the past again, a little boy catching sight of the untasted supper tray outside the closed door and knocking on the panels to enquire if he could eat the food which she had ignored.

He stood rigid, not moving, the memories taut in his mind.

'Come in!' called the woman again, and even as he moved to turn the handle on the door she was opening the door for him so that a second later they were facing each other across the threshold.

No hint of recognition showed in her face. He caught a glimpse of disappointment, then of irritation, and he felt his ears burn scarlet in a sudden rush of embarrassment.

'You must want one of the lodgers,' he heard her say shortly. 'Who are you looking for?'

He swallowed, all his careful words of introduction forgotten, and wondered vaguely in the midst of all his panic how on earth he had had the nerve to come. He stared down at her toes. She wore white sandals, cool and elegant, and in spite of his confusion he was aware of thinking that her smart, casual clothes were much too chic and well-tailored for that little holiday resort far from London.

'Wait a minute,' she said. 'I know you.'

He cleared his throat. Presently he had enough confidence to glance up into her eyes. She looked bewildered but not hostile, and he began to feel better.

'You're Justin,' she said suddenly.

He nodded.

For a moment she made no move, and then she was opening the door wider and turning back into the room.

'You'd better come in,' she said over her shoulder.

He followed her. The room beyond was small with a

view from the window of rooftops and a distant glimpse of the sun sparkling on blue sea.

'You're not much like either of your parents, are you?' she said absently, sitting down on the stool of the crowded dressing table and flicking ash into a souvenir ashtray. 'I hardly recognized you. You've lost such a lot of weight.'

He smiled warily, easing himself on to the edge of the bed.

'Well,' she said at last when the silence threatened to become prolonged. 'Why have you come? Have you got a message from your father?'

'No,' he said, 'he doesn't know you're here. Your note reached me by mistake and I didn't show it to him. I didn't see why you should bother my father when he's still more or less on his honeymoon.'

She was annoyed. As she swivelled round to face him, he could see the anger in her eyes. 'Just what the hell do you think you're playing at?' she demanded coldly.

He had forgotten his panic and shyness now. He stared back at her defiantly. 'You wanted to talk about what happened at Buryan ten years ago,' he said. 'You wanted to talk about Max.'

'To your father. Not to you.'

'I know more than you think I do.'

She smiled, looking sceptical. 'How can you?' she said. 'You were just a child at the time. You couldn't have understood what was happening so how can you know anything about it?'

'Because I saw my mother's death,' he said, and even as he spoke he saw her eyes widen and her expression change. 'I saw it all, don't you see? I followed the murderer up on to the cliffs that night and saw him push my mother down the cliff path to her death . . .'


2


Sarah left the beach soon after five and walked up to the house to see if Jon had returned from his visit to

Penzance. Alexander stayed behind in the cove. When she reached the drive she saw that a blue Hillman was parked behind Max's silver-grey Rolls-Royce and she wondered who the visitors were and whether they had been there long.

The hall was cool and shadowed after the shimmering brilliance of the early evening, and she paused for a moment before the mirror to adjust her hair before crossing the hall and opening the drawing-room door.

Marijohn was sitting at the desk by the window. There was a pen in her hand. Behind her, slightly to her left so that he could look over her shoulder was a tall man, unobtrusively good looking, with quiet eyes and a strong mouth. Both he and Marijohn looked up with a start as Sarah came into the room.

'Oh, it's only you.' Marijohn put down the pen for a moment. 'Michael dear, this is Sarah . . . Sarah – Michael Rivers.'

'How do you do,' said Rivers, giving her a pleasant smile while looking at her with lawyer's eyes. And then as she echoed the greeting, the lawyer's cautious scrutiny faded into a more formal appraisal and there was warmth in his eyes and kindness in the set of his mouth. 'May I offer my congratulations on your marriage? I expect belated congratulations are better than none at all.'

'Thank you,' she said shyly. 'Thank you very much.'

There was a pause. She said awkwardly, as if to explain her presence, 'I – I just wondered if Jon was back yet? He didn't say what time he would be returning from Penzance, but I thought perhaps—'

'No,' said Marijohn, 'he's not here yet.' She turned to Michael. 'Darling, how many more of these do I have to sign?'

'Just the transfer here . . .' He bent over her again and something in the way he moved made Sarah stop to watch them. Phrases of Justin's sprang back to her mind. 'It was obvious he loved her. He kissed her in public and gave her special smiles – oh God, you know? The sort of thing you notice and squirm at when you're a small boy . . .'

It seemed strange to know they were divorced.

'Fine,' said Rivers, gathering up the papers as Marijohn put down her pen. 'I'll take these back with me to London tomorrow.'

'Are you staying near here?'

'With the Hawkins over at Mullion.'

'The Hawkins! Of course! Do they still live in that funny little cottage by the harbour?'

'No, they—' he stopped, listening.

Marijohn was listening, too.

Sarah felt her heart begin to thump faster as she too turned to face the door.

From far away came the sound of footsteps crunching on the gravel of the drive.

'That'll be Jon,' said Rivers. 'Well, I must be going. I'll phone you about the outcome of those transfers and contact Mathieson in the City about the gilt-edged question.'

But Marijohn was still listening. The footsteps echoed in the porch and then moved through the open front door into the hall.

There was an inexplicable pause – the footsteps halted.

'Jon!' called Marijohn suddenly.

The latch clicked; the door swung wide.

'Hullo,' said Jon, unsurprised and unperturbed. 'How are you, Michael? Hullo, Sarah darling – feeling better now?' And as the others watched he stooped to give her a kiss.

'Much better,' she said, clasping his hand tightly as he kissed her and releasing it only when he moved away towards the desk.

Jon turned to Rivers. 'Why didn't you ring up to tell us you were coming, Michael? Are you staying to dinner?'

'No,' said Rivers. 'I'm spending a couple of days with friends at Mullion, and just called in to discuss one or two business matters with Marijohn.'

'Phone your friends and say you're dining out tonight. They wouldn't mind, would they? Stay and have dinner with us!'

'I'm afraid that's not possible,' said Rivers pleasantly. 'But thank you all the same.'

'Marijohn!' said Jon to his cousin, his eyes bright, his frame taut and vibrant with life. 'You'd like Michael to stay to dinner, wouldn't you? Persuade him to stay!'

Marijohn's eyes were very clear. She turned to Rivers. 'Won't you, Michael?' was all she said. 'Please.'

He shrugged, making a helpless gesture with his hands, and then she gave him a warm, brilliant, unexpected smile and he was lost. 'When did you last have dinner with me?'

He shrugged again, not replying, but Sarah saw him bend his head slowly in acquiescence and knew that he had agreed to stay against his better judgement.

'Where's Max, Sarah?' said Jon to her, making her jump.

'He's – he's still down by the cove sunbathing.'

'And Justin?'

'Still in St Ives presumably,' said Marijohn, moving over to the french windows. 'Michael, come out and sit on the swing-seat and forget all those dreary legal documents for a while. I expect Jon wants to be alone with Sarah.'

That was said for effect, thought Sarah instantly and unreasonably. All this is for effect to make some definite impression on Michael. This is all for Michael. And Jon is playing the same game; he's set the key for the evening and she's responding note for note. The key involved inviting Michael to dinner, giving the impression that the past is buried and forgotten, and now they want to show him that everything is normal and that there's nothing to hide.

Her thoughts raced on and on, no matter how hard she tried to stem her rising feeling of panic. How could Jon and Marijohn be working in conjunction with one another when Jon hadn't even known Michael was calling in that evening? But he had known. He had walked into the room and said 'Hullo, Michael' although he could not have known before he opened the door that Michael would be there . . . Perhaps he had recognized Michael's car. But the car wasn't ten years old. Jon could never have seen the car before. And yet he had known, he had known before he had opened the door that he would find Michael with Marijohn in the room . . .

'Come upstairs and talk to me, darling,' said Jon, putting his arm round her waist. 'I want to shower and change my clothes. Come and tell me what you've been doing.'

So she went upstairs and sat on the edge of the bath as he had a shower and then rubbed himself vigorously with the rough towel. He told her about his friend in Penzance and described the motor-boat and the afternoon spin on the sea in detail. Finally as he returned to the bedroom to dress he paused to smile at her.

'Now tell me what you've been doing! You've hardly said a word to me all day! Do you still love me?'

There was a lump in her throat suddenly, a deep unreasoning ache that only deepened against her will. 'Oh, Jon,' was all she could say, and then the next moment she was in his arms and pressing her face against his chest and he was crushing the sobs from her body and kissing her eyes to stop her tears.

'Sarah,' he said, upset. 'Sarah, darling Sarah, what is it? What's the matter? What have I said?'

'I—' she summoned together all her strength and managed to look straight into his eyes. 'Jon,' she said. 'Jon, I want something very badly. Could you—'

'Tell me what it is,' he said instantly, 'and you shall have it. Just tell me what it is.'

She took a deep breath, checked her tears. 'I – I want to go back to Canada, Jon – I don't want to stay here. I just want to go home. Please Jon, let's go. I don't want to stay here. I'm terribly sorry, but I—'

'I don't understand,' he said. 'Why don't you want to stay? I was planning to stay another week.'

She couldn't cry now. She could only stare into his face and think: it's all true. There *is* something. Max wasn't lying. There's something intangible, something impossible to describe, just as he said there was. It's all true.

'I thought you liked it here,' he said. 'What's wrong? What is it?'

She shook her head dumbly. 'Marijohn—'

'What about Marijohn?' he said. He spoke much too quickly, and afterwards looked annoyed with himself for betraying his feelings.

'She doesn't like me.'

'Rubbish. She thinks you're pretty and just right for me and she's very glad I've married someone so nice.'

She twisted away from him, but he held her tightly and wouldn't let her go. 'Come here.'

The towel slipped from his waist. He pulled her down on the bed and suddenly she clung to him in a rush of passion and desire which was terrible to her because she was so afraid it would strike no response in him.

'Sarah . . .' He sounded surprised, taken aback but not indifferent. And suddenly his passion was flowing into her own, and the more she poured out her love to him in movement and gesture the more he took her love and transformed it with his own.

When they parted at last the sweat was blinding her eyes and there were tears on her cheeks and her body felt bruised and aching.

'I love you,' she said. 'I love you.'

He was still trying to find his breath, still trembling, his fists clenched with his tension and his eyes tight shut for a second as if in pain. He can't relax, she thought, and neither can I. There's no peace. We should be able to sleep now for a while but we won't. There's no peace here, no rest.

'Jon,' she said. 'Jon darling, take me away from here. Let's go tomorrow. Please. Let's go back to London, back to Canada, anywhere, but don't let's stay here any more.'

His fists were clenched so tightly that the skin was white across the knuckles. 'Why?' he said indistinctly into the pillow, his voice truculent and hostile. 'Why? Give me one good reason.'

And when she was silent he reached out and pulled her towards him in a violent gesture of love. 'Give me another couple of days,' he said. 'Please. If you love me, give me that. I can't go just yet.'

She tried to frame the word 'why' but it refused to come. She got up, went into the bathroom and washed, but when she returned from the bathroom she found that he was still lying in the same position. She started to dress.

Time passed.

At last, sitting down in front of the mirror, she began to do her hair but still she made no attempt to speak, and the silence between them remained unbroken.

'Sarah,' Jon said at last in distress. 'Sarah, please.'

She swivelled round to face him. 'Is Marijohn your mistress?'

There was utter silence. He stared at her, his eyes dark and opaque.

'No,' he said at last. 'Of course not. Sarah—'

'Has she ever been your mistress?'

'No!' he said with sudden violent resentment. 'Never!'

'Were you having an affair with her when Sophia was killed?'

'No!' he shouted, springing off the bed and coming across the room towards her. 'No, no, no!' He took her by the shoulders and started to shake her. 'No, no, no—'

'Jon,' she said gently. 'Shhh, Jon . . .'

He sank down beside her on the stool. 'If that's why you want to leave, you can forget it,' he said tightly. 'There's nothing like that between us. She—' He stopped.

'She?'

'She detests any form of physical love,' he said. 'Didn't you guess? She can't even bear being touched however casually by a man. Did you never notice how I've always avoided touching her? Did you never notice how I didn't kiss her when we met? Didn't you notice any of those things?'

She stared at him. He stared back, his hands trembling.

'I see,' she said, at last.

He relaxed, and she knew in a flash that he had not understood. He thought she understood only the key to Marijohn's remoteness, and he never knew that all she understood was the despair in his eyes and the physical frustration in every line of his tense, taut frame.


## 3


When Sarah went downstairs the hall was dim and quiet and she decided the others must still be in the garden. There was no sign of Max Alexander. After pausing by the open front door to glance up the hillside and listen to the rushing water beyond the gateway she crossed the hall and opened the drawing-room door.

She had been wrong. Rivers and Marijohn were no longer in the garden. As she entered the room, Rivers swung round abruptly to face the door and Marijohn glanced up from her position on the sofa.

'I – I'm sorry,' stammered Sarah. 'I thought—'

'That's all right,' Rivers said easily, lulling her feeling of embarrassment. 'Come on in. We were just wondering whether Max has been washed away by the tide down in the cove.'

Marijohn stood up. She wore a plain linen dress, narrow and simple, without sleeves. It was a beautiful colour. She wore no make-up and no jewellery, and Sarah noticed for the first time that she had even removed her wedding ring.

'Where are you going?' said Rivers sharply.

'Just to see about dinner.' She moved over to the door, not hurrying, her eyes not watching either of them, and went out into the hall.

There was a silence.

'Drink, Sarah?' said Rivers at last.

'No, thank you.' She sat down, twisting the material of her dress into tight ridges across her thighs and wondering what Rivers had been saying before she had interrupted him. She was just trying to think of some remark which might begin a polite conversation and ease the silence in the room when Rivers said, 'Is Jon upstairs?'

'Yes – yes, he is.'

'I see.' He was by the sideboard, his hand on the decanter. 'Sure you won't join me in a drink?'

She shook her head again and watched him as he mixed himself a whisky and soda.

'How long,' he said presently, 'are you staying here?'

'I don't know.'

He turned to face her abruptly and as she looked at him she saw that he knew.

'You want to go, don't you?'

'No,' she said, lying out of pride. 'No, I like it here.'

'I shouldn't stay here too long if I were you.'

She shrugged, assuming indifference. 'Jon wants to stay here for a day or two longer.'

'I'm sure he does.' He took a gulp of his drink and she saw his fingers tighten on the stem of his glass. 'I didn't realize you would both be coming down here,' he said evenly at last. 'I didn't think he would be seeing Marijohn again. She had made up her mind not to see him again, I know. I supposed he persuaded her to change her mind.'

She stared at him blankly. From somewhere far away she heard the clatter of a saucepan in the kitchen.

'He wanted to see her again – I know that because he came to me in an attempt to find out where she was. Naturally I didn't tell him. I knew she had made up her mind that it would be much better for her not to see him again, and I knew too that it would be disastrous if—'

He stopped.

There were footsteps on the stairs, Jon whistling the old American country song *You Win Again*.

'Listen,' said Rivers suddenly. 'I must talk to you further about this. It's in both our interests, don't you understand? I must talk to you.'

'But I don't see. Why should—'

'You have to get Jon away from here. I can't persuade

Marijohn to leave – we're not even married any more. But you can persuade Jon. God, you're all but on your honeymoon, aren't you? Get him away from here, right away. Back to Canada, anywhere – but get him away from this place.'

'From this place?'

'From Marijohn.'

The whistling stopped; the door opened.

'Sarah? Ah, there you are! Come on down to the cove with me and rescue Max!'

'I think,' said Rivers, 'that he's just walking up to the gateway.'

'Well, so he is!' Jon moved out on to the lawn. 'Max!' he shouted, his hand raised in welcome. 'Where've you been, you bastard? We thought you'd drowned yourself!'

Rivers was already beside her even as she stood up to follow Jon on to the lawn.

'Come for a walk with me after supper and I'll explain.'

'I—'

'You must,' he interrupted. 'I don't think you understand the danger you're in.'

She felt the colour drain from her face as she stared into his eyes. And then Jon was blazing across the silence, bursting back into the room to mix a round of drinks, and Alexander was crossing the threshold of the french windows with a lazy, indolent smile on his face.

'Why, Michael! Fancy that! Just like old times! How are you these days? Still soliciting?'

There was brittle, empty conversation for a few minutes. Max started to expound the virtues of his latest car. Jon, moving across to Sarah, kissed her on the mouth with his back to the others and sat down beside her on the sofa.

'All right?'

When she nodded he put his hand over hers and kept it there. She stared blindly down at his fingers, not hearing Max Alexander's voice, aware of nothing except that Jon was a stranger to her whom she could not trust. It occurred to her dully to wonder if she had ever imagined unhappiness to be like this; it's not the raw nagging edge of desolation, she thought, but the tight darkness of fear. The pain is convex and opaque and absolute.

Marijohn returned to the room a quarter of an hour later.

'I suppose Justin's coming back to dinner, Jon?'

He shrugged. 'I've no idea. I imagine so.'

'Can I get you a drink, Marijohn?'

'No . . . no thanks. I think I'll go out for a while. Dinner will be in about half an hour.'

On the sofa Sarah felt Jon stir restlessly.

'Another drink, Jon?' offered Max Alexander from the sideboard.

Jon didn't answer.

'Jon,' said Sarah, pressing against him instinctively. 'Jon.'

'Do you want to come, Michael?' said Marijohn. 'I don't want to walk far, just down to the cove and back.'

'No,' said Rivers. 'I'm in the middle of a perfectly good whisky and soda and I want to finish it and have another one to follow.'

'Don't look at me, Marijohn,' advised Max Alexander. 'I've staggered down to the cove and back already this afternoon. I've had my share of exercise today.'

Jon stood up, hesitated and then reached for the cigarette box to help himself to a cigarette.

'Do you want to go, Jon?' said Rivers pleasantly.

'Not particularly.' He lit the cigarette, wandered over to the fireplace and started to straighten the ornaments on the mantel shelf.

Marijohn walked away across the lawn. She walked very slowly, as if savouring each step. Jon glanced after her once and then abruptly turned his back on the window and flung himself down in the nearest armchair.

'Why don't you go, Jon?' said Rivers. 'Don't feel you have to stay here and entertain us – I'm sure Sarah would make an admirable hostess. Why don't you go with Marijohn?'

Jon inhaled from his cigarette and watched the blue smoke curl upwards from between his fingers. 'We've been down to the sea already today.'

'Oh, I see . . . Not to the Flat Rocks, by any chance?'

'I say,' said Alexander suddenly, 'what the hell's Justin doing in St—'

'No,' said Jon to Rivers. 'Just down to the cove.'

'How strange, Marijohn told me she hadn't been down to the cove today.'

'Sarah,' said Max. 'Do you know what Justin's doing in St Ives?'

'Do you often come down here?' said Jon idly to Rivers. 'It must take up a lot of your time if you have to visit Marijohn personally whenever it's necessary to discuss some business problem with her. Or do you like to have a good excuse to visit her as often as possible?'

'At least,' said Rivers, 'my excuse for coming here is a damned sight better than yours.'

'Look,' said Max, spilling his drink slightly on the carpet, 'for Christ's sake, why doesn't one of you go down to the cove with Marijohn now? Michael, she asked you – why the hell don't you go if you've come down here to see her?'

Jon flung his cigarette into the fireplace and stood up. 'Come on, Sarah, we'll go down together.'

There was a silence. They were all looking at her.

'No,' she said too loudly, 'no, I don't want to come. I'd rather stay here.'

Jon shrugged his shoulders. 'Just as you like,' he said shortly, sounding as if he couldn't have cared less, and walked through the open french windows across the lawn without even a hint of a backward glance.


4


In St Ives the white houses were basking in the golden glow of the evening and the sea was still and calm. In the little house in one of the back alleys near Fish Street,

Justin was holding a mug of steaming coffee in his hands and wondering what had possessed him to tell this woman the story of his life. It was her fault. If she had not questioned him so closely about the aftermath of that terrible weekend at Buryan he would not have needed to explain anything about his grandmother and the parting from his father, but for some reason he had wanted to explain. At first he had been guarded and cautious, but when she had seemed to understand he had lost some of his reserve. She hadn't laughed at him. As the afternoon slid gently away from them, he began to trust her sufficiently to be able to talk more freely.

'And you never told anyone what you saw that night?' she said at last. 'You said nothing?'

'I didn't think it would help my father.'

'But you're sure now that he didn't kill her?'

'He told me he didn't. Someone else must have killed her. I have to find out who it was.'

She thought about it for a long moment, and the smoke from her cigarette curled lazily upwards until it was caught in the slanting rays of sunlight and transformed into a golden haze.

'I thought at the time that Jon had probably killed her,' she said at last. 'But it was a mere suspicion backed up by the knowledge that he had more than enough provocation that weekend . . . And then last week Max phoned me and asked me out to dinner. As soon as I saw him I realized he was itching to discuss his meeting with Jon earlier and speculate why Jon should return to Buryan. We talked for hours, recalling all our memories, and in the end he said Jon had half-invited him down to Buryan and he had a good mind to accept in order to have the chance of finding out what was going on. He was convinced that Jon had killed Sophia and he thought it curious, to say the least, that Jon should take his new wife back there ten years later. I'd planned to take a few days' holiday anyway at around this time, and I suddenly thought it might be rather interesting to come down here so that I would be close at hand if Max should discover anything . . . But the more I thought about Jon and his connexion with Sophia's death, the more I felt—' She stopped.

'Felt?'

'I – I felt that it was better to let sleeping dogs lie . . . After all, it was ten years ago, and Jon's married again now. I suddenly disliked the thought of Max deliberately going down to Buryan with the idea of probing a past which was better buried and forgotten.'

'So you wrote to my father to warn him.'

'Yes, I thought he should know Max's motives in returning to Buryan.' She leant forward and stubbed out her cigarette. 'Odd how convinced Max was that she had been murdered . . . After all, murder was never mentioned at the time, was it? And the jury at the inquest decided it was an accident. But maybe we all knew she'd been murdered although we were too frightened to say so. That's ironic, isn't it! We all had a motive, you see, each one of us. We all had a reason for killing her, so we all kept silent and accepted the verdict of accident because we were afraid of casting suspicion on ourselves by speaking our suspicions aloud to the police . . . What's the matter? Didn't you guess I might have had a motive for wishing your mother dead?'

He shook his head wordlessly, watching her.

'I was an outsider from the first,' she said, lighting another cigarette and shaking out the match as she spoke. 'They all belonged to a different world – all of them except Sophia, and even her world of Soho cafés wasn't exactly mine. I was only eighteen then; I hadn't been working in London for very long. I met Max by accident at some party which I and a few friends had gate-crashed and I didn't know the kind of man he was. I just knew he was rich and moved in an expensive, exciting world, and I didn't find it difficult to fall in love and start to imagine all kinds of exotic, romantic pictures. It's so easy when one's only eighteen to live with one's head in the clouds, isn't it? Anyway, we had an affair, and eventually he took me to Buryan for that weekend.

'I was still in love with him then, still dreaming my romantic little daydreams.

'I think I hated Buryan from the first moment that I saw it. As for the other people, I didn't understand them at all – God, how baffling they seemed at the time! I found Jon interesting but he scarcely seemed to notice I existed – he was entirely engrossed with his wife and his cousin, and cared for nothing else. As for his cousin – well, I had nothing to say to her; we simply didn't even begin to talk the same language. The solicitor-husband was nice but too polite to be friendly, and anyway he too seemed to be almost entirely wrapped up in his personal problems. I disliked Sophia straight away, but it wasn't a very active dislike. I remember thinking that she just seemed rather common and vulgar.

'She started to flirt with Max about an hour after we'd arrived. I didn't take her seriously at first because I thought she surely couldn't flirt with one of her guests under her husband's nose, but that was my mistake. She meant it all right. The next morning Max and I quarrelled violently and he went off with Sophia to St Ives on a – quote "shopping expedition", unquote. I don't think I've ever been so unhappy either before or since. I stayed in my room all morning and until the early evening when I heard them come back from St Ives. After a while I went to look for Max and you told me – do you remember – that he'd gone down to the cove with your mother for a swim. So I went out, taking the path down to the beach.

'I heard them talking before I saw them. She was saying in that ugly foreign voice of hers that she had a wonderful scheme all planned. She was sick to death of Buryan and wanted to get away from Jon and go back to London, and Max was to be her saviour. She had it all worked out – a cosy little *ménage à deux* with just the right-sized luxury flat in Mayfair and maybe a cosy little divorce at the end of the rainbow. It sounded wonderful. God, how I hated her! I can't describe how much I hated her at that moment. And then I realized that Max wasn't exactly enthralled with all these beautiful schemes and I suddenly wanted to laugh out loud. He tried to put it tactfully at first but when she refused to understand, he spoke more frankly. He didn't want a *ménage à deux* in Mayfair or the scandal and the publicity of being co-respondent in his best friend's divorce suit! The last thing he wanted was to have Sophia permanently on his hands in London! He didn't really want an affair with the woman at all and the thought of her shouting from the rooftops that she was his mistress was enough to make his blood run cold. "Look," he said to her, "I can't and won't play your game the way you want it played. You'd better find yourself another lover." And then just as I was closing my eyes in sheer relief I heard the woman say, "I have to get away from here – you don't understand. I'll go mad if I have to stay here any longer. If you don't take me to London and give me money and somewhere to live I'll make you the most famous co-respondent in town and blow your friendship with Jon to smithereens."

'And Max said with a laugh, "You wouldn't have a hope in heaven of doing either of those things!"

'"Wouldn't I?" she said. "Wouldn't I? Just you try and see!"

'And after a moment Max said, "I'd better have time to think about this and then I'll have to talk to you again. I'll meet you out at the Flat Rocks after dinner this evening and we can discuss the situation in detail."

'I moved then. I came round the rocks towards them and Max saw straight away that I'd heard what they'd been saying. When he lost his temper with me and asked me what the hell I thought I was doing spying on him, I turned on Sophia and called her all the names I could think of. I blamed her for everything – Max's changed attitude towards me, my own misery, his violent loss of temper which upset me more than anything else in the world. And she just laughed. I stormed and raged and poured out abuse and all she did was laugh.

'I found my way back to the house somehow. I went to my room and stayed there while I shed enough tears to fill the Atlantic Ocean. I knew then that everything was finished as far as Max and I were concerned, and that I meant no more to him than Sophia – or any other woman – did. I'd been deceiving myself for weeks that he cared for me, and I knew then that I'd been both incredibly blind and incredibly stupid. But I was only eighteen . . . It's so easy to make mistakes at eighteen, isn't it?

'I knew what time he was going to meet Sophia. I thought that if I could see him for a few minutes alone, if I could meet him by the Flat Rocks before Sophia arrived, I could perhaps persuade him not to listen to her, to call her bluff, and perhaps I could show him how much I still loved him. But I didn't know where the Flat Rocks were or how one reached them. In the end on an impulse I went out of my room and moved downstairs. It was late. There was a hell of a row going on in the music room, but I didn't stop to listen. I went outside to the gate to see if there was any sign of Max leaving for the Flat Rocks, and just as I reached the gate I saw him; he was walking down towards the beach. At the head of the cove he paused to watch the sea for a few minutes, and then he turned to retrace his steps and he saw me straight away. When I asked him where he was going he shrugged and said he was going back to the house.

'"I thought you'd gone to keep your rendezvous with Sophia," I said. "Why have you come back?"

'"It's colder than I thought," he said. "I've come back for a sweater."

'I tried to talk with him then, pleading with him to ignore Sophia and begging him to take me back to London straight away, but it was no good. He wouldn't listen, and just told me not to try to organize his life for him as he was perfectly capable of organizing it himself. When we reached the house again, he left me while he went inside to fetch his sweater, and I waited in the bushes by the gate, meaning to follow him when he came out again.

'He came out again almost at once.

'I followed him a little way, but he must have seen me for he lay in wait and stepped out in front of me as I reached the point where the path forked to go up to the cliffs. We had one final bitter useless row there and then he went on out towards the Flat Rocks while I sat down on a rock near the fork in the path and tried to pull myself together.

'When I finally went back to the house there was a light on in the music room where I had heard them all quarrelling earlier, but the door was open now and no one was there. I was just standing in the hall and wondering where they all were when Jon came down the stairs. "Marijohn," he called, seeing my shadow on the wall and thinking I was his cousin, and then he saw it was me. "Where's Marijohn?" he said. "Where's she gone?" I shook my head. He was very white. "I have to find her. I have to find Marijohn." He kept saying it over and over again. "Where is everyone?" he said at last. "Where's Max?" I told him then, and he went straight away to the front door, stopping for a moment by the chest as if he were pausing to look for something, but there was nothing there. The next moment he was in the drive and I was alone again in the hall.'

She shook ash from her cigarette on to the carpet. 'I didn't kill your mother,' she said at last. 'I could have done it, but I didn't. I went up to my room again and stayed there until Max came up to tell me the news.'

There was a silence in the room. When she next glanced at him she saw to her surprise that he was leaning forward and his eyes were dark with concentration.

'My father was at the house when you returned to it from the cove?'

'Why, yes,' she said. 'I told you.'

'What was he wearing?'

'What was he wearing? God, I haven't the faintest idea! I wasn't in the mood for noticing clothes that night. Why?'

'Was he wearing a red sweater?'

'I don't think so – no, I'm sure he wasn't. When I saw him he was wearing only a shirt and a pair of trousers – I remember noticing that his shirt was open at the neck and I could see the sweat glistening on the skin at his throat.

God, he did look shaken! He was white as a sheet and all he could do was ask for Marijohn . . .'

## chapter 5

1

As soon as it was dark that evening Sarah made an excuse to go up to her room, and then slipped outside into the cool night air to wait in the shadows by the gate. She didn't have to wait long. As she plucked a leaf from the rhododendron bush nearby and tore it to shreds in her fingers she saw the front door open noiselessly and the next moment Rivers was crossing the drive towards her.

'Sarah?'

'Yes,' she said. 'I'm here.'

'Good.' He drew closer to her and she was conscious of his air of authority. He could cope with the situation, she thought with a rush of relief. He's spent his life dealing with other people's problems and her own problem was something which probably he alone was fully able to understand. 'The first thing to do,' he said, 'is to walk away from the house. I don't want to run the risk of anyone overhearing our conversation.'

'Shall we go down to the cove?'

'No,' he said, 'that would be the first place they'd look for us. We'll go up on to the cliffs.'

They set off along the path, Rivers leading the way, and the night was dark and clouded, muffling the roar of the sea.

'Don't let's go too far,' said Sarah suddenly.

'We'll stop around the next corner.'

It was much too dark. Sarah found her feet catching in the heather and jarring on the uneven ground.

'Michael—'

'All right,' he said. 'We'll stop here.'

There was an outcrop of rock below the path and he

helped her down the hillside until they could sit side by side on a rocky ledge and watch the dark mass of the sea straight in front of them. Far below them the surf was a fleck of whiteness on the reefs and lagoons of the shore.

'Cigarette?' said Rivers.

'No, thank you.'

'Mind if I do?'

'No, not at all.' How polite we are, she thought. We should be in a stately London drawing room instead of on Cornish cliffs at night far from the formalities of civilization.

'How did you meet Jon?' he said suddenly, jolting her away from her thoughts.

She tried to concentrate on the effort of conversation.

'We met through a friend of mine,' she said. 'Frank's business was connected with Jon's, and one night we all had dinner together – Frank and I, Jon and some girl whom I didn't know. It never occurred to me at the time that Jon was the slightest bit interested in me, but the next day he phoned and asked to take me out to a concert. I went. I shouldn't have because of Frank, but then . . . well, Frank and I weren't engaged, and I – I wanted to see Jon again.'

'I see.' The cigarette tip glowed red in the darkness and flickered as he inhaled. 'Yes, that sounds like Jon.'

She said nothing, waiting for him to go on, and, after a moment, he said, 'I met both Jon and Marijohn when old Towers died. I was then the assistant solicitor in the firm which had looked after his legal affairs and I was helping the senior partner in the task of proving the will and winding up the estate. Marijohn was eighteen. I'll never forget when I first saw her.'

The cigarette tip glowed again.

'I managed to take her out once or twice, but there were about ten other men all wanting to take her out and there are only seven evenings in a week. They had more money and were older and more sophisticated than I was. She always chose the older men; the ones that mattered were all over thirty-five, but I was still fool enough to go on trying and hoping . . . until I went to a party and heard people talking about her. It was then for the first time that I realized she was completely and utterly promiscuous and slept with any man who would give her the best time.

'I left her alone for a while after that, but then I met her again and it was impossible to put her out of my mind. I had to keep phoning her, finding out who she was living with, going through a self-induced hell every day and night. And it was all for nothing, of course. She didn't give a damn.

'Then, quite suddenly, everything changed. One of her affairs went very, very wrong and she had to have an abortion. She had no money and was very ill. And she came to me. It was I who helped her, I who put up the money, arranged the abortion, paid off the necessary doctors – I, a solicitor, committing a criminal offence! But nobody ever found out. Gradually she got better and I took her away to a quiet corner in Sussex for a while to convalesce, but she wasn't fit enough to sleep with me even if she'd wanted to, and after a week she left me and went back to London.

'I followed her back and found she was planning to go down to Cornwall. "I want to see Jon," she said to me. I can see her now, standing there, her eyes very blue and clear. She was wearing a dark-blue dress which was too big for her because she'd lost so much weight. "I don't want you to come," she said. "I want to be alone with Jon for a while and then when I come back perhaps I'll live with you and you can look after me." When I said – for the hundredth time – that I wanted to marry her she said that she didn't even know if she could live with me let alone marry me, and that I would have to wait until she had seen Jon. I said, "What's Jon got to do with it? How can he help you?" And she turned to me and said, "You wouldn't understand even if I tried to explain."

'She came back from Cornwall a month later and said she would marry me. She was transformed. She looked so much better that I hardly recognized her.

'We had a very quiet wedding. Jon and Sophia didn't

154

come and although I thought at the time that it was strange, the full significance never fully occurred to me. For a while we were very happy – I suppose I had six months of complete happiness, and even now when I look back I would rather have had those six months than none at all. And then Jon came up to town one day from Penzance, and nothing was ever the same again.

'It was a gradual process, the disintegration of our marriage. For a time I didn't even realize what was happening and then I realized that she was becoming cold, withdrawn. Ironically enough, the colder she became the more I seemed to need her and want her, and the more I wanted her the less she wanted me. In the end she said she wanted a separate bedroom. We quarrelled. I asked her if there was some other man, but she just laughed, and when she laughed I shouted out, "Then why do you see so much of Jon? Why is he always coming up to London? Why do we always get so many invitations to Buryan? Why is it you have to see so much of him?"

'And she turned to me and said, "Because he's the only man I've ever met who doesn't want to go to bed with me."

'It was my turn to laugh then. I said, "He'd want to all right if he wasn't so wrapped up in his wife!"

'And she said, "You don't understand. There's no question of our going to bed together."

'It was so strange, the way she said that. I remember feeling that curious sickness one gets in the pit of the stomach the second after experiencing a shock. I said sharply, "What the hell are you talking about?" And she just said, "I can't describe how peaceful it is. It's the most perfect thing in all the world."

'I suppose I knew then that I was frightened. The terrible thing was that I didn't know what I was frightened of. "You're living with your head in the clouds," I remember saying to her brutally, trying to shatter my own fear and destroy the barrier between us which she had created. "You're talking nonsense." And she said untroubled, as if it were supremely unimportant, "Think that if you like. I don't care. But no matter what you think, it doesn't alter the fact that sex for me has long since lost all its meaning. It just seems rather ridiculous and unnecessary." And as if in afterthought she added vaguely, "I'm so sorry, Michael." It was funny the way she said that. It had a peculiar air of bathos, and yet it wasn't really bathos at all. "I'm so sorry, Michael . . ."

'I still couldn't stop loving her. I tried to leave, but I had to go back. I can't even begin to describe what a hell it was. And then we had that final invitation to Buryan, and I resolved that I must talk to Jon and lay my cards on the table. I knew he was absorbed with his wife, and I thought at the time that his relationship with Marijohn would be a much more casual, unimportant thing than her attitude towards him.

'We hadn't been five minutes at Buryan before I realized that Sophia was driving him to the limits of his patience and testing his love beyond all the bounds of endurance. And suddenly, that weekend, his patience snapped and he turned away from her – he'd had enough and could stand no more of her petulance and infidelity. And when he turned away, it was as if he turned to Marijohn.

'It was the most dangerous thing that could have happened; I was beside myself with anxiety, and tried to get Marijohn away, but she refused to go. I tried to talk to Jon but he pretended he hadn't the faintest idea what I was talking about and that there was nothing wrong between him and Sophia. And then – then of all moments – Sophia had to stumble across what was happening and drag us all towards disaster.

'She'd been having an affair with Max and they'd driven into St Ives for the afternoon. Jon was in the music room with Marijohn, and rather than make an unwelcome third I went out fishing and tried to think what the hell I was going to do. I didn't come to any conclusion at all. The child came, I remember, and sat talking to me and in some ways I was grateful to him because he took my mind off my troubles. When he went

I stayed for a little longer by the shore and then eventually I went back to the house for dinner.

'Sophia and Max were back, and Sophia was looking very uneasy. She talked too much at the start of the meal, and then, when Jon and Marijohn were silent she made no further efforts at conversation. When Jon and Marijohn began to talk to each other at last, ignoring the rest of us entirely, I saw then without a doubt that Sophia had realized what was happening and was going to make trouble.

'The child seemed to sense the tension in the atmosphere for he became very troublesome, and suddenly I felt I had to get out of the room and escape. I took the child upstairs. It was the only excuse I could think of which enabled me to get away, and I stayed upstairs with him for about half an hour, putting him to bed and reading to him. I can't even remember what we read. All I could think of was that Sophia believed Jon intended to be unfaithful to her, and was going to make trouble. My mind was going round and round in circles. Would she divorce Jon? What would she say? How much would come out? How much would it affect Marijohn? Would it succeed in driving Jon and Marijohn more firmly together than ever? What was going to happen? And I went on reading to the child and pretending to him that everything was normal, and inside my heart felt as if it were bursting . . .

'When I went back downstairs, they were alone in the music room and there was a record playing on the gramophone. Sophia was in the kitchen with Max. I closed the door and said to Jon, "Sophia knows – you realize that?" And he said, looking me straight in the eyes, "Knows what?"

'I said there was no sense in pretending any longer and that the time had come to be perfectly frank with each other. Marijohn tried to interrupt, telling me not to make such an exhibition of myself, but I shut my mind to her and refused to listen. "You may not be technically committing adultery with my wife," I said to Jon, "but you're behaving exactly as if you are, and

Sophia isn't going to accept all these airy-fairy tales about a relationship with no sex in it. She's going to believe the worst and act accordingly, and in many ways she'd be justified. Whatever your relationship with my wife is, it's a dangerous one that should be stopped – and it must be stopped."

'They looked at each other. They looked at me. And as they were silent, thinking, I knew instinctively what it was that was so wrong. They were sharing each other's minds. Sophia, close as she might have been to Jon as the result of physical intimacy, was as a stranger to him in the face of that uncanny intangible understanding he shared with Marijohn. Sophia was being forced into the position of outsider – but not by any means which she could recognize or label. For because their relationship was so far beyond her grasp – or indeed the grasp of any ordinary person – it was impossible for her to identify the wrongness in the relationship although it was possible to sense that wrongness did exist.

'Jon said, "Look Michael—" but he got no farther. The door opened and Sophia walked into the room.'

He stopped. The sea went on murmuring at the base of the cliffs, and there was no light as far as the eye could see. The darkness made Sarah more conscious of her dizziness and of her hot, aching eyes.

'Don't tell me any more,' she whispered. 'Don't. Please.'

But he wasn't listening to her.

'What is it?'

'I thought I heard something.' He went on listening but presently he relaxed a little. 'There was a terrible scene,' he said at last. 'I can't begin to tell you what was said. It ended with Jon leaving the room and walking out across the lawn. Marijohn went up to her room, and I was left alone with Sophia. I tried to reason with her but she wouldn't listen and in the end she went upstairs to change her shoes before going out. There was some rendezvous with Max on the Flat Rocks, although I didn't know that at the time. I stayed in the drawing room until I heard her go, and then I went up to my room to find Marijohn but she was no longer there. I stayed there thinking for a long while.

'After Sophia's death, I thought for a time that everything was going to work out at last, but I was too optimistic. Marijohn and Jon had a very long talk together. I don't know what was said, but the upshot of it was that they had decided to part for good. I think Sophia's death – or rather, the scene that preceded her death – had shaken them and they realized they couldn't go on as they were. Jon went to Canada, to the other side of the world, and Marijohn returned with me to London, but she didn't stay long and we never lived together as man and wife again. She went to Paris for a while, came back but couldn't settle down in any place with anyone. I wanted to help her as I knew she was desperately unhappy, but there was nothing I could do and the love I offered her was useless. In the end she turned to religion. She was living in a convent when Jon returned to England a few weeks ago.'

He threw away his cigarette. The tip glowed briefly and then died in the darkness.

'So you see,' he said slowly at last, 'it's quite imperative that you get Jon away from here. It's all happening again, can't you realize that? It's all happening again – we're all here at Buryan, all of us except that woman of Max's, and you've been assigned Sophia's role.'

Stone grated on stone; there was the click of a powerful torch, a beam of blinding light.

'Just what the hell are you trying to suggest to my wife, Michael Rivers?' said Jon's hard, dangerous voice from the darkness beyond the torch's beam.


2


'Stay and have dinner with me,' said Eve to Justin. 'I don't know a soul in this town. Take me somewhere interesting where we can have a meal.'

'No,' he said, 'I have to get back to Buryan.' And then, realizing his words might have sounded rude and abrupt, he added hastily, 'I promised to get back for dinner.'

'Call them and tell them you've changed your mind.'

'No, I—' He stopped, blushed, shook his head. His fingers fidgeted with the door handle. 'I'm sorry, but I have to get back – it's rather important. There's something I have to talk about with my father.'

'About your mother's death?' she said sharply. 'Was it something I said? You're sure now that he didn't kill her, aren't you?'

'Yes,' he said, and added in a rush: 'And I think I know who did.' He opened the door and paused to look at her.

She smiled. 'Come back when you can,' was all she said. 'Tell me what happens.'

He thanked her awkwardly, his shyness returning for a moment, and then left the room to go downstairs to the hall.

Outside, the golden light of evening was soothing to his eyes. He moved quickly back towards Fish Street, and then broke into a run as he reached the harbour walls and ran down the steps towards the car park. The sea on his right was a dark blue mirror reflecting golden lights from the sky and far away the waves broke in white wavering lines of foam on the sand-dunes of Hayle.

He was panting when he reached the car and had to search for his keys. For one sickening moment he thought he had lost his key-ring, but then discovered the keys in the inside pocket of his jacket and quickly unlocked the car door. He suddenly realized he was sweating and fear was a sharp prickling tension crawling at the base of his spine.

St Ives was jammed with the summer tourist traffic leaving the town at the end of the day. It took him quarter of an hour to travel from the car park through the town and emerge on to the Land's End road.

He had just reached the lonely stretch of the wild

coast road between Morvah and Zennor when the engine spluttered, coughed and was still. He stared at the petrol gauge with incredulous eyes for one long moment, and then, wrenching open the car door he started to run down the road back to Zennor with his heart hammering and pounding in his lungs.


3

Rivers stood up. He didn't hurry. 'Put out that torch, for God's sake,' he said calmly with a slight air of irritability. 'I can't see a thing.'

The torch clicked. There was darkness.

'Sarah,' said Jon.

She didn't move. She tried to, but her limbs made no response.

'Sarah, what's he been saying to you?'

Rivers took a slight step nearer her and she sensed he had moved to reassure her. Her mouth was dry as if she had run a long way with no rest.

'Sarah!' shouted Jon. 'Sarah!'

'For God's sake, Jon,' said Rivers, still with his calm air of slight irritability. 'Pull yourself together. I suggest we all go back to the house instead of conducting arguments and recriminations on the top of a cliff on a particularly dark Cornish night.'

'Go – yourself,' said Jon between his teeth and tried to push past him, but Rivers stood his ground.

'Let me by.'

'Relax,' said Rivers, still calm. 'Sarah's perfectly all right but she's had a shock.'

'Get out of my—'

They were struggling, wrestling with one another, but even as Sarah managed to stand up Michael made no further attempts to hold Jon back, and stepped aside.

'Sarah,' said Jon, trying to take her in his arms. 'Sarah—'

She twisted away from him. 'Let me go.'

'It's not true about Marijohn! Whatever he said to you isn't true!'

She didn't answer. He whirled on Rivers. 'What did you tell her?'

Rivers laughed.

'What did you tell her?' He had left Sarah and was gripping Rivers's shoulders. 'What did you say?'

'I told her enough to persuade her to leave Buryan as soon as possible. Nothing more.'

'What the hell do you—'

'I didn't tell her, for instance, that Sophia's death wasn't accidental. Nor did I tell her that she was pushed down the cliff-path to her death by someone who had a very good motive for silencing her—'

'Why, you—' Jon was blind with rage and hatred. Rivers was forced to fight back in self-defence.

'For Christ's sake, Jon!'

'Jon!' cried Sarah suddenly in fear.

He stopped at once, looking back at her, his chest heaving with exertion. 'Did he tell you?' he said suddenly in a low voice. 'Did he tell you?'

She leaned back against the rock, too exhausted to do more than nod her head, not even sure what she was affirming. From far away as if in another world she heard Rivers laugh at Jon's panic, but she was conscious only of a great uneasiness prickling beneath her skin.

Jon whirled on Rivers. 'How could you?' he gasped. 'You love Marijohn. We all agreed ten years ago that no one should ever know the truth. You said yourself that it would be best for Marijohn if no one ever knew that she and I were—' He stopped.

'Jon,' said Rivers, a hard warning edge to his voice. 'Jon—'

'Yes,' cried Sarah in sudden passion. 'That you and she were what?'

'That she and I were brother and sister,' said Jon exhausted, and then instantly in horror: 'My God, you didn't know? . . .'

**4**

Justin managed to get a lift to a garage, and had just enough money to pay the mechanic for taking him back to his car with a can of petrol.

It was after sunset. The dusk was gathering.

'Should do the trick,' said the mechanic, withdrawing his head from the bonnet. 'Give 'er a try.'

The starter whined; the engine flickered briefly and died.

'Funny,' said the mechanic with interest. 'Must be trouble in the carburettor. Petrol not feeding properly. Did the gauge say you was dead out of petrol?'

'No,' said Justin. 'According to the gauge there was still a little in the tank. I just thought the gauge must have gone wrong.'

'Funny,' said the mechanic again with a deeper interest, and put his head cautiously back under the bonnet. 'Well, now, let me see . . .'


**5**

Sarah was running. The heather was scratching her legs and the darkness was all around her, smothering her lungs as she fought for breath. And then at last she saw the lighted windows of Buryan and knew she would be able at last to escape from the suffocation of the darkness and the isolation of the Cornish hillsides.

Max Alexander came out into the hall as she stumbled through the front door and paused gasping by the stairs, her shoulders leaning against the wall, her eyes closed as the blood swam through her brain.

'Sarah! What's happened? What is it?'

She sank down on the stairs, not caring that he should see her tears, and as the scene tilted crazily before her eyes she felt the sobs rise in her throat and shudder through her body.

'Sarah . . .' He was beside her, his arm round her

shoulders almost before he had time to think. 'Tell me what it is . . . If there's anything I can do—'

'Where's Marijohn?'

'In the kitchen, I think, clearing up the aftermath of the meal. Why? Do you—'

'Max, can you – would you—'

'Yes?' he said. 'What is it? Tell me what you want me to do.'

'I – I want to go away. Could you drive me into St Ives, or Penzance, anywhere—'

'Now?'

'Yes,' she whispered, struggling with her tears. 'Now.'

'But—'

'I want to be alone to think,' she said. 'I must be able to think.'

'Yes, I see. Yes, of course. All right, I'll go and start the car. You'd better pack a suitcase or something, hadn't you?'

She nodded, still blind with tears, and he helped her to her feet.

'Can you manage?'

'Yes,' she said. 'Yes, thank you.'

He waited until she had reached the landing and then he walked out of the open front door and she heard the crunch of his footsteps on the gravel of the drive.

She went to her room. Her smallest suitcase was on the floor of the cupboard. She was just opening it and trying to think what she should pack when she sensed instinctively that she was no longer alone in the room.

'Max,' she said as she swung round, 'Max, I—'

It wasn't Max. It was Marijohn.

The silence which followed seemed to go on and on and on.

'What is it?' said Sarah unsteadily at last. 'What do you want?'

The door clicked shut. The woman turned the key in the lock and then leaned back against the panels. Somewhere far away the phone started to ring but no one answered it.

'I heard your conversation with Max just now,' she said after a while. 'I knew then that I had to talk to you.'

There was silence again, a deep absolute silence, and then Marijohn said suddenly, 'If you leave Jon now it would be the worst thing you could possibly do. He loves you, and needs you. Nothing which happened in the past can ever change that.'

She moved then, walking over to the window and staring out at the dark night towards the sea. She was very still.

'That was Sophia's mistake,' she said. 'He loved and needed her too but she flung it back in his face. It was an easy mistake for her to make, because she never really loved him or understood him. But you do, don't you? I know you do. You're quite different from Sophia. As soon as I saw you, I knew you were quite different from her.'

It was difficult to breathe. Sarah found her lungs were aching with tension and her fingernails were hurting the palms of her hands.

'I want Jon to be happy,' Marijohn said. 'That's all I want. I thought it would make him happy to come down here with you to stay. I thought that if we were to meet again here of all places nothing would happen between us because the memories would be there all the time, warning us and acting as a barrier. But I was wrong and so was he, and there can never be another occasion like this now. He's leaving tomorrow – did you know that? And when he leaves I know I shall never see him again.'

She took the curtain in her hands, fingering its softness delicately, her eyes still watching the darkness beyond the pane.

'I don't know what I shall do,' she said. 'I haven't allowed myself to think much about it yet. You see . . . how can I best explain? Perhaps it's best to put it in very simple language and not try to wrap it up in careful, meaningless phrases. The truth of the matter is that I can't live without Jon, but he can live perfectly well without me. I've always known that. It's got nothing to do with love at all. It's just something that *is*, that exists. I do love Jon, and he loves me, but that's quite irrelevant. We would have this thing which exists between us even if we hated one another. I can best describe it by calling it colour. When he's not there, the world is black and grey and I'm only half-alive and dreadfully alone. And when he is there the world is multi-coloured and I can live and the concept of loneliness is nothing more than a remote unreal nightmare. That's how it affects me, but Jon I know isn't affected in the same way. When I'm not there, he doesn't live in a twilight black-and-white world as I do. He lives in a different world but the world is merely coloured differently and although he may miss me he's still able to live a full, normal life. That's why he's been able to marry and find happiness, whereas I know I can never marry again. I should never even have married Michael. But Jon told me to marry. I was unhappy and he thought it was the answer to all my difficulties. I was always unhappy . . .

'I can't remember when I first discovered this thing. I suppose it was after Jon's parents were divorced and I was taken away from Jon to live in a convent. I knew then how strange the world seemed without him . . . Then when I was fourteen his father took me away from the convent and I was able to live at his house in London and Jon came back into my life. We both discovered the thing together then. It was rather exciting, like discovering a new dimension . . . But then his father misunderstood the situation and, thinking the worst, decided to separate us again for a while. That was when I began to have affairs with as many men as I could – anything to bring colour back to my grey, black-and-white world . . . Jon married Sophia. I was glad he was happy, although it was terrible to lose him. I wouldn't have minded so much if I'd liked her, but she was such a stupid little bitch – I couldn't think what he saw in her . . . I went on, having affair after affair until one day things went wrong and I had a great revulsion – a hatred of men, of life, and of the whole world. It was Jon who cured me. I went down to Buryan to see him and he brought me back to life and promised he'd keep in touch. I married Michael after that. Poor Michael. He's been very good to me always, and I've never been able to give him anything in return.'

She stopped. It was still in the room. There was no sound at all.

'Even Michael never understood properly,' she said at last. 'Even he tended to think I had some kind of illicit relationship with Jon, but it wasn't true. Jon and I have never even exchanged an embrace which could remotely be described as incestuous. The thing we share is quite apart from all that, and I can't see why it should be considered wrong. But Michael thought it was. And Sophia . . . Sophia simply had no understanding of the situation at all. My God, she was a stupid little fool! If ever a woman drove her husband away from her, that woman was Sophia.'

A door banged somewhere in the distance. There were footsteps on the stairs, a voice calling Sarah's name.

Marijohn unlocked the door just as Jon turned the handle and burst into the room. 'Sarah—' he began and then stopped short as he found himself face to face with Marijohn.

'I was trying to explain to her,' she said quietly. 'I was trying to tell her about us.'

'She already knows. You're too late.'

Marijohn went white. 'But how—'

'I told her myself,' said Jon, and as he spoke Sarah saw them both turn towards her. 'I thought Michael had already told her. I'm sure she must have guessed by now that we both had a first-class motive for murdering Sophia.'

6

It was dark on the road but fortunately the mechanic had a torch and could see what he was doing. Justin, glancing around in an agony of impatience, caught sight of a lighted window of a farmhouse a few hundred yards from the road and began to move over towards it.

'I won't be long,' he called to the mechanic. 'I have to make a phone call.'

The track was rough beneath his feet and the farmyard when he reached it smelled of manure. The woman who answered the door looked faintly offended when he asked her politely if he could use her telephone, but showed him into the hall and left him alone to make the call.

He dialled the St Just exchange with an unsteady hand. It seemed an eternity before the operator answered.

'St Just 584, please.'

Another endless space of time elapsed, and then he could hear the bell ringing and his fingers gripped the receiver even tighter than before.

It rang and rang and rang.

'Sorry, sir,' said the operator at last, cutting in across the ringing bell, 'but there seems to be no reply . . .'

# 7

They were still looking at her, their eyes withdrawn and tense, and it seemed to her as she watched them that their mental affinity was never more clearly visible and less intangible than at that moment when they shared identical expressions.

'What did Sophia threaten to do?' she heard herself say at last, and her voice was astonishingly cool and self-possessed in her ears.

'Surely you can guess,' said Jon. 'She was going to drag Marijohn's name right across her divorce petition. Can't you picture the revenge she planned in her jealousy, the damage she wanted to cause us both? Can't you imagine the longing she had to hurt and smear and destroy?'

'I see.' And she did see. She was beginning to feel sick and dizzy again.

'Marijohn is illegitimate,' he said, as if in an attempt

to explain the situation flatly. 'We have the same father. Her mother died soon after she was born and my father – in spite of my mother's protests and disgust – brought her to live with us. After the divorce, he naturally took her away – he had to. My mother only had her there on sufferance anyway.'

The silence fell again, deepening as the seconds passed.

'Jon,' said Sarah at last. 'Jon, did you—'

He knew what she wanted to ask, and she sensed that he had wanted her to ask the question which was foremost in her mind.

'No,' he said. 'I didn't kill Sophia. You must believe that, because I swear it's the truth. And if you ask why I lied to you, why I always told you Sophia's death was an accident, I'll tell you. I thought Marijohn had killed her. Everything I did which may have seemed like an admission of guilt on my part was in order to protect Marijohn – but although I didn't know it at the time, Marijohn thought *I'd* killed her. In spite of all our mutual understanding, we've both been suffering under a delusion about each other for ten years. Ironic, isn't it?'

She stared at him, not answering. After a moment he moved towards her, leaving Marijohn by the door.

'The scene with Sophia came after supper on the night she died,' he said. 'Michael was there too. After it was over, I went out into the garden to escape and sat on the swing-seat in the darkness for a long while trying to think what I should do. Finally I went back into the house to discuss the situation with Marijohn but she wasn't there. I went upstairs, but she wasn't there either and when I came downstairs again I met Eve in the hall. She told me Sophia had gone out to the Flat Rocks to meet Max, and suddenly I wondered if Marijohn had gone after Sophia to try and reason with her. I dashed out of the house and tore up the cliff path. I heard Sophia shout "Let me go!" and then she screamed when I was about a hundred yards from the steps leading down to the Flat Rocks, and on running forward I found Marijohn at the cliff's edge staring down the steps. She was panting as if she'd been running – or struggling. She said that she'd been for a walk along the cliffs towards Sennen and was on her way back home when she'd heard the scream. We went down the steps and found Max bending over Sophia's body. He'd been waiting for her on the Flat Rocks below.' He paused. 'Or so he said.'

There was a pause. Sarah turned to Marijohn. 'What a coincidence,' she said, 'that you should be so near the steps at the time. What made you turn back at that particular moment during your walk along the cliffs and arrive at the steps just after Sophia was killed?'

'Sarah—' Jon was white with anger, but Marijohn interrupted him.

'I could feel Jon wanted me,' she said simply. 'I knew he was looking for me so I turned back.'

Sarah scarcely recognized her voice when she next spoke. It was the voice of a stranger, brittle, hard and cold. 'How very interesting,' she said. 'I've never really believed in telepathy.'

'What are you suggesting?' said Jon harshly. 'That I'm lying? That Marijohn is lying? That we're both lying?'

Sarah moved past him, opening the door clumsily in her desire to escape from their presence.

'One of you must be lying,' she said. 'That's obvious. Sophia before she fell called out "Let me go", which means she was struggling with someone who pushed her to her death. Somebody killed her, and either of you – as you tell me yourself – had an ideal motive.'

'Sarah—'

'Let her go, Jon. Let her be.'

Sarah was in the corridor now, taking great gulps of air as if she had been imprisoned for a long time in a stifling cell. She went downstairs and out into the drive. The night air was deliciously cool, and as she wandered farther from the house the freedom was all around her, a vast relief after the confined tension in that upstairs room.

He was waiting for her by the gate. She was so absorbed

in her own emotions and her desire to escape that she never even noticed, as she took the cliff path, that she was being followed.

## 8

'It's a funny thing,' said the mechanic when Justin reached the car again, 'but I can't make her go. T'ain't the carburettor. Can't understand it.'

Justin thought quickly. He could get a lift to St Just and a lift out to the airport, but he would have to walk the mile and a half from the airport down into the valley to Buryan. But anything was better than waiting fruitlessly by the roadside at Zennor. He could try another phone call from the square at St Just.

'All right,' he said to the mechanic. 'I'll have to try and get a lift home. Can you fix up for someone from your garage to tow away my car tomorrow and find out what's wrong?'

'Do it right now, if you like. It only means—'

'No, I can't wait now. I'll have to go on ahead.' He found a suitable tip and gave it to the man who looked a little astonished by this impatience. 'Thank you very much for all your trouble. Goodnight.'

'Goodnight to you,' said the mechanic agreeably enough, pocketing the tip, and climbed into his shooting brake to drive back along the road towards St Ives.

## 9

Sarah first saw the dark figure behind her when she was half a mile from the house. The cliff path had turned round the hillside so that the lighted windows were hidden from her, and she was just pausing in the darkness to listen to the sea far below and regain her breath after the uphill climb when she glanced over her shoulder and saw the man.

Every bone in her body suddenly locked itself into a tight white fear.

You've been assigned Sophia's role . . .

The terror was suffocating, wave after wave of hot dizziness that went on and on even after she began to stumble forward along the cliff path. She never paused to ask herself why anyone should want her dead. She only knew in that blind, sickening flash that she was in danger and she had to escape.

But there was no cover on the stark hillside, nowhere to shelter.

It was then that she thought of the rocks below. In the jumbled confusion of boulders at the foot of the cliffs there were a thousand hiding places, and perhaps also another route by the sea's edge back to the cove and the house. If she could somehow find the way down the cliff to the Flat Rocks . . .

The path forked slightly and remembering her exploring earlier that day, she took the downward path and found the steps cut in the cliff which led to the rocks below.

Her limbs were suddenly awkward; the sea was a roar that receded and pounded in her ears, drowning the noise of her gasps for breath.

She looked back.

The man was running.

In a panic, not even trying to find the alternative route down the cliff, she scrambled down the steps, clinging to the jutting rocks in the sandy face and sliding the last few feet to the rocks below. She started to run forward, slipped, fell. The breath was knocked out of her body and as she pulled herself to her feet she looked up and saw him at the head of the steps above her.

She flattened herself against the large rock nearby, not moving, not breathing, praying he hadn't seen her.

'Sarah?' he called.

He sounded anxious, concerned.

She didn't answer.

He cautiously began to descend the steps.

Let him fall, said the single voice in her mind drowning even the noise of the sea. Let him slip and fall. She couldn't move. If she moved he would see her and she would have less chance of escape.

He didn't like the steps at all. She heard him curse under his breath, and a shower of sand and pebbles scattered from the cliff face as he fumbled his way down uncertainly.

He reached the rocks below at last and stood still six feet away from her. She could hear his quick breathing as he straightened his frame and stared around, his eyes straining to pierce the darkness.

'Sarah?' he called again, and added as an afterthought: 'It's all right, it's only me.'

She was pressing back so hard against the rock that her shoulder blades hurt. Her whole body ached with the strain of complete immobility.

He took a step forward and another and stood listening again.

Close at hand and surf broke on the reefs and ledges of the Flat Rocks and was sucked back into the sea again with the undertow.

He saw her.

He didn't move at all at first, and then he came towards her and she started to scream.

## chapter 6

1

Justin was running, the breath choking his lungs. He was running past the farm down the track to Buryan, not knowing why he was afraid, knowing only that his mother's murderer was at the house and that no one knew the truth except Justin himself and the killer. He didn't even know why his mother had been killed. The apparent motivelessness of the crime nagged his mind as he ran, but he had no doubts about the murderer's correct identity. According to Eve it could only be one person . . .

He could hear the stream now, could see the bulk of the disused water-wheel on one side of the track, and suddenly he was at Buryan at last and stumbling through the open front door into the lighted hall.

'Daddy!' he shouted, and the word which had lain silent in the back of his vocabulary for ten years was then the first word which sprang to the tip of his tongue. 'Where are you? Marijohn!'

He burst into the drawing room but they weren't there. They weren't in the music room either.

'Sarah!' he shouted. 'Sarah!'

But Sarah didn't answer.

He had a sudden premonition of disaster, a white warning flash across his brain which was gone in less than a second. Tearing up the stairs, he raced down the corridor and flung open the door of his father's bedroom.

They were there. They were sitting on the window-seat together, and he was vaguely conscious that his father looked drawn and unhappy while Marijohn's calm, still face was streaked with tears.

'Justin! What in God's name—'

'Where's Sarah?' was all he could say, each syllable coming unevenly as he gasped for breath. 'Where is she?'

There were footsteps in the corridor unexpectedly, a shadow in the doorway.

'She's gone for a walk with Michael,' said Max Alexander.

2

'It's all right,' Michael Rivers' voice was saying soothingly from far away. 'It's all right, Sarah. It's only me . . . Look, let's find a better place to sit down. It's too dark here.'

174

She was still shuddering, her head swimming with the shock, but she let him lead her farther down towards the sea until they were standing on the Flat Rocks by the water's edge.

'Why did you follow me?' she managed to say as they sat down on a long low rock.

'I saw you leave and couldn't think where on earth you were going or what you wanted to do. I believe I thought you might even be thinking of committing suicide.'

'Suicide?' She stared at him. 'Why?' And in the midst of her confusion she was conscious of thinking that in spite of all that had happened, the thought of suicide to escape from her unhappiness and shock had never crossed her mind.

'You've been married – how long? Two weeks? Three? And you discover suddenly that your husband has a rather "unique" relationship with another woman—'

'We're leaving tomorrow,' she interrupted. 'Marijohn told me. Jon's decided to leave and never see her again.'

'He decided that ten years ago. I'm afraid I wouldn't rely too much on statements like that, if I were you. And what do you suppose your marriage is going to be like after this? He'll never fully belong to you now, do you realize that? Part of him will always be with Marijohn. Good God, I of all people should know what I'm talking about! I tried to live with Marijohn after Jon had first disrupted our marriage, but it was utterly impossible. Everything was over and done with, and there was no going back.'

'Stop it!' said Sarah with sudden violence. 'Stop it!'

'So in the light of the fact you know your three-week-old marriage is finished, I don't see why you shouldn't think of committing suicide. You're young and unbalanced by grief and shock. You come out here to the Flat Rocks, to the sea, and the tide is going out and the currents are particularly dangerous—'

She tried to move but he wouldn't let her go.

'I thought of suicide that weekend at Buryan,' he said. 'Did you guess that? I went fishing that afternoon by the sea and thought and thought about what I could do. I was out of my mind . . . And then the child came and talked to me and afterwards I went back to the house. Marijohn was in our bedroom. I knew then how much I loved her, and I knew that I could never share her with any man, even if the relationship she had with him was irreproachable and completely above suspicion. I foresaw that I would be forced to have a scene with Jon in an attempt to tell him that I could stand it no longer and that I was taking Marijohn away . . . So after dinner we had the final scene. And I was winning . . . It was going to be all right. Jon was shaken – I can see his expression now . . . And then, oh Christ, Sophia had to come in, threatening divorce proceedings, threatening exposure to anyone who would listen – God, she would have destroyed everything! And Marijohn's name smeared all across the Sunday papers and all my friends and colleagues in town saying, "Poor old Michael – ghastly business. Who would have thought . . ." and so on and so on . . .

'All the gossip and publicity, the destruction of Marijohn, of everything I wanted . . . Sophia was going to destroy my entire world.'

'So you killed her.'

He looked at her then, his face oddly distant. 'Yes,' he said. 'I killed her. And Jon went away, saying he would never have any further communication with Marijohn, and I thought that at last I was going to have Marijohn back again and that at last I was going to be happy.'

His expression changed. He grimaced for a moment, his expression contorted, and when he next spoke she heard the grief in his voice.

'But she wouldn't come back to me,' he said. 'I went through all that and committed murder to safeguard her and preserve her from destruction, and all she could do was say how sorry she was but she could never live with me again.'

The surf broke over the rocks at their feet; white foam flew for a moment in the darkness and disintegrated.

'Sophia knew they were brother and sister,' he said.

'Not that it mattered. She would have made trouble anyway. But if she had never known they were brother and sister, the scope of her threats would have been narrower and less frightening in its implications . . . But she knew. Very few people did. The relationship had always been kept secret from the beginning in order to spare Jon's mother embarrassment. Old Towers made out that Marijohn was the child of a deceased younger brother of his. And when they were older they kept it secret to avoid underlining Marijohn's illegitimacy. I always did think it would have been best if Sophia had never known the secret, but Jon told her soon after they were married, so she knew about it from the beginning.'

There was another pause. Sarah tried to imagine what would happen if she attempted to break away. Could she reach the cover of the nearby rocks in time? Probably not. Perhaps if she doubled back . . . She turned her head slightly to look behind her, and as she moved, Rivers said: 'And now there's you. You'll divorce Jon eventually. Even if your marriage survives this crisis there'll be others, and then it'll all come out, the relationship with Marijohn, your very natural jealousy – everything. Marijohn's name will be dragged across the petition because like Sophia, you know the truth, and when the time comes for you to want a divorce you'll be embittered enough to use any weapon at your disposal in an attempt to hit back at both of them. And that'll mean danger for Marijohn. Whatever happens I want to avoid that, because of course I still love her and sometimes I can still hope that one day she'll come back . . . Perhaps she will. I don't know. But whether she comes back or not I still love her just the same. I know that better than anything else in the world.'

There was no hope of escape by running behind them across the rocks. The way was too jagged and Sarah guessed it would be too easy in the dark to stumble into one of the pools and lagoons beyond the reefs.

'It would be so convenient if you committed suicide,' he said. 'Perhaps I could even shift the blame on to Jon if murder were suspected. I tried to last time. I planned the death to look like an accident, but I wore a red sweater of Jon's just in case anyone happened to see me go up the cliff path and murder was suspected afterwards. I knew Sophia was meeting Max on the Flat Rocks. I heard Sophia remind him of their rendezvous after supper, and saw Max leave the house later. Then after the scene in the drawing room when we all went our separate ways, I didn't go up to my bedroom as I told you earlier this evening. Jon went into the garden, Marijohn went to the drawing room, Sophia went upstairs to change her high-heeled shoes for a pair of canvas beach shoes, and I took Jon's sweater off the chest in the hall and went out ahead of her to the cliffs. I didn't have to wait long before she came out from the house to follow me . . .

'But they never suspected murder, the slow Cornish police. They talked of accident and suicide, but murder was never mentioned. Nobody knew, you see, of any possible motives. They were all hidden, secret, protected from the outside world . . .'

'Michael.'

He turned to look at her and she was close enough to him to see in the darkness that his eyes were clouded as if he were seeing only scenes of long ago.

'If I said that I wasn't going to divorce Jon and that the secret was safe with me—'

'You'd be wasting your breath, I'm afraid, my dear. I've confessed to you now that I'm a murderer and that's one secret I could never trust you to keep.'

She swung round suddenly to face the cliffs. 'What's that?'

He swung round too, swivelling his body instinctively, and even as he moved she was on her feet and running away from him in among the rocks to escape.

He shouted something and then was after her and the rocks were towering tombstones of a nightmare and the roar of the sea merged with the roaring of the blood in her ears. The granite grazed her hands, tore at her stockings, bruised her feet through the soles of her shoes.

She twisted and turned, scrambling amongst the rocks, terrified of coming up against a blank wall of rock or falling into a deep gully. And still he came after her, gaining slowly every minute, and her mind was a blank void of terror depriving her of speech and voice.

When she was at the base of the cliff again she caught her foot in a crevice and the jolt wrenched her ankle and tore off her shoe. She gave a cry of pain, the sound wrenched involuntarily from her body, and as the sound was carried away from her on the still night air she saw the pin-prick of light above her on the cliff path.

'Jon!' she screamed, thrusting all her energy into that one monosyllable. 'Jon! Jon!'

And then Rivers was upon her and she was fighting for her life, scratching, clawing, biting in a frenzy of self-preservation. The scene began to blur before her eyes, the world tilted crazily. She tried to scream again but no sound came, and as the energy ebbed from her body she felt his fingers close on her throat.

There was pain. It was a hot red light suffocating her entire brain. She tried to breathe and could not. Her hands were just slackening their grip on his body when there was a sound far above her, and the pebbles started to rattle down the cliff face, flicking across her face like hailstones.

She heard Rivers gasp something, and then he was gone and she fell back against the rock.

The blackness when it came a second later was a welcome release from the swimming nightmare of terror and fear.


3


When she awoke, there was a man bending over her, and although it seemed that an eternity had passed since Rivers had left her, she learned afterwards that she had been unconscious for less than a minute. The man was frantic. There was sweat on his forehead and fear in his eyes and he kept saying, 'Sarah, Sarah, Sarah' as if his mind would not allow him to say anything else.

She put up her hand and touched his lips with her fingers.

'Is she all right?' said another vaguely familiar voice from close at hand. 'Where the hell is Rivers?'

The man whose lips she had touched stood up. 'Stay here with Sarah, Max. Have you got that? Don't leave her alone for a moment. Stay with her.'

'Jon,' her voice said. 'Jon.'

He bent over her again. 'I'm going to find him,' he said to her gently. 'Justin's gone after him already. Max'll look after you.'

'He – he killed Sophia, Jon . . . He told me—'

'I know.'

He was gone. One moment he was there and the next moment he had moved out of her sight and she was alone with Alexander. He was breathing very heavily, as if the sudden violent exercise had been too much for him.

'Max—'

'Yes. I'm here.' He sat down beside her, still panting with exertion, and as he took her hand comfortingly in his she had the odd instinctive feeling that he cared for her. The feeling was so strange and so illogical that she dismissed it instantly without a second thought, and instead concentrated all her mind on the relief of being alive.

And as they waited together at the base of the cliffs, Jon was sprinting over the Flat Rocks to the water's edge, the beam of the torch in his hand warning him of the gullies and the crevices, the reefs and lagoons.

By the water's edge he paused.

'Justin!'

There was an answering flicker of a torch farther away, a muffled shout.

Jon moved forward again, leaping from rock to rock, slithering past seaweed and splashing in diminutive rock pools. It took him two minutes to reach his son.

'Where is he?'

'I don't know.' Justin's face was white in the torchlight, his eyes dark and huge and ringed with tiredness.

'You lost sight of him?'

'He was here.' He gestured with his torch. They were standing on a squat rock, and six feet below them the sea was sucking and gurgling with the motions of the tide. 'I saw him reach this rock and then scramble over it until he was lost from sight.'

Jon was silent. Presently he shone his torch up and down the channel below, but there was nothing there except the dark water and the white of the surf.

'Could he – do you think he would have tried to swim round to the cove?'

'Don't be a bloody fool.'

The boy hung his head a little, as if regretting the stupidity of his suggestion, and waited wordlessly for the other man to make the next move.

'He couldn't have fallen in the darkness,' said Jon after a moment. 'When you reach the top of a rock you always stop to look to see what's on the other side. And if he had slipped into this channel he could have clambered out on to the other side – unless he struck his head on the rocky floor, and then we'd be able to see his body.'

'Then—'

'Perhaps you're right and he went swimming after all . . . We'd better search these rocks here just to make sure, I suppose. You take that side and I'll take this side.'

But although they searched for a long while in the darkness they found no trace of Michael Rivers, and it was many weeks before his body was finally recovered from the sea.

4

'What'll happen?' said Justin to his father. 'What shall we do?'

They were in the drawing room at Buryan again. It

was after midnight, and the tiredness was aching through Justin's body in great throbbing waves of exhaustion. Even when he sat down the room seemed to waver and recede dizzily before his eyes.

'We'll have to call the police.'

'You're mad, of course,' said Alexander from the sofa. 'You must be. What on earth are you going to say to the police? That Michael's dead? We don't know for sure that he is. That Michael tried to kill Sarah? The first question the police are going to ask is why the hell should Michael, a perfectly respectable solicitor, a pillar of society, suddenly attempt to murder your wife. My dear Jon, you'll end up by getting so involved that the police will probably think we're all in one enormous conspiracy to pull wool over their eyes. They'll ask you why, if you *knew* your first wife had been murdered, you didn't say so at the time. They'll ask you all sorts of questions about Marijohn and your reasons for wanting to protect her. They'll probe incessantly for motives—'

'For Christ's sake, Max!'

'Well, stop talking such God almighty rubbish.'

'Are you scared for your own skin or something?'

'Oh God,' said Alexander wearily, and turned to the boy hunched in the armchair. 'Justin, explain to your father that if he goes to the police now Sophia – and probably Michael too – have both died in vain. Ask him if he really wants Sarah's name smeared all across the Sunday papers. "Canadian millionaire in murder mystery. Horror on the honeymoon." God, can't you imagine the headlines even now? "Sensation! Millionaire's first wife *murdered*! Millionaire helping police in their enquiries." It would be intolerable for you all, Jon – for Sarah, for Justin, for Marijohn—'

The door opened. He stopped as Marijohn came into the room.

'How is she?' said Jon instantly. 'Is she asking for me? Is she all right?'

'She's asleep. I gave her two of my sleeping tablets.' She turned away from him and moved over towards the boy in the corner. 'Justin darling, you look quite exhausted. Why don't you go to bed? There's nothing more you can do now.'

'I—' He faltered, looking at his father. 'I was wondering what's going to happen. If you call the police—'

'Police?' said Marijohn blankly. She swung round to face Jon. 'Police?'

'Tell him he's crazy, Marijohn.'

'Look, Max—'

There they go again, thought Justin numbly. More arguments, more talk. Police or no police, what to tell and what not to tell, Michael's death or disappearance and what to do about it. And I'm so very, very tired . . .

He closed his eyes for a second. The voices became fainter and then suddenly someone was stooping over him and there was an arm round his shoulders and the cold rim of a glass against his lips. He drank, choked and opened his eyes as the liquid burnt his throat.

'Poor Justin,' said the voice he had loved so much ten years ago. 'Come on, you're going to bed. Drink the rest of the brandy and we'll go upstairs.'

There was fire in his throat again. The great heaviness in his limbs seemed to lessen fractionally and with his father's help he managed to stand up and move over to the door.

'I'm all right now,' he heard himself say in the hall. 'Sorry to be a nuisance.'

'I'll come upstairs with you.'

There seemed more stairs than usual, an endless climb to the distant plateau of the landing, but at last they were in the bedroom and the bed was soft and yielding as he sank down on it thankfully.

'I'm all right,' he repeated automatically, and then his shirt was eased gently from his body and the next moment the cool pyjama jacket brushed his skin.

'I'm afraid I've been very selfish,' said his father's voice. 'I haven't said a word of thanks to you since you arrived back and all I could do down on the Flat Rocks was to be abrupt and short-tempered.'

'It – it doesn't matter. I understand.'

'I'll never forget that it was you who saved Sarah. I want you to know that. If Sarah had died tonight—'

'She'll be all right, won't she? She's going to be all right?'

'Yes,' said Jon. 'She's going to be all right.'

The sheets were deliciously white, the pillow sensuously soft and yielding. Justin sank back, pulling the coverlet across his chest and allowing his limbs to relax in a haze of comfort and peace.

He never even heard his father leave the room.

When he awoke it was still dark but someone had opened the door of his room and the light from the landing was shining across the foot of his bed.

'Who's that?' he murmured sleepily, and then Marijohn was stooping over him and he twisted round in bed so that he could see her better. 'What's happened?' he said, suddenly very wide awake, his brain miraculously clear and alert. 'Have you called the police?'

'No.' She sat down on the edge of the bed and for a moment he thought she was going to kiss him but she merely touched his cheek lightly with her fingertips. 'I'm sorry I woke you up. I didn't mean to disturb you. Jon's just gone to bed and Max is still downstairs drinking the last of the whisky. We've been talking for nearly three hours.'

He sat up a little in bed. 'Haven't you decided anything?' She looked at him and he thought he saw her smile faintly, but the light was behind her and it was difficult for him to see her face.

'You're leaving tomorrow – you and Sarah and Jon,' she said and there was a curious dull edge to her voice which he didn't fully understand. 'You'll go straight to London and catch the first plane to Canada. Max and I are going to handle the police.'

He stared at her blankly. 'How?' he said. 'What are you going to tell them?'

'Very little. Max is going to drive Michael's car up past the farm and abandon it on the heath near the airport.

Then tomorrow or the day after I'm going to phone the police and tell them I'm worried about Michael and think he may have committed suicide – I'm going to say that Max and I have found Michael's car abandoned on the heath after you all departed for London. Our story is going to be that Michael came down here in the hope of persuading me to go back to him, and when I refused – finally and for ever – there was a scene which ended in him leaving the house and driving away. We shall say he threatened suicide before he left. Then the police can search for him as thoroughly as they wish, and when his body is eventually recovered – as I suppose it must be, even on this rocky coast – it'll lend support to our story.'

'Supposing Michael isn't dead?'

'He must be. Jon is convinced of it. Michael had nothing left to live for, nothing at all.'

'But . . .' He hesitated, trying to phrase what he wanted to say. Then: 'Why is it so vital that the police don't know the truth from start to finish?' he blurted out at last. 'I mean, I know the scandal would be terrible, but—'

'There are reasons,' she said. 'Your father will tell you.'

'But why did Michael try to kill Sarah? And why did he kill my mother? I don't—'

'He wanted to protect me,' she said, her voice suddenly flat and without life. 'It was all for me. Your father will explain everything to you later when you're all far away in Canada.'

He still stared at her. 'I couldn't see why he was the murderer,' he repeated at last. 'I knew he must have been the murderer but I couldn't see why.'

'What did Eve tell you? What did she say that suddenly made you realize Michael was guilty?'

'I – I persuaded her to talk to me about her own memories of that weekend at Buryan, and her memories, when I pieced them together with my own, spelled the real sequence of events.' He paused to collect his thoughts, thinking of Eve and the little room in St Ives above the blue of the bay. 'I thought my father had killed my mother because I followed a man with a red sweater up the cliff path and saw him push my mother to her death in the darkness . . . As soon as I'd seen her fall I ran away up the hillside and over the hill-top to Buryan. I didn't take the cliff path back to the house because I was afraid my father would see me, so I never discovered that the man in the red sweater wasn't my father at all. But I think Michael must have returned to the house by a similar route to the one I took, because neither you, coming from Sennen, nor my father, coming from Buryan along the cliff path, saw either Michael or myself. My father told me tonight that you and he had met by the steps soon after my mother fell.

'When I left the house to follow the man in the red sweater I met Eve – she was coming up the path from the beach just as I was about to take the fork which led up on to the cliffs. I hid from her, and she didn't see me.

'This afternoon she told me what had happened to her that evening. She said that when she reached the house again after I'd seen her she met my father. That proved to me that the man in the red sweater couldn't have been my father, and she also remembered he wasn't wearing a sweater when she saw him and that the red sweater he'd worn earlier in the evening had been removed from the chest in the hall.

'That meant the man had to be either Michael or Max. And according to Eve, it couldn't possibly have been Max because she'd seen him go off along the cliff path to the Flat Rocks some while before she passed me on her way back to the house. She said they had quarrelled at the spot where the path from Buryan forks, one track leading up on to the cliffs and one leading down to the cove, and afterwards he had gone off up the cliff path to wait for my mother – Eve saw him go. Then she sat down by the fork in the path to try to pull herself together and decide what she should do. She would have seen Max if he had come back from the cliffs, but he didn't come back. And the man in the red sweater, whom I followed had started out *from the house* a few minutes before I saw Eve coming back up the path to Buryan where she was to meet my father. So the man had to be Michael. My father was still at the house and Max had already gone out to the Flat Rocks. There was no one else it could possibly be.'

'I see.' She was silent for a moment, and he wondered what she was thinking. And then she was standing up, smoothing the skirt of her dress over her hips automatically, and moving towards the door again. 'You'd better get some more sleep,' she said at last. 'I mustn't keep you awake any longer.'

She stepped across the threshold, and as she turned to close the door and the light slanted across her face, something in her expression made him call out after her.

But she did not hear him.


5

Max had just finished the whisky when Marijohn went downstairs to lock up and switch off the lights. A half-smoked cigarette was between his fingers and as she came into the room the ash dropped from the glowing tip to the carpet.

'Hullo,' he said, and he didn't sound very drunk. 'How's my fellow-conspirator?'

She drew the curtains back, not answering, and reached up to fasten the bolt on the french windows.

'You know why I'm doing it, don't you?' he said sardonically. 'I'm not doing it for you or for Jon. Between you you've destroyed a good man and were indirectly responsible for Sophia's death. You deserve all you get. So I'm not doing this for you. I'm doing this for the girl because I don't see why she should suffer any more than she's suffered already. Quixotic, isn't it? Rather amusing. But then I've always been a fool over women . . . Lord, what a fool I was over Sophia! I wanted her dead just as much as everyone else did, did you ever realize that? I told Sarah this afternoon that I felt sorry for Sophia, and so I did – to begin with. But I left several details out of my story to Sarah; I never told her that Sophia was trying to force me into taking her away to London with me, never mentioned that Sophia was threatening me, never hinted that it was I, not Sophia, who suggested the rendezvous on the Flat Rocks so that I could try and make her see reason . . . And once she was dead, of course, I said nothing, never breathing a word of my suspicions to anyone, because I had a strong motive for wanting her dead and in any police murder enquiry I would naturally be one of the chief suspects . . . And even now you won't have 'zto worry in case I decide to change my mind and say too much to the police sometime in the future, because I know for a fact that I haven't long to live and when I die you'll all be quite safe, you and Jon, Sarah and the boy . . . The boy will have to know the full story, of course. I can't say I envy Jon having to explain . . . You're fond of the boy, aren't you? I suppose it's because he reminds you of Jon.'

Yes, said a voice in her brain instantly in a sudden flare of grief, and no doubt I shall always have to share him just as I've had to share Jon. Aloud she said, 'I've no mental affinity with Justin at all. He doesn't remind me of Jon as much as all that.'

There was a pause before Alexander said, 'And what will you do? You won't stay here longer than you can help, will you?'

'No,' she said. 'Jon wants me to sell Buryan. He says he never wants to see the place again.'

'Poor old Jon,' said Alexander inconsequentially, swallowing the dregs of his whisky. 'Who would have thought the day would have come when he would say he never wanted to see Buryan again? He'll be saying next that he never wants to see you again, either.'

'He doesn't have to say that,' said Marijohn, and the tears were like hot needles behind her eyes. 'I already know.'

# 6

When Sarah awoke it was dim and she could see that there was a white mist swirling outside the window beyond the chink in the curtains. She stirred. Memory returned suddenly in sickening flashes of consciousness, and even as she reached for him instinctively, Jon was pulling her close to him and burying his face in her hair as he kissed her.

'How are you feeling?'

She pressed against him, savouring his nearness and her own security. 'Jon . . . Jon . . .'

'I'm taking you away from here,' he said. 'We're leaving with Justin after breakfast. Then as soon as we get to London we're flying home to Canada. I'll explain later how Max and Marijohn are going to cope with the police – you don't have to worry about anything at all.'

She put her hand to his face and traced the outline of his jaw as she kissed him on the mouth.

'I love you,' he said in between her kisses, and his voice was unsteady so that it didn't sound like his voice at all. 'Do you hear? I love, love, love you, and you're never never going to have to go through anything like this again.'

'Will we come back to England?' she murmured. The question didn't seem very important somehow but she had a feeling it should nevertheless be asked.

'No,' he said, his voice firm and positive again. 'Never.'

'Oh.' she sighed, half-wondering why she had no feeling of sadness. 'We must find time to say goodbye to your mother before we leave,' she said as an afterthought. 'I feel sorry for her in some ways. I'm sure she'll miss Justin terribly.'

'She'll get over it.' His mouth was hardening again. 'Like most beautiful women she's egocentric enough to care for no one deeply except herself.'

'That's nonsense, Jonny, and you know it!' She felt almost cross. 'It's obvious to any outsider that she cares very deeply for you – no, I don't care what you say! I know I'm right! We must invite her out to Canada to visit us. She's got plenty of money so she'll be able to come whenever she likes. And anyway I think Justin should have the opportunity to keep in touch with his grandmother – after all, she brought him up, didn't she? In spite of the row they had when you offered him the job in Canada, I'm sure he must be very fond of her. Before we fly back to Canada we must call on her and arrange something.'

Jon's mouth was still a hard stubborn line. 'Sarah—'

She slipped her hand behind his head and pressed his face to hers to kiss the stubbornness from his expression. 'Please, Jon!'

The victory came in less than five seconds. She felt him relax, saw his eyes soften, felt his mouth curve in a smile, and she knew then for the first time that there would be no more dread of the Distant Mood, no more tension and worry because she did not understand or could not cope with his changes of humour. When he bent over her a moment later and she felt the love in every line of his frame flow into hers, she knew he would never again belong to anyone else except her.

# *epilogue*

When they had all gone and she was alone in the still, quiet house, Marijohn sat down at the desk in the drawing room and took a clean sheet of notepaper and a pen.

She sat thinking for a long while. It was very peaceful. Outside the sky was blue and the stream rushed past the water-wheel at the end of the drive.

She dipped her pen in the ink.

'My darling Jon,' she wrote quickly at last with firm, resolute strokes of the pen. 'By the time you read this, you will be home in Canada in the midst of your new life. I know there's so much for you there, more now than ever before, as both Sarah and Justin will be with you and in time Sarah will have children of her own. I want you to know first and foremost how glad I am about this, because almost more than anything else on earth I want you to be happy and to lead a rich, full, worthwhile life.

'I have decided to go back to the only world I think I could ever live in now, the world of Anselm's Cross – or of any convent anywhere. I did think of avoiding this by travelling abroad, Jon, just as you suggested, but I don't think I would find peace abroad any more than I would find peace here at Buryan.

'When I look back I can see how clearly the fault was mine. In a way, it was I who killed Sophia and I who killed Michael and I who almost killed Sarah. I ruined Michael's life and very nearly yours as well. You could forgive me for both I expect, but I know you'll never really forgive me for what happened to Sarah that night. Max always said *you* were the one who was the constant source of danger to everyone around you, but he was wrong. I was the source of danger, not you. Everything I touch seems to turn into a disaster. If you're honest with yourself you'll see that as clearly as I see it now.

'You did talk when we parted of perhaps seeing me again in the very distant future, but Jon darling, I know you so well and I know when you're lying to save me pain. I shall never see you again, not because you think it's better for us to be apart or because you owe it to Sarah or for any other noble reason, but because you *don't want* to see me – because you know, just as I know, that it was through me that Sarah was nearly killed and your second marriage nearly wrecked as utterly as your first, and you never want to run the risk of that happening again. I don't blame you; in a way, the knowledge that I'll never see you again helps me to see more clearly which course I now have to take.

'I've just three things left to say. Don't pity me, don't blame yourself, and don't ever try to communicate with me, even out of kindness, in the years to come.

'All my love, darling, now and always, and all the happiness you could ever wish for.

'Your own,
'Marijohn.'

# The Waiting
# Sands

## prologue

There were still times when Rachel thought of Daniel. She would think of him at the height of summer when the city sweltered beneath the hazy summer skies to bring back memories of another land where the sun was cool and the sea breathed white mist over remote shores. She would think of him sometimes at night when she awoke for no reason and sat up listening to the restless city around her, the city so many thousand miles from the past she had no wish to remember. She would think of him when the other girls in the apartment talked of love and romance and happy endings, and she would say to herself how strange it was that she should think of him so often when she knew for certain now that she had never loved him.

She had not always lived in New York, but now she had been there nearly five years. Her home was in England, in Surrey, not far from London; she was the only child of an elderly Anglican parson and his wife, and for the first twenty-two years of her life she had moved in the orderly, old-fashioned circles of the world of the country vicarage. She had gone to a local day school, progressed from there to secretarial college where she had acquired the necessary skills without undue difficulty and then had gone abroad to Geneva for six months. On her return, she had begun to earn her living in London.

It had all been typical, a career duplicated by a great many other girls. She had several good friends, was happy at home, enjoyed tennis at weekends during the summer and in general was perfectly content with her life; certainly if anyone had ever suggested to her then that she would alter her entire circumstances radically by emigrating to a foreign country she would have been astonished and then indignant that anyone could suggest such a thing.

The only extraordinary and unusual element in her otherwise normal existence was her relationship with her friend Rohan Quist.

It seemed to her often that Rohan had been the most consistent thread in her life, his presence flickering across the pattern of the years like quicksilver darting over shifting sands. For Rohan had always been there. He had shared her past and she had shared his. She could remember clinging to the stays of her play-pen while he had ridden his tricycle up and down the drive to show off to her that he was free and mobile while she was still behind the bars of infancy. But later he had taught her to ride the tricycle, led her hand in hand to kindergarten, drawn her into all the intricate games of childhood, the societies, the sworn oaths, the pacts which led to adventure. 'And nobody's to say Rachel's too young,' he had shouted to his adherents in the pack he led. 'Because she's my friend!' She could see him now, eight years old, thin and wiry with thick straw-coloured hair and enormous blazing grey eyes.

Rachel's my friend . . .

And Rohan was good to his friends. Long afterwards when they were grown up it was he who would provide an escort whenever she wanted to go out, he who had the little red Volkswagen to take her on weekend drives into the country, he who had invited her to the May Ball at Cambridge where she had met a whole host of eligible young men. 'We'll say we're cousins,' he had ordered authoritatively. 'Then no one will get the idea that I have any possessive rights over you.' And no one had. She had danced the night away and drunk a little too much Heidsieck '59, and after breakfast at dawn in Grantchester when she was quite exhausted, Rohan had materialized from a punt on the river and had ferried her safely back to town.

There had been quarrels, of course, times when they were not on speaking terms. Rohan was an emotional extrovert who preferred to give vent to his grievances in a splendid display of rhetoric, and Rachel, who had more of an Anglo-Saxon temperament, found such exhibitions annoying. But the moods passed; the words were forgotten, and soon they were picking up the threads of their friendship as if nothing had happened and life continued as usual.

But they were getting older, and Rohan's grievances in a certain direction were becoming more acute.

'It's all very well,' he had said crossly, 'but I'm always the one who makes the effort, I'm the one who takes you around and introduces you to all the good-looking men. What do you ever do for me? When have you ever introduced me to a pretty girl? When? Just answer me that!'

'That's not fair!' Rachel had retorted, rising to an argument with spirit. 'What about all my schoolfriends? I constantly introduced them to you!'

'Hardly my type, were they? I mean, seriously—'

'Helen's very pretty!'

'But poor Helen,' Rohan had said in the tired voice he used when he wanted to annoy her. 'Absolutely no sex appeal.'

'How the hell am I to know how you define the term sex appeal?'

'No swearing, please. I always hate to hear women swear.'

'You're impossible!' Rachel had blazed. 'Quite impossible!' But she had felt guilty all the same. And then, when she had gone abroad to study French for six months she had met Decima in Geneva, and Decima was very different from the kind of girls Rachel had known at school.

When the six months had come to an end, Rachel and Decima had returned to England together and Rachel had introduced her new friend to Rohan at the earliest opportunity. Decima was staying with Rachel for a few days before returning to her home in Scotland; the three of them had planned an exciting weekend together before her departure. 'We'll have a grand time,' Rohan had said, jaw stuck out to show his aggressive determination to enjoy life to the full. 'My cousin Charles is coming down from Oxford and we'll make up a foursome. You remember Charles, the professor in medieval history, don't you, Rachel? He would do very nicely for you – you're always saying how much you like older men . . . Yes, that would be a good foursome. You and Charles, Decima and me . . .'

Decima and Charles had married less than four months later. After the engagement was announced, all Rohan had said was: 'It's just as well. She wasn't really my type – much more suitable for Charles, and I'm sure they'll be very happy . . . I wonder if they'll live at Oxford all the year round? Charles used to spend the university vacations in Edinburgh.'

And Rachel had said: 'Maybe they'll stay at Ruthven.'

Ruthven . . . Rachel had never been there, but Decima had talked so often of her home that Rachel had evolved a clear picture in her mind of the house to which no road led, its grey walls imprisoned between the mountains and the sea, the savage coast of Western Scotland, remote, vast and unmarked by time. She had thought on more than one occasion how nice it would be to visit Decima there.

But Decima and Charles had been married well over two years before an invitation came, and long before then Rachel had resigned herself to the fact that she would never be invited since Decima had not bothered to keep in touch with her and their correspondence had soon lapsed. Rohan thought nothing of inviting himself to Ruthven now and then for a few days of fishing and shooting with his cousin Charles, and couldn't understand why Rachel did not merely arrive on Decima's doorstep, but Rachel was proud; if Decima wanted to see her, then Decima should write and ask her to come; until then Rachel had no intention of turning up where she was apparently not wanted.

Then finally after two years the invitation arrived out of the blue, and the chance came for Rachel to visit Ruthven at last. It was late summer; Rachel had just come back from a holiday in Florence and happened to be between jobs, so the invitation could hardly have come at a better time.

The postmark was Kyle of Lochalsh, the handwriting unquestionably Decima's. Rachel ripped open the envelope with a pleasant feeling of anticipation and eagerly began to read the letter inside, but a second later bewilderment had displaced her eagerness, and presently even the bewilderment had vanished, leaving her feeling both uneasy and disturbed.

'Dearest Raye,' Decima had written, 'I'm so terribly sorry I've been such a hopeless correspondent, and please don't think that just because I've not written much I never think of you. I have thought of you so much, especially when it's seemed that there's no one I can turn to, and I'm writing to ask if you can possibly come up to Ruthven for a few days. My twenty-first birthday falls next Sunday, and it would be such a relief if you could stay until after the celebration dinner party which Charles is giving for me on Saturday night. Please come, Raye. I may be behaving very stupidly by panicking like this, but I would feel so much less frightened if I knew you were beside me at Ruthven till after midnight on Saturday. I can't say any more than this now as I'm just about to leave for Kyle of Lochalsh to meet Rohan, but please, please come as soon as possible. I'll explain everything when I see you and meanwhile much love,
'Decima'

# Part 1:
# Ruthven

## chapter 1

1

Shortly before the long-awaited invitation was sent, or even thought of, Decima Mannering was sitting on the window-seat of her bedroom overlooking the ocean and thinking of her friend Rachel. Rohan Quist was due to arrive that day at Ruthven to begin two weeks' holiday, and Decima always thought of Rachel whenever Rohan was due. The two seemed to be inseparable in her mind; it was as if they were husband and wife, she thought, or, to describe the relationship more accurately, brother and sister. It was odd how an unrelated man and woman could know one another since infancy and yet never become sexually involved with each other. It was not even as if it were a casual childhood friendship long since outgrown. They were nearly always together, almost inseparable, and yet it was quite evident there was no sexual attachment of any kind uniting them. It was really most curious. But then, remembering Rachel, one might perhaps conclude that the situation was only to be expected. Rachel had such an unfortunate attitude where men were concerned; she either frightened them right away or else she de-sexed any possible relationship by being apparently cold and withdrawn. There was some basic inferiority complex, of course; she had to be constantly reassured that a man was interested in her, and the need for reassurance led her to set up impossibly high standards which any admirer could not conceivably hope to attain. Or maybe there was no inferiority complex and Rachel was simply old-fashioned, desiring her various beaux to be pure knights in shining armour riding to court her on spotless white chargers.

Poor Rachel . . .

She could remember when she had first met Rachel in Geneva. Rachel had worn a very English tweed suit which was a little too big for her, and still wore her dark hair in braids coiled around the top of her head. Quaint,

Decima had thought. Pretty in a way. If one liked that kind of thing.

It was odd how they had become such friends when they had nothing whatsoever in common, but Decima had been lonely and unhappy away from her father, and Rachel, separated from her parents for the first time, was kinder and more sympathetic than anyone else. Rachel's peaceful world of vicarage tea-parties and lawn tennis at weekends was such a different world from any Decima had ever known. For Decima was a child of high society, the daughter of a Scottish aristocrat and an Italian princess long since divorced, and until the age of fourteen Decima, in the custody of her erratic, volatile mother, had been shuttled to and fro across the continent and twice round the world while her mother took part in the endless social whirl of the current international set. And then her mother had died of an overdose of sleeping pills taken incontinently after a surfeit of alcohol, and Decima had been extricated from her cosmopolitan whirlpool and withdrawn by her father to the west coast of Scotland.

Decima had loved Ruthven from the first moment she had seen it. Her father had worried in case she had hated to come to such a backwater after the glamour of a dozen different cities, but to Decima, saturated with the sophistication of city life, Ruthven was a fairy-tale, a miraculous escape from that other world where she had been a forced onlooker at her mother's feverish pursuit of gaiety. She had loved it better than any place on earth.

Her father had been delighted by her marriage to Charles Mannering, an Oxford professor and author of two books on medieval history. He had liked Charles from the first, and had made him a trustee in administering Ruthven for Decima if she inherited the estate while still under age. He even inserted a clause to say that if Decima died before her twenty-first birthday the estate should pass to her children and, if there were no children, then title to the land should pass to Charles outright. But this was only to happen if Decima were to die before attaining her majority. Once she was twenty-one the trust ceased and the property became hers entirely to dispose of or retain as she wished. The house itself, being so remote, was in fact of little financial value, but the timber forests on the land were worth a small fortune and were leased to the Forestry Commission at an extremely profitable annual rate.

When her father died six months after her marriage, Decima found herself a wealthy heiress. She was nineteen at the time.

And now she was nearly twenty-one.

She sat for a long time on the window-seat that morning and stared out over the dark sea as she considered her problems. The difficulties were quite clear in her mind. It was the task of solving them which was so hard. Surely there must be some perfectly simple solution which was staring her in the face. It was a pity Rohan could not help her, but he was after all Charles' cousin. Rohan . . .

Rachel.

Decima was very still. If Rachel came, it might be the solution. Conventional, solid, dependable Rachel. It would be perfect. She had to come.

Moving swiftly over to the small secretaire in one corner of the room she found pen and paper and began to write in a small, neat, flowing hand.


2

Charles Mannering was sitting in his study which faced east to the mountains, and thinking of his wife. On his desk in front of him was a portrait of Decima on her wedding day, and after a while he took the frame in his hands and stared at the picture for a long time. It was hard to believe it was a mere two and a half years since he had first seen her. But then it had been a very eventful two and a half years.

Leaning back in his chair he closed his eyes for a moment. He saw himself at thirty-six, a scholar highly regarded in intellectual circles, a bachelor snugly ensconced in his rooms at Oxford. He had almost everything he wanted by then, success in his work, personal freedom and a large circle of friends. It would have been entirely perfect, he had thought at the time, if he had had enough money to retire from teaching, which took up a good deal of his life, and to give him complete personal independence. He could have travelled, spent more time on research, had more time for writing books. But then one could not expect life to be entirely perfect, and he had on the whole been very fortunate. It would have been wrong to complain.

And then he had gone down to London one weekend to stay with his cousins, the Quists, and Rohan, with the air of a conjuror producing two white rabbits out of a top hat, had appeared triumphantly with two girls. He could remember vaguely seeing Rachel on a previous visit several years ago, but the other girl with her slanting blue eyes and silky black hair was unknown to him.

Of course she was absurdly young. It went without saying that a man of thirty-six would necessarily find a girl of eighteen a mere child. But suddenly after a few words with her he was struck with her sophistication and the knowledge which lay hidden in those slanting, watchful eyes. This girl was not as young as her years implied. There was something about her which was as old as time itself, and she knew it all too well.

Charles was fascinated, intrigued. He had always been attracted to older women before and this was the first time he had felt even a remote interest for a woman so young.

When he was sure he had not the slightest chance of being refused, he asked her to sleep with him.

Never had he more badly miscalculated. For one most unpleasant moment he thought he had ruined all his chances with her, but presently she forgave him and seemed anxious to see more of him. But any deviation from conventional morality was quite out of the question. If that was all he was interested in, he could forget about her.

Charles, like most clever men, fancied himself as being

irresistible to women when he put his mind to it, and his *amour propre* had suffered a severe blow. In fact it was so badly bruised that on his return to Oxford he found it difficult to concentrate on his work and was completely unable to write any more of his book on *Richard Coeur de Lion*. Presently he sent a letter to Ruthven and received a charming reply inviting him up for the weekend. Charles was on the next plane to Inverness almost quicker than he could escape from his lecturing schedule.

He had liked Ruthven. Hopelessly primitive, of course, and completely impracticable (imagine having no road connecting it to the nearest town!) but a good place for a holiday and ideal for working quietly on a book or doing concentrated research. Decima's father, only a few years older than he, seemed a nice chap. He was pleased because he had just renewed the lease of part of his land to the Forestry Commission and thus ensured a comfortable income for himself for the next few years. Useful things, trees. Timber was valuable these days. Since the coming of the Forestry Commission Ruthven's value had increased from barely two thousand to well over one hundred thousand pounds . . .

'I'm surprised you don't sell out,' Charles had said, thinking that so much money could be much more sensibly invested – a villa on the Costa Brava, perhaps, or a house in the Canary Islands. 'But then, of course,' he had added adroitly, 'it's your home and of great sentimental value to you.'

'Exactly!' said Decima's father, pleased that his guest should have understand his sentiments so well. 'Decima and I both feel the same way about that.'

'I quite understand,' said Charles, not understanding at all. 'I agree with you absolutely.'

Surely Decima could not really feel so attached to such a rambling, remote, ranshackle old house miles from anywhere! Decima with her background of international society, her education in Paris, Rome and Geneva – it was inconceivable that she could ever want to cling to this little corner of Western Scotland for any length of time. When she inherited the land she would no doubt change her mind about retaining it . . .

But she hadn't. That was what was so extraordinary. He replaced the photograph of her carefully on his desk and looked out of the window again at the bleak mountainside and moor which stretched to the forestry plantation. 'I'll never sell this,' she had told him bluntly, 'so you may as well forget about it. This is my home now and for all time.'

'But it's so remote, Decima!' he had protested. 'So cut off! A young woman like you should travel and meet interesting people and—'

'I had enough travel when I was a child to last me a lifetime,' she had said, 'and I'm tired of meeting so-called interesting people. God, I have enough of boring social life stuck down at Oxford with you in term-time, don't I? After a few weeks of that it's a relief to get back here.'

'I know you dislike the life at Oxford,' he had said carefully. 'God knows I'd be much happier if I didn't have to teach to supplement our income. But if I – you – were to sell Ruthven we could have enough money to invest to enable me to retire and we could easily settle in another part of Scotland near here—'

And she had said in contempt: 'I'm not selling Ruthven just so that you can live on my money for the rest of your life.'

It hurt even now to remember the tone of her voice. *I'm not selling Ruthven so that you can live on my money.* As if he were a gigolo or opportunist instead of a self-respecting Englishman with a great deal of pride.

Things had been very bad after that. They had gone for a whole week without speaking to one another and he had been miserable, unable to write or read, unwilling even to go fishing up the burn. But she hadn't cared. She had gone riding every day over the moors, or taken brief swims in the icy sea when the sun shone a little warmer than usual, and when the time had come to order the month's provisions she had taken the boat alone into Kyle of Lochalsh to do the shopping.

He could remember her very clearly coming back from the town. She wore a dark-blue sweater which reflected the blue of her eyes and her dark hair was streaming behind her in the wind. He had never seen her look so beautiful or more hopelessly beyond his reach. And then as he came down to the jetty to help her unload the provisions she spoke to him for the first time since their quarrel a week ago and said:

'There's a letter for you. It's addressed in an exquisite gothic handwriting and the postmark is Cambridge.'

There was only one person who could be writing to him from Cambridge in a a gothic script. In the midst of his depression Charles was aware of pleasure, a quick pang of anticipation.

'Who is it from?' said Decima. 'I've never seen such a remarkable handwriting.'

'It's from a former student of mine,' he said mechanically. 'He went from Oxford on a scholarship to Cambridge to do postgraduate work; he's now making a study of the economic and social position of the monastic orders in England in the thirteenth century.' And even as he spoke he was ripping open the envelope and unfolding the single sheet of paper within.

'My dear Charles,' someone had written with elegant strokes of a pen dipped in black ink. 'My sister and I will shortly be in Edinburgh for the Festival, and I wondered if there was any possibility of meeting you there? Alternatively, if you do not intend to go to the Festival this year, I would very much like to visit you; Rebecca and I plan to hire a car after the Festival and see a little of Scotland, so it would be easy enough to drive up to Kyle of Lochalsh. If such a visit would inconvenience either you or your wife in any way, please don't hesitate to say so, but I would very much like to see you again and you always wrote such enthusiastic letters in praise of Ruthven that I find myself more than anxious to go there. Hoping, therefore, to see you again in the near future, I remain . . .' etc.

Charles folded the letter and put it away in his wallet.

'What's his name?' said Decima casually. 'Have I ever met him?'

'No,' said Charles. 'He left Oxford before I met you. His name is Daniel Carey.'

That had been two months ago. The Careys had now been six weeks at Ruthven and showed no sign of leaving.

Charles was still sitting in his study and thinking of the past when there was a soft knock on the door and the next moment a young woman of about twenty-four was slipping into the room. She hesitated as she saw he was deep in thought, and then as he looked across at her and smiled she stepped forward towards him.

'Am I interrupting anything?'

'No,' he said, still smiling. 'Sit down and talk to me for a while. I was just wondering how I could write of King John's obsession with the young Isabella of Angoulême without giving the impression I was writing a medieval version of *Lolita*.'

Rebecca laughed. 'You're teasing me as usual!'

'Why do you say that?'

'Historians of your calibre aren't concerned with the sexual obsessions of middle-aged potentates.'

Now it was his turn to laugh. 'Yet this particular infatuation had widespread consequences . . .' Really, he thought, looking at her, she was a most unusual girl. Possibly too intelligent for most men's tastes, but none the less attractive in a dark, fine-drawn, unusual way . . . And it was pleasant for once to talk to a woman who was well aware that Isabella of Castile and Isabella of Angoulême were very far from being the same person.

For some reason he thought of his cousin. Perhaps Rohan would take a fancy to her. On the whole he hoped not. Rohan was much too much of an extroverted young philistine to appreciate the fine qualities of a woman such as Rebecca Carey.

'Have you seen Decima this morning?' he enquired. 'I hope she hasn't forgotten that my cousin Rohan is arriving today.'

'No, she was talking of going into Kyle of Lochalsh

to meet him this afternoon. I understand she has some shopping to do.'

'I see. And Daniel?'

'I believe he volunteered to go with her.'

'I see,' said Charles, and idly began to picture how he would spend the long peaceful afternoon at Ruthven . . .


3

When Rebecca left Charles she went upstairs to her bedroom and flung herself face downwards on the bed, her hands crushing the pillow fiercely and pulling it against her breast. Her whole body was trembling, alive with a million vibrations, and after a while she could lie still no longer but ran from her room and out of the house to the sea. The sun was warm; there was no one about and, if she had not seen the boat moored to the jetty, she would have assumed Decima and Daniel had already set off for Kyle of Lochalsh. Charles was no doubt still in his study which faced east over the mountains.

When she was about two hundred yards from the house she sank down behind a rock out of the wind and paused to regain her breath. For a moment she wondered whether to go swimming; the cold would be acute at first, she knew, but after a moment it would become more tolerable, and she loved fighting the high waves which pounded into surf on the deserted beach. She was just considering going back to the house for a towel and a bathing suit when she saw Daniel coming towards her across the sands.

Daniel was her only brother, and there were no sisters. Her parents had died soon after she was born; she could remember neither of them, only the cousins who had brought her up in Suffolk, near Bury St Edmunds. Consequently, because Daniel was the only close member of her family she had ever known, it was not surprising that she should have relied so much upon his companionship and derived such a sense of security from sharing his interests. As she had grown older she had conscientiously modelled herself on him, straining to keep up with all his interests and follow the development of his thoughts and philosophies. He liked to talk to her and all she wanted was to be a worthy companion to him on such occasions. She admired his mind so much that she felt it a compliment when he tried to share it with her. She was, after all, only his young sister. A lesser man would have ignored her or else merely talked to her in a patronizing manner, but when Daniel talked to her it was as if she were his equal.

She felt the most important person in the world on those occasions; she could even forget she was merely a thin, sallow girl with plain features and a moderate intellectual capacity which would always fall short of brilliance.

Her looks had improved as she entered her twenties and she found men were beginning to take an interest in her, but she had no patience with anyone less clever than herself and so her friendships never lasted long. Charles Mannering, however, was very different from the young men she was accustomed to discarding in impatient disappointment; she soon realized not only that Charles was exceptionally clever but also that he was the first man she had ever honestly admired – apart from Daniel, of course, but Daniel was only her brother. She wondered idly why Daniel had not yet married; there had been plenty of opportunities she knew, but no woman ever seemed to interest him for long.

As he came within earshot she called a greeting and he raised his hand in response, his footsteps soundless on the soft sand, the wind whipping the words from his mouth as he tried to reply. She saw him smile, shrug his shoulders in resignation; his dark eyes were narrowed against the sun, his hands thrust casually into the pockets of his trousers to confirm his air of nonchalance, and when he reached her a moment later his voice was low and cool and unhurried.

'Are you coming into Kyle of Lochalsh with us?' he asked. 'We're going in ten minutes.'

'No,' she said. 'There's nothing I want there.'

He looked at her for a moment and she had the feeling he could see right into her mind and knew exactly why she had no interest in going. Presently he said:

'You like it here, don't you? It's a pity you can't marry Charles and live here with him.'

'Ruthven doesn't belong to Charles.'

'It would if Decima died before she was twenty-one.'

'I hardly think she's likely to die within the next eight days!' Then, suddenly: 'How did you find that out?'

'She told me.' He turned aside. 'Are you sure there's nothing you want at Kyle of Lochalsh?'

'Quite sure, thanks, Danny.'

'I'll see you later, then,' he said and moved away from her on his way across the shore to the jetty. As she watched him, she saw Decima leave the house with a basket over her arm and step into the waiting motor-boat.

Decima always looked so smart. This afternoon she was wearing dark slacks and a pale-blue sweater with a turtle-neck. Daniel too would think she looked smart. Rebecca always knew how Daniel would feel about women.

After a while she moved slowly back to the house. The sun was already overcast, and she knew the best of the day was gone. For the first time she wondered vaguely what Charles' young cousin would be like and then, when she entered the house a moment later, she forgot about Rohan Quist until his arrival at Ruthven several hours later.

4

Rohan was drinking Scotch and water in a pub overlooking the harbour when they arrived. He had reached the town an hour earlier after an uneventful journey from Inverness in the red Volkswagen, and after garaging the car had decided to have a drink to pass the time. He recognized the motor-boat at once as it nosed its way through the fishing boats to the quay, and he recognized Decima at the wheel almost as soon as he saw the boat, but the dark man in the black windcheater was a stranger to him, someone whom he had not expected to see.

He was conscious instantly and inexplicably of jealousy.

They moored the boat and stepped on to the quay. The man was not as tall as he had at first anticipated, but he had a broad, powerful build. Rohan's slight frame tautened. Instinctively his scalp started to prickle; if he had been a dog the hackles would have risen on the back of his neck, and yet there was no logic in his reaction, no reason for his distrust.

The man touched Decima's arm without taking it and they walked along the quay side by side. They were talking. Rohan saw Decima laugh.

Who was this man?

They came nearer and nearer. Within minutes they had reached the door of the pub and were walking inside to look for him, but he was still so absorbed with the force of his reaction that he made no move from his chair. He felt cold suddenly, chilled by a series of emotions he had never experienced before. It was as if he had felt someone walking over his grave.

'Why, there you are!' cried Decima. 'Silly thing, why didn't you call out when you saw us come in? How are you? It's such a long time since you've been up here.'

'Yes,' he said. 'It is.' But he wasn't looking at her. He was looking right past her over her shoulder but, even as she turned to make the introductions, the stranger stepped forward of his own accord and held out his hand.

'My name is Daniel Carey,' he said with an unexpectedly charming smile. 'Welcome back to Ruthven, Mr Quist.'

## chapter 2

1

It was Thursday when Rachel arrived at Ruthven. She reached Kyle of Lochalsh in the early evening and found Rohan waiting for her at the little station. He wore two sweaters, a jacket and a pair of heavy tweed trousers, and still contrived to look cold.

'Decima's in the boat to avoid the current breeze from the Arctic,' he told her. 'I hope you brought your winter clothes with you, because if you haven't you'll freeze to death in twenty-four hours. The weather changed yesterday, and I've never been so cold in all my life . . . Is this your luggage? OK, let's go . . . Yes, it was quite warm till yesterday and then the mist started to blow in from the sea and the thermometer dropped twenty degrees or so. I think it's more the damp than the actual cold that's so chilling – it seems to get right into your bones and stay there till you shiver it out again . . . Did you have a good journey?'

'Fair.' She followed him as he left the station, a suitcase in either hand, and as they walked out into the street the damp chill of the wind blew across the sea from Skye towards them. 'I can hardly believe Decima really lives right out here,' she said to Rohan, drawing up the collar of her raincoat. 'Decima of all people! I can only visualize her in town against sophisticated backgrounds. I can picture Charles playing the role of country gentleman but the very idea of Decima playing the outdoor country-tweeds type is too much for me altogether.'

'Yes?' said Rohan with vague interest. 'And yet, curiously enough, it's Charles who seems ill at ease in his role and Decima who seems perfectly relaxed and content at Ruthven . . . there's the boat across the harbour – can you make it out? And there's Decima in the wheelhouse – you can just see her blue jacket.'

They walked on and were soon at the jetty by the water's

edge. There were fishermen attending to their nets, white gulls soaring aloft on the wind currents, the sounds of water and Gaelic voices and the occasional throbbing of an engine. Rachel was aware of strangeness, as if she were a traveller in a foreign land. This remote corner of Britain might have been a thousand miles from the Britain she knew, the soft verdant slopes of the Surrey hills with their tall, swaying beech trees and blazes of gorse and rhododendron. A world removed from the graceful houses and shining roads and half-hour train service to the throbbing metropolis of London. Perhaps, she thought, it was not so strange that Decima should feel at home here while Charles did not; Decima, with her cosmopolitan upbringing, would see nothing strange and hostile about this land while Charles would always be conscious that he was an Englishman in foreign territory, an intellectual far removed from Oxford's spires, a product of civilization adrift among barbarous surroundings.

'Is Charles really so ill at ease here?' she asked Rohan curiously.

'Well, perhaps that's a slight exaggeration, because I know he enjoys fishing and the opportunity to work in peace, but I think he's always anxious to get back to Oxford after a while. I can see his point of view, God knows. This place is all very fine for a holiday but to remain here for any length of time would be too much of a good thing. That's why I'm surprised the Careys have stayed so long. They've been six weeks at Ruthven now.'

A gull screamed overhead and dipped towards the sea. The sun shone briefly through the clouds for a moment; the grey landscape seemed to glow in response, and then harden as the sun disappeared again.

'Who are the Careys?' said Rachel.

'Didn't Decima mention them in her letter? How odd! I would have thought she'd have been sure to mention them.'

'But who are they? Some friends of Charles?'

'My dear R., they're the most extraordinary couple – I can't imagine what on earth you'll make of them.

Rebecca Carey is one of these frighteningly intellectual women with a curious dramatic intensity which I find rather unnerving. Everything she does, she does with a passionate zeal which quite takes one's breath away. Rather tiring, actually.'

'Not your type, from the sound of her!'

'Well, she could be if she had a sense of humour, but unfortunately she's too busy taking everything – including herself – much too seriously.'

'You mean,' said Rachel, 'she doesn't find your jokes amusing.'

'I mean nothing of the kind! All I was saying was—'

'Yes, I see. And what about her husband? Is he full of passionate humourless zeal too?'

'He's her brother, not her husband, and a former pupil of Charles now doing research at Cambridge.' Rohan was watching the boat. They were two minutes away from it now. Decima had caught sight of them, he noticed, and was waving to them.

'How dull,' said Rachel, waving back with a smile. 'Whatever made Charles invite them to Ruthven? Ah, here comes Decima! Lord, she looks prettier than ever and I feel so untidy and travelstained . . .'

Decima was already stepping off the boat and moving swiftly towards them. The wind tore for a moment at her black hair and she swept it out of her eyes with a laugh. She wore no make-up, and as the result of many weeks spent in the damp, moist climate of the Highlands, her complexion was flawless, her skin pale but not pallid, her cheeks faintly glowing with a mere trace of rose. She wore loose-fitting slacks and a bulky windcheater and still contrived to look beautiful.

'Raye! How lovely to see you!' She had a low, soft voice with a slight indefinable hint of a foreign accent. It was a voice which needed few words to convey whatever emotion she chose to put in it. 'I'm so glad you could come.'

There was no sign of nervousness, none of the anxiety which had shown itself so clearly in the hurried letter. She was composed, effortlessly poised. She might have been a mature woman nearly thirty instead of a girl not yet twenty-one.

'It's most exciting to be here,' said Rachel politely, suddenly smitten with the full force of her inferiority complex. 'I've never been to the Highlands before.'

'All aboard!' sang out Rohan, detecting the stiltedness in her voice and at once rushing to the rescue. 'Next stop Ruthven! Do you want to take the wheel, Decima?'

'We'd soon be aground if *you* took it!' the girl retorted, and they laughed, the moment of awkwardness forgotten. 'Are you cold, Rachel? Do you want to go below to the cabin out of the wind? You must be so tired after your journey.'

And as Rachel hesitated, not wishing to appear unsociable but dreading the chill of the wind, Rohan said: 'I'll call you just before Ruthven comes into sight – go and sit in the cabin and peer through the portholes and sip some of Decima's best Scotch.'

'Yes,' said Decima, 'get her a drink, Rohan. I can manage up here once you've helped me cast off.'

'I'm sure you can,' said Rohan, and added to Rachel: 'Decima handles a boat as well as she drives a car – better than most men.'

Decima laughed. 'Only the British can say a woman's masculine and mean it as a compliment!'

'My dear Decima,' said Rohan, 'only a man who was blind, deaf and dumb could ever doubt your femininity . . . I'll be with you in a moment, Rachel. Go down to the cabin and make yourself at home.'

Rachel did as she was told. The cabin was warm and snug and had two bunks, one on either side of the gangway. As she sat down on the nearest one she was suddenly conscious of weariness, and leaning back against the wall of the cabin she closed her eyes for a moment as the engines roared into life. She could hear Rohan's voice shouting something, then a thud from somewhere on deck, and gradually she could feel the boat moving, swaying away from the jetty and out to sea.

She sat up and glanced out of the porthole. The harbour

was already receding and Kyle of Lochalsh a mere huddled collection of grey stone buildings below the bare, grey mountains inland.

Footsteps clattered above her. 'Found the whisky yet?' said Rohan, entering the cabin amidst a draught of cool air. 'No? You will have some, won't you?'

'Please.' She watched him take a bottle from a cupboard above the bunk and then go aft into the tiny galley for a glass and some drinking water. A minute later the liquid was fire in her throat and she was beginning to feel better.

She glanced out of the cabin again. There was nothing to be seen at all now except the rocky coast and the bleakness of the moors and hills inland. Once more the sun shone for a moment, and its light flickered fitfully over the dark landscape.

'How odd,' she said, 'to see no houses, no trees, no roads. It's almost unnerving. I must be more over-civilized than I thought I was.'

'I don't know about being over-civilized,' said Rohan. 'Even the Highlanders themselves find it oppressive – aren't they always drifting south to the lowlands and the towns? And you can understand why. Imagine trying to make a living from land like that! Even the crofters around Ruthven drifted south in the end with their sheep.'

'And yet in a way, it's very beautiful.'

'Certainly,' said Rohan, 'for a little while.' He went back into the galley to mix himself a drink. When he returned she moved up on the bunk so that he could sit down beside her, and she thought how curious it was that she, who was so often shy with men, should always be perfectly at ease when she was with him.

'Well,' she said with a smile, 'tell me all the details. What's been happening?'

He shrugged. 'Not too much. I've been fishing a few times on my own. Charles came with me once, but he's very involved in his book at the moment and I think he decided to fish more out of politeness than anything else.'

'And have you been riding with Decima?'

'No,' he said, taking a gulp of his Scotch. 'But I've

been out a couple of times alone – and nearly galloped into Cluny Sands without realizing I'd come so far. For God's sake don't go riding on your own, Rachel – if you ride inland you'll probably get lost on the moors and if you ride along the sea-shore you'll go straight into dangerous quicksands. You won't even know they're quicksands till your horse starts to flounder. They look so white and beautiful and inviting, just like any other stretch of deserted sea-shore around here.'

'Why didn't Decima go with you? I'm sure she'd have kept you out of dangerous territory.'

'She seems to have lost interest in riding lately.'

'So you've been having a solitary sort of holiday!' she teased. 'Charles won't fish with you and Decima won't go riding! What about the Careys?'

'They don't ride or fish.'

'No? What on earth have they been doing with themselves for six weeks, then?'

'Rebecca swims.'

'*Swims*? In this climate?'

'It was warmer a little while ago. And she spends the rest of the time reading Jean-Paul Sartre and imagining herself to be a second Simone de Beauvoir.'

'And her brother?'

'Daniel? I really don't know. I never seem to see much of him.' He offered her a cigarette and gave her a light. 'I think I'll just see how Decima's managing on deck,' he said suddenly, standing up. 'We can't be too far from Ruthven by now. I'll be back in a minute.'

She was just closing her eyes in a moment of drowsiness a short while later when he called down the hatch to her. Rousing herself with an effort, she left the cabin and went up on deck.

The wind struck the side of her face as soon as she stepped outside the deck-house, and she felt her body tighten in an attempt to lock out the cold. The sea was a swaying grey shot with white flecks and the sky was a pale ragged blue streaked with banks of stormy clouds. At the wheel Decima's face was glowing, her long hair streaming behind her, her eyes bright, and beside her Rohan, hunched in his coat, called out something which was lost in the hum of the engine and the roar of the wind.

Rachel turned to face the wind, and as she did so, the boat rounded the peninsula and she saw Ruthven.

The wind whipped at the foam; there was salt on her lips, spray in her eyes, a mist of water billowing from the prow of the boat. And through it all, there were the turrets and towers of Ruthven, grey walls clearly etched against the vast background of the moors, while beyond the walls seemingly encroaching almost to the water's edge to the north and south of the bay, were the mountains wreathed in billowing mist.

Decima was at her elbow suddenly; Rohan had taken the wheel.

'Isn't it beautiful?' she said, and her eyes blazed with a passion which Rachel had never seen her show for any man. 'Isn't it the most perfect place in all the world?' And as she laid her hand on Rachel's arm, Rachel could feel the nervous strength flowing through those slim fingers, the vibrant tremor of joy.

'It's unique, Decima,' she heard herself say. 'I've never seen anything like it before.'

The landscape was so powerful that it was almost overwhelming. She wondered if she had ever felt as far from civilization as she felt at that moment, and the pang of fear, unexpected and ridiculous, made her stiffen for a moment before she pulled herself together.

Decima had returned to the wheel; as they approached the shore, Rachel could see the house more clearly, the rugged stone, the blank, dark windows, the partially cultivated garden. There was a jetty with a boat house, stables and out-buildings beyond the house. A cow nibbled tranquilly in a grassy field to the right, and six little pigs frolicked in an enclosure beyond the cow. Hens wandered near the front door, and an enormous St Bernard who was snoozing on the porch with lofty disregard for fowls, opened his eyes at the sound of the motor-boat and began to pad down towards the jetty.

The domesticity of the scene in close-up was oddly reassuring after the wildness of the long-distance view.

The boat curved towards the jetty, nudged it neatly and swayed to a halt as the motors died. The enormous dog put out a paw and patted it vaguely.

'Careful, George,' said Decima, jumping down on to the jetty and turning to help Rachel. 'Rohan, can you manage those suitcases? I can see Charles coming, so he'll be able to give you a hand with them.'

Rachel scrambled on to the jetty. The damp air felt deliciously cool and fresh now that they were out of the wind. She took a deep breath, half-closing her eyes, and when she looked up again she saw Decima's husband crossing the sands towards them.

There was a girl with him, a dark woman in a thick green sweater and a tweed skirt.

'That's Rebecca Carey,' said Decima's voice carelessly. 'I don't think I mentioned to you that we had guests at Ruthven, did I, Raye?'

'Rohan told me.'

The St Bernard rose with vast dignity and advanced towards Charles. His bulk filled the jetty.

'Out of the way, George,' Rachel heard Charles say good-naturedly. 'That's better . . . Why, Rachel, how very nice to see you again! Did you have a good journey? You did? Splendid . . . May I introduce you to one of our guests? Rebecca, this is Rachel Lord. Rachel – Rebecca Carey.'

The girl's hand was limp. Rachel took it but soon let it go. 'How do you do?' she said politely.

Something else had caught the attention of the St Bernard. He was plodding majestically over the sands and his long tail was waving with unhurried grace.

'Can I give you a hand with those suitcases, Rohan?'

'. . . come up to the house. All right?'

'. . . sea's a bit choppy . . .'

'Not so good for swimming, Rebecca! Decima, why don't you . . .'

A man had come out of the house and was walking

down towards them to the beach. When he reached the St Bernard, he paused to put a finger lightly on the dog's head and the dog looked up at him as if that one caress signified immeasurable honour.

'This way, Rachel,' said Decima, walking along the jetty away from the boat.

The man and the dog reached the edge of the sands together. The St Bernard was moving surprisingly fast without giving the appearance of making any extra effort. The man, though, was moving slowly yet gave the impression of speed. He wore a dark pullover and dark trousers and his hair was as dark as his eyes.

'Ah, there you are!' said Decima, and her voice rang out across the sands. 'I was wondering where you'd gone to!' She turned to Rachel, and her eyes were as vivid as a southern sky in high summer. 'This is Rebecca's brother, Raye,' she said. 'This is Daniel Carey.'


2


Daniel saw a tall, slim girl with soft brown hair and shy eyes and a wide, beautiful mouth. Because he was an observant man he also noticed that she was badly dressed in a raincoat which did not suit her, and wore ugly shoes in a style which might just possibly have been fashionable some years previously. Her smile was hesitant but full of warmth, and he knew at once that she was honest and would find any insincerity distasteful. Beside her, Decima's poised brilliance seemed strangely artificial and cold, an exercise in perfection which was as empty as it was unarousing.

'Have you much luggage, Miss Lord?' he asked her, scrupulously polite. 'Can I help bring it up to the house?'

'Charles and Rohan are seeing to that,' said Decima before Rachel could speak. 'Come on up to the house with us, Daniel.'

Perhaps it was her tone of voice which made him at once want to do exactly the reverse of any suggestion she happened to make, or perhaps he was too conscious of the knowledge that she did not attract him at that moment and that he wanted to escape from her. Whichever it was, he stepped past them towards the jetty and called back over his shoulder: 'I'll just see if there's anything I can do.'

The St Bernard lumbered after him placidly, brushing Rachel's raincoat with his waving tail.

'George!' called Decima sharply.

But the dog pretended not to hear her.

'I can't think why George likes you so much, Daniel,' observed Charles, descending from the jetty with one of Rachel's suitcases. 'You never pay any attention to him.'

'You sound almost jealous, Charles!' said Rohan from behind him. He was smiling, but the smile never reached his eyes. 'I thought you were above feeling jealous of things in your possession.'

My God, thought Daniel. This is a stupid man.

He felt himself go ice-cold with rage.

But Charles was laughing, deaf to all insinuations, happily oblivious of any emotional undercurrents in the atmosphere. 'I wouldn't grudge anyone a dog's affection! But I've never known George to be so friendly towards a stranger before – Daniel must have a way with animals, I suppose.'

'Daniel has a way with all kinds of things,' said Rohan Quist, but Charles had moved on down the jetty and wasn't listening to him.

Rebecca spun round. 'What's that supposed to mean?'

'He's merely paying tribute to my many talents,' said Daniel very quickly before Quist could open his mouth. 'Let's go back to the house.'

As they stepped off the jetty, Rebecca began to say something to him but he cut her off abruptly with a single movement of his hand and she was silent at once. Really, he thought in irritation, Rebecca was unusually sensitive these days. Dangerously sensitive, in fact. He must have a word with her later.

When they reached the house he went into the living room while the others took the luggage upstairs, and moved over to the sideboard to mix himself a drink. He had just gone over to the window with his drink in his hand when his sister came into the room.

'Shut the door, please.'

She shut it. 'Danny—'

'What's the matter with you?' he said angrily. 'Why couldn't you have ignored Quist altogether? You played right into his hands!'

'But Danny, when he said—'

'Ignore it. Forget it. Can't you get into the habit of ignoring anything Quist says which might conceivably have a *double entendre*?'

'But—'

'He's out to make trouble, that man – you know that as well as I do. Why give him the satisfaction of knowing he's succeeding?'

'But Danny, supposing Charles—'

'The hell with Charles!' said Daniel, and then stopped dead as Charles walked into the room.

Quist was right behind him.

'Can I get either of you a drink?' he heard himself offer, giving them his most charming smile.

'Thank you,' said Rohan, 'but no.'

'Charles? Will you drink some Scotch on the rocks with me?'

'Thanks,' said Charles cheerfully. 'That's exactly what I need.' He sat down in a chair and stretched out his legs before the hearth in a picture of relaxed ease. 'What about you, Rebecca?' he added. 'Will you have a drink?'

'Not at present, thank you, Charles.' Her voice was taut and uneasy.

There was a silence. Daniel served cubes from the ice-bucket into the glass, and stirred the whisky carefully without any apparent trace of tension.

'Here you are, Charles,' he said at last, turning to face his host, and even as he spoke he wondered if Charles was really unaware of Rohan's attitude, of Rebecca's nervousness, of his own mixed emotions of disillusionment, scorn and contempt. Daniel had a sudden painful memory of those days not so long ago when he had been a freshman at Oxford and had waited eagerly to gain admission to the hall where the celebrated historian Charles Mannering was lecturing. It was hard to believe it was such a short time since he had admired and respected Charles. No doubt, Daniel thought, it would have been different if he and Rebecca had never come to Ruthven.

Ruthven had changed everything.

The silence was threatening to become prolonged again when the door opened and Decima came into the room.

'Why, how quiet it is in here!' She was so poised, so apparently unaware that anyone should be ill at ease in that plain, cheerful room that her very presence seemed to mock the tension among them. Rohan said, 'I think I will have a drink after all,' and Charles was already reaching for his pipe; over by the window Rebecca picked up an old magazine to take over to the armchair in the corner, while Daniel sat down opposite Charles by the hearth with the massive St Bernard at his feet.

'Dinner will be in about an hour,' said Decima. 'I thought that would give Rachel sufficient time to have a bath and change and recover a little after her long journey.'

The talk became desultory; after a while Decima departed to see if the cook was coping satisfactorily with the meal, and soon after she returned Rachel came downstairs from her room to join them. She was wearing a grey dress in a style that was too old for her, and a plain elegant brooch which even the best-dressed woman in the world would have been pleased to wear. Her short hair had been carefully brushed and shone in the ray of sunlight which slanted into the room. She still looked shy.

Everyone made a great fuss of her, Daniel thought. Charles immediately offered her a drink. Rohan insisted that she sit next to him on the couch. Decima immediately assumed the role of perfect hostess, anxious, solicitous, exerting every surreptitious means to make her guest perfectly relaxed and at ease.

He still couldn't understand why Decima had suddenly invited her to Ruthven.

'. . . haven't really had the chance to talk to you about the celebrations for my twenty-first,' Decima was saying with animation. 'It's all rather exciting – I'm so glad you could come, Raye – I do hope you'll enjoy it . . .'

The birthday party seemed to have given Decima an excellent excuse for issuing her unexpected invitation. But an excuse for what?

'. . . Charles is giving a dinner party for me on Saturday. There'll be sixteen guests and we'll light the fires in the hall and get out the long dining table and if Willie – that's the gamekeeper – and the men have luck shooting, we'll be able to roast venison on the spit . . .'

Daniel thought of his own twenty-first birthday five years earlier on the eve of his last term at Oxford. There had been a party which had made the Dean blanch and the townsfolk complain, and he had almost decided to get married. Luckily, even in spite of a surfeit of champagne, he had avoided committing himself. The next morning a letter had arrived from his parents' lawyers to the effect that he was now fully entitled to the money which had been held in trust for him since childhood.

Decima would come into money too, of course. And, once she was twenty-one, she could do as she pleased with Ruthven.

'Who will the sixteen guests be?' the girl was asking.

'Oh, Rebecca and Daniel, of course, you and Rohan, Charles and I – and the MacDonalds and Camerons from Kyle of Lochalsh, and the Kincaids from Skye, and my father's lawyer, old Mr Douglas of Cluny Gualach and his daughter Rosalind; we had to ask Mr Douglas as he wrote me an enormously long legal letter the other day all about my father's will and inheriting all the money and all the sordid little details about that . . .'

'You would hardly describe the ownership of Ruthven as a sordid little detail, would you, Decima?' Daniel could not resist saying.

'Well, no, I agree!' She laughed carelessly, took a sip

from her glass. 'But lawyers somehow succeed in taking the romance out of becoming twenty-one and reduce it to such mundane levels . . . May I have some more wine, Charles?'

Daniel wondered idly if Decima was aware that she drank too much. The preliminary glasses hardly seemed to affect her, and even after that the effect was barely noticeable.

In contrast, the other girl scarcely seemed to touch her wine at all. Yet she appeared to enjoy the meal, for she smiled often and seemed to lose much of her reserve. Once or twice she glanced at him and caught him watching her, and he saw her blush faintly after she had looked away and pretended to interest herself in something else.

He wondered what kind of relationship she had with Rohan Quist, but decided it was probably true that there was nothing between them except ordinary friendship. Quist, even though only a year younger than Daniel himself, seemed a mere child still, excitable, over-emotional and immature, and those qualities were hardly sufficient to attract any woman, let alone a woman with such unusual simplicity of manner as Rachel Lord.

When she and Decima rose at last to leave the men alone with their liqueurs, he realized to his astonishment that he had been thinking about her continually throughout the meal, and as he watched her leave the room, he was aware of wondering curiously whether she too had been thinking of him.

3

Rachel excused herself early, saying that she was tired after the long journey and, with a lamp in her hand, found her way up the curving staircase to her room. Someone, presumably the housekeeper, had lit the fire in the grate and the flames had already taken the chill from the air, but outside the rain hurtled in from the Atlantic and dashed itself against the windowpane, and as she knelt on the hearth to warm her hands she could hear the wind rasping against the outer walls.

It was strange to remember that it was only September and that, far away in the south, people would be wearing summer clothes and perhaps taking a stroll in the evening sunlight.

The wind hummed through the eaves again; she shivered and drew closer to the warmth of the fire.

The flames were flickering, spiralling columns of light, distorted patterns, fragments of vitality. She stared at them for a long time, and as she watched she thought of Daniel Carey and wondered why it was that she was so shy with men and lacked all trace of her usual self-confidence. With any man whom she did not know she was always painfully ill at ease.

Carey had no doubt thought her very gauche.

She was just recalling Decima's perfect poise and maturity of manner, and thinking that self-confidence was undoubtedly easy if one happened to be beautiful, when there was a knock on the door. At first she thought she was imagining it or confusing it with the soughing of rain and wind outside, but even as she started and turned her head uncertainly towards the door, the knock came again.

'Rachel?' said a soft voice urgently, and the next moment the door was opening and Decima was slipping into the room. 'Ah, there you are.' She shut the door behind her and moved swiftly over to the hearth where Rachel was still sitting. 'Thank God I've at last got a chance to talk to you alone.'

Rachel looked blank, and then realized she had been so absorbed in remembering the conversations at dinner that she had temporarily forgotten the letter which had brought her to Ruthven.

'I've been waiting for a chance to talk to *you* alone,' she said lightly to Decima. 'What on earth were you hinting at in your letter? I couldn't make head or tail of it except that you seemed to be in a rather panic-stricken state – and yet here you are as cool as a cucumber and just as balanced as you always were! Just what exactly's going on?'

Decima had a fur stole over the midnight-blue dress she had worn at dinner, and as she sat down on the floor beside Rachel she drew the stole more closely round her shoulders. Her face looked white and pinched suddenly; the firelight flickered across the violet circles beneath her eyes and glinted in an expression which made mockery of Rachel's light, amused remarks.

Rachel suddenly felt her heart beating uncertainly, and the shock of recognition prickled beneath her scalp. 'Something's very wrong,' she heard herself say. 'That's it, isn't it, Decima? Something's very wrong.'

Decima didn't answer.

'Tell me what it is.'

There was a silence. And then as the wind sighed again in the eaves and the rain hissed in the darkness beyond, she heard Decima whisper:

'I think Charles is planning to kill me.'


*chapter 3*


1

The fire was still dancing, wrapping greedy tongues of red and yellow around the logs. And the light danced on Decima's face so that the fear shone in her eyes and her knuckles gleamed white as she clasped her hands tightly together.

Rachel said: 'Charles?'

'I've suspected it for some while.'

Rachel's mind at that moment seemed incapable of anything except recalling odd random memories. She thought of Geneva where she had first met Decima and how little she had suspected at the time that the meeting would lead to this moment at Ruthven years later; she thought of the spires of Oxford and an adolescent Rohan boasting of his celebrated cousin Charles; she thought of her first meeting with Charles Mannering, the occasion when he had first seen Decima; she thought of his charm and erudition, his wisdom and wit, his vanity and conceit and pride.

It came as a shock to realize fully, for the first time, how much she had always disliked him!

'You can't believe it, can you?' Decima was saying. 'You can't believe that it could ever be true. You've only seen Charles in his role of academic celebrity, respected and admired by countless intellectuals, the pillar of Oxford society, the perfect English gentleman. You don't believe, do you, that he could ever be otherwise than charming and good-natured and generous.'

'I—'

'Well, I didn't believe it either! When I married him he seemed everything I could ever want, an older man whom I could trust and lean upon, a clever man whom I could respect, the kind, considerate husband I felt sure could make me happy. But I was wrong. He never loved me! He married me because of my looks, because I would cause a stir wherever I went in Oxford and he could bask in my reflected glory and listen to other men congratulate him on his wife! I soon discovered how selfish and vain he was, soon realized that the only person *he* cared about was himself! However, I too was proud and I didn't want to run to my father and admit that I'd made a terrible mistake in marrying this man, so I said nothing and pretended all was well when all the time disillusionment followed disillusionment and I wished to God I'd never met him.'

There was a silence. The warmth of the firelight seemed strangely incongruous in contrast to the stormy darkness without and Decima's low unsteady voice close at hand.

'But it wasn't until after my father died, that I realized the main reason why Charles married me. I can't think why I never saw it before – I must have been blind, but it wasn't until Father was dead and the lawyers were trying to decide what his will meant, that I realized Charles had married me for my money.

'Charles is basically very lazy. He's not interested in teaching students – or in doing any formal work! He pretends he likes free time to write and do research, but he doesn't write much! He just enjoys being a gentleman of leisure, and if I sold Ruthven and invested the proceeds, he'd never have to teach again. When he married me he thought I'd sell it as soon as I reached twenty-one – he couldn't conceive that I could ever really *like* living here, that I wouldn't sell it for all the money in the world. He didn't understand what it meant to me to have a home I loved after so many years of traipsing from one hotel to the next with my mother throughout my childhood. He made no pretence of even trying to understand. He was angry because he wanted the money and I was quite determined that it should never get into his hands.

'I don't suppose you have any idea of the terms of my father's will. My father, like everyone else, was deceived by Charles' superficial charm and thought he would be the ideal person to look after my interests if I was left an orphan before I was twenty-one; so in his will, my father made Charles, as well as the lawyer Mr Douglas and his partner, a trustee of his estate if he died leaving me a minor. He inserted a clause to say that if I died before I was twenty-one the estate should pass to my children, and if I had no children then it should pass to Charles. If I died after I was twenty-one, and had left no will disposing of the estate as I wished, Ruthven would still pass to Charles as my next-of-kin.'

'And have you made a will?'

'It's all drafted and ready to be signed as soon as I'm twenty-one. I have to be twenty-one before I can make a valid will, as I expect you know. But if I die before I'm twenty-one, the terms of the trust will come into effect and Ruthven will pass to Charles. There's nothing I can do to alter that.'

'Has he already tried to force you to sell it?'

'Soon after my father died Charles tried to urge the other trustees to sell on my behalf, but they wouldn't when they knew I was very much opposed to the idea of the sale. As trustees they have a power of sale, but in practice they would never force a sale without my consent. Mr Douglas was an old friend of my father's.'

'So—'

'Charles wants Ruthven – or rather the money that the sale of Ruthven would bring him. He knows damn well that I would never leave him a square inch of it in any will I might make after I'm twenty-one, and so his only chance to acquire it would be if I were to die before my twenty-first birthday.'

'But Decima, your birthday's Saturday and this is Thursday evening—'

'My birthday's on Sunday. The dinner party is on Saturday so that everyone can drink my health as the clock strikes twelve and my birthday officially begins. The idea was Charles', not mine.'

'But that means he has only forty-eight hours left—'

'That's why I invited you to Ruthven – because I couldn't face it any longer on my own. My nerves weren't strong enough, and there was no one I could trust—'

'Not even Rohan?'

'Charles' cousin?' said Decima ironically. 'No, I wouldn't trust Rohan.'

'And the Careys?'

'I don't trust the Careys,' said Decima.

'Why? Because they're Charles' friends?'

'Because they've outstayed their welcome without any apparent reason and are both determined to stay until after my twenty-first birthday party . . . Because Charles likes them and begged them to stay. Because . . . of many things.' She looked into the flames, and her eyes were bright and hard. 'Rebecca is the kind of woman I despise, and Daniel—'

She stopped.

'Daniel?'

'Daniel isn't interested in women,' said Decima. 'History and learning and books are all he cares about. Do you think he would listen even if I did tell him my suspicions about Charles? Of course not. He would smile politely but think me a mere neurotic female highly unworthy of any attention he could spare me . . . And anyway, I could never confide in Daniel.'

'But Decima, has Charles made any move, given you any hint that he might try to—'

'He hasn't mentioned selling Ruthven since the Careys came,' Decima interrupted. 'That in itself is unusual. And his behaviour in general has been strange. He's been so extraordinarily nice to me! He really has taken trouble over the dinner party arrangements, and he's promised to give me a beautiful diamond necklace for my birthday (which he can't afford, incidentally), and he's even suggested—' She bit her lip and glanced at Rachel from beneath her lashes. 'We haven't lived together for over a year,' she said after a moment, glancing back into the flames. 'Recently I've been locking my door at night when I go to bed. Charles suggested that I started sleeping in his room again as I did when we were first married.'

'But—'

'And he has debts,' she said suddenly, as if rushing away from a subject she had no wish to discuss. 'I – I looked among his papers once when he was out fishing . . . We lived far beyond our income after we were first married – I think he was relying on the money from Ruthven's sale to help him with the bills . . . He has even borrowed money to pay his earlier debts. And yet he talks of buying me a diamond necklace as if he had all the money in the world! Besides, we're always quarrelling over money. Before the Careys came we used to quarrel almost every other day and the subject of Ruthven's sale was always cropping up.'

'Why should the Careys' arrival make him drop the subject, I wonder?'

'I don't know, but I think he has some scheme, and the Careys have some leading part in it. I don't know why else he would drop the subject entirely, unless he had decided that reasoning with me was useless and it was necessary to make other plans.'

'Have you never thought of leaving Ruthven? You must have been very frightened these last few days.'

'Of course I've thought of it! But there are two things which have always deterred me. The first is simply that I've no proof that Charles is planning violence and it *is* possible that I may be mistaken about his intentions – this doesn't reverse anything I've just said against him, because I'm still convinced he married me for my money and would love to get his hands on it. But I've no tangible proof that he plans to kill me. Supposing I was wrong? If I left him now when he may well be genuinely eager to be generous towards me and to organize such lavish celebration for my birthday, I don't think a judge would be very sympathetic if I tried to get a divorce; Charles won't divorce me. It would reflect too badly on his ego and pride – to have to confess that he, the great success, had made a failure of marriage, and couldn't hold on to his much-displayed wife! And with his job and background he's not going to smear himself by providing the evidence for any adultery petition of mine. My one hope of a divorce is being able to prove he drove me into desertion. Besides, who knows? If he is innocent and I've misjudged him, perhaps the situation may improve once I'm twenty-one and he no longer has a hope of getting his hands on my money . . . But perhaps I'm expecting too much. Certainly, as things stand at the moment that's a hopelessly optimistic view.'

'I see . . .'

'My other reason for staying is minor in comparison but not unimportant. Ironic though it may seem, at present I've no money of my own and couldn't afford to go away – all my income from the Forestry Commission is used by the trustees in seeing to Ruthven's upkeep and giving me a ridiculously small allowance; the balance is put into the trust fund for me to inherit when I'm twenty-one.'

'So Charles can't even borrow money from you?'

'He can get nothing whatsoever unless I die before midnight on Saturday.'

Rachel stared at her. 'But Decima—' She paused, trying to marshal her thoughts into a sensible pattern and ignore the knowledge that she was far from the protective shields of civilization, but the howl of the wind and the hammering of the rain outside seemed to undermine her reserves of strength with horrifying thoroughness. She could only think that she was ten miles by sea from the nearest town, imprisoned between the vast mountains and the stormy sea, and that the danger in that still house suddenly seemed immensely alive and vital. This was no half-imagined illusion conjured up by any neurosis of Decima's; this was a reality in which she herself was personally involved. 'But what I can do?' she whispered to Decima. 'Tell me what can I do.'

'Stay with me. Don't leave me alone with Charles. And be on your guard for me.'

'Why, yes . . . of course. It'll only be till Sunday, won't it? Once you're twenty-one, you're no longer in danger because Charles would have nothing to gain from your death.'

There was a silence. At last Decima glanced at her watch. 'I must go back before they start wondering why I'm staying here so long . . . I shall go down and tell them I feel tired and have decided to follow your example in going to bed early. Then I'll go to my room and lock my door and try and get some sleep.'

'Would you like to sleep in here? One of us could sleep on the couch . . . But no, I suppose that would cause suspicion if we were found out.'

'Yes, I think so, and I want to avoid letting Charles know I'm afraid and suspect him of anything . . . Once he thinks I suspect something, he'll be on his guard.'

'Didn't he think it suspicious that you'd asked me to stay when we'd more or less lost touch with each other?'

'No, you were a friend of Rohan's and he thought inviting you was a clever idea on my part to make the numbers even for the dinner party . . . Oh, and he was probably glad you could come because he would feel you would divert Rohan's attention from me.' She stood up, automatically straightening her dress, her fingers working nervously over the material. 'Charles is convinced that Rohan and I are having an affair,' she said with a laugh which held no trace of mirth. 'Amusing, isn't it? As if I would! Anyway, I'd be more than glad if you could occupy Rohan for me, if only to allay Charles' ridiculous suspicions . . . Now I really must go – I'll see you tomorrow morning, of course. Perhaps you'd like to have breakfast with me in my room at nine-thirty? Mrs Willie, the housekeeper, always brings breakfast up to me in the mornings . . . And thank you for listening to me so well, Raye – I feel better already, just through talking about all my fears and worries to someone . . . Till tomorrow, then – I hope you sleep well, by the way. Do you have everything you want here?'

'Yes, I think so, thanks. Goodnight, Decima – and try not to worry too much.'

Decima smiled faintly; there was a draught as she opened the door and the next moment her footsteps were receding down the passage and Rachel was alone once more by the fire in the darkened room.

She threw another log into the flames. Sparks flew up the chimney. She sat for a long time while watching the wood burn and then very slowly she began to get undressed. But even as she got into bed sometime later and drew the blankets tightly around her, she found she was still wondering what part Daniel Carey played in any plans Charles might have for Decima's future.


2


When she awoke the sun was shining through the curtains and, on moving to the window, she saw that the sea was a rich, dark, swaying blue which stretched to the clear line of the horizon. The sky was pale and cloudless, bearing no trace of the stormy evening before, and the white sands shone invitingly in the light of early morning.

It was eight o'clock, long before the time for the promised breakfast with Decima at nine-thirty. The memory of Decima and the conversation of the previous evening made her pause motionless by the window for several long seconds and then, on realizing she was cold, she retreated to the warmth of her bed once more.

But she was uneasy, restless. After a time she recognized the impossibility of falling asleep again, and she got up, found a pair of slacks and a thick sweater, and started to get dressed. Within ten minutes she was slipping out into the corridor. At the head of the stairs she paused to listen but the house was quiet and she supposed everyone else was still sleeping. She reached the hall. She could hear faint sounds now, but they came from the kitchens far away where the housekeeper was already at work. Moving in the other direction, Rachel opened the front door and stepped into the clear cool air outside.

The landscape seemed different in sunshine. As she walked downhill towards the jetty she could see that the mountains beyond the house were shimmering in green and purple shades, and now that there was no mist covering the scene she could see the dark line of the trees forming the edge of the forestry plantation far away across the moors. Above the jetty she paused to look around her; to the left the sands stretched south along the black cliffs which rose abruptly from the harbour of Ruthven, and to the right the sands were curtained by the rocky arm of a peninsula thrusting out into the ocean.

Rachel turned south.

The breeze was cool, but no longer damp and chill. The sunlight, though pallid, was faintly warm. Gulls swooped above the roar of the surf and soared high over the black cliffs, and their screams carried shrilly on the air currents to echo among the rocks.

Rachel was conscious suddenly of loneliness. She glanced back over her shoulder at the house, but Ruthven was gone, hidden by a jutting corner of the cliffs, and there was no sign of civilization. She hesitated uneasily, and then pulled herself together with a smile at her city-dweller's reactions and walked on.

The cliffs were taller now, great scarred walls of granite with rocks piled at their base and embedded in the sand. There were caves too, some enormous caverns the size of a church, some mere holes barely high enough for upright stance. Rachel, venturing nearer the cliff-face, found deep pools left behind by the tide and an assortment of shellfish and seaweed clustered in the water among the rocks.

She was just stooping to examine a large shell when she suddenly felt she was being watched. She swung round abruptly, but there was nothing there, only the roar of the surf and the screaming of the gulls. Her heart was pounding in her lungs so hard that even her movements away from the cliffs were stiff and awkward, but once she was close to the breaking waves and away from the dark, gaping mouths of the caves she felt better. She started walking again and soon she had rounded another rocky peninsula and was standing before another expanse of wide white sands, unmarked, untouched, effortlessly beautiful. She stepped out towards them quickly, forgetting her absurd nervousness of a few minutes before and feeling unexpectedly light-hearted.

There was a howl from behind her. An enormous throaty baying echoed among the cliffs and as she spun round in shock she saw the vast St Bernard pounding towards her, his jaws gaping as he bared his teeth.

Like most people unaccustomed to even small dogs, Rachel was too frightened to move. And then as the dog reached her and she stepped back automatically in self-defence, she felt her heels sinking and realized in a flash of understanding that she had wandered right to the very edge of the quicksands of Cluny.

She froze in her tracks, and the dog stopped too, still baying in warning. Then, very delicately he stepped forward, tail swaying and took the cuff of her jacket between his teeth to lead her away from the sands to safety. Rachel automatically wrenched her shoes free to follow him, and presently the dog released his hold on her jacket and looked up at her sadly as if incredulous that anyone could be so stupid and careless.

She was just stroking the top of the dog's head when she saw Daniel.

He was standing at the entrance to one of the caves, but

as she saw him he began to walk over to her. He walked slowly, not hurrying, his hands in the pockets of his old dark corduroys, and when he drew nearer she saw that his eyes were watchful and his mouth was unsmiling.

'Did no one tell you,' he said, 'about Cluny Sands?'

'Why, yes,' she said, stumbling over the words just as she had always done at school. 'Yes, Rohan told me. But I didn't think – I didn't remember—'

'I see.' He whistled to the dog. 'Here, George.'

The St Bernard lumbered over to him obediently and sat down on the sand, his tail still swaying.

'Why didn't you call out to me sooner?' Rachel heard herself demand. 'Why did you let me get right to the edge before you sent the dog after me?'

'I thought you were certain to know about the sands and would stop before you reached the edge. Besides, the tide's out and the sands are less dangerous; the danger comes when the tide is on the turn.' He was still motionless and there was something about his eyes which brought her back to the rawness of adolescent emotions, a world she thought she had outgrown long ago.

She glanced away out to sea. 'I still think you might have called out sooner,' she said abruptly.

Some indefinable element in his manner was at once erased; he smiled, and his voice when he spoke was full of charm and warmth.

'I do apologize,' he said. 'It was wrong of me, I see that now, and you must have had a bad shock. Let me take you back to the house and brew you some coffee to make amends.'

She glanced at him briefly but lowered her eyes even before she smiled in return. 'Thank you,' she murmured. 'But I'm quite all right.'

'But you'll accept my offer of coffee all the same, I hope.'

'I – I've promised to have breakfast with Decima.'

'Decima never looks at a breakfast tray before nine-thirty,' said Daniel, 'and we'll be back at the house long before that. However, it's as you wish, of course.' His shoe knocked against a pebble and he stooped to pick it up and fling it out to sea. 'How do you find Decima, by the way? Has she changed much since you last saw her?'

'No, she doesn't seem to have changed. But then I've hardly seen her yet.'

'You never actually knew her very well, did you?'

'Why, yes,' said Rachel, astonished enough to glance up into his eyes. 'I knew her very well indeed! We were at school in Geneva together for nine months and were the closest of friends.'

'Oh?' said Daniel. 'You surprise me.'

She couldn't help asking him why.

'You seem very dissimilar types.'

'You hardly know me,' she heard herself say, 'and you've known Decima little more than six weeks, I understand.'

'I see I've expressed myself badly,' he said. 'Let me put it this way: I've seen enough of Decima to enable me to form an opinion of her, and it wouldn't take five minutes' conversation with you to determine that you could never in a thousand years be placed in the category in which I should place Decima.'

'And what category is that? Or aren't I supposed to ask?'

'It would be better if you didn't, certainly. If I told you, you might feel bound to tell Decima as she's such a close friend.'

'And as you seem to think this would be a bad thing,' said Rachel, 'I assume your opinion of her can't be very high.'

'I didn't intend to imply that. Decima is very beautiful and very charming and an admirable hostess. I don't think anyone would quarrel with that.'

'No, indeed . . . She must have caused quite a stir in Oxford circles after she married Charles.'

'Yes, I believe she did. I'd left Oxford by that time so I never met her, although I continued to keep in touch with Charles after I left.' He was watching the St Bernard paddling at the water's edge. 'You knew Charles before he married Decima, I suppose?'

'Yes, Rohan introduced me to Charles when we – Rohan and I – were quite young. But we only saw him occasionally. He didn't come down to visit Rohan's family very often.'

'Charles is a remarkable man,' said Daniel, still watching the dog. 'Academically he's one of the most gifted men I've ever met.'

Rachel said nothing.

'Strange, isn't it,' said Daniel, 'how a very clever man should be quite so foolish?'

The waves crashed on the beach in a roar of surf, but she did not hear them.

'He should never have married Decima, of course. I'm only surprised he didn't see at the time how unsuited they were. Lord knows it must have been obvious enough.'

After a moment Rachel said: 'He – regrets the marriage?'

'Didn't Decima tell you their marriage was a mere formality?'

'Yes, but—'

'That was the main reason why my sister and I have stayed so long – the Mannerings begged us not to leave! They were both so bored with each other's company that they welcomed us with open arms. Didn't Decima tell you that? I'm sorry if I've said too much but I was under the impression you were in her confidence.'

It was only then that she realized he was trying to discover how much she knew and why she had come to Ruthven.

'There's been so little time,' she said, suddenly confused. 'Decima's hardly touched on the subject of either why you were here or why you had stayed so long.'

'Well, it's easy enough to explain.' He gestured towards a flat slab of rock near the cliffs. 'Shall we sit down for a moment? Rebecca and I had decided to visit the Edinburgh Festival together – she'd just taken her postgraduate Diploma of Education exams and had planned to have a long holiday before looking around for a job, and my time is my own during the long vacation. Remembering that Charles had written to tell me of Ruthven during the years we had corresponded, I thought it might be interesting to hire a car after the Festival and drive up to the Highlands and over to the west coast. I wrote to Charles, telling him of the plans, and he wrote back by return mail to ask us to stay.

'I was intrigued by this place as soon as I saw it. I suppose every civilized man dreams from time to time of finding somewhere completely isolated and free from all the trappings of city and suburban life, but most of the time he never comes within a thousand miles of such a place. But Ruthven for me was the place of my dreams.' He stooped to run his index finger softly down the back of the dog at his feet. The wind from the sea flicked unseen fingers through his dark hair. 'But something happens to people,' he said after a while. 'Something happens to them when they're imprisoned between the mountains and the sea, cut off from other human beings and forced through necessity and circumstance to have more contact with each other than would otherwise be the case. One finds oneself being sucked into a vortex; personality grates on personality in an ever-shifting pattern; everyone gets to know everyone else much too well for comfort.

'Rebecca and I should have left long ago, but we did not. For one thing Decima begged us to stay for her birthday, and for another . . . well, Charles too was anxious that we should stay, and I suppose the wish to leave wasn't strong enough.' He stopped. There was a pause. Then:

'I don't quite understand your remarks about a vortex,' Rachel said slowly. 'But surely Rohan's arrival – and now mine – must have eased matters if things were getting strained.'

'It would have been better if Quist had never set foot in this place,' said Daniel abruptly. 'And as for you . . . I can only advise you to leave as soon as you can. There are things going on here which I couldn't even begin to explain to you. Leave before you too get drawn into the vortex and find yourself unable to escape.'

Spray flew from the crashing surf. The tide was creeping farther towards them and from the south she could hear the roar of the undertow sucking over Cluny Sands.

'I don't understand you,' she said woodenly. 'What are you trying to say?'

A voice sounded above the roar of the surf. As they both swung round abruptly they saw Rebecca Carey walking towards them and, when she saw that they had noticed her, she raised her hand in greeting.

'But for God's sake,' said Daniel to Rachel, 'don't go repeating what I've said to Charles or Decima or Quist. I spoke for you and you alone.'

'Of course,' she said sharply, annoyed that he even considered it necessary to give her such a warning, and then she realized that her mouth was dry and her limbs stiff with tension.

Rebecca was already within earshot.

'This is the best morning we've had for days,' she called out, as she came up to them. 'You've brought good weather with you, Rachel.' The wind blew her short hair into her eyes, and she pushed it back impatiently. She wore a tweed skirt and an olive-green sweater, and the plain clothes were the perfect foil for the strong lines of her face and the glow of her eyes. It was a good-looking face, neither pretty nor beautiful, but Rachel thought her good looks were marred by a trace of aggression which seemed to hint that Rebecca had been accustomed all her life to reach out to grasp things she wanted, as they never came to her of their own accord. Rachel, who had gone to a large girls' day school before being exported to Geneva, had met a great many girls during her life and had no difficulty at all in placing Rebecca in the appropriate category. Rebecca was the one who sat in the front of the class and always knew all the answers, the girl whose tongue was as sharp as her brain and made enemies as fast as she tried to make friends, a lonely person in spite of her militant air of self-sufficiency.

With Rachel pity always outweighed dislike.

'You're up early,' she said pleasantly to Rebecca. 'Do you always go for a walk before breakfast?'

'I certainly don't wallow around in bed till ten with a breakfast tray, if that's what you mean. Danny, Charles is talking of going into Kyle of Lochalsh this morning to arrange for food for the dinner party. Didn't you say you wanted to go into town before Saturday evening to get Decima a present?'

'I'd thought of it.' He turned to Rachel. 'Do you have a present for Decima?'

'Yes, I've brought a small present up from London.'

'In that case, since you've had the experience of choosing a present for her, perhaps you'd care to come with us into town and help me select something? I've no idea what to buy for her and I'd appreciate some advice.'

'It will hardly be as difficult to choose as all that,' Rebecca said sharply before Rachel could reply. 'And I don't suppose Rachel wants to go back into Kyle of Lochalsh today.'

'I – I'm sure Rebecca could advise you just as well, Daniel—'

'As you wish.' He turned abruptly and set off at a brisk pace across the sands, the St Bernard padding in his wake.

'You'll probably find some very good Gaelic jewellery in town,' Rachel heard herself say in an instinctive attempt to gloss over the moment of awkwardness. 'It shouldn't be too difficult to find something suitable.'

'Exactly what I thought,' said Rebecca crisply. 'I'm surprised he asked you to come. He should have realized you would be too tired after your journey to want to do much today. How are you feeling, by the way? You look tired.'

'I—'

'As you're up so early, I suppose you didn't sleep well?'

'Well, actually, I—'

'It's always difficult getting used to a strange place, isn't it? And Ruthven must seem so primitive after the London suburbs . . . Tell me, how did you come to meet Daniel this morning? I was looking for him everywhere.'

Rachel wondered for a fleeting moment why she always felt so irritated with people who prefaced all their questions with the words, 'Tell me.'

'I just met him down here on the beach,' she said shortly and noticed in surprise that her feeling of irritation was growing with every second that passed; she very seldom allowed herself to be ruffled by a person's manner, but Rebecca seemed to have the most unfortunate effect on her.

'But why did you walk so far south? Cluny Sands—'

'Yes,' said Rachel politely. 'I've heard all about Cluny Sands.'

'You have? That's just as well . . . They remind me of that novel by Sir Walter Scott – which was the one where the hero had trouble with quicksands? *Bride of Lammermoor*, was it? Or *Redgauntlet*? But of course, those quicksands were by the Firth of Forth.'

'Of course,' said Rachel, who had never read either novel. 'So they were.'

'You read Scott? Charles has a complete collection. What a wonderful library he has! It seems such a pity that Decima never reads anything except those ghastly women's magazines . . . But then I believe she only had a very superficial education.'

'I expect she finds it adequate enough.'

'You think so? But then she's not really too clever, is she? And, of course, she's not too well either, I'm convinced of it.'

The cool hard drift of the conversation was suddenly crystallized into the ice of innuendo.

'What do you mean?' said Rachel sharply. 'Decima's as well as you or I!'

'Oh, but you haven't been living here these past few weeks as I have! She's really been acting in such a strange way – that's why we all encouraged her to have you to stay. Charles especially thought you would be good for her, a stabilizing influence . . . She was getting rather – well, rather neurotic, although I hate to use a word with such unfortunate connotations. She's been giving poor Charles such a very difficult time.'

'I don't quite—'

'I can say all this to you, you see, because I really feel you should know the truth of the situation in order to be able to cope with Decima as you think best . . . Ah, there's Ruthven! How fast Daniel's been walking! He's nearly by the jetty already . . . And there's Rohan in the doorway – look, he's waving to you! What a strange man he is, so foreign, so unusual. Tell me, he's not entirely English, is he?'

'His father came from Sweden. But about Decima—'

'Sweden? Oh well, of course, everyone knows the Swedes are a very strange race . . . Yes, it's really a great pity about Decima. I've made countless efforts to be sociable and friendly towards her, but she simply refuses to make any effort at all. Ever since we came here she's been hostile and trying to make things difficult for Charles – it's really been a constant source of embarrassment.'

'I'm surprised you stayed so long, then,' said Rachel, 'if you were unpopular with your hostess.'

'But my dear, there was no reason for her attitude! It was quite without motivation! Charles has confided to me once or twice that Decima is convinced that she's being persecuted in some way or another . . . As soon as they go back to Oxford he's arranging for her to see a doctor – you understand? I mean, it's not normal, is it? All she wants to do is hide from the world here in the back of beyond – she doesn't even want to go back to Oxford. Imagine not wanting to see Oxford again! I think she's afraid of meeting people, of showing herself. It's quite a common nervous complaint, I believe.'

'Decima seems eminently sane to me,' said Rachel, 'and I also disagree with your earlier remark about her intelligence. She was very clever indeed at school. Just because she's not intellectual doesn't mean to say she's not clever.'

'Well, of course,' said Rebecca, exactly as if Rachel hadn't spoken, 'the longer you stay here, the more apparent her state of mind will become to you. All I can say is that she's been acting very strangely lately.'

There was a small uncomfortable silence. Then:

'Rohan seems to want to talk to you,' Rebecca said as they watched him reach the beach and again wave to attract their attention. 'Will you excuse me? I want to find out what time Daniel plans to go into Kyle of Lochalsh.' And she was gone, her footsteps quickening across the sands.

Daniel was aboard the boat moored to the jetty, and as Rachel watched he came up from below deck and waited by the wheelhouse as he saw his sister coming. He seemed far away and remote, a minute part of the vast landscape of sea, sky and mountains.

'Ah, *there* you are!' said Rohan, stating what must have been obvious to him for at least five minutes. 'What's the matter with you, getting up so early?' He was still some way away from her, but his voice carried clearly on the still morning air. 'And why the secret rendezvous with Daniel?' he added as he came closer. 'I saw him follow you out of the house and across the sands! Rebecca looked most insulted when she came outside later and saw her beloved brother had walked off without her – usually they go together for their early morning stroll. What did Carey say to you anyway? What did he want?'

'It was nothing,' said Rachel automatically, her thoughts still on her conversation with Rebecca, and then as she thought of Daniel, she added a shade too positively, 'Absolutely nothing at all.'

'Ah-*ha*!' said Rohan at once. 'Ah-ha! My dear girl, don't tell me you find Carey irresistibly attractive! Don't tell me—'

'No, of course I shan't tell you, because it isn't true! Shut up, Rohan, for God's sake. It's too early in the morning for such nonsense . . . Listen, I want to talk to you – let's sit down here for a moment before we go on up to the house.'

'All right,' said Rohan agreeably, moving over to a long

rock and subsiding on to it without argument. 'What's the matter? Did Carey—'

'Forget Daniel for a moment, would you? I want to talk to you about Rebecca.'

'Really? Do we have to? All right, all right, all right! Don't get huffy and walk off with your nose in the air! I was only joking. What's all this about Rebecca?'

'We've just had the most extraordinary conversation. She was saying such fantastic things that I was quite speechless.'

'Such as?'

'That – that Decima had a persecution complex—'

'Oh God!'

'– and was mentally ill—'

'What did you say?'

'What do you think I said? I told her as politely as possible that I thought she was the one who needed the psychiatrist, not Decima.'

'You didn't!'

'Well, no, to be honest, but I did deny it and say that Decima was as sane as we were.'

'Hm.'

'Well, isn't she? Don't be silly, Rohan! Look, what's been going on? Why should Rebecca say a thing like that? What happened here before I arrived yesterday?'

Rohan was silent. As she watched him she saw the amused lines about his mouth smooth themselves away and his grey eyes seemed to darken with his change of mood. 'There are several reasons why Rebecca should say a thing like that,' he said at last. 'First of all, Decima dislikes Rebecca and makes no effort to hide it. Secondly, Rebecca dislikes Decima for a good many reasons, the first and foremost of which is probably because Rebecca would always despise a woman less intellectual than herself. And thirdly, Decima really has been behaving very oddly.'

'I hadn't noticed. She seemed very normal to me.'

'Well, yes, naturally,' said Rohan. 'She was most successful at creating an atmosphere of normalcy when you arrived last night.'

After a moment Rachel said, 'I don't understand.'

'Things have been very far from normal, Rachel, and it all stems from Decima. I wouldn't say this to you if I hadn't known you all my life, because I know you and she were close friends for a while and as far as you're concerned you're still friends even though perhaps not such close friends as you were once. But I know you too damn well, Rachel, for insincerities, and I would be insincere if I didn't tell you that Decima's the last person who should ever be a friend of yours.'

'But I thought you liked Decima! When you first met her—'

'I didn't know her then, just as you don't know her now, but she's no good, Rachel. She's given Charles one hell of a time and I can tell you here and now he's at his wits' end with her. I keep telling him to divorce her, but they haven't been married three years yet, and it's not easy to get a divorce before then. Besides, he's against a divorce purely from a social point of view; divorce today hasn't the stigma it used to have, but he moves among elderly circles governed by a strict morality, and a divorce would certainly do him no good. However, it must obviously come to that in the end. I don't think she'll leave Ruthven to return to Oxford with him this time when term begins, and that'll mean a public acknowledgement of the rift between them.'

'He'll miss Decima's money if they're divorced, won't he?'

'Charles has enough money! He doesn't have to worry about that!'

'Nobody ever has enough money,' said Rachel ironically. 'No matter how much you have, it's never quite enough.'

'But Charles didn't marry Decima for her money, Rachel! He married her because he was infatuated with her looks, personality, sex appeal – call it whatever you like! Perhaps you didn't see much of him before they were married and while they were engaged, but he was up to his eyes in his infatuation – and when a man's in love with a bank account instead of a pretty woman he hardly goes around with a moonstruck look in his eyes, unable to eat or sleep.'

'But when did the disillusionment begin? Wasn't it when he found she wouldn't consent to Ruthven's sale?'

'Is that what she says? Didn't she tell you anything about her marriage?'

'She mentioned that she'd been unhappy.'

'*She'd* been unhappy! My God! What about Charles? I don't know why she married him, but it certainly wasn't for love. Maybe she was attracted by the fact that he was an older man and a well-known name in academic life. Or maybe she was impressed by his charm and found the idea of marriage appealing. But she didn't love him! She may be beautiful and exotic and seductive but she's as cold as that northern sea out there, as empty and sterile as these desolate mountains around us. As far as any form of physical intimacy is concerned, she simply isn't interested. Whose idea was it, do you think, that they should have separate bedrooms? Certainly not Charles'! Charles is a man, just like any other, when it comes to sex. He would even like children now, I think. But is Decima interested in children? Of course not! She doesn't care about anything except herself. Charles was a novelty to begin with, but she was soon bored. She yawned at the social occasions she had to attend with him, embarrassed him with her extravagances, humiliated him by making no attempt to fit into his world. She even flirted with the undergraduates in an effort to annoy him – but then she'd flirt with any man! Decima thrives on admiration.'

There was a long moment of silence. Then:

'There are two sides to everything,' said Rachel slowly at last, 'so I'm not surprised to hear there are two sides when it comes to the Mannerings' marriage. But here there are such wide discrepancies that one or the other party must be lying! According to Decima—'

'Yes, what on earth's Decima been saying? I didn't realize you'd already had the chance to speak to her.'

'We talked for a little while after dinner last night, and

she implied she wasn't happy and that Charles had married her for her money. She also said that *he* had been acting strangely, and that—'

'Charles? But that's nonsense!'

'Is it? Anyway, she said she was glad I had come because I would act as a diversion by keeping *you* occupied. Then Charles wouldn't go on suspecting that you and Decima were having an affair.'

Rohan was suddenly white. 'Decima and I – but that's preposterous! Ridiculous! Absurd!' He stared at her, his grey eyes wide and dark, and for the first time since her arrival she saw through the mask of his light-hearted manner to the tension and fear which lay beneath. So Rohan too had somehow been drawn into the vortex which existed at Ruthven. Daniel's warning of the vortex rang once more in her ears, but before she could speak again Rohan was saying in a tight, controlled voice which she scarcely recognized: 'Decima was lying to you. Why should Charles suspect me of trying to have an affair with her when it's perfectly obvious that she's much more interested in Daniel Carey?'

## chapter 4

1

Daniel was watching Rohan and Rachel from the wheel-house of the boat. They had been sitting on the rock together for ten minutes and still appeared to be deep in conversation.

'I don't like that girl,' Rebecca said from beside him.

'So I observed.' He lit a cigarette and the flame of the match was reflected for a moment in his eyes. He was thinking of Quist, wondering what game the man was playing, what he was saying to Rachel Lord a hundred yards away across the beach.

'Why on earth did you ask her to help you choose a present for Decima?'

He felt annoyed suddenly. 'Why not?' he said, wishing she would go back to the house and leave him alone for a while with his thoughts. 'I like her.'

'I wouldn't have thought she was your type.'

'Then I must be tired of my type – whatever that may be.' He went out on deck, but she followed him. He was reminded suddenly of the times when they had been children and Rebecca had always followed him faithfully wherever they had gone. It occurred to him vaguely that he was becoming a little tired of this childhood echo shadowing him wherever he went.

'I'm going back to the house,' he said shortly.

'I'll come with you.'

They returned in silence, not speaking till they reached the hall. Then: 'I'll call for you when I'm ready to leave,' he said over his shoulder and moved swiftly up the stairs to his room. On reaching the door he flung it shut behind him thankfully and did not at first notice that someone was waiting for him in the chair by the fireplace.

'Danny—'

He swung round. She stood up, graceful and poised as ever, and the folds of her pale-blue peignoir seemed to float for a second in the draught of movement. 'Danny, I had to see you—'

'There's nothing to say.'

But she wasn't as meek as Rebecca, not as willing to accept the finality of his retorts. 'Listen, Daniel, I've changed my mind—'

'Then you've changed it too late, Decima. I'm sorry.' She was very close to him now; he noticed how she took a deliberate step nearer to him so that he could see how thin her peignoir was and how much excitement lay just beneath the lace surface. 'Please, Danny,' she said and her blue eyes were misty. 'Please . . .' It was cleverly done, he thought. In her own way she was an artist. And much to his anger and disgust he felt his pulses quicken as he allowed himself to look at her for a long moment. He would have turned away but she put a hand on his arm and halted him. 'I've treated you badly, I know, Danny; it was wrong of me and I realize that now. But I was frightened, anxious, scared . . .' She paused, searching his face for some glimmer of capitulation.

'You were none of those things,' he heard himself say. 'You were amused, flattered and diverted. Diverted because my attention provided a variation from the normal course of events at Ruthven, flattered because any woman likes being paid the kind of attention that I paid you, and amused because you're too cold to find anything except amusement in your power to interest a man when you yourself feel nothing at all.'

'That's not true!' she stormed, passionate and tempestuous now as if in a full demonstration of her emotional range. 'Just because I said no, just because I allowed myself one instant of loyalty to Charles, just because for a moment I was frightened by the depth of my feelings for you—'

'You didn't care, Decima, and no matter how hard you try now to play the role of the loyal young wife beset with temptations, you'll never make the part convincing. You refused because you didn't care, and once I realized that and saw your masquerade for what it was, I didn't care either.'

'But I do care, I do! I'll do whatever you want, Danny, I swear it – just say what you want me to do and I'll do it!'

'You don't understand,' he said coldly as the hot sweat moistened the palms of his hands. 'You're making the situation much more complex than it really is. The position was simply this: I saw you, wanted you, just as I'd want any other attractive woman. After you'd played around and successfully kept me at arm's length while you amused yourself watching my growing frustration, it eventually dawned on me that you were never going to be interested enough to say yes and, even if you did, you probably wouldn't have much to offer in the end. I'm not interested in cold women. And as soon as I lost interest in you sexually, I'm afraid that was the end of your power over me. Next time I'd advise you to play your cards a little differently if you want your fun to last longer.'

She was very white. For a moment he had the unnerving impression that he had misjudged her and that she was, after all, capable of caring, and so strong was the impression that he instinctively drew closer to her.

The next thing he knew was that she was in his arms and her mouth was beneath his own.

Her lips were very far from being cold.

After a long moment she said, 'Take me away from Charles.'

He looked at her. It did not seem preposterous at all, merely the most natural thing in the world. He was still looking at her when there was a soft knock at the door and they both spun round.

'Daniel?' called Charles softly. 'May I come in?'


## 2

Daniel took several seconds to answer the door. It vaguely occurred to Charles to wonder why he was taking so long and then, before he could question it further, the door was opening and Daniel was on the threshold.

'I'm sorry, Charles, I wasn't sure whether I heard you . . . Won't you come in?'

'No, I was only going to tell you that I plan to leave for Kyle of Lochalsh at ten-thirty – will that be convenient for you?'

'Fine. I'll tell Rebecca.'

'I've already told her,' said Charles, moving on down the corridor. 'I'll see you later, Daniel,' and he was gone.

Daniel closed the door just as Decima emerged from her hiding place behind the long curtains.

'I keep thinking he suspects something,' she said. 'Supposing he knows. Or supposing he suspects—'

'How can he when there's nothing to suspect?' He had himself tightly in control now. He knew exactly which course he was going to take and exactly how he was going to manage the situation. It was as if the brief interval with Charles had sharpened his sensibilities and frozen the heat in his body to ice. 'There's nothing between us now, Decima, and as far as I'm concerned there never will be.'

'But just now—' Her eyes were brilliant with anger, her face white with fury. 'Just now—'

'Just now I was a fool, Decima, but I'm not such a fool as to make the same mistake twice. If you want to escape from your marriage, you must find someone else to help you, for the help won't be coming from me.'

She still stood looking at him. 'But why?' she said at last. 'Why? I thought a few days ago that you felt quite differently.'

'I'm sorry if I misled you,' he said, turning abruptly as if to terminate the conversation, 'but I'm afraid there's nothing more to be said.'

He waited for her to speak again, to demand a further explanation or even to lose her temper, but she was silent. And then very slowly she said: 'You're sure you won't regret that, aren't you?'

He swung round. Her face was still white but her mouth was smiling.

'Regret what?' His voice was cool and casual in his ears.

'You don't want to get a bad reputation in academic circles, do you?' she said, turning from him to open the door. 'They're really so fussy about professors nowadays, I've heard.'

And she was gone, closing the door lightly behind her and leaving him alone at last in the solitude of his room.


3


Decima was not in her room when Rachel called for breakfast at nine-thirty. The large light room was neat, the bed already made, and from the window Rachel had an uninterrupted view south-east to the moors and mountains and south-west to the sea. She was just wondering whether to seek Decima downstairs when the door opened and Decima herself came quickly into the room.

'Ah, there you are!' Her cheeks were flushed and her eyes very bright, as if she were very excited. Or very angry. 'I'll call for Mrs Willie to bring up the breakfast tray. Did you sleep well?'

'Fine, thanks. I awoke early and went for a walk along the beach . . . Is anything the matter, Decima? You look a little uneasy.'

'No, it's nothing. Just nervousness . . . I think we'll all be going into town this morning, by the way, so I hope you'll come with me and keep me company. Daniel and Rebecca have to do some personal shopping and I have to go with Charles to order the food for the dinner party. As there's been no shooting party I'm afraid we'll have to buy the venison. You wouldn't mind coming, would you?'

'Not in the least. It's a beautiful morning for a boat trip . . . What time is Charles planning to go?'

'About ten-thirty – if I can be ready by then. I'm so bad at getting up in the mornings.'

This turned out to be perfectly true. In the end it was after eleven o'clock by the time everyone was aboard the boat and Charles was starting up the motor.

The sun was pleasantly warm; Rachel, sitting near the stern with the soft wind caressing her skin, found it hard in the light of day to recall her fears of the previous evening after dark or even fears of that same morning during her conversation with Daniel by Cluny Sands. Everyone seemed perfectly normal. Charles and Rohan were in the wheelhouse, Decima was beside her on the seat and the Careys were in the prow of the boat, near enough to talk to each other but each appearing to maintain silence. She watched the back of Daniel's head and then Rohan came out of the wheelhouse to join them and she glanced out to sea abruptly.

'Are you all right, Decima? You look a little chilled.'

'No, I'm fine.'

Something was definitely wrong with Decima. Rohan and Rebecca had been right after all. Glancing at her friend, Rachel noticed the nervous workings of her fingers on the material of her skirt, the restlessness of her eyes, the tenseness in every line of her slim body. She had had nothing for breakfast except a cup of coffee, and had talked rapidly in fits and starts on any random topic which came to her mind. It had been an uncomfortable meal and Rachel had been glad when it was over.

Rebecca was moving. As Rachel watched, she left Daniel in the prow and went into the wheelhouse for a word with Charles before slipping below decks and out of sight.

Rachel began to watch Daniel again.

'Let's go below,' Rohan was saying. 'I'll make you some coffee, Decima.'

'No, thanks.'

'Sure? How about you, Rachel?'

'What?'

'Would you like some coffee?'

'Oh . . . no thanks, Rohan.' Daniel had turned around and was coming towards them. The breeze was suddenly icy-cool against her hot cheeks.

'Wait, Rohan,' said Decima clearly. 'I think I will come below with you.'

'You will? Fine. Sure you won't change your mind, Raye?'

She hardly heard him. Daniel was smiling at her, sitting down in the seat which Decima had just left. 'I'm sorry I was rather abrupt with you this morning,' he was saying. 'I'm afraid I left you very suddenly with my sister.'

He was sitting next to her in a casual, relaxed position, his legs stretched out and crossed at the ankles, one elbow on the back of the seat to ease the pressure on his spine so that his body was turned slightly towards her. She felt stiff and awkward suddenly, wanting to relax and yet afraid of betraying her taut muscles by one careless movement, wanting to look at him, yet not trusting herself to meet his eyes. Her awareness of him was so immense that she thought that even if he had held her in his arms it would have been impossible for her to have felt more at the mercy of her own emotions. And for Rachel, who had always prided herself on the level-headed advice she had given, when requested, to her love-lorn friends, such a complete reversal of her self-possession seemed to strip her of all vestiges of confidence.

She looked at him suddenly, determined that he should never know the effect he had on her, and said with candour, 'Decima doesn't seem herself at all this morning. I was wondering what was the matter with her, but she says nothing is wrong.'

He shrugged. 'She's easily upset, it seems . . . How calm the sea is today! The landscape looks almost at peace. Have you been to Scotland before, by the way, or is this your first visit?'

She answered him readily enough, but she had noticed how deftly he had avoided a discussion of Decima. He asked her more questions about her life in London, even about her recent visit to Florence and, while she answered, she was wondering if he had had an affair with Decima and abused Charles' hospitality in the most shameful of all ways possible. Yet Rohan had not said positively that Daniel and Decima were having an affair, only that Decima was much too interested in her guest . . . And Decima had said the previous evening that she disliked Daniel Carey and that she didn't trust him.

Either Rohan was mistaken, thought Rachel, or Decima was lying. Probably Decima was lying because she wanted Rachel's support against Charles and feared Rachel might disapprove of a confession of infidelity; she wouldn't have wanted to risk losing Rachel's sympathy at that particular moment.

Probably, too, they were having an affair. She doubted very much whether Decima would be cold and remote if she were strongly attracted to a man, and surely Daniel would have left Ruthven days ago if he had failed from the outset to get what he wanted. A man like Daniel Carey would probably always get what he wanted from women with very little trouble.

'I often go down to London from Cambridge for a weekend,' he was saying. 'We must arrange to meet some time. Did you say you enjoyed the theatre?'

And then she was lost again, lost to the cool clear voice of her reason appraising the situation, lost to all her sensible powers of judgement. Yes, she loved the theatre, she went as often as possible, as often as she could afford it . . .

'Afford it?' said Daniel, his fine eyes alive with surprise. 'Are your escorts so mean they allow you to pay your own way?'

Normally she would have been too proud to admit that she seldom had the opportunity of an escorted visit to the theatre, but some strange instinct made her be honest with him just when she most wanted to be dishonest.

'It's only girls like Decima who have a string of escorts lining up to take them out every night of the week!' she said lightly. 'The rest of us aren't so fortunate. If I had to wait for a generous escort every time I wanted to see a play I wouldn't go to the theatre nearly as often as I like.'

He was so astonished that she almost laughed. 'You mean you go on your own?'

'Yes, of course – why not? Or perhaps I may go with a girl friend. But I don't sit around at home like a modern Cinderella if I haven't got someone to take me out.'

He stared at her.

This time she did laugh. 'You look as if I've just destroyed all your conventional ideas about young single women!'

He laughed too, 'No. it's hardly as drastic as that, but nonetheless . . .' He glanced away, and she did not at first realize that he was checking that no one else was within earshot. 'Nonetheless, it confirms my original impression of you.'

'And what was that?'

'That you're a most unusual and interesting woman.' He was on his feet, not looking at her, and the breeze tore at his dark hair for a moment as he stepped over to the wheelhouse.

'May I borrow a cigarette from you, Charles? I seem to have used my last one . . . Thanks.'

She was watching him, noticing every movement, her mind teeming with every echo of their conversation and recalling every inflection of his voice. Charles gave him a cigarette and he paused in the shelter of the wheelhouse to light it. And then, before he could return to her, Rebecca emerged from below decks and the chance to renew the conversation was gone.

Rachel turned away and stared across the sea at the inland mountains.

It was after one when they reached Kyle of Lochalsh. After they had found a place for the boat in the harbour, Charles suggested they have lunch before doing anything further, but Daniel had little enthusiasm for the idea and in the end he and Rebecca separated from the others and walked off into the town on their own. Daniel again asked Rachel to come with them, but Decima at once said that Rachel had agreed to help her buy food for the dinner party. Daniel had shrugged and said nothing further.

It was curious, Rachel thought, how everyone seemed to relax once the Careys had gone. Charles became more jovial, Rohan more loquacious and Decima less painfully ill at ease. Rachel could even feel her own tenseness evaporate once Daniel had gone, but her thoughts were still in such turmoil that it was hard for her to concentrate afresh on Decima's troubles and the situation surrounding her. Making a great effort, she managed to answer the remarks that were addressed to her, but all the time she was thinking of Daniel and remembering how he had already suggested travelling from Cambridge to London to see her.

And suddenly she didn't care what his relationship with Decima was or had been, didn't even care whether in fact it had ever existed. With something of a shock she realized she didn't care about Decima any more either. In a moment of honesty with herself she saw vividly that her world had assumed new and frightening dimensions; it was as if quite without warning she had been swept off her feet by a strong current, borne turbulently along on the crest of a huge, silent tide over which she had no control. *I'm no longer an outsider looking in at the scene being played before me*, she thought, *but part of the scene itself*.

And she felt not only a strange sense of exuberance but also a sharp pang of dread.

She had been drawn into the vortex.


4

Daniel said to his sister: 'Things are getting dangerous.'

'With Decima?'

'The situation's getting out of hand. I was a fool ever to get involved with her.'

Rebecca was shocked. Daniel never made a fool of himself over a woman. 'What do you mean, Danny? Why do you say that?'

He told her. They were walking up the High Street past the shops selling tweeds and tartans, past the butcher, the baker, the greengrocer, but by the time they reached the little shop selling Gaelic silverware and jewellery, Rebecca had long since ceased to be conscious of her surroundings.

'My God, Danny—'

'So you can see how dangerous it is.'

'But she'll have to be stopped! Something will have to be done!'

'That's my worry, not yours.'

'But of course it's my worry too! She could ruin you, Danny – do you think I would stand by and see that happen? How can you say it's not my worry?'

'You've problems of your own without involving yourself in mine.'

'But I'm already involved! Danny, the associate professorship you were hoping to get – supposing Decima should—'

'Precisely.'

'But what shall we do?'

'You will do nothing at all,' said Daniel quietly, 'what I shall do remains to be seen.'


5


They had bought all that was necessary for the dinner party after lunching at one of the inns near the harbour; Rachel had gone with Decima to buy the venison and the rest of the food while Rohan had gone with Charles to attend to buying the champagne and an assortment of other bottles that were considered necessary. By the time all the purchases were safely on board it was after three-thirty and there was still no sign of the Careys.

'I think I'll stroll over to the pub at the jetty, and coax the landlord to serve me a pint of beer outside licensing hours,' said Rohan. 'Then I'll see the Careys when they arrive back at the boat. Will anyone come with me?'

'Perhaps I will,' Charles said. 'Decima?'

'No, I'm too tired. I'll wait here.'

'I'll stay with Decima,' said Rachel, before she could be asked. 'You two go off and have your beer.'

When they had gone Decima complained of a headache and went aft to make herself coffee in the tiny galley. 'Do you want some, Raye?'

'No, thanks. I'm going up on deck, I think. Will you be all right down here?'

'Yes, I'll have some coffee and then lie down for a minute. I hope the Careys won't be too long. I feel like going home now.'

'I'll give you a call when I see them.' She went up on the deck and moved into the wheelhouse to escape the increasing chill of the sea breeze. It was cloudier now, the best part of the day already over, and the sea was swaying restlessly as if in anticipation of rain to come.

She began to wonder where Daniel was and what he was doing.

She had scarcely been five minutes in the wheelhouse before she saw him. He was walking towards the jetty with Rebecca, and as they passed the pub Rohan and Charles must have attracted their attention, for they stopped and looked at one of the downstairs windows. Presently Rebecca went inside the pub, but Daniel remained outside and as Rachel watched he started walking away from the building towards the jetty and the boat.

There was a tightness suddenly beneath her heart, a hollow in the pit of her stomach. She sat perfectly still, watching him walk the length of the jetty, and as she watched it seemed to her that she had been waiting for many years without knowing what she was waiting for, knowing only that she would recognize the moment when it came.

He reached the boat, saw her, smiled. The hull shifted in the water as he climbed aboard.

'I thought I'd find you here,' he said. 'Where's Decima?'

'Down in the cabin, resting.'

'I see.' He stepped into the wheelhouse beside her and glanced down the jetty towards the pub but no one was in sight. 'The others should be here in a minute.'

'Yes, I saw Rebecca go in to fetch them.'

There was a silence.

Rachel was steadfastly watching the grey stone walls of the pub with its swaying sign above the doorway. Presently she felt Daniel's hand on her arm, and as she glanced round at him instinctively, he began to speak. 'Don't believe—' But he stopped.

The sentence was never completed.

Afterwards all Rachel could remember was the grip of his fingers on her wrists and the harsh warmth of his lips on her mouth. There was heat, a blaze of power, the pressure of hard muscles taut in a hard, strong body, and then suddenly it was over and the dark dizziness was ebbing before her eyes so that she could see at last past Daniel to the deck where Decima stood frozen in immobility as she watched them.

Rachel felt her lips move.

Daniel spun round.

'Well, well,' said Decima politely in her softest, sweetest voice. 'It seems as if I underestimated you, Raye. You certainly don't waste much time, do you? So sorry to interrupt you both at such a terribly awkward moment but I thought I'd just tell you that the others have left the pub and are on their way over here . . .'

# 6

It was raining by the time they reached Ruthven. Heavy clouds had sunk over the mountain summits and laid dark fingers across the moors behind the sands. After making her escape as quickly as possible to her room, Rachel found that the fire was already lit and the housekeeper had just put a ewer of hot water on the washstand for her.

She undressed thankfully, stripping off the clothes which had become sodden in the short journey from the jetty to the house, and huddled herself in the quilt from the bed for a moment before taking advantage of the warm water.

She was just putting on her wool dress some minutes later when there was a soft tap at the door.

'Who's that?'

'Decima.'

Oh God, thought Rachel. She could already feel the crimson of embarrassment suffusing her neck and creeping upwards to her face. Decima was the last person she wanted to talk to.

'I'm just dressing for dinner, Decima – can it wait?'

'No, I want to talk to you.'

The zip fastener at the side of the dress jammed in her hot fingers. 'Just a moment.'

The zip refused to go either up or down. 'Oh hell!' muttered Rachel at last, abandoning it, and wrenched open the door much more violently than she had intended.

Decima was dressed for dinner. She wore black, a plain, simple dress, and above her left breast was a diamond brooch which glittered in the dim glow of the lamp and firelight.

'Yes?' said Rachel abruptly.

Decima moved into the room without speaking. Then as Rachel closed the door: 'I just wanted to warn you about Daniel.'

Rachel suddenly felt very angry indeed. After all, what right did Decima have to enable her to act so possessively where Daniel was concerned? Decima, a married woman, had much less right to Daniel than she had and certainly no right at all to criticize Rachel's behaviour with him. 'I've nothing to say about Daniel,' she heard herself say coolly. 'I'm only surprised that you should want to talk about him.'

Decima raised her eyebrows slightly. 'You're very quick to take offence all of a sudden, aren't you? Why should you feel so guilty just because I saw you kissing Daniel this afternoon at Kyle of Lochalsh? Is a kiss such a novel experience for you that you're overcome with remorse and shame for days afterwards?'

'I—'

'I only wanted to warn you that Daniel has a very accomplished way with women. Charles tells me that when Daniel was an undergraduate at Oxford—'

'I'm not interested,' said Rachel furiously, 'in past gossip. I don't care how many affairs Daniel has had and, even if I did care, it's certainly none of my business. But what I *am* interested in is why you deliberately misled me last night when you came here to tell me about Charles! Why did you lie and say that Daniel wasn't interested in women and that you didn't trust him when you'd been secretly having an affair with him for the past few weeks?'

The light was uncertain but she thought she saw Decima turn very pale. 'I – I was too ashamed . . . I thought if I could avoid telling you—'

'How much else have you avoided telling me, Decima?'

There was a long, still silence. 'What do you mean?'

'I couldn't help wondering how much the failure of your marriage was Charles' fault and how much was yours.'

Another silence. Then, 'I—' Decima hesitated. 'I suppose we were both to blame in some ways . . . I was so angry when I saw Charles had married me for my money that I didn't behave very well at Oxford . . . There was nothing wrong, you understand, but once or twice I drank too much at the sedate cocktail parties, and embarrassed Charles. And I flirted now and again with a couple of students, just out of boredom . . . But I was never unfaithful! Even now, with Daniel, even though he begged me and begged me to be unfaithful to Charles, I always somehow managed to keep my head and refuse him. Rachel, you've no idea what a strain I've had to endure these past few weeks! I was genuinely attracted to Daniel but was terrified in case Charles should find out. Then I began to wonder if Charles was secretly encouraging Daniel, so that once I was proved unfaithful he would have the excuse for any kind of revenge. I could hardly believe, you see, that Daniel would behave so shamefully to Charles, whom I knew he respected and liked.'

'That certainly seems hard to believe, but how much encouragement did you give him?'

'None at all, I swear it! But I find him attractive, I admit it, and sometimes it was very hard – in fact, impossible – to keep aloof from him. Perhaps it's hard for you to understand, but—'

Rachel found it all too easy to understand. She was beginning to feel slightly sick; her head ached dully. 'I'm surprised Charles didn't realize what was happening.'

'That's why I began to think he was secretly conniving at Daniel's behaviour. He even encouraged the Careys to stay at Ruthven as long as possible! And then I began to think – imagine – all kinds of things; I thought they might all be in a plot against me, manoeuvring me into some terrible position from which there was no retreat

. . . I – I've been so frightened, Raye, it's all been such a nightmare . . .' She was trembling; she had to sit down. 'I'm sorry if I behaved badly to you this afternoon when I saw you with Daniel, but my nerves were in such shreds that I couldn't even think clearly. It just seemed to me that you, the only person I could trust, were being gradually prised away and turned against me, and the thought was so shattering and frightful that I lost control of myself altogether. You do believe me, don't you, Raye? You're not against me, are you?'

'Of course not,' said Rachel shortly. 'Don't be silly.' But beneath her reassuring manner, she was badly shaken; her mind a mass of conflicts and doubts.

It was undeniably true that everyone she had spoken to that day had tried to turn her against Decima. It was probably also true that Daniel was so accustomed to getting his own way with women that he couldn't resist amusing himself with her. No doubt he had thought her quaint and old-fashioned and had enjoyed seeing how much he could disconcert her and disrupt her conventional behaviour.

The headache had become a tight pain behind the eyes.

'Have you got some aspirin by any chance, Decima?'

'Aspirin? Yes, of course . . . Listen, why don't we have dinner together in my room? I don't want to face the others again tonight. We could have a quiet dinner and talk for a while and then have an early night.'

'Wouldn't that look rather suspicious? Anyway, I'm well enough – it's just a slight headache. I really think I'd better dine with everyone else.'

In spite of everything, she still had no wish to miss an opportunity to see Daniel. As she returned from Decima's room with the aspirin bottle five minutes later she wondered how she could still find him attractive when she knew beyond any doubt that he could not care for her.

Daniel cared only for Decima; the entire scene in the wheelhouse that afternoon had probably been enacted with the specific intent of making Decima jealous in the hope of increasing her interest in him.

Twenty minutes later, her headache eased, she went down to the dining room for dinner.

Decima made no appearance at dinner, but Charles and Rohan were talkative enough and spent most of the meal discussing plans for the dinner party on the following evening while recalling their own twenty-first-birthday celebrations years earlier; in contrast, Rebecca said little and Rachel too found she had less than usual to say. Daniel did not look at her once throughout the entire meal and said no word to anyone. At the earliest opportunity he excused himself and withdrew from the room.

Rebecca at length went off to the library to read; Charles retired to his study to look at his manuscript for a while, and Rachel and Rohan were left facing each other across the table.

Rohan leant forward to move the candelabra. 'Why didn't Decima come down tonight?'

'She said she was tired.'

'And what do you say she was?'

'She certainly looked tired. She really is in a very nervous state, Rohan. I feel quite worried about her.'

'If her nerves are in a bad way,' said Rohan, 'she has only herself to blame.'

'Oh? And what's that remark supposed to mean?'

'She could leave tomorrow if she wanted to.'

'Don't be a fool! How could she possibly walk out on this celebration dinner party which has been so carefully arranged and planned? She's committed to staying here at least until the morning of her birthday. And she tells me she hasn't the cash in hand to leave before then anyway.'

'You're attracted to Daniel, aren't you? No, don't try and tell me that's nonsense! I know when you like a man and when you don't. But you can forget Daniel. He's totally absorbed in Decima.'

'I—' Rachel began, but Rohan wasn't listening.

'Do you think I didn't notice as soon as I came to Ruthven how things were between them?' he interrupted. 'Do you think it wasn't obvious to me that he wanted her and was trying every trick he knew to get her to go away with him?' His voice was a little unsteady. As if to cover up his lack of self-possession, he reached for the carafe of wine and clumsily poured some more into his glass. But his hand was trembling; the wine spilt into dark red pools on the white cloth. 'I told Charles,' he said. 'But he didn't believe me. Can you imagine that? This morning after I left you I saw Decima slip into Daniel's room to wait for him to come back from the boat, and I knew damn well what she was waiting for. I went to Charles and said—'

'You had no right to do that, Rohan. It's no concern of yours,' Rachel interrupted sharply.

'Charles is my cousin, isn't he?'

'That's got nothing to do with it. You had no right to interfere.'

'Christ Almighty!' shouted Rohan, setting down his glass with such a crash that the frail stem seemed to shiver. 'Don't preach to me! Don't get up into your little Victorian pulpit and preach sermons to me about what to do and what not to do! What do you know about life anyway? You've never been in love, never gone to bed with anyone, never—'

'What on earth's that got to do with you sneaking to Charles to tell him that his guest's trying to seduce his wife? Good God, if Charles hasn't the perception to see when a guest of his is behaving disgracefully, he deserves to have his wife seduced! I'm not surprised he didn't welcome you interfering in his affairs!'

'But if he knew Daniel was trying to seduce Decima, why the hell didn't he throw Daniel out of Ruthven? And besides, he didn't believe me when I told him about them! He was so vain, so incredibly pompous and conceited that he thought it was impossible that Decima should ever think of being unfaithful to him! And all along he's insisted that the Careys stay at Ruthven!'

'Then either he's a fool or else he has special reasons of his own for keeping the Careys here.'

'What reasons?' demanded Rohan. 'Give me one good reason why he should continue to keep his wife's lover in his house!'

'According to Decima, they're not lovers.'

'If they're not, it's not for want of trying on Daniel's part!'

'How do you know?'

He stared at her. 'I've been watching them.'

'Spying on them, you mean, don't you?'

'I—'

'For God's sake, Rohan, what on earth are you trying to do? Are you Charles' self-appointed private eye, or something? To be quite blunt, what is it to you whether Decima goes to bed with Daniel or not?'

Rohan pulled back his chair and stood up so abruptly that the chair fell over backwards. 'It's quite obvious,' he said, striding over to the door, 'that you haven't the slightest grasp of the situation at all.'

She allowed him thirty seconds for his rage to cool and then followed him into the little drawing room off the great hall. He was standing by the blazing log fire, and in his hands was a carved ivory paper-knife which he had apparently picked up from the desk in his agitation. The ivory was curved like a tusk, and the upper half of the tusk was the sheath into which the blade of the knife could be inserted, while the lower half of the tusk was the handle in which the blade was embedded. Rachel could not remember seeing it before.

'Where did that come from?'

'It's Rebecca's. She bought it in Edinburgh just before she came to Ruthven.' He put it down abruptly, and she saw that the carvings on the ivory surface were of Chinese figures, each perfectly executed and designed.

She picked it up idly.

'There are two questions I should like to see answered,' said Rohan suddenly. 'First, why should Charles tolerate Daniel's behaviour and in fact actively encourage the Careys to stay, and second, why should Decima have chosen to stay here when she had the means and opportunity to escape earlier?'

'Ruthven *is* her home, Rohan. Why should she allow herself to be driven away?' She pulled the tusk apart absentmindedly, and ran her index finger along the edge of the blade. 'Goodness, this knife's sharp! You could dissect an Aberdeen Angus with it.' She sucked her finger where a faint line of red was already showing, and put the knife back on the table.

'But surely,' Rohan was saying, 'if Decima was really in such a state of nerves as the result of her relationship with Daniel or Charles or both of them, would she care much about leaving Ruthven for a while? Wouldn't she be merely glad to escape?'

'But what chance has there been for her to escape?'

'Daniel—'

'I'm quite sure that Daniel wouldn't have been so foolish as to commit himself in that way.'

'How do you know?' said Rohan. 'He's little more than a stranger to you. How do you know what he might or might not do?'

The knife was a mere white blur on the polished surface of the table. Rachel picked it up again blindly, her fingers working over the cool surface. Everything Rohan said was true. What did she know of Daniel? How did she know that Daniel hadn't asked Decima to go away with him and then, on her refusal, had paid Rachel attention to make Decima jealous? Wasn't it obvious that the scene in the wheelhouse had merely been to incite Decima to re-examine her feelings for him? It had clearly been a successful manoeuvre, for that same evening at Ruthven Decima had come to her to try to turn her against Daniel so that she might have him for herself once more.

Decima, with her money and beauty and her effortless, graceful poise . . . It was so easy to picture her with Daniel, much easier to picture her with him than with Charles. It seemed that Decima was playing some game of her own, planning all the time to go away with Daniel eventually.

'Is anything the matter, Rachel? You look very white.'

Decima had always had what she wanted. Life was very easy for people like Decima who were constantly beset with favours and attention, admiration and compliments.

Daniel would seem just like any other man to her, another name to add to the long list of men who had stopped to look at her more than once. Decima didn't need Daniel except to use him in obtaining whatever it was she wanted. Decima didn't care.

But Rachel cared. 'No,' she said. 'Nothing's the matter.'

'Has Daniel—'

'I don't want to talk about Daniel any more.' The knife slipped from her hands and fell loudly on the table. 'I think I'll go to bed early. My headache seems to be getting worse.'

'If you want some aspirin—'

'No, Decima gave me some already, thanks. Goodnight, Rohan.'

'Goodnight,' he said slowly, and she knew, even though she did not glance back at him, that his grey eyes were sharp and watchful as he noted her withdrawal and drew his own conclusions from her behaviour. Rohan always saw too much.

Moving swiftly, hardly knowing where she was going, she found her way across the hall and stumbled upstairs to the comforting privacy of her room.


7

She awoke very suddenly just after midnight. The wind was whispering at the window again and humming in the eaves, and the rain was a light, stealthy patter against the pane. It was pitch dark. All she could see was the luminous dial of her little travelling clock and the white strip of the sheet turned down over the quilt.

She sat up listening.

The house was still, yet something had woken her. Maybe she had been dreaming and, on awakening, had confused the dream with consciousness.

She went on listening but heard nothing, and presently she slipped out of bed and moved across to the door without lighting the lamp. She was just about to ease the door open when she heard the creak of a floorboard in the corridor outside. Unreasonably, her scalp tingled. Her limbs froze, and movement was impossible. She was suddenly and uncontrollably frightened.

It was hard to judge how long she stood there in the darkness waiting, but after a minute of complete silence she managed to edge noiselessly back to her bedside table and find the matches to light the lamp. The glow of light was reassuring. With the lamp in her hand she turned back to the door. No doubt she was being foolish and would laugh at herself in the clear light of morning, but she knew she would be unable to fall asleep easily again unless the door was locked.

It was not until she reached the door that she discovered that there was no key in the lock.

Perhaps it was on the other side.

It was at least two minutes before she could bring herself to turn the handle and pull the door slowly inward towards herself. There was no one outside. Stepping into the corridor quickly, she saw it was empty.

There was still no sign of a key. She paused, uncertain of what she should do, and as she hesitated she saw that there was a faint glow at the far end of the corridor, as if a large lamp was still burning downstairs in the hall. Suddenly making up her mind she blew out her lamp, leaving it in her room, and returned to the passage.

Decima's door, farther down on the right of the corridor, was closed and, although Rachel knocked lightly on the panels and called out softly to ask if she were asleep, there was no reply. She tried the handle but the door was locked. Decima at least had a key for her room.

Rachel moved on. The gallery when she reached it was in darkness but, as she glanced over the banisters, she saw that one of the large lamps was indeed burning on the table in the hall below. Again she paused. Her knowledge of the house was still slight, but she knew that her room was in the south wing of the house and that Decima's room was in the south-east turret with windows which overlooked both the mountains and moors in the east and the sands and cliffs to the south. Charles apparently had rooms in the west wing which faced the sea, and she could remember Rohan mentioning that his room also faced the ocean. The north wing was no longer used, the game-keeper and his wife now preferring to live in the small croft a hundred yards from the house. This meant that the Careys had probably been given rooms in the east wing which faced the mountains and moors, and it was in the east wing that Rachel now stood. Unlike the other wings of the house, the corridor was open on one side so that it was possible to look over the banisters into the great hall below, and halfway down the corridor the twin staircases linking the two floors curved to meet in a wide landing. At the far end of the corridor, a more insignificant staircase spiralled upwards in the north-east turret to lead to empty rooms on higher, deserted floors, but the main staircase, beginning as it did in the great hall itself, had more style and elegance. On the side of the corridor which did not face the hall and stairs, six doors led into the six rooms of the east wing. As she moved towards the landing and the head of the stairs, she saw that one of the doors was ajar.

She stopped.

The room was in darkness. After a moment's hesitation she tapped the panels, but when no one responded she pushed the door open wider and glanced into the room.

The bed was unslept in, the curtains of the windows still undrawn, but the embers of a fire burnt in the grate and from their glow there was sufficient light for her to see without the aid of a lamp.

Daniel kept his room neat. A pair of masculine slippers stood near the bed; a dressing gown lay precisely across one of the high-backed armchairs where it had been placed, not thrown, by its owner. There was a pair of silver clothes-brushes on the high dresser, a large plain comb beside them, and by the washstand was an old-fashioned razor set incongruously beside a modern tube of shaving cream.

Not wanting to pry among his belongings she withdrew quickly to the corridor again, but not before she was aware of her curiosity to explore further, to strain to discover more about him than the facts she already knew. After the scene in the wheelhouse that afternoon, she was conscious of an immense desire to find other evidence of his personality, other clues of his past. How had his life been spent when he was away from his books and his research? What had his childhood been like, his adolescence? Had there been disappointments and disillusionment or had the path of his success been so clearly marked from the beginning that he had never known the pain of failure or the pangs of frustration? Had he many friends at Cambridge? Did he live alone there, or—

But she decided not to pursue this line of thought. She had already told Rohan in indignation that she was not concerned with Daniel's past relations with the opposite sex, and to dwell upon the subject now would make her earlier remark seem hypocritical.

Moving quickly as if to shake off all thought of Daniel's possible associations, she left the room and went out on to the landing again.

There was still no one in sight.

Then where was Daniel? And who had left the light burning in the hall?

It was not until she was halfway down the stairs that it occurred to her to wonder if Decima really had been sleeping so soundly behind her locked door. She stopped, her hand on the banisters as she glanced back over her shoulder at the silent gallery she had just left.

It was then she heard the sound of voices. They seemed far away, a mere murmur sighing through the vast silence of the hall, but on reaching the last stair she found the sound was coming from one of the rooms leading off the hall to the left of the staircase. She stepped over to the library, and then realized that the voices came from Charles' study next door, the ground floor of the south-east turret.

She drew nearer. The door was almost shut and the occupants of the room obviously believed that it was completely closed; having been about to knock and enter to find out who was up so late, Rachel instinctively hesitated as the first snatches of conversation reached her ears.

'No,' Charles Mannering was saying strongly. 'That would be out of the question. My dear, you've attended University. You know how things are. Of course, if I were free it would be a different matter.'

A woman spoke – Rebecca's strong, resonant voice, hushed now and low. 'But Charles, supposing Decima—'

'Decima knows nothing, suspects nothing.'

'Then why did she invite that girl here?'

'A mere foil to divert attention from herself.'

'But supposing Decima should suspect—'

'My dear, Decima is totally absorbed in herself and always will be. Do you suppose she has any time for suspicions?'

'Charles . . .'

And then a silence broken only by a sharp intake of breath, a stifled exclamation and seconds later a small spent sigh.

Rachel took a step backwards in retreat. Her limbs were stiff and awkward as if suddenly released from a long paralysis, her thoughts spinning in shocked staccato patterns. Her first coherent reaction was that whatever happened they must not find her in the hall, must never guess that she had overheard Charles talking of a time when he might be 'free', speculating on Decima's suspicions, referring to her with such casual contempt.

She must hide. She had to think. Her mind was whirling dizzily and all she was aware of was that Charles cared nothing for his wife's activities and would not risk losing Rebecca by making any move which might result in Daniel taking her away.

She opened the door of the drawing room where she had talked to Rohan earlier and stumbled inside. Something moved on the hearth. As she jumped and stifled a cry of shock, a draught from the chimney made the dying fire throw out a shaft of light and she saw that the St Bernard had been stretched out on the hearthrug in slumber and that she had awoken him.

He gave a deep growl.

'It's all right, George,' she whispered. 'It's only me.'

He still growled, but now his tail was swaying from side to side. The firelight glinted in his eyes and made them look glazed and fierce.

She sank down in an armchair. Presently the dog relaxed too, still watching her, and they faced each other across the hearth. Beyond the dog stood the desk, its polished surface smooth, the red leather blotter glowing, the small calendar showing a date which was already three days old, the glass paperweight reflecting odd beams of the firelight.

Presently she stood up, moved restlessly over to the desk and altered the date on the calendar. It was now the morning of Saturday, the twelfth of September. Tonight at eight the dinner would begin to celebrate Decima's coming of age, and the next time the clocks struck midnight it would be to herald the beginning of Decima's twenty-first birthday. If anything were to happen to her, it would have to happen within the next twenty-four hours.

She replaced the calendar and then stopped to look at the desk. Surely something was missing. The top of the desk looked different in some way. She recalled her talk with Rohan in that same room a few hours ago, and as the scene came back into her mind she glanced at the smooth, empty surface of the table by the chair on the other side of the hearth.

Memory returned; the white ivory paper-knife with the razor-sharp edge was gone.

There was a void suddenly in the pit of her stomach; her hands were clammy. Steady, she told herself. Don't jump to conclusions. Rohan probably moved it absentmindedly after I was gone.

She thought again of her conversation with him, the

memory running through her mind like a strip of film. The knife had been on the desk by the paperweight and then Rohan had picked it up in his agitation, only to put it down again on the table a moment later. Then Rachel herself had picked it up and handled it for a short time. But she could clearly remember replacing it on the table by the chair.

She looked around, checking the mantelpiece, opening the drawers of the desk, even going over to the window-seat on the far side of the room. She was just pausing to examine the bric-à-brac in a small cabinet by the window when she suddenly knew beyond any doubt that she was no longer alone in the room.

She whirled round, her hand flying to her mouth as she saw the dark shadow watching her.

'Looking for something, Rachel?' enquired Daniel's cool voice from the doorway.


# Chapter 5

1

He came into the room, his feet soundless on the soft carpet and closed the door behind him. The dog's tail thumped on the hearth in recognition, but Daniel ignored him.

'What are you doing down here at this hour?' His voice was still polite but the hard edge to it was unmistakable. Rachel was aware suddenly of the power of his presence, his ability to take command of a scene merely by entering a room.

'I couldn't sleep.' Her fingers were automatically drawing her dressing gown closer around her. 'I came downstairs to look for a book I thought I'd left here.'

'I see,' he said and she knew he disbelieved her. 'And have you found it?'

'No. No, I—'

'What was it called?'

There was a small, deadly pause. She was completely unable to think of any title whatsoever.

'It was just a novel,' she stammered. 'I don't remember the title. It had a dark-green cover with black lettering.'

'I'll help you look for it.'

'No, please . . . I'm not even sure that I left it in here.' Her self-possession was ebbing so fast that she almost felt she might turn and run from the room if he persisted in questioning her about the book. Emotional claustrophobia overwhelmed her; she began to move swiftly over to the door, but he was nearer the doorway than she was and in three strides he was there before her.

She stopped.

'What's the matter?' he said. 'You look very shaken. What's been happening?'

The impossibility of telling him that she had eavesdropped on Charles and Rebecca made her say the first thing that came into her head. 'What are *you* doing down here?' she demanded. 'Why were you still up?'

'I never go to bed before midnight,' he said shortly. 'I've been in the library reading and when I left to go upstairs just now I thought I heard sounds from this room.'

She found to her horror that she had nothing to say. She felt the colour suffuse her neck and creep upwards to her face, and it seemed as if all the self-consciousness of the past had combined in one enormous moment of embarrassment and diffidence. The brass handle of the door was cool against her palm. She tried to turn it but he put his hand over hers and stopped her.

'I want to talk to you.'

This was no scene played for Decima's benefit. Decima was upstairs behind her locked door. No matter how ambiguous his attitude might have seemed that afternoon in the wheelhouse, there could be no ambiguity this time in the drawing room with the door closed to the world beyond and the fire dying in the grate.

'Perhaps it could wait till tomorrow,' she said, the old

mixture of pride and fear and a dozen other muddled emotions making her withdraw from him although she longed for him to contradict her and force her to stay. 'I'm very tired.'

During past encounters with other men this had always been the point at which her involuntary coolness had resulted in her being left alone to regret her words. The man would have been either offended or disheartened; either he had never cared sufficiently to persist in overriding her request, or else he had never had the perspicacity to see that the apparent rejection was not a rejection at all but merely a craving for reassurance. Every man she had ever known well before had always chosen this moment to turn and walk away.

'Tired?' said Daniel. 'I thought you said you were so restless you had to come downstairs for a book? Come and sit down for a moment and tell me why you look as if you'd seen a ghost.'

'I – it was nothing.' But she allowed herself to turn from the door and sink down on the sofa beside the hearth. 'The house was so still that I became foolish and started imagining I heard noises and saw shapes in the shadows.'

He sat down on the sofa beside her; the springs creaked softly beneath his weight and then were still.

'Did Decima say anything?' he said at last.

'About the scene in the wheelhouse? No, nothing.'

'Nothing at all?'

'Nothing.'

So perhaps after all he was merely interested in Decima, curious to find out her reaction to the scene in the wheelhouse. Standing up blindly she moved back to the door. 'You'll excuse me, but I really mustn't stay . . . I'll find my book in the morning.'

But he was already standing up to follow her. Wanting only to escape from him now, she stepped quickly into the hall and was already past the threshold when she saw to her horror that Charles and Rebecca were just leaving the library.

She stopped.

Behind her Daniel too was motionless and she heard his sharp intake of breath. Across the hall Charles hesitated, his fingers still on the doorhandle as he drew it shut, and Rebecca, her cheeks hot, stared at Rachel.

There was a silence. Then:

'So you two are up late as well,' said Charles. 'Or did something bring you downstairs, Rachel?' He had noticed her shabby dressing gown.

She suddenly realized that her face was still flushed from the encounter with Daniel. No doubt both Charles and Rebecca would think that she and Daniel had had some kind of rendezvous in the drawing room . . . She could feel the colour deepening in her cheeks and then Daniel was stepping past her towards his sister, his movements easy and relaxed.

'Rachel was looking for a book she'd left behind earlier this evening.' He was composed and untroubled. Once again he had entered a scene and blandly assumed control of the situation.

'Are you coming upstairs now, Rebecca? Or shall I see you tomorrow morning?'

The words drew an innuendo which was a mere nuance as thin as a razor-edge but the tone of his voice gave the implication an uncomfortable depth.

'I don't know what that remark's supposed to mean,' said Charles much too quickly. 'What are you trying to imply, Daniel?'

'Why, merely that I'm going to bed myself and wondered if she intended to do likewise! What else could I mean?' He was mocking Charles, entangling him in verbal snares. 'Goodnight.'

'Wait!'

'Yes?'

Charles suddenly became aware of Rachel's presence and stopped. There was another awkward pause.

'If you'll excuse me . . .' Rachel muttered, and hurried past the group with her eyes on the ground. She could feel their eyes watching her as she ran upstairs and stumbled along the corridor to her room, and then as she reached the sanctuary she wrenched open the door and slammed it shut after her in her relief.

She sat down, still breathing unevenly, but presently when she had recovered her breath she opened her door again and went back into the passage. Decima must be told of the overheard conversation between Charles and Rebecca. Moving cautiously back down the passage Rachel hesitated outside the door of Decima's room and then hearing the sound of voices she moved on to the gallery. There was no one in the hall but she could hear voices raised in argument. They must have gone back to the study, or perhaps to the library, for although she could hear the voices she was still too far away to distinguish what was being said.

She hesitated and then, realizing that this was a good opportunity to see Decima without danger of discovery, she went back to the locked door.

'Decima! Decima, are you awake?' She knocked swiftly on the panels. 'Decima, wake up!'

There was movement within, the flare of a match, the flickering of light beneath the door.

'Rachel?' called Decima nervously.

'Yes – can you let me in?'

'Just a moment.'

More noises, the soft padding of slippers, the turning of the key in the lock, and then Decima was facing her across the threshold.

'What is it?' Her voice was almost hostile. 'What do you want?'

This was not the welcome Rachel had expected. 'Can I come in for a moment?' she said uneasily. 'It's difficult to talk out here.'

Decima opened the door without a word.

'Has something happened, Decima?'

'Nothing.' She turned aside and went back to the bed. 'I've just decided to open the door to no one either tonight or tomorrow evening before the party.'

'Not even to me?'

'Not even to you.'

'You mean you no longer trust me?' Rachel was both astonished and angry. 'Oh come, Decima! Just because Daniel—'

'Deny you're attracted to him, then!' Decima flared, whirling round to face her. 'Deny it! But you won't deny it, because it's true. And if it's true then I no longer trust you.'

'You're being absurd,' said Rachel coolly. 'For goodness' sake, Decima, pull yourself together! You're being both melodramatic and hysterical.'

'Who are you to talk of melodrama?' Decima exclaimed furiously. 'You with your adolescent infatuation, your schoolgirl's crush—'

Rachel turned aside abruptly. 'There's nothing more to be said.'

'I'm beginning to think Rohan's the only one I can trust,' Decima blazed, still trembling, her blue eyes narrow and hard. 'He at least hates Daniel.'

Rachel didn't listen. She was so angry that she went out and slammed the door violently behind her, and it was not until she was back in her room again that she realized she had mentioned not one word to Decima of the conversation she had overheard between Charles and Rebecca.

And as she thought of Charles and Rebecca she remembered the sounds of argument she had heard a few minutes ago, and it occurred to her to wonder what was happening in the library where Charles had gone with his guests.


2

Rachel awoke early again and lay listening for a long while to the still house. At last, unable to bear her immobility a moment longer, she got up and went over to draw the curtains. The morning was pale and cool, the sun visible but remote. Soon the clouds would creep in from the Atlantic and form a grey world of sky and sea, but at present the sunlight was strong enough to give a greenish tinge to the moors and a blue darkness to the swaying sea.

Rachel dressed and went downstairs. The housekeeper was busy in the scullery and, after taking some hot water, Rachel withdrew to one of the rooms near the kitchen to wash. There was a supply of running water on the ground floor of the house and two bathrooms near the kitchen, but hot water still had to be heated in the kitchens and transported gallon by gallon to the nearest bathroom. It occurred to Rachel as she staggered beneath the weight of two enormous jugs of steaming water that people who deprecated the modern comforts of the twentieth century should try living for a time in a house with no hot running water and no electricity. When she had finished dressing it was still early, too early for Decima to have stirred from her bed. Rachel wondered if anyone else was up. After hesitating for a while she went downstairs again to the kitchens. No one was about. The housekeeper had disappeared. Rachel found some porridge simmering on the range, helped herself to a bowlful and put the kettle on for tea, but even by the time she had finished her meal no one had come to interrupt her. She was just about to take the dirty dishes out of the scullery to wash them when there was the sound of footsteps in the hall and the next moment Charles walked into the room.

He stopped abruptly when he saw her. He looked tired, she thought. His mouth was drawn and there were lines of exhaustion about his eyes so that he looked closer to fifty than a man not yet forty years old.

'Oh, it's you,' he said. 'Is Mrs Willie about? I want to talk to her about the arrangements for the dinner party tonight.'

'No, she seems to have disappeared.'

'Perhaps she went back to her croft to cook Willie his breakfast.' He went through into the scullery and looked at the saucepan of porridge without enthusiasm. Presently he came back into the kitchen and stared out of the window at the backyard beyond.

Rachel waited awkwardly, wanting to escape yet not

knowing how to do so without appearing rude. She was just rising to her feet a moment later when Charles said suddenly: 'I'd like to talk to you. Would you have any objection if we walked out a little way over the moors?'

Rachel was astonished. 'Why, yes – yes, if you like, Charles,' she managed to say. 'Do you want to go now?'

'If you don't mind.'

'No, of course not. I'll just run upstairs and get my coat.'

There was still no one about, no sign of movement from upstairs. In her room once more she found her coat and slipped it over her shoulders. Then, still wondering what Charles could intend to say to her, she went downstairs to the kitchens to rejoin him.

He was still standing by the window, his hands in his pockets. As she came in he turned to face her. 'All right?'

She nodded.

'Good.' He led the way outside and the cool soft air of the Highland seas fanned her cheek as she stepped into the sunlight. She drew a deep breath, savouring the breeze's freshness, and then followed Charles across the yard and up the hillside to the north of the house, past a cow nibbling at the short grass and a sow with six piglets in the meadow beyond. There was a potato patch and a row of cabbages by the small croft where Willie the gamekeeper lived with his wife, and then Charles was leading the way out to the moors and up on to the cliffs which rose above the sands.

'I wanted to get out of the house,' he said. 'Then there's no chance of anyone eavesdropping.'

Remembering how she herself had eavesdropped yesterday evening, Rachel immediately felt herself blush scarlet, but fortunately he was ahead of her and did not notice. They walked on until the ground no longer tilted uphill but ran evenly along the top of the cliffs. To their left came the roar of the sea as the surf thundered on the beach and to the right loomed the nearest of the mountains, its bare slopes arid and rocky in the clear light.

There was a ragged stone circle ahead, the relic of some ancient tribe. Charles selected one of the stones that had fallen to the ground and sat down on it.

'Cigarette, Rachel?'

'No, thanks.'

She watched him light the cigarette and then toss the match away on to the damp ground. The flame smouldered, flared for a minute and then died in a thin curl of smoke.

After a long moment, he said: 'Why did Decima invite you here?'

Rachel searched desperately for a plausible explanation. 'I – I was an old friend . . . I suppose – as it was her twenty-first birthday she felt she would like to see me again—'

'I don't believe that,' said Charles. 'I don't mean to say that you're lying, but I think you've been misled. You're so utterly dissimilar from Decima that I can't visualize her wanting to resurrect a schoolgirl friendship.'

'But—'

'Decima hadn't contacted you since her marriage, had she? Why would she suddenly decide to do so?'

'I'm sorry, Charles, but I just don't understand what you're driving at. As far as I know—'

'But you know so little, don't you?' he said. 'You don't know anything at all.' His fingers were unsteady, she noticed with a shock; the hand which held the cigarette was shaking. There was a long pause. Then: 'I've been very foolish,' he said at last. 'I must have been quite mad. But it's not always easy to be as clever and wise as one always imagines oneself to be, is it? Sometimes you don't even realize how foolish you've been until it's too late to draw back.'

She could think of nothing to say. Below them the ocean roared far away beneath the cliffs and the clouds were billowing towards them from the horizon.

'I've been having an affair with Rebecca,' he said suddenly. 'I know you're aware of that because Daniel told me last night that he had seen you outside the library listening to the conversation I was having with her.'

'I—' Guilt and horror made speech impossible. She could only stare at him with burning eyes while rage against Daniel throbbed through her mind.

'Daniel was angry,' said Charles as if this explained everything. 'We were all angry. We had an exhausting, abortive, endless quarrel which left us all drained of any vestige of emotion.' He drew on his cigarette. 'After it was all over, I felt as if I'd been shaken to my senses after six weeks of foolish illusions. And then I began to wonder what Decima had said to you and why you were here and I resolved to speak to you as soon as I could to tell you the truth and find out how far this situation had been misrepresented to you.'

His sincerity was almost painful. Rachel could hardly bear to look at him.

'I love Decima,' he said. 'I always have. I think it would be true to say that I loved her even more after we were married than before. Perhaps you find it hard to understand why I love her so much when we really have very little in common; we share no interests, come from different backgrounds, even different generations. But that makes no difference. After that terrible quarrel with the Careys last night I realized that in spite of all that had happened nothing had changed. I would never consent to losing her. How could I? Our marriage at the moment is a mockery, but I would rather have her on those terms than not have her at all.' He was staring down at his cigarette, his shoulders hunched, his limbs tensed and motionless. 'Besides,' he said after a moment, 'the situation as it exists now between us could hardly get any worse. After thinking about it all night, I came to the conclusion that if I made a great effort and did all I could, things might still work out. If I could take Decima abroad for a while – if we could get away from this place, this prison, this enforced confinement far from any normal civilized way of life, then I think there might be some hope for us. Shut away up here one tends to forget what a normal life under normal conditions is like. If we could go abroad for a while and come to know one another again, then perhaps there could be children. We could settle in the country near Oxford, perhaps. There are some beautiful houses north of Banbury.'

'Decima will never leave Ruthven,' Rachel heard herself say.

'No, she doesn't want to leave – she doesn't want to face the normal world, can't you see? She had such an appalling childhood and adolescence trailing round the world in the wake of her promiscuous mother that she wants nothing but to retreat from anything that remotely resembles that way of life. But if only she could be shown that life in the outside world is nothing to be feared, then I think she would be happy to settle somewhere away from Ruthven. At the moment she is rejecting all the values of a normal world and burying herself in this tomb – she's destroying herself, destroying me, destroying everything I've ever wanted.'

'But Charles, you talk as if Decima was mentally unhinged! Surely—'

'Not mentally unhinged, but there's something definitely wrong in her psychological make-up, can't you understand?' His eyes were wide and dark, his face strained. 'What girl of twenty-one, who could have the world at her feet, would choose to seclude herself in a place like this? Why should any normal girl refuse to live with her husband barely six months after they were married? I wanted her to consult a doctor, but she refused and seemed to withdraw from me still further until it seemed she was building up a store of mythical grievance against me in her mind. And yet I loved her! I tried and tried to reason with her, but there was nothing I could do. I gave her everything she wanted, spent much more money than I should have done, and still all she did was complain about our brief term-time life at Oxford and criticize my Oxonian friends. She seemed to take pleasure in embarrassing me, in making me as unhappy as possible. Last winter I let her go home to Ruthven early to prepare for Christmas before I arrived, but I missed her so much while she was away that I couldn't bear to be separated from her again. I can't begin to describe to you the misery and frustration and hopelessness of it all. I didn't know it was possible to be so unhappy.

'But we went on from day to day, still together. Some days were better than others. And then, this summer, when Daniel wrote to say he and Rebecca were in Scotland, I asked them to Ruthven in the hope that a glimpse of the outside world which they might present would in some way help Decima. And so the Careys came to Ruthven.

'I suppose it wasn't surprising that I should be attracted to Rebecca. She was everything that Decima was not, intellectual, passionate and intense. She was interested in my work, enjoyed my company and – it was obvious – admired me. You can imagine the effect this would have on me after the life I had been living with Decima. No doubt I shouldn't offer excuses for myself, but Rebecca gave me all that I had lacked for the past two years. I lost all hold on my restraint, my common sense, my self-control. I lost sight of everything. I never even noticed that Daniel found Decima attractive or that she had decided to play around with him. I was well accustomed to ignore all her empty gestures of flirtation at Oxford, and well used to the fact that most men found my wife attractive. Even if I had noticed I might not have taken it seriously, and as it was I was too absorbed with Rebecca to notice anyone else.

'So Decima became involved with Daniel – and found she had taken on more than she bargained for. Daniel wasn't one of the fresh-faced students she'd been so accustomed to dazzling at Oxford! And Daniel was the last man to allow her to call the tune and set the pace of their relationship. Daniel knew what he wanted and if Decima wasn't interested in playing the game by his rules, then he certainly wasn't going to bend over backward to do as *she* wished!'

'So Daniel never had an affair with Decima.' She was

dizzy suddenly, faint with the vastness of relief. 'He never had an affair with her.'

Charles raised his eyebrows. 'No, you misunderstand – I see I explained myself badly. Decima wanted a flirtation with Daniel for her own satisfaction and amusement – in other words, an attachment which would never get as far as the bedroom. But Daniel wasn't interested in getting involved merely to gratify Decima's ego. So he took control of the situation and dictated his own terms and Decima, caught off balance, no doubt, and taken by surprise, allowed herself to be dictated to.'

'But you said Decima was cold – cold and withdrawn! I don't believe she would ever have had an affair with Daniel! I just don't believe it!'

'My dear, he told me last night that they were lovers. He told me himself.'

The roar of the surf suddenly seemed much too close. The oppressiveness of that welling of sound made the sea blur before her eyes and she turned away instinctively to stare inland over the barren moors and the harsh lines of the mountains.

'Last night after you'd left us in the hall we went back into the study. Daniel had made it clear that he knew all about Rebecca's affair with me, but I had been so blind as to imagine he had no idea what was going on. I was angry with him for implying as much in your presence and once we were in the library I told him so. It was then that Daniel said you knew anyway as he had seen you listening at the door – he said it was perfectly obvious to anyone what was going on. That, of course, made me even angrier and we started to quarrel. Rebecca tried to speak up for me from time to time, but he wouldn't let her and she would rather argue with God than argue with Daniel. So Daniel began to speak as if he were the prosecuting counsel at a trial and I the prisoner at the bar.

'To begin with I was so furious that I could hardly listen to a word he said. Then gradually I began to realize that much of what he said was true, and I began to feel sick and ill. He told me that I was to blame for the situation at Ruthven, that it was my fault that Decima had behaved the way she had, that I had behaved like a middle-aged fool over his sister. "You moan to my sister of how your wife misunderstands you," he said, "but how much effort have you made to correct the situation? Aren't you just too content to sit back and let Decima go her own way while you go yours? You weep that you loved your wife and got nothing in return, but how far did you go to offer anything apart from the honour of bearing your name and the dubious pleasures of your narrow academic social circles? Did you protest at Decima's flirtations at Oxford? Oh no, you were too busy sitting back and getting a vicarious sense of enjoyment by watching her play with her admirers and eventually send them packing! You were so smug and self-satisfied with your beautiful wife, so damned sure she was too cold ever to be actually unfaithful to you! You basked in the reflected glory of other men's admiration for her! You were too vain to care that she was driven to amuse herself with others because you couldn't keep her fully amused yourself!

'I couldn't contain myself any longer. I shouted at him: "Who are you to preach to me, Daniel Carey? You come here at my express invitation and yet think nothing of abusing my hospitality in the most shameful way imaginable! Do you think I hadn't noticed that Decima has been flirting with you?" To be honest, I hadn't noticed this until Rohan pointed it out to me yesterday morning, but even then I assumed it was a mere casual flirtation and I was far too involved with Rebecca to ask Daniel to leave. "Just deny that you haven't tried to persuade Decima to have an affair with you!" I shouted at him. "Just try to deny it!"

'And he said coolly, with such scorn as I could never put into words, "Of course I don't deny it. Why should I? I decided to teach you both a lesson, Charles! I thought it was high time someone showed Decima what it was like to be used as a pawn, a means of amusement – I thought it was high time she had a dose of her own medicine! And I thought it was high time someone knocked down the walls of egoism and vanity you've built around yourself, time someone showed you that your wife wasn't as cold as you liked to think she was!"

'I couldn't quite grasp what he was saying at first. I said: "What do you mean?"'

'And he said, "You don't think I'd let any woman use *me* as a plaything, do you? I dictated my own terms, and Decima hardly paused to question them. She became my mistress some time ago.'

'I stared at him. I couldn't even think coherently. And suddenly all I knew was that this man had taken my wife and I had stood by and let it happen because of a temporary infatuation with another woman. I felt ill and dizzy, as if someone had taken an axe and smashed my world to smithereens. After a while I managed to say to them both, "You will leave this house on Sunday morning and I never want to see either of you again." And I left them together in the library and somehow managed to find my way upstairs to my room.

'I tried to sleep, but all the time I kept thinking of what Daniel had said and every time I went over his words again, the more truth I seemed to see in them. I resolved that once the Careys were gone I would take Decima away and try to start all over again. I realized that I loved her and wanted her still, and in the light of this realization my attraction to Rebecca seemed very shallow and meaningless.'

He stopped. The world was still. The clouds had blotted out the sun now and were wreathing the mountain-tops with soft, ghostly fingers.

'But what was Rebecca's reaction when you told them both to leave?' Rachel heard herself ask. 'Wasn't she very upset?'

'I didn't stay to see her reaction. All I knew was that I never wanted to see either of them again.' He buried his head in his hands for a moment. 'Rohan was right,' he said after a while. 'He distrusted them from the first. There are some people like that, I suppose. They're destructive, dangerous people leaving a trail of disaster behind them. Once they're out of our lives, perhaps we'll at last be able to return to normal.'

It was raining, the light sea mist fresh against Rachel's skin. The damp moistness was somehow soothing, and she faced towards the sea to meet it.

Charles stood up. 'We'd better go back.'

They left the stone circle and started back along the cliffs. For a time neither of them spoke.

'I'm sorry to have burdened you with all this,' Charles said at last, 'but I didn't know what you were thinking or what conclusions you had drawn from the knowledge that you had, and I felt it important that you should know the truth.'

'Yes,' said Rachel. 'Yes, I quite understand. Thank you.'

'I seem to be totally unable to communicate with Decima at the moment. She refuses to talk to me. I was wondering if she'd said anything to you.'

'No, she was very reluctant to talk to me last night. I only noticed that she seemed very upset over Daniel.'

'Well yes,' said Charles. 'I've no doubt she is . . . I'm hoping to God everything will be better after the Careys have gone. I wish now we could put off this damned dinner party tonight, but we've invited too many people from outside and it's too late now to get in touch with them.'

'Couldn't you phone them and cancel it?'

'Ruthven's not on the phone.'

'Oh no, how stupid of me. I forgot.'

They walked on for a few yards. Then:

'You asked me in the beginning why Decima invited me to Ruthven,' Rachel said. 'Why do *you* think she invited me, Charles?'

'I think possibly she may have fancied the notion of leaving me and marrying Daniel. She would have assumed I'd be most reluctant to divorce her and so she wanted a witness that I was committing adultery with Rebecca. Rohan, being my cousin, would naturally be averse to being a witness against me, so she found herself in need of inviting an outsider to Ruthven.'

'But did she know about you and Rebecca? I always had the impression she had no idea of this.'

'No, she knew all the time. Daniel said last night that she had known almost from the beginning – and found my infatuation amusing,' he added bitterly. 'Yes, she knew all right. I suppose I was so wrapped up in my feelings for Rebecca that it must have been patently obvious to everyone, even to Decima, who's usually too absorbed in her own affairs to notice the affairs of others.'

In Decima's eyes, Rachel thought, this would give Charles yet another motive for wanting to kill her, for he would then inherit her money and marry Rebecca. It was only surprising that she had never once mentioned it to Rachel. Perhaps she had been held back by some obscure pride; the fact that her husband was being unfaithful to her must have been a blow to her ego, no matter how amused she might have pretended to be to Daniel about the situation.

Yet it was almost impossible now for Rachel to imagine Charles planning to kill Decima. Perhaps it had all been some terrible figment of Decima's imagination. Perhaps Decima really was mentally disturbed.

They'll turn you against me, Decima had said. They'll try to prise you away from me, because you're the one person I can trust . . .

'I don't know what to think,' Rachel said aloud in despair. 'I simply don't know what to do.'

Charles swung round startled. Was it her imagination or did she really see a flash of suspicion in his eyes? Perhaps the whole scene had been played for calculated effect, to deceive her. Perhaps it was all a masquerade.

'It's nothing,' she said. 'I suddenly felt so confused.'

'I understand – I'm sorry. I almost forgot you would be fond of Decima. It must be very upsetting for you to hear bad reports of her.'

Rachel said nothing.

They were in sight of the house now, following the

path down the hillside past the croft, the pigsty and the cow. The housekeeper was in the yard taking in some washing. As they approached she caught sight of them and withdrew to the shelter of the back porch to wait till they were nearer.

'Mrs Willie looks worried,' said Charles. 'I hope nothing's wrong.'

They reached the yard and crossed it to the porch. The housekeeper started to speak almost as soon as they were within earshot. 'I was never so glad to see you, Professor,' she was saying, and anxiety made her soft Highland accent broader so that it sounded Irish. 'What should I be doing about preparing the dinner for tonight? Mrs Mannering's just taken the boat and gone off to sea without telling me what arrangements she wanted me to make, and—'

'Gone off to sea?' cried Charles in amazement. 'When was this, for God's sake?'

'Maybe ten minutes ago, sir. I heard the engine of the boat and saw her at the wheel heading away from the shore.'

'Was she alone?'

'No, sir. She went with your cousin, Mr Quist.'


3


Charles was quick to pull himself together. Moving forward into the kitchens with the housekeeper, he surveyed the food in the pantry and then embarked on a discussion of how the venison should be cooked. After a moment's hesitation Rachel went outside again and walked round to the front of the house, but the motor-boat was nowhere to be seen and the vast expanse of the ocean stretched uninterrupted to the horizon. She stood still, undecided what she should do, and as she paused she wondered in astonishment where Decima and Rohan had gone and why they had chosen to walk out of the house on the very morning of the party, when their help would be needed in making the necessary preparations. If she were Charles, Rachel thought, she would be very angry indeed.

Someone was calling her name. Turning abruptly she saw Charles coming towards her from the back of the house and she retraced her steps to meet him.

'There's no sign of them, is there?' he demanded, and when she shook her head he said tightly: 'I don't know what the hell they think they're doing but I can only assume they've just gone for a short spin and will be back before long. I think the best we can do is merely to carry on with the preparations and do as much as we can.'

'Yes – yes, of course . . . What would you like me to do?'

'Well, I hate to ask one of my own guests to do anything at all, but I wonder if you could possibly pick some flowers and arrange them in the hall? We'll be dining in the hall tonight, of course. I must find Daniel and ask him to help me set up the long banquet table . . . Do you think you can manage the flowers?'

'Yes, don't worry, Charles. And if there's anything else I can do, just let me know.'

After he had gone, she walked down into the overgrown garden and examined the selection of flowers, but it was late in the year and summer had already left the Highlands so that there were few flowers to choose from. There were some hardy blue-petalled shrubs beneath the shelter of the stone wall at one end of the garden but the stems were tough beneath her fingers and in the end she decided to go back into the house for a pair of scissors. It was already beginning to rain again; the sky was heavy with billowing clouds blowing in from the sea and the few streaks of blue which remained were pale and cold and far away.

Charles and the housekeeper were still in the pantry; Rachel found a pair of heavy shears in one of the drawers of the kitchen table and wandered back into the hall. She felt curiously abstracted from reality, as if she were moving in a dream and was powerless to control her own fate. It was as if forces around her were manipulating her at will, pulling her this way and that and finally tossing her adrift on the strong current of a swift-flowing river which was rushing her headlong towards some destination as terrible as it was unknown. She could feel her own helplessness as clearly as she could feel that dreadful propulsion towards the hidden future which lay waiting for them all. She paused again in the huge hall and listened to the silence, and even as she realized at last how frightened she was, she heard the sound of weeping coming from the drawing room close at hand.

The door was ajar. With her fingers pressing against the panels she opened it still wider and glanced into the room.

'Danny?' said Rebecca sharply as she saw the door open and then, as she realized it was Rachel, she turned aside without a word and buried her face in her arms again.

Rachel did not know whether to move forward or to retreat. In the end she remained where she was, one hand still on the door handle, and said hesitantly: 'If there's anything I can do – shall I find Daniel for you?'

Rebecca lifted her head so fiercely that Rachel had a stab of shock. Her eyes, brilliant with tears, were suddenly blazing with anger, and her limbs were trembling. 'You!' she cried. 'You! You've caused enough trouble! You leave Daniel alone! Why did you come to this place anyway, except to spy and cause trouble? That's why Decima asked you to come, wasn't it? To spy on me and Charles so that she could drag Charles' name through the mud in a divorce petition! And now you've turned Charles against me and towards Decima again because you want to keep Decima from Daniel – because you want Daniel for yourself! Why, you silly, stupid fool! Do you think Daniel cares a damn for either of you? Do you think he cares for Decima's shallowness, her coldness, her boring trivial feminine mind? And do you think he cares any more for you with your dreary old clothes and your spinsterish mannerisms, your gaucheness and pseudo-intellectualism? And now because of you and what you've done, Charles has told us to leave and my whole world is over and finished—'

Rachel at last found her tongue. The rage was so vast within her that it impaired her speech and her voice was low and harsh and uneven. 'You're being melodramatic, over-emotional and utterly absurd, only you're so in love with your role as rejected heroine that you can't bear to look at the situation as it really is!' Her hands were clenched so tightly that they hurt; her nails dug into her palms. 'I've never spied on you and Charles! I don't care how much of a fool you care to make of yourself over a married man in the name of free love or whatever quasi-intellectual line of philosophy you happen to believe in – why should I care? It's nothing to do with me! And if you think Decima asked me up here to spy on you two, you must be mad! Decima was far too engrossed in Daniel to care what you did with her husband when her back was turned – she merely invited me here to keep Rohan out of her way. And if you think I would ever be interested in a man who sleeps with his host's wife – or any other woman who happens to be available – you couldn't be more wrong! You can keep your precious brother! Let him take you as far away from Ruthven as it's possible to go, for I don't care if I never see either of you again!'

Rebecca was on her feet, her face white, her movements unsteady, her eyes wide and dark and hard. 'That's what Charles said.' Her voice was little more than a whisper. And then suddenly she was screaming, her face distorted, her eyes narrow slits of rage: 'I hate you all, do you hear? I hate every one of you! I hate Decima and I hate you and I hate that fool Quist and I hate Charles – Charles more than any of you! Charles Mannering, the noble, distinguished, celebrated professor, the lying, weak, cowardly bastard who tells me that he's so sorry – yes, *so sorry*, but he's made a mistake and he doesn't want to divorce Decima after all and marry me – he's *so sorry*, but actually he doesn't want to see me again because I've served my purpose, just as if I were some tart or some harebrained little student who had a crush on him at Oxford! "I'm so sorry," he says! My God, I'll make him sorry! I'll teach him what it is to be sorry. I'll—'

She stopped.

Behind Rachel the door was softly closed.

'You'd better go to your room, Rebecca,' said Daniel without emotional inflection. 'You forget that we're not leaving till tomorrow.'

There was a long silence. Rebecca was staring at him, and Rachel suddenly found she had to sit down. Daniel was motionless. Presently he held out his hand to his sister.

'I'll take you upstairs.'

'It's all right.' She was crying, pushing past Rachel and stumbling towards Daniel.

He opened the door for her. 'I'll come upstairs presently.'

She made no reply. They could hear the harshness of her sobs as she moved across the hall to the stairs, and then Daniel closed the door and there was silence.

After a while he said: 'It seems I was mistaken.'

She stared at him, not understanding, and outside the squall broke and the rain hurled itself against the window-pane in an ecstasy of violence.

'I misjudged the kind of person you were.' He crossed to the fireplace and was still again, looking at her. 'You told Charles about Decima and myself, didn't you?'

She was wild-eyed, mesmerized by his stillness, appalled by his controlled anger. 'No,' she heard herself say, 'Rohan told Charles. I had nothing to do with it. It was Rohan.'

'Rohan or you – it's the same thing, isn't it? For a long time I was puzzled about why you had been asked to Ruthven and then at last I realized that Quist had manoeuvred it. He thought you could be useful to him – and of course you were.'

'Useful?' She felt dizzy, confused. 'I don't understand.'

'Don't tell me you hadn't realized that Quist is infatuated with Decima and would do anything to drive a wedge between her and any man she happened to be interested in?'

'I—'

'He hated me from the first but was powerless to do anything about the situation. To make matters worse, Charles was so absorbed in Rebecca that he didn't care what his wife was doing with me! So Quist conceived the idea of inviting an outsider here whom he could use and manipulate to play the four of us off against each other with the result that Decima and Charles would be reconciled and Rebecca and I would be sent away. Which is exactly what has happened.'

'But what you say isn't true!' said Rachel loudly, struggling with the tangled web in which she found herself. 'It was Decima who invited me here – Rohan had nothing to do with it! Nothing! It was Decima, Decima, Decima! Can't you understand! And Rohan isn't infatuated with her anyway – you're the one who's so infatuated with her that you're driven to imagine these preposterous schemes and ideas!'

'So you *are* jealous,' he said, 'I thought you were. You told Charles that Decima had been having an affair with me and Quist backed you up to the hilt. And Charles is so weak and so easily swayed that the two of you managed to convince him that he'd have no peace of mind till Rebecca and I left this house.'

'It's not true – not true—'

'You hate Decima's guts, don't you? You'd see her dead if you could!'

'No, no – I'm not like that—'

'Well, you've been wasting your energy being jealous! Decima's not my mistress and never has been. I told Charles last night that she was but it was a lie because I wanted to shake him . . . He's so damned smug, so damned self-righteous, so bloody satisfied in the belief that his wife would never be unfaithful to him! I saw that he had made up his mind to be rid of us so I didn't care what I said or how much I hurt him so long as I dragged him down from the pompous little pedestal he had built for himself. I was tired of the way he was using my sister, tried of his affectations and complacency!'

'You hate him because he's Decima's husband!'

'Decima! I care nothing for Decima! All I ask is to be rid of her – she's a danger to me, a menace to my future plans. If she gets Charles to use his influence in revenge—'

'I don't believe you,' Rachel heard herself say, and her voice was no longer steady. 'You had an affair with Decima, and now you suspect her of preferring Rohan – or even Charles. You're so unaccustomed to a woman losing interest in you before you lose interest in her that you have to resort to wild flights of imagination—'

'You don't know what you're talking about.'

'I just don't believe you never had an affair with Decima!'

'I don't care what you believe! Why should I? What are you to me? I thought at first you were different, but now I see you're the same as a thousand other women, petty, jealous and mundane. The hell with you! Go on back to your so-called platonic friend Rohan Quist and vent your stupid small-minded jealousy on his obsession with Decima Mannering, for God knows I've no further use for you.'

And he was gone as quietly as he had come, leaving nothing behind him but the squalling of the rain on the windows and the howl of the sea wind far away.


4


She went to her room and stayed there. She shut the door and pushed a chair against it to hold it fast in lieu of a key, and she drew the curtains to shut out the tortured convulsions of the weather and the appalling bleakness of the barren landscape. And then she lay down on her bed in the cool twilight and cried till her throat ached and her eyes were too swollen to see. Her face became hot and flushed with her tears, but after a while she became aware of how cold she was and how much she longed for the heat of a fire.

She got up, stooped to examine the grate, but there was nothing there but ashes and the scuttle by the hearth had only a few small pieces of wood in it. Shivering, she drew back the curtains and stared dry-eyed at the scene before her. It had stopped raining. The squall had died, but there was a mist clinging to the mountains and she could hear the hum of the strong wind as it swept in from the sea.

She shivered again. Perhaps there would be more fuel in Decima's room, and some matches too to set the fire alight. She started to wonder if Decima and Rohan had come back from their trip to sea, but that only made her think of Daniel again and her eyes filled with tears. She tried to dash them away, but they only fell the faster and she was still crying as she pulled aside the barricade, opened her door and stepped out into the corridor.

It was very quiet. Stifling her sobs, she went down the corridor to Decima's room at the far end and fumbled with the latch.

There were glowing embers in the grate; evidently Decima had lit the fire that morning, and the room was still warm and comfortable. Rachel closed the door behind her and locked it before sinking down on the hearthrug to build the fire to a warmer blaze, and within minutes the flames were leaping up the chimney and the cold was slowly ebbing from her limbs.

She sat there for a long while. There was a curious burning in her mind, as if some rich and valuable vein of thought had been hacked off and obliterated by some frenzied act of destruction. Her other thoughts were dim and unresponsive, her other emotions dulled by pain and anaesthetized by shock. All she was conscious of was this great searing sense of loss for which there was no cure, no solution. 'I never loved him,' she said to herself again and again. 'It was an infatuation. He was right and I was jealous and foolish and stupid. He despises me.'

But she had loved him. She had timidly reached out towards him, her longing overcoming all her shyness and reserve and fear, and her love had been wrenched from her, twisted by cruel hands and flung back, a crippled, shameful, distorted thing, into her face. She felt too crushed, too humiliated and too full of pain even to acknowledge that the love she had felt had been as deep as any of which she was capable. She could only acknowledge the twisted distortion which had been flung back at her, and could only tell herself numbly that she had been deluded and absurd.

'It was an infatuation,' she said aloud to the hard tongues of flame in the grate. 'I was foolish. I never loved him.'

And the pain of loss was a raw gaping wound from which it seemed the throbbing would never die, and the grief was a great barren waste which stretched as far as the eye could see.

'I wasn't in love,' she said. 'I was infatuated. I was mistaken. It was all a mistake.'

And it seemed to her even as she listened to the words that the house around her and the landscape beyond the window perfectly represented the desolation of her mind, the negation of all warmth and light and the presence only of arid starkness and a waste of isolation.

She got up and went to the window, as if by gazing out on that bleak landscape she could somehow gaze into her own mind, and as she moved she brushed the cushion from the window seat to the floor. She stooped automatically to pick it up and then she noticed that on the window seat there was a slim leather-bound volume which the cushion had concealed.

It was a diary.

She picked it up, but her fingers were still unsteady and it slithered through them to the floor and fell open at her feet. She stooped, and as she picked up the book she saw that the writing was not Decima's at all but a stormy tempestuous scrawl forming emotional uneven sentences.

Her eyes read isolated words even before her mind could stop them. 'Charles said . . . I told Charles I felt . . . Charles and I made love . . . Charles promised . . . Charles . . .'

There were intimate descriptions, passages of avowed love, ecstatic words of praise.

Rachel shut the book tightly and put it back beneath

the cushion. It was only when she turned away once more towards the fire that it occurred to her numbed brain to wonder why Rebecca Carey's diary should be so carefully concealed in Decima's room.

## chapter 6

1

Rohan and Decima didn't come back. The long morning drifted into a cold grey afternoon and still there was no sign of them. At some time after three Rachel slipped into an exhausted sleep on the hearthrug in Decima's room but no one interrupted her and no one came to see where she was.

When she awoke it was dark and the fire was dying in the grate. For one long moment she lay still, too stiff and cramped to move, and then memory flooded back into her mind with a stab of pain and she sat up, ignoring the ache in her limbs and the dry burning of her eyes. Tonight was the night of the dinner party, the night when sixteen guests at eight-thirty would be arriving at Ruthven to dine in the great hall below. Tonight was the eve of Decima's twenty-first birthday, the last night of the Careys' stay at Ruthven, the last time that Rachel would see Daniel. Tonight was the night of masquerade, of playing a part, of letting no one know that her mind was still in the grip of that great aching sense of loss that cast out all other thought and emotion.

No one must ever know, was all she could tell herself. No one must ever find out.

She stood up painfully, and moved to the door. It was so dark in the corridor that she had to pause for a moment to get her bearings, and then she set off in the direction of her room with one hand against the wall so that she would know when she reached the door. A minute later she was sitting on her own bed and struggling to light the lamp.

Mrs Willie had obviously been much too busy cooking to go around lighting fires in the bedrooms; the ashes were still grey in the grate and the room seemed bitterly cold and damp. Rachel drew on her overcoat and looked at herself in the mirror.

She saw a stranger with dishevelled hair and bloodshot eyes swollen with weeping. Her skin seemed blotched, her expression empty of all feeling. She stared at herself for a long time and then, lamp in hand, went back to Decima's room for a box of matches and a log for the fire.

It was six o'clock when she managed to get the fire alight. She desperately wanted hot water to bathe her face but she was afraid of meeting the housekeeper in the kitchen, afraid of anyone seeing her before she had had a chance to mend her appearance a little. Presently she used some of the cold water in the ewer to wash her face, and then she spent some time combing and rearranging her hair before venturing downstairs to fetch hot water.

The hall looked beautiful, the long banquet table aglow with white linen and silver cutlery and red candles waiting to be lit. Someone had completed the task which Charles had allotted to her, for there were flowers in tall vases on the chest and tables at the side of the hall and a small arrangement on the banquet table among the two epergnes. Four lamps were burning and huge fires were blazing in the enormous twin fireplaces on either side of the hall.

Charles came out of the library just as she stepped into the hall and paused to look at the scene. There was no escaping him.

'Hullo,' he said. 'Where have you been? I tried to find you a while ago and had no success.'

'I'm so sorry, Charles – I – I didn't feel too well . . . Please forgive me for not doing the flowers—'

'No, that doesn't matter. I picked them later and Mrs Willie arranged them when she had a spare minute. I say, are you all right? You look very pale.'

'Yes, I'm much better now, thank you. I was just going to get some hot water to wash with before I change. Are Decima and Rohan back yet?'

'No, they're not. I don't know where the hell they've got to. I can only suppose that the storm caught them at sea and forced them to head for Kyle of Lochalsh for shelter. The storm's stopped here but it may still be strong over at Kyle and forcing them to stay in harbour there. I hope to God they get back before the guests start to arrive. It was a damnfool thing to do today of all days anyway – Decima at least, if not Rohan, ought to have been here to help with all the preparations . . . Rachel, are you sure you're all right? You certainly don't look well.'

'Yes, really, Charles, I'm quite all right now . . .' She made her escape, obtained her supply of hot water and set off back to her bedroom again before she should meet anyone else. There was a glow of light beneath Daniel's door as she passed it, but Rebecca's room was in darkness.

Perhaps Rebecca intended to spend the evening on her own.

It was only when Rachel reached her room again that she became aware of panic. How could she possibly face all those people whom she did not know and act as if nothing had happened? How could she be sociable and friendly and hospitable just as if nothing were wrong? And how could she even begin to think of facing Daniel again after all that had been said between them that morning?

Because no one must ever know, she thought. No one is ever going to know unless I'm weak and give myself away. And I'm not going to be weak and give in and hide myself in my room because I haven't enough courage to face the world at this particular time.

No one must ever know. The evening loomed before her, an enormous obstacle which had to be surmounted before the tranquillity and relief of the day ahead. All she had to do was to get through this evening somehow.

Once the evening was over she would be able to relax and recover herself.

She didn't know then how wrong she was. Afterwards, looking back, she decided that this was just as well, for if she had known then what was going to happen that evening she would never have left her room.

## 2

'But where are they?' cried Charles in exasperation. 'Why aren't they here? What's happened to them?'

The clock chimed half-past seven. Rachel, seated tensely before the hearth of one of the big fires in the hall, made no reply, and presently Charles in an agony of suspense paced to the front door and opened it to stare out to sea.

'There's a boat coming in now . . .' He stepped outside, shutting the door behind him, and Rachel was left alone before the hearth in the silent hall.

A door closed somewhere far away upstairs; there were voices, a murmur of conversation, the sound of footsteps on the stairs.

Rachel did not turn around. At last when they were behind her she glanced up and tried to force out a stiff 'good evening' but Daniel moved past her without a glance in her direction and Rebecca went over to the table on a pretence of examining the silverware.

Rachel stared back into the flames.

'Someone's arriving,' said Daniel to his sister. 'There's a boat down by the quay.'

'Rohan and Decima?'

'I don't know. There's another boat out at sea heading in this direction. The guests are starting to arrive.'

'Supposing Decima doesn't come back?'

'Then Charles will look like a bloody fool, won't he?' said Daniel and opened the front door to stand outside on the porch.

The St Bernard, which had been closeted in the kitchen

out of the way until he had escaped through the back door, lumbered solemnly into the room and settled himself comfortably at Rachel's feet before the fire. Mrs Willie, scurrying into the hall at the same moment with two large ashtrays, caught sight of him and gave an exclamation of annoyance.

'George, what are you doing in the hall? Come here at once, you bad dog!' And she stooped to smack his head and lay a firm hand on his collar.

The St Bernard growled.

'Let him be,' called Daniel from the door. 'He's no trouble. I'll see he's not a nuisance.'

'Just as you like, Mr Carey,' said the housekeeper with a shrug and disappeared again in the direction of the kitchen while the dog returned to his slumbers on the hearthrug.

'It's neither Decima nor Rohan,' said Rebecca who had been watching from the window. 'It must be the first contingent of guests.'

And the next moment Charles had entered the room with the MacDonalds and Camerons from Kyle of Lochalsh and the party had begun.

Afterwards, Rachel's memories of that last dinner at Ruthven were blurred and she could remember only isolated scenes which seemed to have little or no connexion with each other. She could remember Charles saying – how many times? Three? Four? – that Decima had gone into Kyle of Lochalsh to do some last-minute shopping and had apparently been delayed there with Rohan. She could remember Robert Cameron saying that he had noticed the Ruthven boat moored in the harbour at Kyle, and the look of relief on Charles' face changing to one of anger as he began to wonder why Decima was deliberately delaying her return.

The Kincaids arrived from Skye soon after eight and finally Decima's lawyer, old Conor Douglas, from Cluny Gualach with his daughter, but still there was no sign of Decima and Rohan. Half-past eight struck. Then a quarter to nine.

'We'd better dine, I think,' said Charles abruptly. 'There's no use in spoiling the dinner, and I've no doubt you're all hungry after your journey.'

Rachel could remember the glow of candles in silver candlesticks and the sparkle of champagne in the elegant glasses, but not the taste of the food, nor the order of the menu. She was sitting between one of the MacDonalds, a young man of about twenty-seven, and old Mr Douglas the lawyer, and all the time she was conscious of Decima's empty chair at one end of the long table and Rohan's vacant place directly opposite her. Daniel was far away, hidden from her almost entirely by one of the epergnes and a candelabrum of red candles, but sometimes during a lull in the conversation she could hear his voice travelling towards her from the other end of the table.

The dinner was finished at last, the speeches left unsaid. The guests lingered at the table over coffee and liqueurs, and the conversation rippled on inconsequentially, the guests mellow with good food and drink and almost forgetting that the guest of honour had never appeared to receive them. To Rachel, longing for the solitude of her room and an escape from the torture of making sociable conversation, it seemed as if the party would never end.

It was some time after ten when Decima and Rohan came back. They were laughing together up the garden path from the jetty, and it was not until Rohan flung wide the front door and strode into the room that Rachel realized they were both dead drunk.


3


'Good evening, everyone,' said Decima, mocking them all. 'How kind of you to come. Please excuse me not being here to greet you but Rohan wanted to make love to me and I had to explain that I can't be unfaithful to my husband, even though he's been sleeping with Rebecca Carey for the last few weeks, because he wants a reconciliation with me and he's promised to send the Careys away tomorrow. Why, Charles darling, how beautiful the hall looks! So sorry I wasn't here to help . . . Rachel, you look awful! What's the matter? Hasn't Daniel bothered to give you his best smile today? Daniel, you really should be more considerate!'

'Charles,' said Daniel to his host, 'your wife's as drunk as a barmaid. You'd better take her upstairs.'

'Why, listen, Charles!' jeered Rohan. 'Listen to who's giving you advice! It's the guest who tried to seduce your wife under your own roof, Charles! Why don't you ask him to put Decima to bed for you? I'll tell you why you don't ask him, Charles. It's because you're so god-damned proud, Charles, that you can't admit you could ever be in the position of the fooled husband! You think you're God, don't you, Charles, God's gift to culture, to academic life, to women, to the whole world, but hell to all that, Charles, you're not God's gift to your wife!'

Charles was white to the lips, shocked speechless.

Daniel was on his feet, his hands gripping Rohan's arms as he tried to lead him away. Around the table the guests were frozen with shock, as silent and motionless as if they had been carved out of stone.

'Let go of me, you—' Rohan was fighting, but he was no match for Daniel's strength.

Over on the hearth the St Bernard began to bark.

'Charles darling,' said Decima, 'did you give George any champagne?'

The noise of the barking seemed to send great shafts through Rachel's consciousness until she began to feel that she was waking at last to reality after a long hypnotized sleep. She stood up suddenly, her feet carrying her around the table to where Rohan was shouting abuse at Daniel, and suddenly it seemed that Daniel didn't exist at all and Rohan was the only one who was real.

'Rohan, you idiot, stop making such a fool of yourself!' Her voice was curt and cold. 'Stop it, do you hear? Stop it!' And when he took no notice of her, she slapped him hard across the mouth.

The crack of the impact of hand against flesh seemed

to echo throughout the length of the hall. There was a hideous silence. No one moved. No one spoke. And then Decima yawned and said idly to no one in particular: 'Lord, how tired I am! Goodnight, everyone,' and curled herself up on the hearthrug before one of the fireplaces and went immediately to sleep, her head resting on the St Bernard's massive body as he lay beside her.

'Well,' said old Conor Douglas, the lawyer of Cluny Gualach, rising briskly from the table as if nothing had happened, 'I think we should be on our way, Rosalind.'

'Yes, we too must be going,' said Robert MacDonald for all the world as if the dinner party had ended with perfect normalcy. 'Thank you so much, Charles, for a most excellent meal.'

'Most delightful . . .'

'We did enjoy ourselves . . .'

'Thank you again for your hospitality . . .'

The endless stream of conversation trickled on with a remorseless inevitability until finally the last goodbye had been said, the front door closed and bolted after the last guest, and Ruthven was alone at last with those who lived within its walls. Without a word Charles went straight to the library and slammed the door shut behind him.

'Exit Charles,' said Rohan, 'thinly disguised as an insulted English gentleman.' And he laughed.

'Exit Rohan,' said Rachel unsmiling, 'appearing undisguised as a very drunk, very foolish overgrown schoolboy. This way.'

'Which way? Here, take your hand off my arm, Raye! What do you think you're doing?'

'We're going upstairs.'

'But—'

'Don't argue.'

'Yes, but look here—'

'Shut up.'

'What about Decima?'

'She's passed out. Daniel and Rebecca will see to her.'

'Oh no,' said Rohan forlornly, 'no, don't leave her with the Careys. Don't leave her with them.'

'Don't be silly.'

Halfway up the stairs he said: 'I'm crazy about her, Raye. I always have been. I never told you.'

'No,' she said. 'You never told me.'

'I'd do anything for her,' he said. 'Anything at all.'

'Yes.'

'I'd marry her but Charles won't give her a divorce.'

'No, I understand he's set on a reconciliation.'

'But at least I made her leave Daniel. She saw that she could trust me more than she could trust him.'

'Yes.'

'Daniel doesn't give a damn for her. I'm the one who really loves her. She knows that now.'

'Yes.'

'She's going to come away with me. She's promised. She's going to be mine for ever and ever and ever . . .'

'Mind the corner. It's dark down here.'

'. . . ever and ever and ever . . .'

They walked on down the south wing past the south-west turret room to the west wing that faced the sea.

'Which is your room, Rohan?'

'This one. No, this one. I can't remember.'

It was the second room. Rachel found the lamp, but he had fallen across the bed in a stupor even before she had managed to light the wick. After pulling off his shoes and arranging the quilt on top of him as best she could, she blew out the lamp again and went back past the south-west turret room to her own room in the south wing. She shut the door in exhaustion, lit the lamp on the table and sank down in the chair before the hearth.

After ten minutes or so she remembered she had left Decima sleeping downstairs. Perhaps she should go and see if she was all right. No, let someone else look after Decima for a change! Decima with her sneering tongue and cool hateful remarks . . . What was it she had said? *You look awful, Raye! What's the matter? Hasn't Daniel given you his best smile today?*

It was an unforgivable taunt to be made in front of a gathering of strangers, and Rachel had no intention of forgiving. Decima could go to the devil as far as she was concerned.

'Don't leave Decima with the Careys!' Rohan had said, maudlin with his surfeit of liquor. 'Don't leave her alone with them . . .'

'I don't trust the Careys,' Decima had said. 'They're against me – everyone's against me – don't let them turn you against me too, Rachel . . .'

All that nonsense about Charles wanting to kill her so that he might inherit Ruthven . . . Absurd. Charles wouldn't kill anyone, although God knows he certainly must have felt like killing Decima when she humiliated him before all his friends . . .

Decima must have drunk a great deal. Normally, as Rachel well knew, she could drink a fair share of Scotch and still show no trace of having drunk more than a glass of iced water. Rohan too was accustomed to liquor. His bachelor life in London had ensured that.

I wonder, thought Rachel, why they both got so drunk. I wonder what made them drink so much.

She wanted desperately to relax and find peace in sleep, but her mind was vibrantly alive, the thoughts milling through her brain, and after a while she stood up and moved restlessly out into the corridor. There was a light glowing beneath Decima's door, and as she drew nearer she could hear the faint sound of a man's voice and a woman's murmur from within.

She knocked softly on the panels. The murmuring ceased at once.

'Who is it?' called Decima sleepily.

'Rachel. I just wondered if you were all right.'

'Yes, thanks. Daniel brought me upstairs a little while ago. There's no need for you to worry.'

Rachel wanted to ask who was with her but was so convinced that it was Daniel that her courage failed her. 'I'll see you tomorrow, then,' she said, turning away. 'Goodnight, Decima.'

''Night.' Decima sounded a long way off, barely conscious.

Rachel waited for the murmuring to begin again but it did not. At last, not wanting to risk being found listening outside the door, she walked on to the head of the stairs and glanced down into the hall. The remains of the dinner party lay haphazardly on the long banquet table below and, although the candles had been snuffed, the lamps still burned on the chest and side-tables around the room. The twin fires were now mere glowing embers in the great fireplaces, and Rachel noticed that the St Bernard had left his favourite place on the hearth and was stretched out in slumber before the door of the small drawing room across the hall.

Rachel went over to the library door and knocked softly. 'Charles?'

There was no reply.

She tried again. 'Charles, it's Rachel. May I come in?'

There was still no reply, but she could see the light shining beneath the door. Perhaps he had fallen asleep. Cautiously she turned the handle, pushed open the door a little way and began to walk into the room.

Her feet stopped just after she had crossed the threshold. Paralysis flickered through her body with lightning speed, taking from her even the power to draw a breath, and then suddenly the gasp of shock was tearing at her lungs and her throat was dry as she tried to scream. For Charles lay slumped back in his chair with Rebecca's ivory dagger in his chest and she knew at once, even before she moved forward again towards him, that he was dead.

4

She could not bring herself to touch him. He lay there still and silent in death, his face tilted downwards, his arms hanging over the arms of the chair behind the desk, and all she could do was look down at him in horror and try to think what she could do. The white ivory of the dagger gleamed in the lamplight. The carved sheath lay neatly on the window seat close at hand where the murderer had discarded it.

The murderer. Charles had been murdered.

There was a fire in the grate, the flames flickering so feebly that they were almost moribund. There were papers burning, the trace of scorched dark leather. When she knelt down on the hearth a second later she saw that someone had tried to burn Rebecca's diary in the dying fire a short while ago.

A door slammed somewhere. There were footsteps crossing the hall, getting louder and louder as they drew nearer to the library. Propelled by fears and instincts which she didn't even begin to analyse, Rachel sprang to her feet and stepped swiftly behind the long red curtains which stretched from the floor to the ceiling in front of the french windows.

She was just in time.

She heard the door open even though she didn't dare look to see who had entered, heard the abrupt silence which came the next moment, heard the click of the latch as the door was shut quietly again.

The silence after that seemed to go on and on and on. The only thing she could see was the red velvet of the curtains before her, but she knew just as surely as if she could have seen him face to face that it was Daniel who had entered the room. She could imagine him beside the body, noticing the dagger, seeing the sheath, catching sight of the scorched diary just as she had done.

He was very silent, she thought; it was almost as if he had known what he was going to find . . . But that was impossible of course.

Or was it?

She heard a small noise then, the crackling of scorched papers, and guessed he must be pulling the diary from the grate. She heard him throw on another log and use the bellows to work up the flames to a blaze which would effectively destroy everything he had been unable to remove.

After that there was another silence. What would he be doing now? Hardly daring to breathe she found the chink in the curtains and glanced through them into the room beyond.

He was wiping the handle of the dagger with his handkerchief. As she watched he picked up the sheath from the table and wiped that too before replacing it again where he had found it. Then, very carefully, he wrapped Charles' fingers around the hilt of the dagger and rearranged the body so that Charles' weight was thrust forward still farther on to the blade in his chest.

She edged farther to the right of the chink in the curtains for safety, and as she shifted her position the curtain rings far above gave a small, almost inaudible squeak of movement as she touched the material in front of her by accident.

She froze.

There was nothing then, nothing at all. She tried to hear his breathing but the room was as silent as a tomb and she could only hear the thump of her heart and the roar of blood in her ears.

She went on waiting, hardly able to breathe. And then, just as she began to think she was safe after all, he flung back the curtains with a quick flick of his wrists and she was staring up into his eyes.


5


'What are you doing here?'

'I wanted to talk to Charles. I came here about a minute ago and then I heard you coming so I hid here.'

'Why?'

'I don't know.'

He stared at her, his eyes wide and dark, and she leant back against the french windows as her strength deserted her and her limbs began to tremble.

316

'You'd better make up a better story than that to tell the police,' he said after a while. 'It doesn't sound very convincing.'

'Perhaps it would be more convincing,' she heard herself say in a shaking voice, 'if I told them I saw you take your sister's diary from the grate where it lay burning, wipe her fingerprints from the dagger, and rearrange the body to make it seem as if Charles had committed suicide.'

'Rebecca didn't kill him,' he said again flatly.

'Then who did?'

He turned from her abruptly and moved across the room. 'Why, Decima, of course,' he said. 'Who else?' He wrenched open the door. 'You'd better come and help me find her.'

'Decima didn't kill him,' said Rachel.

'Why do you say that?'

Instinct made her say nothing.

'Why do you say that?' repeated Daniel, but she would not answer him.

The St Bernard was at the foot of the staircase, his tail swaying gently, as he followed Daniel up the stairs to the gallery above.

'Shouldn't we get the police?' Rachel said suddenly.

'Yes, we'll have to take the boat into Kyle of Lochalsh. Or maybe Quist can go if we can wake him up. Did you put him to bed?'

'More or less. Shall I go and try to wake him?'

'No, we must find Decima first.'

'Why not Rebecca?'

'Because Decima was Charles' wife,' said Daniel, 'and whether she killed him or not she has the right to be told first of his death.'

Rachel's mind was spinning. The shock made her thoughts jumbled and confused so that all she was aware of thinking was that Charles had been killed and that one of his guests had killed him. It must be Rebecca, she thought. Decima was in her room. Rohan was drunk in his bed. Daniel . . . But where had Daniel been? With

Decima in her room? Had she been confessing to him that she had killed Charles and framed Rebecca, and had Daniel then immediately come downstairs to rearrange the scene of the crime so that Rebecca would be cleared? But Decima had been drunk. Decima had been carried upstairs to her room . . . by Daniel.

They were outside the door.

'Decima,' said Daniel in a low voice and knocked on the panels.

There was no answer.

'Decima?' He opened the door slightly and glanced inside. The next moment he was crossing the room swiftly and Rachel was following him across the threshold.

The bed was empty, as empty as the room itself. It was bitterly cold and the lamp was smoking in the draught from the huge window which was flung open as wide as it would go.

Understanding came to Rachel so quickly that she was conscious of neither shock nor horror, only of a dim, unreal surprise. 'My God—'

'Keep back,' said Daniel suddenly, but she was already beside him at the window and staring down through the darkness at Decima's lifeless body on the stone terrace below.

Somewhere far away in the hall, the grandfather clock began to strike midnight.

Decima had died before her twenty-first birthday.

# Part 2:
# Cluny Sands

# chapter 1

1

Afterwards, all Rachel had wanted to do was to bury herself in the midst of some teeming civilization. She was obsessed with the desire for traffic and huge buildings and throngs of people, some foreign city far south of Ruthven where the sun would scorch the concrete pavements and burn out the memory of silky mists and soft sea breezes. Even London, six hundred miles from those grey stone walls, eventually seemed too close, and even though Daniel was by that time far away in Africa the memory of him lingered with each memory of Ruthven.

She thought of Ruthven often. She knew she would never forget that moment at midnight when she had faced Daniel in Decima's room.

'Can't you see?' he had said to her by that open window with the damp night air chilling the room. 'I've just rearranged Charles' body to look as if he deliberately pressed forward on that dagger and killed himself. The police are going to think he murdered Decima – God knows he had enough provocation after the way she behaved tonight – and then committed suicide. If they think that, there'll be no repercussions for the rest of us. They've got to think that Charles killed Decima and then himself.'

She had stared at him, trying to read his mind and decipher the meaning which lay behind what he had said. After a while she had said, shaken: 'But how can we say that? I spoke to Decima on my way down to the library to find Charles. Her door was closed but I called out from the passage to ask if she was all right and she said she was. Charles died before she did.'

'But no one else knows that,' he had said. 'Just you and I. We know that Decima killed Charles and framed it to look as if Rebecca had killed him, but nobody knows that except you and I.'

She had hesitated a long time. She thought of Charles, the evidence that Rebecca had killed him, the proof that Daniel had been so quick to destroy. Daniel must have killed Decima too, unless Daniel himself . . . Every muscle in Rachel's body tightened in an agony of nervousness and suspense.

'Don't you understand?' he had said very deliberately. 'It's the easiest way out. All you would have to do would be to omit any mention of the fact that you spoke to Decima before you found Charles dead, and omit all mention of the fact that you saw me rearrange the body. Then once the police accept that explanation, the rest of us won't come under suspicion.'

And still she had hesitated, torn between fear and doubt, knowing what she should do yet not knowing whether she had the strength to do it. At last he had said without emphasis: 'The police could suspect you, you know. If they thought that you were jealous of Decima, that you hated her because she humiliated you, they might think you killed her. They might think Decima had killed Charles and then you killed Decima.'

He had wanted to ensure her silence, her acquiescence in his desire to suppress the truth. She wondered if he had ever realized that even after their quarrel and his rejection of her she would still have done anything to protect him.

'I think I understand,' she had heard herself say at last, her voice seeming strained and distant in her ears. 'Yes, we'd better do as you suggest.'

So she had committed herself and after that there could be no turning back. He had not seemed grateful, she noticed, but only infinitely relieved, as if he had somehow managed to overcome some insuperable obstacle threatening his own security.

The local police had been slow and rustic; when the CID men arrived later, they had found the trail cold and the case a formality. At the ensuing inquest the coroner had been a retired doctor from Fort William, the jury mostly fishermen from Kyle of Lochalsh, and it had seemed obvious to all of them after hearing evidence from the dinner-party guests that Charles had killed his wife and then in despair committed suicide. The papers had made a great splash of it for a couple of days on the front pages, and Charles had had his obituary in *The Times*, but after that the case had been soon forgotten, dismissed as one of the more newsworthy tragedies of the year, and the press had passed to other matters to feed to their voracious readers.

As Decima had died before attaining twenty-one, Charles should have inherited Ruthven under the terms of her father's will, but since by law a murderer cannot profit from his crime, it was held that the estate would revert to Decima's next-of-kin. Since Decima was an orphan with no relatives, this in fact meant that the house and estate of Ruthven passed into the hands of the Crown. The profitable forestry estates were sold to the Forestry Commission, and the house, which no estate agent had been able to sell, was in the end left to fall gradually into decay. As for Willie the gamekeeper and his wife, they had accepted a post on a large estate further south near Lochaber and when they moved from Ruthven some two months after the inquest they had taken George, the St Bernard, with them.

The incident was closed; the nightmare was over. Rohan, Rachel, Rebecca and Daniel went their separate ways.

For a short time Rachel had stayed in London, not really wanting to leave it, for she loved the city better than any other, and then one day she had met Rebecca by chance in Mayfair. She was teaching, Rachel discovered, lecturing in economics. And Daniel? Yes, he was happy. He had gone out to Africa to teach English and English history in one of the new African states. He seemed to have found his vocation, for apparently he wanted nothing except to remain in the new life he had chosen for himself.

It was then that Rachel realized how empty England was, how unbearably dreary her life had become. The longing to escape became an obsession. She felt she could only begin to live again if she were in a new country, in new surroundings and among new people, and finally she made the decision to go to America where, she had heard, English secretaries were in great demand. She arrived in New York three months later, found a job without difficulty, and quickly made friends at the women's hotel where she was staying. Soon she was sharing a luxury apartment with three other girls in midtown Manhattan just west of Fifth Avenue, and four years later was surprised to look back and find how quickly the time had passed.

It was then that Rohan arrived. He had been working in England for an automobile concern, and now wrote to say that he was to be transferred to his firm's New York branch. He had, he disclosed, requested the transfer.

She met him at the airport. It was rather absurd because she felt like crying at the sight of someone from home, and he, emotional as ever, was obviously overcome with pleasure at seeing her again. He looked tired after the journey, but his grey eyes were as brilliant as ever and his hair, still straw-coloured, rose up in a tuft above his forehead where he had pulled it in his excitement.

In the cab on the way back into the city she said: 'But I still don't understand why you requested the transfer.'

'Maybe for the same reasons as the ones which persuaded you to leave England,' he answered, staring out of the window at the approaching skyline of Manhattan. 'And I'm not as English as most Englishmen. There's a lot of foreign blood in me. I didn't think I would find it hard to live abroad for a while.'

'It's funny,' she said. 'I don't know why, but I half thought you might be getting interested in Rebecca. When you wrote to tell me you were coming to the States I thought you were writing to tell me you were engaged. You mentioned her quite often in your letters.'

'I saw a little of her now and then,' he said, very casual, almost uninterested. 'It was nice, but . . . she wasn't really my type. And besides—' He stopped.

'Besides?'

He turned towards her and she saw that his face, usually so mobile and expressive, was very still.

'There were too many memories,' he said. 'For both of us. It was better to go our separate ways.'

She nodded silently, making no comment. It was the one and only reference that either of them made to Ruthven, and it was never mentioned between them again.

Yet still she thought of Daniel.

Daniel in Africa, Daniel abandoning career and home and country to teach African children in a gesture which was as out of character as it was striking. She could never understand what had taken him to Africa, for Daniel was not the kind of man who offered his services to welfare organizations for a nominal salary, and still less the kind of man who would feel any desire to teach children in a new country with poor facilities. With his background of scholarship he might have ultimately attained all the academic honours he could have wished for; she could see him so clearly at Cambridge with its ancient beautiful buildings, visualize him so easily accepting a good academic post and lecturing to brilliant gifted students; there would have been a professorship waiting in the future, a successful business and social life, a life in England among English people in an English university town.

But he had turned his back on all that. The absoluteness of the gesture with its sweeping implications was something she could understand, even if she did not understand the gesture itself. Daniel had always seemed so vivid and positive to her that she could easily imagine him reaching a decision to change his entire life and then having the courage to keep to his decision and follow it through to its conclusion. That at least was in character. But to go to Africa, to seek the steamy torrid climate of the Equator, to bury himself as an obscure teacher far from home was a decision which seemed both bewildering and bizarre.

She wanted to talk to Rohan about it, but Rohan was

always so scrupulously careful never to mention the subject of Ruthven now that they were so far from the past that she never managed to broach the subject with him. Rohan quickly settled down in the city, soon gathered a host of friends around him, and before long he was again the leader of the crowd, just as he had been long ago, as far back as she could remember, and after a while she began to feel that her life had swung back to normal again after some nightmare deviation from its appointed course.

But all she was aware of thinking whenever she met another man was: he is nothing compared to Daniel.

Her mother wrote to her from England: 'So you're meeting such a lot of people, dear. It must be lovely to have Rohan there with you. Is there anyone special at the moment? It's so amazing to think that next September you'll be twenty-eight. . . .'

Her mother was thinking of tomorrow, and tomorrow for Rachel did not exist. Tomorrow was a great emptiness, a desert stretching into nothingness before the oasis of today, and the landscape was so desolate that she did not even dare to look at it.

I shall never marry, she thought. Not while Daniel's image is still so strong in my mind.

But Daniel had preferred his life to take a different course. He had never loved her, just as she had never really loved him, and she could see now that her whole attitude to him was a romantic attachment, a young girl's infatuation which she had never fully outgrown; it was surely best to pretend even to herself that the whole episode was already forgotten, and then perhaps she would find it easier to obliterate him from her mind for all time.

It was evening. She was going out to dinner and had just had a bath. There was a long mirror in the living room next to the desk, and she had always sat in front of it to put on her make-up because the light from the desk lamp was perfect for applying cosmetics. As she began to put on her make-up the phone on the desk started to ring.

She picked up the receiver without interest. 'Hullo?'

'Rachel,' said Rohan, and his voice sounded thin and far away as if he were speaking from a great distance. 'I had to call you.'

Rohan was always dramatic. His reason for calling was probably trivial.

'I'm just going out,' she said. 'Can I call you back later?'

'No,' he said, 'no, I have to tell you. I had a letter from England today.'

She thought she heard his voice tremble. Her fingers suddenly tightened on the receiver. 'From England?'

'From Rebecca, Rachel. From Rebecca Carey.'

She could see her expression in the long mirror, watch the colour ebb from her face. It was as if she were watching a film, seeing a stranger whom she did not know.

'I got the letter this morning,' he was saying. 'I couldn't think why she was writing, as we only exchanged addresses as a formality.'

'What did she say?'

'Can't you guess? It's Daniel, Rachel – Daniel's returning from Africa, coming back into our lives . . .'


2


Daniel had often asked himself why he had gone abroad. He, who had always lived his life in the most English of environments, who had lived in the oldest and most English parts of England, who had worked in such a peculiarly English world of academic research – why should he of all people have suddenly decided to turn his back on it all and try instead to teach in a hostile foreign land for little money and little prestige? He had gone back to Cambridge after Ruthven fully prepared to resume his life where he had left it, to pick up the threads as if he had never been away and to slip back with ease into the intellectual satisfaction of his work and his life amongst those ancient, beautiful surroundings. He had never anticipated what had happened when he went back. He had never once thought that the world he loved would have changed so that it seemed to him yet another Ruthven in its arid, desolate sterility; he could never once have imagined that he would ever pause on the Bridge of Sighs and look at the smooth waters of the Cam below and think to himself: 'I have no place here any more. I'm a stranger knocking on the door and trying to gain entrance, but I've come to the wrong door. There's nothing here for me.'

His work suddenly seemed a mere mechanical exercise of his brain, and even his ambition had died. He had waited, hoping his apathy was some form of reaction from the events at Ruthven, but the state of mind persisted and at last he realized clearly that he had to get away – away from Cambridge, away from England, and most of all away from Rebecca. It was true they had never spoken of Ruthven, and Rebecca had shied away from all mention of Charles and Decima, but Daniel, convinced as he was that she had killed them both in a burst of frenzied rage and revenge, found it impossible to be at ease with her. Several times he tried to force himself to speak of it to her, but each time he had failed. She must know, he thought, that he had covered up for her; she must realize that he knew . . . But if she did, she seemed determined not to speak of it, and the awkwardness between them became more pronounced. When he had decided to go abroad she was very distressed and for a time tried to persuade him to stay, but when she saw he was determined she gave up her attempts at persuasion and appeared resigned to the situation.

A voluntary educational organization had seized on the opportunity to enlist a graduate capable of teaching English; within three months he had a class of forty African children in Accra and was learning to live in the country which had once been called the White Man's Grave.

He found he enjoyed teaching more than he thought he would, and, contrary to what he had always imagined, the younger his pupils were the more he enjoyed teaching them. *When I eventually return to England,* he thought, *this is what I shall do. I'll get a school of my own and teach young children, not vegetate in some great university lecturing to pseudo adults who think they're God's gift to society.*

The decision pleased him; he was happy. Perhaps he would even have stayed longer in Accra if he had not begun to think more and more of Rachel Lord.

He didn't know why he thought of her so often. Perhaps it was because he had never really been able to make up his mind about her. She had seemed so full of candour and sincerity, so honest and unspoilt and unsophisticated, that it had sickened him to discover she had stooped to spying and telling tales in the violence of her jealousy of him. And then later . . . It was Rohan, Rachel had said, I never told Charles. It was Rohan . . .

But Decima had said Rachel was the one who had told Charles. 'Can't you see she's beside herself with jealousy?' she had blazed to Daniel. 'Can't you see she has this schoolgirl crush on you and is as jealous as hell?'

He had never even considered that it might be Quist, and yet it was much more likely that Quist would have been the one to cause trouble. But why had Decima lied? Because it was *she* who was jealous, *she* who was spiteful enough to want to hurt Rachel and pay her back for capturing Daniel's attention? Perhaps after all Rachel had been speaking the truth, and if so perhaps she was still everything he had first imagined her to be. The more he considered the situation, the more convinced he became that he had misjudged her, and the more he became convinced that he had judged her wrongly the more he wanted to see her. Now, five years after he had left England, he found he was thinking of her all the time. He thought of her when his students asked him questions about English places and English people; he thought of her whenever he received his three-week-old copy of the *Sunday Times* and saw the theatre news and the book reviews; he thought of her when he was introduced to other women and above all he thought of her each year on the anniversary of those terrible days at Ruthven when he relived the memories he would carry with him to the end of his life. Sometimes it seemed to him that he would only have to close his eyes to be back again at Ruthven and facing her beside the open window of Decima's room.

He was not sure when it first became clear to him that he would have to see her again. Perhaps the turning point came when he received a letter from his sister mentioning that she had met Rohan Quist again by chance in London and that he was about to leave England to work in New York.

'Apparently Rachel is working in New York already,' Rebecca had written, 'so I suppose this will give them the opportunity to revive their platonic friendship again.'

It was then that he had started to wonder whether Quist and Rachel would ever discuss Ruthven when they met. Unless Rachel was very careful such a discussion could be extremely dangerous.

He thought about it for a long time, remembering every detail of those last hours at Ruthven, but the more he thought about it the less convinced he was that everything was perfectly safe. Supposing Rachel betrayed to Quist that she knew the coroner's verdict had been wrong . . . Quist had loved Decima. Suppose he got it into his head to resurrect the entire business . . .

It was then that Daniel first conceived the idea of seeing Rachel again to warn her not to talk, and once the idea of seeing her was in his mind there was no putting it aside.

Several of Rebecca's letters had referred to Quist after that first meeting when he had told her he was planning to join Rachel in New York.

'Rohan rang up,' she had written in the next letter, 'and asked me out to dinner. I nearly refused and then I thought; hell why not? So I went. We went to an extremely good restaurant, and much to my surprise I rather enjoyed myself. He seems to have matured a great deal and it was hard to believe he was the same person as the Rohan Quist we knew at Ruthven . . . He didn't refer to Ruthven at all, or to Charles or Decima, but for me at any rate, if not for him, the memories were there like a great wall between us. . . .'

Rohan had taken her out several times after that. Then later she had written:

'Saw Rohan again last night. It was his birthday and he said he wanted to go out and have a few drinks somewhere, so we went to the Dorchester and got rather tight on vodka martinis. After the fourth he started to talk about Rachel, and by the time he had finished the fifth he was talking of Ruthven. "It's a funny thing," he said, "but I'm sure Rachel knows something." And I said: "Knows what?"

'"About Ruthven," he said. "She won't talk about it, though. She never talks of Ruthven. But I'm sure she knows something."

'I said: "Why do you say that?"

'And he said: "Because I've known Rachel over twenty-five years and I know her better than most men know their own sister, I know when she's keeping her mouth shut and when she isn't."

'Well, I couldn't resist it – I just had to ask him if he hadn't always been a little in love with her. And he said: "A little perhaps." I thought he was going to say more but when he didn't I asked him why he didn't marry her.

'He just laughed. He was very drunk. Then he said suddenly: "Maybe I will! It's about time I got married." And he laughed again suddenly, as if he'd been very clever, and he went on laughing until he knocked over his glass . . . We went soon after that. He said he'd phone me before he left for New York next week, but somehow I doubt if he will."

Rebecca had been correct. Rohan had never phoned.

It was soon after that letter that Daniel had begun to make arrangements for his departure. It was impossible to leave at once, for the summer term was just beginning and he was bound to stay until it was finished, but just over three months later he said goodbye to his students in Accra, boarded the plane for London and began his long, dangerous journey back into the past.

All Rachel could think of was that Daniel was coming. After Rohan had told her the news and had said he would come round to her apartment straight away, she hadn't moved from her position in front of the mirror for a long time, and then at last she picked up the receiver of the phone again and cancelled her date for the evening.

Daniel was coming. It had been five years since Ruthven but now the five years were as if they had never existed at all. Daniel had left Africa and was already in London on his way back into their lives.

'Rebecca said in her letter that he wanted to see you,' Rohan had said to her over the phone. 'I don't understand it at all. You haven't been in touch with him, have you?'

And she had said blankly: 'Of course not.'

'Then why does he want to see you?'

'I – don't know.'

There was a long silence. Then:

'I'll come round right away,' Rohan had said abruptly, and hung up.

Daniel was coming. He wanted to see her. Why else would he want to see her unless it was because of Ruthven?

She saw the house then so clearly in her mind that it seemed to her that she would only have to close her eyes to be back there again breathing the damp pure air and feeling the soft sea breeze moist against her cheek. She saw the bare stretches of the moors ending in the dark lines of the forestry plantation, the desolate mountains, the swaying sea, and there before her eyes were the turrets and towers of Ruthven with their grey walls and blank windows.

Her thoughts, as if liberated at last after five years of constant suppression, went on and on and on. She was recalling each detail of her stay five years ago, reliving the horror of those last hours, the discovery of Charles' body, the realization of Decima's death, the agreement she had reached with Daniel . . .

Daniel. Daniel wanted to see her. Daniel was coming to New York.

When Rohan arrived a few minutes later she could hardly reach the door fast enough to answer the bell.

'We'd better go out, hadn't we?' he said as she let him in. 'There's no privacy here.'

'The others are out. They won't be back for hours yet.'

'Okay, then we'll stay here. Let me get you a drink.'

She asked for a Tom Collins and went into the kitchen to fetch the soda from the refrigerator. Later, when he had mixed the drinks, they sat down together on the couch and he gave her a cigarette. After a moment he said with wry cynicism:

'Perhaps he's coming to propose.'

'Oh, for God's sake, Rohan!' She was too tense to laugh at such a preposterous suggestion. 'You know as well as I do that whatever relationship existed between Daniel and me certainly wasn't on that plane. I don't know why he can possibly want to see me, least of all now, five years after Ruthven.'

There was a silence. Rohan leant forward to flick ash into the tray on the table and the light glinted for a moment on the gold of his cuff-links and the crisp white cuff of his shirt below the sleeve of his suit. He looked well dressed and elegant, and the years had smoothed out the angular thinness of his face and body so that all impression of immaturity had been eliminated from his appearance. His fair hair, which had never lost the shining brightness of childhood, was neat and well cut, his fine eyes reflecting the thoughts of his mind like an opaque mirror. She wondered again why he had never married. Perhaps he had always been too conscious of Decima's memory, just as she herself had always been too quick to remember Daniel . . .

'Raye?'

She suddenly realized he had asked her a question. 'I'm sorry,' she said confused. 'I was thinking of something else. What did you say?'

'I was just asking,' said Rohan, 'if you were quite sure you had no idea why Daniel should be looking for you?'

'What do you mean?'

'It's about Ruthven, isn't it?'

'Honestly, Rohan, I—'

'You shielded him, didn't you?'

There was a dead silence. They looked at one another. Then:

'Shielded him?' said Rachel.

'I always suspected you were keeping something back at the inquest. It had to do with Daniel, hadn't it? There was no one else you would have shielded.'

She didn't answer.

'Was Daniel involved?'

She still didn't answer.

'Raye—'

'It was as they said at the inquest,' she interrupted quickly, a spot of colour flaming in each cheek. 'Charles killed Decima and then committed suicide.'

'Yes,' said Rohan. 'Very convenient.' He watched his cigarette burn for a moment. Then suddenly his eyes were looking straight into hers and she knew at once what he was going to say. 'Did Daniel kill Decima?'

'Rohan—'

'He had a good enough motive. She told me on the eve of her birthday that she had originally wanted him to take her away with him, but he had lost interest in her and refused. She was furious with him and determined to pay him back. "I'll make trouble for him," she said to me, "I'll see he doesn't get that post he wants at Cambridge." She was full of plans to ruin him. Did he kill her?'

'I—' The horror of those last hours at Ruthven made speech difficult. 'I – don't know,' she said desperately at last. 'I just don't know, Rohan. He had the opportunity.

He was in Decima's room talking to her before I went down to the library to find Charles.'

'He was *where*?'

'In Decima's room. I knocked on her door to ask her if she was all right and she said she was. Someone else was with her at the time because I could hear the murmur of voices—'

'You mean,' said Rohan, slowly, 'that Decima was alive then?'

'Yes. Yes, she was alive.'

'But that means—'

'I know. Charles didn't kill Decima. He was the one who died first.'

'But my God, Raye, why on earth didn't you tell the police?'

'It was the easiest way out, Rohan . . .' She told him about Charles then, described how Daniel had destroyed the evidence that Rebecca had committed the murder. 'He said it was obvious that Decima had killed Charles—'

'Obvious?' said Rohan amazed. 'Obvious? Why the hell should Decima have killed Charles? I talked to her that evening! She was full of plans for getting a divorce – I had offered to take her away with me for a while – we had planned to leave Ruthven together the next day. That was why we both got drunk – we were drunk with exhilaration and pleasure! Why should she have murdered Charles? She didn't need to! Isn't it much more obvious that Rebecca killed him? She was out of her mind with frustration and rage. She could easily have killed him in a fit of fury and left Daniel to clear up after her! That to me is much more plausible than to suggest that Decima was the murderess.'

'Daniel said Rebecca had been framed.'

'Well, of course he'd say that! Of course!'

'But Decima – who pushed her from the window?'

'Why, Daniel, of course! Who else? When Rebecca came and told him what had happened, he suddenly saw how he could use the situation to his best advantage. If he were to silence Decima he could make it seem that Charles had killed his wife and then committed suicide. In that way he would extricate Rebecca from a very unpleasant situation and also eliminate the threat Decima presented to his future and prospects. So he went back to Decima's room – which he must have left shortly after you spoke to Decima on your way down to the library – killed her, and then returned to the library to rearrange the body and obliterate all trace of Rebecca from the scene of the crime. Imagine how he must have felt when he found you there! His one chance lay in the fact that you were sufficiently – that you cared for him enough to agree to shield him, so he told you what to tell the police, and gambled on the likelihood that you would do as he said.'

Rachel ground her cigarette to ashes, stood up and moved restlessly over to the window.

There was another long silence.

'Why on earth didn't you tell me this before, Raye?'

What was there to say? That she had never been able to acknowledge to herself the probability of Daniel's guilt? That even after five years she was still in love with the memory of a man who had never loved her in return? There was no logical answer, no easy explanation. 'It seemed the simplest way out at the time,' she heard herself say at last. 'I know it was weak and stupid of me, but it was such a temptation to do as he suggested and make the inquest a simple uncomplicated affair. I'd reached the end of the road by that time – I couldn't have endured more police investigations or the possibility of being detained at Ruthven any longer. I just wanted to leave, to forget, to escape.'

'It might have seemed the simplest way out at the time,' Rohan said, 'but I doubt if it's going to be quite so simple now. You realize of course why Daniel's coming to look for you.'

She stared at him blankly.

'He's heard through Rebecca that I'm in New York. He realizes that I'll be seeing you constantly. He thinks you're going to talk, Rachel – he thinks that in the end you'll tell me the truth. You're a menace to his security.'

The silence then was so acute that it seemed almost audible. The large, softly lit room seemed poised and waiting, and as Rachel stood beside the long mirror and caught sight of her reflection it was as if she saw a stranger with whom she had no connexion, a girl with wide, blank grey eyes in a white frozen face.

'What shall I do?' she said, and suddenly the years fell away and she was a child again turning to Rohan for comfort and advice. 'What shall I do?'

He got up, crossed the room and paused very close to her so that they were a mere few inches apart. 'You don't have to worry,' he said softly. 'You don't have to worry about anything. I'll look after you.' And he took her in his arms.

At first she was so surprised that she had no reaction at all and then she felt a surge of gratitude and a wave of overwhelming relief. Tears pricked her eyes. She slipped her arms around his waist and pressed her face against his shoulders, and presently she felt his lips brush her hair and touch her forehead. She raised her face to his. 'What shall we do?'

'We'll leave New York. I'll say I have to go home for a few days for family reasons – I'm more or less my own boss at work, so no one's going to ask any questions. You'll have to leave your job – or take some unpaid leave. One or the other. Is your passport in order? We'll leave New York tomorrow evening.'

'Supposing Daniel should arrive before then?'

'He doesn't know where you live – he only knows my address through Rebecca. His only way of contacting you will be by first contacting me, and I can stall him off. You're safe for a time, anyway. Have you got enough money for your fare?'

'Yes, I think so.'

'I'll ring up and make the reservations.' His hand was already on the phone. 'We'll try and get on a flight tomorrow evening.'

'Rohan—'

'Yes?'

'Suppose he follows us? Where shall we go when we get to England?'

'Somewhere remote and isolated, where we can set a trap for him. Of course! The obvious place! Why didn't I think of it before? We'll go back to Ruthven . . .'


# 4


Rebecca was at the airport to meet him as the plane from Accra finally touched down on British soil. After the long tedious minutes spent in Customs and Immigration, he passed through the barrier to join her and she was running into his arms.

'Danny . . . oh, Danny . . .' She was hugging him fiercely as if to make up for the five years he had spent away from her, and he pressed her to him tightly in response. Presently she looked up at him with shining eyes and they laughed together in happiness.

'How tanned you are!' she exclaimed. 'You look so well . . . Oh Danny, how wonderful to see you again . . .'

She had her car, a small Mini-Morris, parked outside the building and after they had all his luggage safely stowed away they set off to her tiny flat in Bayswater. They were just turning off the main road into Hammersmith some time later when she asked him the inevitable question.

'What are you going to do now, Danny? Have you any ideas?'

'Yes,' he said without hesitation, his eyes on the road ahead. 'I have a flight to New York booked on Monday. I'm going to spend a week or two in America.'

He heard her gasp, saw her hands swerve on the wheel. 'America?' she said incredulously, as if she could hardly believe her ears. 'New York?'

'I plan to go to the Embassy tomorrow to get a visa.'

After a moment she said: 'Why?'

He made no reply.

'It's not because of Rachel and Rohan, is it?'

He stared straight ahead of him, vaguely aware of all the changes in the Hammersmith he remembered, savouring the English roads and the English houses and the signposts bearing English names.

'If it is,' she said, 'you can save yourself a plane fare. They're back in England.'

The landscape froze before his eyes. He whirled to face her. 'They're back?'

'I was going to tell you—'

'Where are they?'

'Rohan called me yesterday morning soon after they'd arrived. He said they were over here for two weeks' holiday and were on their way north to Scotland.'

He stared at her incredulously. 'You didn't tell him, did you, that I was coming home?'

The car swerved again; she drew into the side of the road and switched off the engine. The traffic roared past.

'Well, yes,' she said. 'I did. I wrote and told him last week soon after you'd told me your decision.' She hesitated uneasily. Then: 'I'm sorry, Danny. I didn't realize—'

'It doesn't matter. It's done now. It was my fault for not anticipating that you'd tell him.' He switched on the engine again for her and pressed the starter. 'Don't let's stop here.'

'But I don't understand,' said Rebecca bewildered, slipping the car into gear and easing out the clutch. 'What do you want with them, Danny? Why do you want to see them now after all this time?'

'It's just something I have to straighten out with Rachel,' he said, and his mouth was dry as he spoke. 'I'd rather not go into details. Whereabouts in Scotland are they going?'

'To Kyle of Lochalsh,' said Rebecca. 'Rohan said they were planning to visit Ruthven.'

# 5

They had taken the night train from London to Edinburgh and had just had lunch on Princes Street by a window which faced the castle. They had already hired a car for a week at one of the local garages and were planning to set off after lunch on the north journey into the Highlands towards Fort William, Inverness and Kyle of Lochalsh. The sun was shining. Outside, the gardens at the foot of the castle were immensely green and the grey castle walls, standing aloft on the black upthrust of volcanic rock, shimmered in the heat haze.

'I still don't see how meeting Daniel at Ruthven will ever induce him to admit anything,' Rachel was saying as the waitress brought them coffee.

'He'll have to admit something,' Rohan said drily. 'He won't follow us all the way to Ruthven for the purpose of keeping his mouth shut.'

'But why couldn't we have met him in London?'

'Because he's more likely to take risks and give himself away in a remote place. In London he'd be too much on his guard.'

'Do you think so? I still can't help wishing we didn't have to go back.'

'Look,' said Rohan, 'who's in charge of this plan – you or me? Right. Well, sooner or later Daniel's going to catch up with you and if he's going to catch up with you, it's best for me to be there too, isn't it? Right. Well, assuming that I'll have to face a potentially dangerous man and deal with him in whatever way the situation demands, I think I have the right to choose a location. And I chose Ruthven.'

'Yes,' said Rachel. 'All right.'

He capitulated at once. 'Look, Raye, I'm sorry – I didn't mean to upset you – I know it's all the most awful strain for you—'

'No,' she said. 'It's all right. Really, Rohan, it's all right.'

They drank their coffee. Then:

'Rohan.'

'Yes?'

'You're not going to kill him, are you?'

'Not unless I have to,' said Rohan, 'but if he tries to harm you I'll break every bone in his body without any hesitation at all.'

'Is that why you have brought the gun?'

'Well, I have to have some protection, don't I? Besides, he may well be armed himself.'

'Yes,' said Rachel. 'I suppose he might.'

Rohan's hand slid across the table and closed on hers. 'You're not still in love with him, are you?'

'No, of course not. That's all over and done with and has been for five years.'

He went on holding her hand beneath his own. After a while he said: 'How much longer do we have to go on pretending to ourselves that we're just good friends?'

She looked up. The sun was slanting right through the window into her eyes and he saw her expression of astonishment before she leaned forward out of the shaft of light and put her face in shadow. 'I'm not sure,' she said at last, 'that I quite understand you.'

'No?' he said. 'It's very simple. Now that I know for certain that you've got over this feeling you had for Daniel, I was wondering if you'd marry me.'

She was silent for a long time, looking into his eyes. In the end she looked away. Her face was grave and still, and it was impossible to tell what she was thinking, but he knew instinctively that she was going to refuse.

'Do you intend to remain unmarried all your life?' he heard himself say quickly. 'We know each other so well, Rachel – we can relax and feel at ease with each other, we suit each other so well. Why go on as we have been doing in an endless attempt to find someone else? I would have asked you before if I hadn't thought you were still emotionally involved with Daniel. I've known for a long while that you're the woman I want to marry.'

'No,' she said. 'I'm just the *kind* of woman you want to marry. It's not the same thing.'

'You don't understand—'

'You don't love me, Rohan! Well, yes perhaps you do in your own way, but not in a way a husband loves his wife.'

'You're a perfectionist,' he said. 'You're waiting for a glamorized, unreal brand of love which doesn't really exist. You'll wait for ever, Rachel, can't you see? You'll wait for ever for the kind of love that doesn't exist outside the pages of romantic fiction!'

'I'd rather wait for ever,' she said deliberately, 'than marry a man I only half-loved.' And then instantly: 'Rohan, it's not because I care nothing for you – I do care a great deal, you know I do – but surely you must see that we wouldn't be suited, that marriage wouldn't really work . . . I'm sorry.' She fumbled with her handbag, almost knocked over her coffee cup. 'Shall we go? There are people over there waiting for tables . . .'

He rose without a word, helped her on with her coat and then went to the cashier's desk to pay the bill.

'I'm sorry, Rohan,' she said again as they went out into the street. 'Please forgive me—'

'There's nothing to forgive.' He smiled at her. 'If you have such qualms about the subject we'd do better not to marry. But in case you should change your mind, the offer still stands.'

They walked down Princes Street, turned up the road where they had left the car. Rachel's mind was in such turmoil that she scarcely knew where she was going. Rohan's proposal had caught her completely unawares and her thoughts, already confused over Daniel, were whirled into greater bewilderment and chaos than ever before. She had answered Rohan instinctively, but even now her logic was beginning to question her instinct. Every reason which Rohan had put forward for marriage was sound; there was every likelihood that they would be as happily married as most couples; he cared for her enough to be with her now when she needed him most of all, and he was always the first person she turned to; she was nearly twenty-eight years old and could certainly do far worse than marry Rohan who at thirty-one was successful in his work, popular with his friends, and good looking in his own unusual way.

Why, then, had she refused his offer so quickly that her reaction was almost an automatic reflex of her mind?

The answer came straight away, flashing across her thoughts before she could even struggle to suppress it, and she knew well enough why she had rejected Rohan.

He was nothing compared to Daniel.

## 6

Daniel and Rebecca had discussed Ruthven in great detail for some time. The subject, unmentioned between them for so long, proved to be so enlightening to both of them that they had recalled with meticulous precision each incident and scene which had preceded the murders. Afterwards Daniel felt so exhausted that he had a bath and slept for a couple of hours before shaving and getting dressed. It was evening, and from the noises in the kitchen he guessed that Rebecca was cooking a meal for them. He picked up the receiver and phoned London Airport.

'When's the next flight to Inverness, please?'

'One moment, sir.'

His call was switched to another extension. There was a click, another voice, and he had to repeat his question.

'The next flight leaves at ten o'clock tonight, sir.'

'Is there a vacancy on it?'

'For how many?'

'Just one.'

'One moment.' Another click, a buzz, a few seconds of empty silence. Then: 'Yes, we have a cancellation so there's a seat available. Would you—'

'Yes,' said Daniel. 'I'll take it. My name is Carey. What time should I be at the airport and where can I pick up my ticket?'

Rebecca had come out of the kitchen but he scarcely

noticed her. Then: 'Thank you,' he said, and hung up the receiver.

'Danny—'

'I'm sorry,' he said to her. 'But I really have to go. I shan't be away long, only for a couple of days or so. I'll explain all about it when I get back.'

'Do you want me to come with you?' She was fighting to overcome her disappointment at the thought of losing him so soon. 'Can I help at all?'

'No,' he said, 'this is something which has to be settled between Quist, Rachel and myself. You stay here. I'll be all right – I know exactly what I'm doing . . .'


7


Rachel and Rohan did not know that while they were spending the night at Kyle of Lochalsh Daniel was sleeping in a hotel at Inverness. They had arrived after dark and found rooms in one of the small hotels near the harbour. After a late supper they had gone to bed and slept until it was time for breakfast at nine o'clock the next morning.

The weather was as unexpectedly fine as it had been in Edinburgh the previous day. Rachel woke to find the sun sparkling on the harbour and glittering on the array of boats moored along the quay. Across the sea loomed the distant heights of Skye and the gulls wheeled and mewed over the stone houses of the town around her. Once she was dressed she paused by the window again to survey the scene, and then Rohan was knocking on her door and they went downstairs to breakfast together.

'How did you sleep?' said Rohan over the toast and marmalade.

'Surprisingly well. I suppose I was very tired after the journey.'

'Yes, I was too.'

They ate for a moment in silence. Then: 'I'll ask the landlord where we can hire a boat from,' Rohan said.

'There shouldn't be any difficulty in getting one.'

'No, I shouldn't think so,' said Rachel, and felt a small core of fear harden noticeably inside her.

She was dreading the return to Ruthven. It had been bad enough returning to Kyle of Lochalsh with its memories of shopping with Decima and the meeting with Daniel in the wheelhouse, but the very idea of seeing Ruthven again was almost more than she could bear. Closing her mind against it resolutely, she poured herself another cup of tea and helped herself to an additional slice of toast, but her nervousness was soon so immense that she had to leave both unfinished.

'Ready?' said Rohan at last. 'Then let's go.'

It took them about an hour to find the type of boat they wanted. Then after they had stocked the small galley with provisions of all kinds, they cast off from the quay and headed out to sea.

They lost sight of the town less than twenty minutes later.

The wave of isolation that hit Rachel then was so immense that she scarcely knew how to control it. She left the deck and shut herself in the galley below in the hope that she would be able to block out her fear if she didn't see the increasing bleakness of the landscape and the appalling loneliness of those barren shores, but the fear persisted and in the end she drank a double Scotch to steady her nerves. After that she felt better. She had another, to be quite safe, and then went back on deck to join Rohan in the wheelhouse.

'How are you doing?'

'Pretty well. It's a beautiful day, isn't it? I've never seen the sea so calm here before.'

The boat sped on through the dark blue waters, and the landscape, basking in the unaccustomed sunshine, seemed to have lost its quality of overwhelming desolation and become breathtaking in its stark magnificence. Rachel found she could look at it now without feeling fear or dread, and when, at last, she saw the promontory which would bring them to Ruthven, she felt her nerves sharpen again in anticipation.

'Isn't it odd?' said Rohan, and she knew then that he too was uneasy. 'It's just as if nothing had changed. It's hard to realize that Charles and Decima aren't waiting to meet us and that Mrs Willie isn't baking bread in the kitchen and that George isn't snoozing before the fire in the hall.'

They rounded the promontory. There was a shower of spray as the boat met a complex of currents, and then they were heading directly inland and Ruthven lay before them across the water. The sun shone on the grey walls and made the background of mountains and moors shimmer in a green-purple haze.

'I've never seen it look so beautiful,' said Rohan. 'Perhaps now at last I can see why Decima loved it so much.'

The blank windows stared at them unseeingly. As they drew nearer they saw the garden was more wild and untended than ever and that the gamekeeper's little croft was already falling into ruins.

They reached the jetty. Rohan manoeuvred the boat into position and jumped ashore to fasten the painter to the bollard.

'The boards of the jetty aren't too secure,' he warned her. 'Careful how you go.'

'Thanks.' She scrambled ashore and stood still for a moment. The sea breeze fanned her cheek; a gull screamed above her. Everywhere was very still.

'I'm going up to the house,' said Rohan. 'You needn't come if you don't want to, but I'm curious as to what's happened and what it looks like now.'

She was glad he gave her the chance to refuse. 'I'll stay here,' she said. 'I don't particularly want to go back.'

'OK. I won't be long.'

She watched him move quickly up the path to the house. When he reached the front door he discovered it was locked and she saw him go round to the back and disappear from sight.

She waited some time in the sunshine, and then slowly

the curiosity began to seep through her until she wished she had gone with him. After dreading the return to Ruthven so violently, it now seemed that the reality of return was not nearly as disturbing as she had feared it might be, and in the relief of realizing this she wanted to go into the house and try to blunt the edge of her worst memories by revisiting the scenes under different circumstances.

Presently she left the deck and stepped ashore on to the creaking jetty again. It took her about five minutes to reach the house. Rohan, she discovered, had climbed in through the kitchen window which might or might not have been broken before his arrival. As she was wearing slacks it was easy enough for her to clamber in after him, and soon she was walking through the huge deserted rooms and making her way into the massive emptiness of the great hall.

'Rohan?' she called uncertainly as she reached the foot of the stairs, but there was no reply.

Presently she mounted the staircase and then paused to listen. It was very quiet, very still. The sunshine streamed through the long windows of the hall, but the house was eerie in its deserted emptiness and Rachel was conscious of the smell of damp and decay.

She moved down the corridor and paused for some time outside the door of Decima's room, but suddenly her courage ebbed and she hadn't enough left to turn the handle and walk in. She went back down the passage to the head of the stairs and all at once it seemed to her as if she were re-enacting her movements on the night of the murders and she had just stopped outside Decima's door to ask her if she were all right. She reached the landing and paused to look down into the hall.

She could see the scene then as if it were yesterday, the long banquet table, the red candles snuffed and gutted, the remains of the dinner still strewn over the white tablecloth, the twin silver epergnes, the drooping flowers. Around the hall were the lamps, still burning, and the red embers in the two fireplaces. George, the St

Bernard, had been asleep before the hearth. Or had he? No, that had been earlier. When she had returned to the hall to find Charles, George had been asleep outside the door of the small drawing room. She could remember wondering why he had chosen to lie in that draughty corner when both fires were still glowing in the grates.

As she began to descend the stairs it suddenly occurred to her to wonder again why the dog had been lying there. If Daniel had been in the drawing room, then it would have explained the dog's presence, for George had followed Daniel everywhere, but Daniel had been upstairs talking to Decima in her room.

Or had he?

She stopped dead.

She was recalling the scene in the library when she had found Charles. There had been the closing of a door far away, the sound of footsteps crossing the hall and then Daniel had entered the room just after she had managed to hide behind the curtains. He had come from the hall, from the drawing room. She would never have heard the door of Decima's room close. It had been the door of the drawing room where the dog was waiting for him.

Daniel hadn't been in Decima's room at all.

Then who had been with her as Rachel passed the door? Rebecca? But it had been a man's low murmur she had heard. Not Daniel. And not Charles, who was already dead. That left Rohan. Rohan had been with Decima just before she died.

But Rohan had been blind drunk. She had had to put him to bed.

Or had he been shamming? She had thought at the time that for two persons accustomed to liquor they had managed to get surprisingly drunk. Supposing it had all been an act, a plan to set the stage – for what?

For Charles' murder . . .

Rebecca had been framed. Rohan, thanks to Rachel's testimony, would be found to be much too drunk to commit a crime. And Decima . . . Daniel had carried Decima upstairs to her room. He would also testify that she had been too drunk to commit murder. But Daniel hadn't stayed in Decima's room because when Rachel reached the hall on her way to find Charles, George was already outside the drawing-room door waiting for Daniel to come out. And Decima, Rachel knew, had at that time been alive and well.

Daniel hadn't killed Decima. Rebecca? No, because the voice talking to Decima had belonged to a man. And Charles was already dead.

Rohan had killed Decima. And either he or Decima had first killed Charles.

*Rohan was a murderer* was all she was conscious of thinking, her frightened thoughts repeating themselves over and over again in a paralysis of horror. *Rohan was a murderer.*

And then the full impact of the situation struck her and she was so unnerved that she could neither move nor breathe.

Rohan was a murderer and she was alone with him at Ruthven.

## chapter 2

1

Daniel rose early, had hired a car by eight-thirty and by nine o'clock had left Inverness behind and was driving west over the Highlands to Kyle of Lochalsh. It was raining. Clouds obscured the mountains, and mist trailed over the vast expanses of sodden moors. There were few other cars on the road. The rain slewed remorselessly on to the windscreen to make driving difficult, as he drove on over that storm-torn landscape it seemed to him that the five hot steamy years in Accra had been a dream and that he had never left this beautiful appalling remoteness with its rains and mists and pale shrouded northern light.

This is the real Scotland, he thought. Glasgow is for the business men; Edinburgh is for the tourists. But up here north of the Highland Line is the Scotland which is for no one, least of all for intruders, the Scotland which made even the Romans turn back unnerved in retreat. No wonder they believed it was the very edge of the world, the remotest corner of land known to man. The mountains are crowded together as if waiting to entomb all trespassers in the valleys, and the moors rise up from the road like the sides of a grave.

The heavy rain continued for some time. He was just wondering if there was any possibility at all of a break in the weather, when the road surmounted a pass and suddenly the clouds lifted from the mountain slopes, the rain lessened, and the sky seemed brighter. Within twenty minutes the highest of the inland mountains were behind him and he had travelled into a different world; the sun shone, the sky was blue and as he descended from the hills to Kyle of Lochalsh he could see that the horizon of the Atlantic was hazy with the promise of good weather.

He drove into the town.

Outside the small inn where he and Charles had often stopped for a beer after a shopping expedition, he parked the car and went inside. The landlord's wife was industriously sweeping out the bar with a long broom.

'Good morning,' she began brightly, and then stopped in stupefaction as she recognized him.

'Good morning,' he said, and waited for her to give him the information he wanted.

'Well!' she said amazed. 'Well!' And when he was silent, she added: 'It *is* Mr Carey, isn't it?'

'It is. You've got a good memory, Mrs MacCleod.'

She was pleased that he remembered her name. 'Well, now,' she said sympathetically. 'What a shame! You've just missed them – they were staying down the road at the Stuart Arms. My husband was over there talking to Ian Black, the landlord, when they arrived last night, and he said— '

'They've already gone?'

'Hired a boat this morning from Duncan Robertson – I saw them walk along the quay just a little while ago—'

'How long ago?'

She looked vaguely surprised by the abruptness of his questions. 'Why, two or three hours ago, perhaps. I'd just lit the fire in the kitchen and then I came in here to listen to the weather forecast on the wireless, and lo and behold, who should I see when I looked out of the window but Mr Quist and the young lady walking past to the quay . . . How long will you all be staying here, Mr Carey? Such a surprise to see you again. I said to my husband—'

'Not long,' said Daniel. 'Thank you, Mrs MacCleod.' And before the woman could even draw breath to say goodbye he was moving swiftly out of the house and down to the quayside and the harbour.

# 2

Rachel's first thought was to find the gun. Blindly, almost without thinking, she went out of the hall and back through the kitchens again to the broken window. As if in a nightmare her movements seemed curiously slow and clumsy; the window through which she had climbed with such ease earlier now seemed a difficult and dangerous obstacle in her path, and she cut her hand slightly on a piece of broken glass as she scrambled over the sill.

*I must get back to the boat,* she thought. *I must find that gun.*

There was no other thought in her mind at all. Her eyes saw the brilliant sparkle of the sun on the sea and clear sky, but they made no impression on her. She ran down towards the jetty, pushing her way through the overgrown garden, and soon she was gasping for breath and her heart was pounding in her lungs.

*I must get to the boat,* said the voice in her mind over and over again. *I must find the gun.*

She went on running. It seemed a long way to the jetty, and again she was reminded of some hideous nightmare in which one ran and ran yet never reached one's destination. Brambles tore at her slacks; giant bushes and unwieldy shrubs leered in her face and then suddenly she was out of the garden and running along the path down to the jetty.

*I must get to the boat*, she kept thinking. *I have to find that gun.*

Her foot stumbled against a rock; she nearly fell, and then at last reached the rotting boards of the jetty and scrambled aboard the boat. She went to the wheelhouse. No gun. He must have left it below. She was beside the hatch suddenly, almost falling down the gangway to the lower deck. She could picture the gun lying on the top of Rohan's suitcase, and the suitcase was tossed across one of the bunks. . . .

She flung open the cabin door with a gasp of relief and then felt the gasp freeze in her throat.

'Hullo,' said Rohan. 'I thought I'd lost you. Where did you go?'

Instinct made her brain miraculously clear; her reactions were suddenly as sharp as a razor-edge.

'I went to the house and couldn't find you.' She made no effort to hide the fact that she had been running, and sank down on the bunk opposite him to regain her breath. 'Then suddenly I had an awful panic and saw ghosts in every corner. I ran all the way back here.'

'So it seems!' He smiled at her reassuringly. He had the gun in his hands and was checking to see that it was loaded correctly. He looked calm and untroubled, and the very familiarity of his expression and attitude gave Rachel a strange confidence. This was the Rohan she had known all her life, her friend of nearly all her life, the man whom she knew better than anyone else.

Rohan wouldn't harm her.

He stood up. 'Daniel won't be here for a while yet,' he said, tucking the gun into his belt. 'Let's take some of the food we bought in Kyle and walk along the beach away from the house. I don't want to sit on deck and look at Ruthven. I'm not surprised you felt panic-stricken when you went inside! I felt much the same myself.'

'Where were you?' she said. 'I couldn't find you anywhere.'

He moved to the door. 'I went to Decima's room,' he said abruptly, and for a moment she thought he wasn't going to add any more. Then: 'I shouldn't have gone. It was horrible.'

He went up on deck and she followed him.

'Why did you go?' she said.

'I don't know,' he said, and his eyes as he turned to look at her were dark and blank. 'I don't know. It was as if she were up there waiting for me, challenging me to come back.' He stepped on to the jetty, and then hesitated. 'We forgot the food.'

'We can always come back,' she said, 'and I'm not hungry.'

'All right.' He walked down the jetty and led the way out to the beach.

The sun was warm; the surf roared in their ears; beneath their feet the sand was firm and smooth. They walked for a long time in silence, and beside them towered the cliffs with the gaping caves and litter of black rocks embedded in the white sand. The tide was still going out. Rohan seemed engrossed in his private thoughts, and Rachel, her initial panic overcome, felt ice-cool and alert. It was not until they rounded the promontory that she was aware of the ache of tension in her body and the fear crawling up and down her spine.

'We're at the quicksands.' Her voice was harsh and abrupt.

'So we are,' said Rohan. He stood still, gazing out over the miles of white beach ahead shining deceptively in the bright light. 'Cluny Sands. Just lying there peaceful in the sun. Waiting.' He turned to face her. 'It's odd,' he said. 'But I feel so strongly as if everything here is waiting. The house was waiting, the shore was waiting and now these sands are waiting too.'

Rachel turned aside sharply. 'That's melodramatic, Rohan, and you know it. Don't be absurd.'

'But don't you feel it?' he said. 'Don't you? Don't you feel that everything is poised and waiting?'

'I could imagine all kinds of things if I wanted to,' she heard herself answer tersely. 'If one stays in these surroundings long enough one could imagine anything. It's that kind of place.'

She hoped he couldn't hear the thumping of her heart, nor see the trembling of her clenched hands.

'Let's sit down,' he said. 'Let's sit down for a while.'

'Why?'

'Why?' he said. 'Why, to wait for Daniel, of course. We're waiting too now, just like everything else. Everything's waiting for Daniel.'


3


Daniel took the boat far out to sea before heading north to Ruthven. He had no wish to be blatantly visible from the beach and he was already trying to decide where to land. If he went to the jetty he would immediately announce his arrival. Perhaps if he were to try and anchor near the beach between Ruthven and Cluny Sands he would run less risk of Rohan seeing him immediately. It might be worth trying, although he was unaccustomed to boats after five years away from them, and did not want to risk running aground in shallow waters.

The boat sped on over the calm sea and left a wake trailing in the dark blue water. The air was full of warmth and peace, and the gulls soared aloft on the soft breeze, their wings white arcs against the sky.

He lit a cigarette.

He was thinking of Rachel again, visualizing her with Quist, unknowing and unsuspecting, being carried deeper and deeper into dangerous waters, manoeuvred into a position from which she could not escape. He was conscious of how his attitude towards her had changed.

He had left Accra to protect his sister, to warn Rachel to say nothing to Quist about the false verdict at the inquest, and had instead discovered that his sister was entirely innocent. She had insisted her innocence and he had believed her; her protests were too genuine to be disbelieved. And then, even before he had time to feel ashamed of his suspicions, he had realized the extreme danger of Rachel's position. If Rachel once revealed the full extent of her knowledge to Quist she would always be a potential source of danger to him. The number of suspects was so small; she had no doubt left Ruthven believing Rebecca to be guilty, probably even suspecting Daniel himself to be in some way involved, but if she once thought them innocent there was only Rohan Quist left to suspect . . .

And Quist was a murderer who had killed before and would kill again. Daniel could remember thinking how ironic it was that Decima, who had been without passion herself, should in the end have been victim of a *crime passionnel*.

And now Rachel was alone with Quist at Ruthven. Perhaps by this time she had guessed the truth. If she were to hint for one moment to Quist that she suspected him . . .

Daniel threw away his cigarette.

There was no time to lose.


4

She was almost sure that Rohan was asleep. He was lying face downwards on the sands, his head pillowed in his forearms, his breathing quiet and even. The gun, which he had taken out of his belt for greater comfort, lay peacefully beside him, its barrel glinting in the sunlight.

She picked it up.

Rohan didn't stir.

How did one remove the bullets from guns? If she could somehow take out the bullets, then Daniel would be safe, and she could return the gun to Rohan so that he would never know she had tampered with it.

She stood up very slowly, gun in hand. The tide had turned, she noticed; the waves were creeping back over the sands and the thunder of the surf seemed more powerful in her ears. She moved nearer the cliffs, and then all of a sudden she was amongst the rocks and Rohan could no longer see her.

She looked down at the gun in her hands and examined it.

It was unnerving not to be able to see Rohan, not to know whether he was still asleep. In a sudden moment of panic she moved back to the shore, but he was still sleeping, his position unchanged, and she felt her body relax slightly in relief.

It was then that she heard the suck of the undertow as the tide crept in over the quicksands.

Withdrawing behind a rock again she struggled with the gun, and at last, just as she was giving up hope, the metal broke open and the bullets spilled into her hands.

She went back to Rohan, stopped just long enough to put the gun down beside him and then went as close as she dared to the sands.

The bullets were soon gone. She had thrown them into the sands in the path of the incoming tide and they only took a few seconds to vanish from sight. She was just wiping the sweat from her forehead and pushing back her hair when his voice said softly from behind her: 'Why the hell did you do that?' and whirling round she found herself face to face with him and her back to Cluny Sands.


5

'So you know,' he said. 'I wondered if you did.'

He stood watching her, his blue shirt brilliant against the background of sand and rock, his fair hair shining in the sun, his eyes dark, opaque, expressionless. After a moment he said: 'How did you know?'

And she said: 'I realized just now in the hall that Daniel hadn't been with Decima just before she died. The scene jogged my memory and I realized then that Daniel had been downstairs in the drawing room when I had gone to the library to find Charles. He wasn't in Decima's room, and yet I'd heard a man's voice there. And then I knew that you had pretended to be drunk earlier and that, after I'd left you, you'd slipped out to the library.'

'I went to Decima's room first to get Rebecca's diary and the knife.' He half-turned so that he faced the sea, and she saw that his hands were clenched as he thrust them into his pockets. Presently he said: 'It's hard for me to explain my feelings for Decima. How can a woman ever understand? I was infatuated with her. She was an obsession with me. For a long time after she married Charles I tried to pretend that there was no infatuation and no obsession, but you can't pretend for ever that black is white and white is black. And every time I went back to Ruthven my hatred for Charles grew and the pretence of not caring for Decima grew harder.

'Do you remember how I used to admire Charles – almost hero-worshipped him, when we were young? My distinguished cousin! My respected, esteemed, learned cousin who taught at Oxford and was one of the great scholars of his day! Charles was everything I knew I could never be. No wonder I admired him so much. And then gradually the beginnings of the long disillusionment set in, and I saw everything I had believed in was a myth, a self-deception. Charles was a brilliant scholar, but he was weak, opinionated, vain and pompous. And worst of all, he had won Decima, the greatest prize for any man to win, and then he had estranged and antagonized her so that she wanted only to be rid of him. Can you imagine how I felt? Can't you see? The more I allowed myself to admit my obsession for Decima the more I hated Charles, and all the while I had to conceal my feelings, to pretend and pretend and pretend . . . Something happens to a man when all the most violent passions are twisted together within him and suppressed again and again. You live in an unreal world and only your thoughts and wishes are reality. I wished Charles dead and that Decima were mine – that was my reality. I lived with that wish for a long time until it was more real to me than anything else in the world. It was a reality even before I began my last visit to Ruthven . . .

'I remember very well the first time I saw Daniel Carey. I had just arrived at Kyle of Lochalsh and was drinking beer in the pub overlooking the harbour when I saw Charles' boat draw up to the quay. Daniel was with Decima. I knew as soon as I saw him that nothing would ever be the same again and, even as I watched them laughing together while they walked down the quay, I was convinced that she loved him.'

The tide crept nearer; a huge wave broke and rushed greedily towards them as it ate into virgin sand.

'And then you came,' he said. 'And miraculously, almost unbelievably, Daniel seemed to tire of Decima and turn to you. It was then, and not till then, that Decima turned to me and it seemed at last that I was going to get everything I'd ever wanted.

'I suppose Decima guessed from the beginning how I felt for her. You remember she told you – to confuse you – that Charles was glad you'd come to Ruthven because it would divert her attention from me, and that Charles suspected us of having an affair? That was untrue, for Charles knew nothing about how I felt, but I got a bad shock when you repeated the story to me! I then realized that Decima had merely told you that to throw you off the scent and conceal from you her involvement with Daniel. At that time, of course, there was nothing between us, but I think she sensed my feelings nonetheless. Women have an instinct for divining how a man cares, I think, no matter how much he may lie and pretend to the contrary out of pride, and so when she realized at last that she could no longer rely on Daniel she came at once to me for help.

'It was the day of the dinner party. She said she wanted the opportunity to talk to me alone, so we took the boat and went out to sea, intending just to cruise around in open waters for a while, but then as you know a storm blew up and we had to head for Kyle for shelter. We spent quite a long time at sea before we had to seek shelter. She let me do exactly as I wished. Later, when we were in Kyle waiting for the storm to die, she told me she would marry me if she were free but that Charles had now quite made up his mind not to divorce her, and it seemed that she was tied to him indefinitely.

'We were drinking by that time. Alcohol seemed to clarify the situation and make everything so obvious.

'"I would kill Charles," she said, "but I'd be too afraid, too frightened . . . And how could I kill him? I haven't the strength or the knowledge." She seemed so powerless, so vulnerable, so young . . .

'I said: "I'd kill him for you, if I could."

'I should have guessed then what was happening, because she had the whole scheme ready and planned – she must have worked it out as soon as she had discarded her plans for using Daniel the day before, and she already had Rebecca's knife and diary hidden in readiness. I should have realized that she was only using me, just as she had tried to use Daniel, but I was long past sane, sensible reasoning, far beyond all sanity and logic.

'"It would be so easy," she said. "Can't you see? Everything is already set perfectly. Rebecca has the ideal motive for murdering Charles. We can use her knife to kill him and set the scene to make it look as if she killed him in a fit of rage – he has, after all, just ended their affair against her will. I saw her this morning weeping and red-eyed, and Charles had told me by that time that he was sending the Careys away. Rebecca is the perfect scapegoat – but we must take care no suspicion falls on us. We'll go back tonight at the end of the dinner party and pretend to be drunk out of our minds. The dinner party will collapse in chaos, and someone will see us to our rooms. As soon as you're sure the coast's clear, you can come back to my room and I'll give you the dagger and Rebecca's diary which I stole from her earlier. Then after it's done you can go back to your room and no one will ever know that we weren't really drunk at all, and after it's all over we can go away together.'"

A gull wheeled and soared high over the sea. Behind them the tide was still sucking over the quicksands but they no longer heard it.

'So it wasn't Decima who killed Charles,' Rachel heard herself say. 'It was you.'

'Yes,' he said. 'I killed him. After you'd led me to bed I waited and then went to Decima's room. Daniel carried her upstairs a few minutes later and I hid in the cupboard till he'd gone. Decima asked him where Charles was and he said that Charles had gone to the library.

'I took the knife and the diary and went down the back stairs to the kitchen. Mrs Willie had gone back to her croft so there was no one about, and when I reached the hall I saw that too was empty – apart from the dog sleeping outside the drawing-room door.

'I went to the library. Charles was just sitting with his head in his hands. He didn't even see the dagger until I was much too close for him to avoid it, and he died almost at once. No one saw me leave the library afterwards. I retraced my steps up the back stairs and went to Decima's room to tell her that all was well, and that was when you passed by in the corridor and heard us talking.

'It was after you'd gone that my whole world collapsed. I started to talk to Decima of when we would go away together, but she wasn't interested. I tried to kiss her, but she was lifeless, cold as a statue, remoter from me than she'd ever been.

'"What's the matter?" I said frantically. "What have I done?" And then suddenly, hideously, I saw the truth.

'She cared for me no more than she cared for anyone else. She was completely egocentric, a narcissus in love with herself, withdrawn from other beings and beyond their reach in her own private world. Charles was an obstacle in her path so he had to be removed. How could she remove him without getting hurt herself? Why, get someone else to murder him for her! Why not? Men were always falling over themselves to do as she wished. At first she thought Daniel would probably be just like all the others. He would do as well as anyone. But first of all she must plan very carefully so that no suspicion could possibly fall on her.

'She was aware that Charles was having an affair with Rebecca, but she didn't plan then, as she did later, to frame Rebecca for Charles' murder. She had planned a scheme long before she knew about Charles and Rebecca, and it was this scheme which she intended to put into operation. She was to act the part of the terrified young wife in fear of her husband but much too nervous and weak to attempt to remove him. Then, after Charles was dead, she could sob on the Chief Detective-Inspector's shoulder and confess that Daniel Carey had been so in love with her that he had killed Charles to prevent her suffering any further and to remove her from all danger.

'But first of all she had to create the impression of the terrified young wife, and to do that she needed an audience.

'So she invited you to Ruthven and spun you the story about Charles wanting to kill her. You were to be her audience, the witness who would later back up her story to the police. That was why you were invited to Ruthven.

'And then everything went wrong with that scheme and got out of hand so that she was forced to reshape her plans. You fell in love with Daniel and she knew she could never trust you to give evidence for her against him. At the same time she realized that Daniel wasn't so infatuated with her that he would kill for her. In fact, he wasn't infatuated at all.

'So she used me. She tore down the façade I had presented to everyone since her marriage and destroyed all my defences and then gathered together all my love and hate and twisted them into her own distorted pattern. And it wasn't until afterwards in her room that I realized what she had done.

'I have no memory after that. I remember staring at her as I recognized the truth and then nothing at all except isolated things – pulling open the window, the rush of cold air, my hand on her mouth as she tried to scream. I flung her from me as if I would smash every ounce of bone and blood in her evil rotten body, and after that there was just a dreadful blankness until I reached my room again and locked the door against the nightmare of what had happened . . . I've been trying to keep my mind locked against it ever since. The last five years have been one long struggle to shut out all the dreadful memories and submerge myself in something new and far away in another world, but there are some things you can't shut out no matter how much you want to, and when I came back here today and went to her room I knew I would never get rid of them, never, no matter how long I lived and no matter where I went.'

The surf broke down the beach and sped swiftly across the sands to their feet. It touched Rohan's shoes but he seemed not to notice for he made no effort to step back.

'I'm glad I've told you,' he said after a while. 'I've wanted to tell you for a long time. Perhaps that's why I asked you to marry me. I'd have been safe if we were married, because a wife can't give evidence against her husband.'

He was still looking out to sea, and suddenly she saw him stiffen. 'There's a boat out there,' he said, pointing behind her over her shoulder. 'A small boat a long way out – can you see it?'

Rachel spun round.

At the same moment a huge wave broke and streaked up to her, knocking her off balance, and even as she stumbled backwards before falling, she heard the roar of the undertow and the greedy sucking of the quicksands beneath her feet.


6


Daniel saw the blue of Rohan's shirt from out at sea, and immediately altered his course to head inland. As he drew closer he strained his eyes to see what was happening on the beach but beyond the fact that Quist and Rachel were by the water's edge and Rachel appeared to be on her knees he had no idea what they were doing.

And then Quist started to run. Almost at the same moment Daniel realized that Rachel, who was still motionless, was on the edge of Cluny Sands.

Pulling out the throttle he revved the engine into a higher speed and headed straight for the beach.


## 7

Rohan saw the boat coming and stopped in his tracks. It came on without faltering and then, just as he thought it must surely come aground, the engines were cut and Daniel, emerging from the wheelhouse, stooped to the deck to pick up the anchor and fling it overboard. Then he stooped again and this time when he straightened his back he had a coil of rope in his hands.

Rohan thought for a moment, his brain suddenly cool, sharp and detached. If he were lucky he could easily deal with Daniel, who would be much too preoccupied with the rescue to notice Rohan's movements. And Rachel . . . Rachel was stuck in the quicksand. He could always say afterwards that he had been unable to reach her. Two victims for the quicksands. He could almost see the newspaper headlines. Dual tragedy on remote Scottish coast, heroism of lone survivor . . .

He stood his ground, waiting.

On the boat Daniel had slung the rope over his shoulder and was lowering himself into the shallows. As he moved swiftly through the water to the shore he made no attempt to speak and Rohan found his silence curiously unnerving.

'I was going back to the house,' he heard himself say rapidly as Daniel came abreast of him. 'There's a ladder there. I thought if I could crawl along the ladder I could reach her. I wasn't running away.'

Daniel pushed past him without a word, and broke into a run.

'Daniel—' Rohan stared after him blankly for a moment, and then pulling himself together he ran back along the beach to where Rachel had left his empty gun.


## 8

'Wait,' said Daniel to Rachel. 'Don't move. The more you struggle the farther in you'll sink.' He was uncoiling the rope as he spoke, his fingers working to tie the last yard into a noose.

'Rohan was going to get a ladder,' she said, and her voice was shaking in spite of all her efforts to keep calm. 'He said there was a ladder in the gardening shed.'

'He told me.' The knot was tied, the rope firm beneath his fingers. 'Now listen,' he said. 'Listen. I'm going to throw this to you. Slip the noose around your body and hold on to the rest of the rope as hard as you can. Can you manage that?'

'Yes.'

Another wave broke. She felt the sands sucking at her legs, pulling them sickeningly downwards, and suddenly the horror of it all was in every part of her and she hardly knew how to stifle her screams.

'Ready?'

'Yes.'

And even as he threw the rope towards her she saw Rohan moving up behind with the butt of the gun glinting in his hand.

'Daniel—'

But he was much too quick for her to complete the sentence. As soon as he saw her expression change he had whirled round, dropping the rope on the sands, and had caught Rohan's upraised arm before the blow could fall.

They struggled. The tide swirled forward over their naked feet, and suddenly Rachel's mind was a mere camera incapable of any emotional reaction as it recorded the scene like a strip of film before her eyes.

The gun spun out of Rohan's hand into the quick-sands and was gone a second later. Rohan took a step backwards. Then another. And as his feet began to sink he lurched forward towards firmer ground and the blow from Daniel's fist caught him so cleanly on the jaw that unconsciousness must have come immediately. He keeled backwards, his feet staggering from the weight of the blow, and even as Rachel opened her mouth to scream, he fell full length into the quicksands and the waves surged forward greedily over his body.

The world spun dizzily. She would have fallen, but the sand was up to her waist so that falling was impossible, and then just as she hovered on the brink of consciousness she felt the rope tighten round her body and Daniel's voice ringing in her ears.

'Hold the rope!' he was shouting. 'Pull as hard as you've ever pulled in your life! Pull, for God's sake!'

The rope was rough and seared her palms. Another wave disturbed the sands and suddenly her hips were free. She clung on, trying to move her feet, and again another wave helped her and shifted the sand. She pulled until she felt she could pull no longer, and suddenly her ankles were free and she was half-skidding, half-floating along the shifting sands.

She felt tears blur her eyes, her limbs lock in a paralysis of exhaustion, and then his hand was reaching for hers, pulling her back out of the long nightmare which had begun five years ago to the peace of another saner world beyond.

# *epilogue*

Three days later, Rebecca Carey received a letter from her brother.

'It seems as if I shall be delayed in Scotland for longer than I thought,' he had written. 'The whole story is much too complicated to put in a letter so I shall have to explain the situation more fully when I see you. However to put it as briefly as possible, I reached Ruthven to find Rachel trapped on Cluny Sands by a rising tide, and managed to pull her to safety by a rope from the boat I'd hired. Quist wasn't so lucky. I'm sorry to tell you this, as I know you were seeing a great deal of him recently, but in trying to rescue Rachel he himself was trapped and died despite our efforts to reach him. I hope you won't be too upset by this. Perhaps when you feel ready to do so you could telephone his family, whom the authorities have already notified, and say that he died trying to save Rachel's life.

'Now perhaps you can guess one of the reasons for the delay, if not the other. When we got back to Kyle of Lochalsh we told the police what had happened and they have asked us to stay for the inquest, which will be held on the day you receive this letter. Then, after the inquest is closed and the matter ended, I shall be driving Rachel back to Inverness (where I hired a car) and travelling from there by train to Edinburgh where we shall be staying for a further seventeen days. You will, of course, be utterly astonished to know that I shall be staying with Rachel in Edinburgh for an apparently arbitrary choice of seventeen days, so I had better explain that one is permitted to be married in Scotland if one has been resident in that country for three weeks. We have so far been resident four days so that leaves seventeen days unaccounted for.

'I do realize that this news will be something of a surprise to you, but I know you're far too intelligent not to realize how fine a person Rachel is and how fortunate I am to be able to marry her. Let me know when you'll be arriving for the wedding, won't you? We'll be staying at the North British Hotel near Princes Street, and you can contact us there.

'Rachel asks rather shyly (I wonder why?) to be remembered to you. I send my love as always, of course, and look forward to seeing you again as soon as possible.

'Your brother,
Daniel.'

# Call in the
# Night

# chapter 1

It was in the afternoon when the phone call came from Europe, one of those long shimmering afternoons of high summer when the distant reaches of the avenue dissolved into a haze and the heat was locked into the streets by the tall buildings. As soon as I had crawled home from an ill-advised window-shopping spree along Fifth Avenue I went to the air-conditioner, pressed the switch and stood for a few moments before the fan as I stared out of the window. Eighteen floors below me pedestrians toiled along the pavement and traffic broiled at the intersections; twenty blocks away to the north-west a helicopter prowled through the sky and tiptoed to a landing on the summit of the Pan-Am building. I was reminded of a fastidious fly examining a piece of angel cake.

I turned, moved away from the window and opened the door of the closet which the owners of the apartment hopefully described as a kitchen. There was a bottle of bitter lemon in the icebox; underneath the sink was the small bottle of gin which I always kept in readiness against the possibility of unexpected guests, although why I bothered to keep such a thing I don't know since none of my girlfriends had a penchant for alcohol and I had hardly reached the stage of being a secret drinker. However, I had fallen into the habit of keeping an unopened bottle of gin in the apartment ever since the time several months ago when I had been in the embarrassing position of being unable to offer a date anything stronger than ginger ale, and habits, unlike male escorts, are easy to acquire and hard to shake off. Now, because I was so exhausted and felt totally limp with the heat, I seized the gin bottle and poured a minute measure into the glass to join the ice and the bitter lemon. I smiled, feeling pleasantly wicked to be drinking alone, and thought how shocked my parents would have been if they could have seen me.

Both had been total abstainers, pillars of a very proper little New England community in New Hampshire; my father had even refused to grow apples on the small farm where we had lived because he disapproved so strongly of cider.

I sighed, half in irritation, half in regret at my memories. That chapter of my life was closed now, and although I missed my parents and occasionally suffered vague pangs of nostalgia for the New Hampshire countryside, I was in fact thankful to be free of that strict New England upbringing. Even now I sometimes wondered if I were completely free of it. After twenty-eight years in the world and three years in New York City I was still smitten with guilt if I bought clothes which were frivolous rather than useful, and worried myself silly if I didn't have a healthy balance at the bank.

'So *sensible*, darling!' Gina always used to say. 'If *only* I could be more like you!'

But she wasn't. Gina was utterly different, so different that I had no idea how we had managed to maintain close contact with one another after our parents' deaths. She was five years younger than I, and so had had five years less of exposure to the New England influences. For a time while she had worked in New York I had conscientiously tried to keep an eye on her, but after a while I gave up. It was much too exhausting, and anyway I had no wish to quarrel with her by criticizing her shortcomings. So we went our separate ways, and later I had my somewhat dubious reward when she went to Hollywood and scribbled reams of rushed letters to me concerning her work and her excessively complicated love life. Evidently my tolerant resignation, which my parents would undoubtedly have judged to be cowardice to tackle a moral issue, had encouraged Gina to cast me for the role of confidante. The mail from California came with great regularity. At first she had tried to phone collect, but I didn't take kindly to that.

'Three minutes only,' I told her. 'I'm sorry but I'm rather broke at the moment and can't afford any more.

I don't want to have to eat yogurt for dinner as well as for lunch.'

'But darling, how *can* you be so poor!' She sounded so upset at the thought of it that I began to feel touched by her concern. 'I mean, you must make such an awful lot of money teaching those terrible children—'

'Not as much as you make in a thirty-second soap commercial,' I said with truth, and then felt guilty lest she should think I was mean, so I encouraged her to talk for ten minutes and postponed buying the 'Antony and Cleopatra' album until another time.

However, she took the hint, and after that the letters started to arrive. I began to feel that perhaps I had missed my vocation in life and that I should have been running an advice column for females in distress. 'I hardly know what to say,' I wrote despairingly in an early letter back to her. 'I don't think you'll find my comments any use to you at all. I can't imagine why you should think that just because I'm five years older than you I have a total, all-enveloping knowledge of human relationships and problems.'

'But you're so sane!' cried Gina's pen, weeping purple ink on to pink paper in reply. 'So sensible! If you only knew how comforting it is in this mad crazy mixed-up beastly city to have *someone somewhere* who can talk sense and behave normally . . .'

In fact I think I had become a parent-substitute for her, a symbol, however inaccurate, of the orderly world she could remember from her childhood, and that although nothing would have induced her to return to the discipline of a New England existence, it comforted her to think that it was always there if ever she needed it.

After a few months of this peculiar correspondence, I found I was becoming much fonder of her than I had been when we had both lived in New York; distance lends enchantment. When she came through New York *en route* to a modelling career in Paris we had a very enjoyable week together, but I could not pretend to myself that I wasn't slightly relieved when the time came for us to part again. I felt like a quiet, placid house in a quiet, tree-lined road of some quiet small town which had suddenly been hit by a tornado, lifted off the ground, spun round three times in mid-air and then dropped back into place with an earth-jarring jolt.

Gina had been six months in Paris on that afternoon in early July when I returned from my window-shopping stroll along Fifth Avenue. I had had lunch with an old college friend, and had left my apartment building before the arrival of the mail, which was never delivered before noon on Saturdays. When I returned exhausted at four o'clock I almost forgot to check the mailbox but fortunately I remembered, and there, waiting for me, was the familiar airmail envelope and the familiar dizzy purple-inked handwriting beneath the familiar French stamps. After I had mixed myself my illicit bitter lemon, I subsided on to the couch, shook off my shoes and put my feet up. Then with my glass in one hand and Gina's letter in the other I settled down to assume my well-worn rôle of guide, philosopher and friend.

It started in the usual way. According to Gina, this was 'just a little note'. Sighing with resignation I began to count the pages of whirling purple loops and curls, and then curiosity got the better of me and I went back to the beginning again.

'. . . this is just a little note, darling, honestly, as I'm so rushed I'm nearly going out of my mind and I'm supposed to be in three different places at once right now and oh! life's so complicated just trying to fit everything in, and sometimes I wish I was like you, darling, honestly, with your nice steady job and your regular salary and your dear little apartment the size of a dime and your view of mid-town Manhattan, and sometimes I really do wish I was back in New York with the luncheonettes and the pizza shops and the bars and the heat that bounces up from the sidewalk to meet you, because although Paris is so glamorous and so exciting and so *soigné*, it does nothing but rain and one does get just a *little* tired of all those dashing French males pinching one's bottom on the Metro. Talking of males, I've just discovered the

most enthralling specimen you could ever imagine, and –
just for a change – he has absolutely nothing to do with
the world of fashion or photography, and he's not even
French either, and let's face it, darling, I'm just about due
for a change of nationality romance-wise after six months
or warding off/egging on would-be Latin lovers. This
latest gem is British, but not the bowler-hatted variety
or even the Carnaby Street variety either (yes, believe
it or not, there *are* other kinds!). His name is Garth
Cooper. He seems to be unmarried, but I can't think
how he's managed to escape for so long because he's about
thirty-five and there's nothing wrong with him, quite the
reverse in fact, as I've been discovering recently when
we've been out on the town together. In fact that reminds
me, we went out together last night and GUESS who we
saw! Just guess! You never will, never in a million years
– Warren Mayne! And if you'll believe it, he came right
up and kissed me as if he was still my fiancé. Some people
have an awful nerve, don't they? I was embarrassed to
pieces and didn't even dare look at Garth but afterwards
he seemed amused and said it looked as if Warren had
come to Paris so that he could get in touch with me
again. Of course I denied it, but I *did* wonder. Oh, it's
just too much of Warren if he has followed me to Paris!
It'll make life so horribly complicated and I just can't
bear it, it's complicated enough already, and sometimes
I can't help wishing you were here to sort it out for me
– incidentally hasn't school finished for the summer yet?
What are you doing about a vacation? Rake those surplus
dollars out of your bulging bank account and buy yourself
a round-trip excursion flight to Paris! Must rush, darling,
no more now, love and take care and all the rest.'

'GINA'.

I sighed again, sipped my gin and reflected
what a mysterious thing sex appeal is. Gina and I look
rather alike – or at least we used to before Gina took
to false eyelashes and the hollow-cheeked look – but
she obviously has a certain mysterious quality which
I lack. I really can't believe the mystery rests on false

eyelashes alone so I suppose some extraordinary fusion of the hereditary quirks of our very ordinary parents must be responsible. Whatever it is, it never seems very fair. But then unless one is a complete *ingénue* one hardly expects life to be fair; I had long ago resigned myself to that basic truth so I was always cross when I caught myself behaving like an *ingénue* again and envying Gina her good luck.

As if, I thought, disgusted with myself, I even wanted to be a model. She was welcome to it all. Paris, men and mink coats! I was perfectly happy with my Shakespeare records and my friends and the Metropolitan museum on Sundays; I had a job I liked, an apartment of my own, and perhaps, if I were careful with my savings and my raise came through shortly, a shining little red Volkswagen . . .

After day-dreaming for several minutes of stepping casually into my very own car as the doorman held open the door for me with an admiring smile, I roused myself, found pen and paper and sat down again to consider a reply. I always found Gina's letters easier to answer if I made the effort to write when her initial impression was still clear in my mind. To write a guide-philosopher-friend letter in cold blood after an interval of several days was much too turgid a task to face.

'My dear Gina,' I began, scratching away nimbly at the paper. 'How you do ramble on, although I'm sure I'm just as bad myself sometimes. Here are my comments in chronological order: (1) you know darn well you'd rather be in Paris in the rain than in a ninety-degrees-ninety-percent humidity New York, so don't ask me for sympathy on *that* issue. (2) If the Metro is such a danger spot for the more vulnerable parts of your anatomy, catch a bus and sit down at once. (3) I don't trust this thirty-five-year-old Englishman. Why should he be (apparently) floating around Paris with money to burn? Also, what do you mean when you say he "seems" to be unmarried. That sounds as if you really think he might be married. If he is, say a tender goodbye now, and then maybe I won't have to offer you my shoulder to cry on long distance in six months' time, when he suddenly strikes a noble pose and decides to go back to his wife. (4) Bad luck about meeting Warren again. However, if you don't want to see him in the future, there's one quite simple remedy. Tell him so. (5) I'd love to come to Paris and see you but am just about to get my little red car which I told you about when you were here last winter. Maybe next year? I'm not having a very ambitious vacation this year, just a week in Boston with Sue and her husband and a week in Martha's Vineyard at Nancy's cottage there . . .'

I paused to reread what I had written before continuing my own news, and swallowed the last of my drink. I was just picking up my pen again to resume the letter when the phone rang.

Reaching backwards I grabbed the receiver and knocked over my empty glass. 'Yes?' I said confused, picking up my glass and retrieving my writing pad which had slid off my knees to the floor. 'Hello?'

'Miss Claire Sullivan, please.'

'Speaking,' I said dimly, puzzled by the unfamiliar man's voice and the hum of the long-distance wire.

'Miss Sullivan, this is London, England. Will you accept a call, please, from a Miss Gina Sullivan who wishes to reverse the charges?'

I was so surprised that I even forgot to be annoyed at Gina's further attempt to call collect. 'London?' I said in amazement. 'London, England?'

'Yes, madam. Shall I—' He paused politely.

There was no mistaking the British courtesy. Or the British accent.

'Yes,' I said rapidly. 'Yes, I'll take the call. Thank you.'

'Go ahead, please, caller.'

'Gina?' I said at once incredulously. 'Gina, what are you doing in—'

But she was already talking, not listening to me, her voice high-pitched and breaking with panic, her breath coming in sobs and gasps, and as I listened her terror communicated itself to me until I too was rigid with her fear.

375

'Oh Claire, Claire, please come,' she was sobbing. 'Please come, Claire. Oh Claire, I'm in such dreadful terrible trouble I don't know what to do – Claire, you just have to come, please – I don't know what to do—'

'Gina listen! Where are you, for God's sake? What's happened? What – Gina, are you there? Gina—'

But there was nothing there any more, just that long empty silence, and then across a distance of three thousand miles I heard the soft stealthy click of the receiver being replaced.

## *chapter 2*

The buzz of the disconnected wire produced a reaction from me of stupefied disbelief. I stared at the silent phone and listened to the dull *purr* as if I were completely paralysed, and then at last I pulled myself together, called the operator, and asked for the international circuits.

'I was speaking to London – I was cut off—' I couldn't think clearly; I heard myself stumble over the questions the operator asked. 'No – no, I don't know the number in London . . . yes, if you could please trace the call for me . . .'

I hung up, waited, mixed myself another gin. At last, just as I thought I could bear waiting no longer, the phone rang again.

'The call came from 16 Hereford Mansions, London W8,' said the operator sedately. 'Number: Kensington 2127. The number is listed under the name of a Mr Eric Jantzen, that's J-A-N-T-Z-E-N. Shall I try the number for you?'

'Please.' My pencil whispered across the paper, recording the information she had given me.

'Whom are you calling, please?'

'Gina Sullivan.' I spelled it.

'One moment, please.'

I waited, listening. Presently I heard the dialling, followed by the sound of the bell ringing far away.

'Trying to connect you,' said the operator.

'Thank you.'

It went on ringing.

'Still trying to connect you,' said the operator.

'Thank you.'

A long pause.

'I'm sorry,' said the operator. 'There's no reply. Can I try the number again for you later?'

I couldn't think what to say. At last I said: 'No, thank you, but could you check the address of the call again?' My sister had never mentioned anyone called Eric Jantzen and I wanted to be quite sure there was no mistake.

'Call you back,' said the operator, impersonal as an automaton, and hung up.

I replaced the receiver and sat staring into my glass. Supposing I kept trying that number and still got no reply? What was I to do? I'll wait till midnight, I thought and then if I haven't managed to contact Gina or if she hasn't called back . . . My scalp prickled. What was I to do then? It would be no good calling the police of the local precinct about something which had happened in London. And if I called the police in London, spoke to Scotland Yard . . . I tried to imagine the conversation.

'My sister called me from London just now,' I would say. 'She sounded very frightened and hysterical. Then we were cut off and the receiver was replaced and now I can't re-establish contact with her. Could you check the address of this apartment belonging to Eric Jantzen and see if she's all right?'

Did one ask Scotland Yard to give reassurance about one's relatives? I mentally tried a more dramatic approach. 'I'm afraid something dreadful has happened to my sister – we were cut off in the middle of our conversation and it sounded as if someone had silenced her . . .'

But that wasn't true. Gina hadn't mentioned that she was in danger, only 'in trouble'. If she had been interrupted by someone who had silenced her and replaced the receiver, she had given no indication of it. There had been no scream, no gasp of horror, only the hysteria and sheer panic which I, perhaps mistakenly, had interpreted as a hysteria born of fear. I rephrased my approach to Scotland Yard and imagined the subsequent conversation.

'I've had a very disturbing phone call from the apartment of a Mr Eric Jantzen,' I would say. 'My sister was hysterical and sounded immensely frightened – I think it's vital that the call should be investigated—'

And Scotland Yard would interrupt: 'What was your sister doing in London? How well did she know this Eric Jantzen?'

'I don't know, but she was friends with an Englishman called Garth Cooper.'

'You say your sister's a model by profession?' Scotland Yard would say instantly. 'Young – smart – presumably attractive to men?'

'Yes, but—'

'Isn't it likely that she was hysterical as the result of a crisis which was possibly brought on by her relationship with either or both of these two men?'

'Well, yes, but—'

'Did she actually say she was afraid? Or in danger?'

'No, but—'

'What were her exact words?'

I winced. I didn't have to imagine Scotland Yard's comment on that particular phrase. I was just wondering if I should call on them anyway, when the phone rang again. It was the operator confirming Jantzen's name and address. I told her I had changed my mind, and asked her to try the number again for me in an hour's time. After I had replaced the receiver, I had a brainwave, and going over to the bureau on the other side of the room I got my writing case and found the phone number of Gina's apartment in Paris. Gina shared the apartment with another American girl, whom I had never met, called Candy-Anna; I particularly remembered the eccentric hybrid of a first name, although I had long since forgotten the second. Presently I was talking to the international department again, and placing yet another call to Europe.

This time I was more successful. A voice as languid as melting maple syrup answered the ringing phone and breathed a tingling hello into the mouthpiece.

'Go ahead, caller,' the operator said.

'Candy-Anna?'

'Ye-es,' said the voice, sagging a little with the realization that I wasn't an escort calling for a date. 'Who's this?'

'Gina's sister Claire in New York. I—'

'Well, *hi!* I've heard so much about you! Gina was saying only yesterday—'

'Yes, I'm trying to find her.' My interruption was hardly very adroit but she appeared not to notice my abruptness. 'Do you know whereabouts in London she is, please?'

'Why, how clever of you to know she's in London! She only decided yesterday to—'

'Do you know where she's staying there?'

'Well, no – no, not really . . . She travelled over with a friend of hers, a wonderful, wonderful man who you'd just love to meet—'

'Garth Cooper?'

'Why, you *know* him! Isn't he the most—'

'No, I haven't met him. Do you know where he lives in London?'

'Gee, no – is it important? Gina'll be back on Monday – she was only going for the weekend and she said—'

'Did she ever mention the name Eric Jantzen to you?'

'Eric who? Honey, I just don't remember! If you knew how many wonderful men Gina has absolutely panting on our doorstep—' Sour grapes tinged the maple syrup sweetness briefly and was gone. 'I'm sorry I just can't remember – honestly. I don't *think* she ever mentioned an Eric, but it's just possible I might have forgotten. I forget terribly easily. My memory's just the most hopeless thing you could ever imagine . . . Say, how's New York? What time is it there? Tell me all about it!'

Not at three dollars a minute, I thought with wry amusement, but I said politely that it was afternoon in New York and the weather was fine and I was so grateful for her help and hoped to meet her one day. Having escaped from the conversation as gracefully as possible I got up and moved restlessly over to the window.

I simply did not know what to do. I glanced at my watch. It was five-thirty in England. In half an hour the operator would try the Jantzen number again. I at least had till six o'clock to decide what to do if I were to unable to make contact with Gina.

I tried to consider the situation quite dispassionately. What did I really think had happened? If I were honest I had to admit I believed Gina had got into some sort of emotional tangle with Garth Cooper and Eric Jantzen. I knew from past experience that Gina had an enormous talent for tying her love life up into the most preposterous knots. She had probably gone to London with Cooper and then discovered from Eric Jantzen, whoever he was, that Cooper was married after all. In her shock she had characteristically dramatized the situation by believing her heart to be utterly broken for all time, and carried away by a sense of tragedy had made the phone call to tell me what trouble she was in.

Then why had she hung up in the middle of the conversation?

I worried over the question until the phone rang again at six o'clock.

'There's still no reply from the London number,' said the operator. 'Shall I call again at seven?'

I made a spur of the moment decision. 'No,' I said. 'Could you please place a call for me to Scotland Yard?'

I suspected that by this time even the automaton of an operator was beginning to doubt my sanity.

'Scotland Yard, London?'

'Yes,' I said. 'The police.'

'Person to person?'

'No, no – anyone will do. I want to report something.'

'Call you back,' said the operator in the kind of voice one uses to the mentally disturbed, and left me listening once more to the dull buzz of a severed connexion.

I began to rehearse my story again and tried to suppress a feeling of mounting nervousness and panic. When I was finally called upon to tell my story some minutes later I found myself, much to my fury, stammering over my carefully rehearsed words while my face burned with my embarrassment.

Fortunately the policeman at the other end of the wire, Detective-Inspector Fowles, listened and commented courteously enough and asked the right questions to straighten out my confused story. When I asked in desperation at last if the police would be able to help, he was reassuringly placid.

'Yes, we'll send someone round to make an enquiry at the Jantzen flat,' he said. 'Don't you worry, we'll look into it straight away. If there's been any funny business going on we'll sort it out and find out what's happening to your sister.'

'Can you let me know any news as soon as possible? I realize these phone calls must be very expensive, but I'd really appreciate it if—'

'Yes, of course, Miss Sullivan. Now I have a note of your number here, don't I? I'll give you a ring myself as soon as the report comes through and I have some news for you.'

I thanked him gratefully, replaced the receiver and then leaned back on the couch and closed my eyes. I felt exhausted. After a while I went to the kitchen and half-heartedly tried to cook myself some supper, but I found I could eat nothing.

I walked restlessly about the room, stood by the window, stared out at the Pan-Am building and the other giant buildings. Another helicopter landed and departed. Seven o'clock came. Lights were pinpricking the dusk; night-time New York was coming alive, and far below me on the Avenue I could see the red tail-lights of the cars as they cruised *en masse* to the midtown restaurants and the glitter of Broadway. Soon it was eight o'clock. Then nine. Twice I nearly picked up the phone in an agony of impatience, but managed to restrain myself; the man at Scotland Yard would call back. It was senseless calling him again when he might not yet have the news I wanted. I was just making myself another cup of coffee shortly before eleven-thirty when the ring of the phone made me spill boiling water over the floor.

'Hello?' I said nervously into the receiver. 'Claire Sullivan speaking.'

It was Scotland Yard, Detective-Inspector Fowles again. My knees were unsteady suddenly; I had to sit down.

'Miss Sullivan, I'm afraid we have no real news of your sister but all seems to be quite in order so perhaps no news is good news. Mr Jantzen had invited her to have a drink with him, but he was delayed and couldn't keep the engagement – he tried to contact her to cancel the evening but couldn't get in touch with her. He was completely unaware that your sister had ever been in the flat.'

'But—' I was confused. 'How did she get in if he wasn't there?'

'He suggested that she might have come with a friend of hers, a Mr Cooper. Apparently this Mr Cooper has a key to the Jantzen flat.'

Somewhere far away at the back of my mind I was conscious of a slight unreasoning stab of fear.

'Did you check with Mr Cooper?' I said uneasily.

'We haven't been able to contact him so far, but I shouldn't worry too much, if I were you, Miss Sullivan. Apparently your sister came over from Paris with this Mr Cooper—'

'Yes,' I said. 'I know.'

'I expect they've gone out on the town tonight – your sister's probably having the time of her life, and enjoying every minute of her visit!' He sounded comforting, reassuring; I could tell that he himself was convinced nothing was wrong. 'Look, I'll tell you what I think happened – she and Cooper went to his friend's flat for a drink and had a tiff about something. Maybe he pretended to walk out. Well, you know these young girls – and your sister probably enjoys a spot of drama now and again. She put through her call to you to weep on your shoulder – and then lo and behold he turns up again all ready to apologize and they go off together quite happily as if nothing had ever happened. You mark my words, you'll have a call from her tomorrow saying she's sorry she gave you such a fright.'

All I could say was: 'Supposing she doesn't call?'

'Well, if she doesn't . . .' He paused to consider this remote possibility. 'Give it till Monday and then check up to see if she got back to Paris safely. If she didn't and if there's still no word from her, then get in touch with me again.'

'All right,' I said slowly. 'All right, I will. And thank you very much for all the trouble you've taken.'

'Not at all, Miss Sullivan. Don't mention it.'

We said goodbye, he very cordial and friendly, I stilted with anxiety and uneasiness.

Presently I sat down on the couch and remained there for a long while, but the more I told myself that it was foolish to go on worrying, the more worried I became. The thought of waiting another forty-eight hours until Monday without doing anything except while away the time was not a pleasant thought. At last, in an agony of indecision and nervousness I got up, went over to my purse and had a look at the balance in my chequebook. After a little simple arithmetic with the balance in my savings account I sat thinking for a long while. I was remembering the car again, my little red Volkswagen waiting patiently for me to save up the money to buy it. I thought of the trips I had planned, the luxury of excursions out of town to the beach in summer without the tedium of the long subway ride, the six-week expedition to the West I had visualized during next year's summer vacation.

I thought for a long time.

'Well,' I said aloud to myself at last, 'perhaps it would all have been rather extravagant. And everyone says that keeping a car in Manhattan is more of a liability than an asset. I can wait a little longer for that sort of extravagance. And I always did want to go to Europe.'

Having reached my decision I felt much better. I went to bed, snatched a few hours' sleep, and as soon as I awoke next morning I dialled Pan-Am to enquire how soon they could offer me a seat on a flight from New York to London.

Fate then took a hand in the proceedings; I discovered that because it was the height of the summer tourist season at that time, all the planes were fully booked on the flights to London. I put my name down on several lists, and then, nearly beside myself with frustration, I paused to consider the situation. It was now Sunday morning. Even if I got a flight that same day I would hardly be able to reach London before Gina left England to return to France – assuming, of course, that Gina was safe and well. That being the case it would be more sensible for me to try to obtain a flight not to London, but to Paris. I went back to the phone again and eventually, by a stroke of luck, found there was a cancellation on a TWA flight to Paris on Monday. Having made my reservation and committed myself positively to my decision to go to Europe I was at last able to relax a little, but there was too much to do to enable me to relax for long. I set out for Forty-second Street to exchange a cheque for a ticket to Paris, and as I walked I found myself again thinking of Gina, her suave Englishman Garth Cooper, Candy-Anna saying in her carefully preserved southern drawl: 'Such a wonderful, wonderful man . . .'

I began to be nervous once more. I could hardly reach the airline's building at Forty-second Street quickly enough.

Half an hour later with my ticket safely in my purse I

returned home and tried to prepare for my journey in an organized manner, but I found I was still too distraught to conform to any careful routine. I checked my passport and smallpox-vaccination certificate; eternally optimistic, I had always kept both valid. The dreary task of packing lay before me. Finally when my suitcases were closed I called a couple of friends to tell them that I had decided to take a surprise trip to Europe. Both friends were suitably amazed. I began to wonder vaguely if I were indeed demented, but pushed the thought out of my mind as I sent a cable to Gina's apartment in Paris to announce my arrival.

Perhaps, I thought, determined to be optimistic and believe that all was well, perhaps Gina would be at the airport to meet me.

But somehow at the back of my mind I remained uneasily convinced that no one would be there when my plane touched down at Orly. I started to worry again, worrying all through Sunday night, and then at last it was Monday and I was rushing to my bank at nine to buy travellers' cheques before taking a cab out to Kennedy to catch the morning flight. Fortunately all went well; there were no delays, no last minute disasters, and within forty-eight hours of Gina's phone call from London I was on my way to Europe to find her.


The flight seemed endless. For hour after hour the plane seemed suspended in a blue vacuum, and at last the time difference between Europe and America manifested itself in a spectacular sunset and an early twilight. By the time we reached Paris it was night, although my watch told me that in New York it was still late afternoon. I thought of the long avenues dissolving into a heat-haze, the stifling sidewalks, the drone of a million air-conditioners, and suddenly that was far away on the other side of the world and the plane was beginning its long downward path to the runway and French soil.

I roused myself from the torpor of the long flight, put away my book, forgot to feel nervous. Below me I could see lights, European lights, pinpricking the darkness of the summer night, and my excitement was such that for a moment I forgot Gina altogether. The plane sank lower and lower; the lights stretched as far as I could see. Presently I saw the lights of the airport, and as the plane sank still lower to meet them I remembered to fasten my safety belt. Within quarter of an hour the plane had landed and I was stepping out into a new and different land.

My excitement rose in a crescendo and then ebbed. I felt alone, foreign, shy. I did have a slight knowledge of French so I was not completely at a loss but the rapid cross-fire of conversation around me was far removed from the simple phrases I had learned at school. Feeling very lost and helpless I filtered through Customs and Immigration and was directed by dual-language signs to the place where I could get a bus to the terminal. I hung back, hoping in spite of myself that there would be some sign of Gina, but there was no face I knew; I remained a stranger among strangers and the airport continued to seem cold and impersonal.

After a delay I managed to cash a travellers' cheque, and was able to pay my fare and board the bus. My second stage of the journey began; the bus roared through the Parisian suburbs, over cobbled streets, past outdoor cafés and shabby houses. And then suddenly the shabbiness was gone and there were wide boulevards, illuminated vistas, floodlit buildings, incredibly familiar landmarks. We seemed to drive through the middle of the city, and soon my excitement was such that I forgot I was alone and thought only that this was Paris and I, Claire Sullivan, was seeing it all with my own eyes.

I reached the terminal, found my baggage again, hailed a waiting cab.

'*Numéro vingt-deux, Rue St Thomasine, s'il vous plaît.*'

The driver nodded, assuming an expression of what I supposed was typical Parisian *ennui*. We shot off like a bullet from a gun, bounced over cobbles, screeched to a halt at an intersection. Finally as we cannoned forward again I became adjusted to this spastic form of transport and instead began to feel nervous in case my cable had failed to reach Gina's apartment.

But it had arrived safely. After I had paid the driver and left the cab I found my way into the apartment building with my luggage and shut myself in a small but modern elevator. Gina lived on the third floor. On emerging into the passage I couldn't find a light and had to strike a match, but at last I was outside the right door and reading Gina's name above Candy-Anna's on the name slot.

I was conscious of immense weariness mingled with relief. I rang the bell, waited, and presently the door opened and I was facing a slim willowy girl with honey-blonde hair and limpid blue eyes.

'Well, he*llo* there!' said Candy-Anna, effortlessly hospitable. 'Welcome to Europe! It's just wonderful to see you but I hope you're not going to be terribly disappointed. Gina must have decided to prolong that weekend in London – she didn't come back last night after all and I just haven't the remotest idea where she is . . .'


## Chapter 3

'Who is this man Garth Cooper?' I said. 'Have you met him?'

Half an hour had passed since my arrival, and we were sitting drinking Swiss coffee in the large dishevelled living room. Candy-Anna had been pardonably curious about the suddenness of my trip to Europe and my concern for Gina, but I am not naturally inclined to confide in complete strangers so I had edited and omitted large sections of the story.

'Gina's been pressing me to come to Europe for a vacation, so I decided I would,' I had said. 'I had a phone call from London on Saturday night in which she sounded very odd, to say the least, but when I called her back I couldn't get in touch with her. That was when I called you to try and find out why she was in London and who she went with.'

'Well, she went with Garth,' Candy-Anna had answered. 'But it wasn't just a wild lost weekend together – my, but you mustn't think that!' Her limpid eyes assumed a carefully cultivated expression of innocence. 'Garth was going back to London after being in Paris on business and Gina decided to go too, just for the weekend and to see a bit of England. But I guess the weekend must have been a real blast and she decided to stay on. Why was her phone call to you so odd? You don't think anything's happened to her, do you?'

'She just didn't seem like herself.' I had finished my cup of coffee, and then asked my question about Garth Cooper. 'I believe you said on the phone that you'd met him,' I added, remembering. 'What kind of a man is he, do you think?'

But I might have known Candy-Anna would be quite incapable of giving a straight answer to such a question.

'Garth? Why, he's just a wonderful, wonderful person! We both absolutely love him to pieces—'

'Yes,' I said, trying not to sound impatient, 'but what does he do? Why was he in Paris? Does he live in London?'

'My, I've no idea! I guess he must. But I think he has a small place in Paris too – I remember him saying he was always travelling back and forth between the two places . . . So glamorous!' She sighed. 'Imagine living and working in London *and* Paris—'

'Yes,' I said again, digging my nails into the palms of my hands. 'But what does he *do?*'

Candy-Anna frowned for a moment, probably from the effort of mobilizing unused machinery for thought. 'Well, gee,' she said at last, vaguely surprised, 'isn't that the strangest thing? I've just no idea at all.'

'Did he seem rich?'

'Oh *yes*! He took cabs everywhere and never used the Metro. And he and Gina went to simply wonderful places to eat and did marvellously glamorous things, like going to the opera and the theatre. It was lovely for Gina! I was so happy for her.'

I had my doubts about that, but kept them to myself. 'How long has Gina known him?'

'Oh . . . about six weeks, I guess. But he hasn't been in Paris for the whole of that time. He was here all last week and they saw each other nearly every night. Then on Friday night they took off for London together.'

'I suppose you don't know when he himself is scheduled to come back to Paris?'

'Gee, no! I've no idea. It could be that he'll stay in London for a while now. I just don't know.'

I wondered what to do. It was beginning to look as if I should take a plane to London as quickly as possible, find this man Cooper and ask him point blank what had happened to Gina. But then . . . I sighed. I was no doubt being melodramatic and foolish. In all probability Gina was hopelessly involved with him by this time and had no intention of returning to Paris while her romance was flourishing so successfully in London. She wouldn't thank me for interfering. I began to feel as if I had made a complete fool of myself. Against Scotland Yard's advice I had taken a melodramatic view of the phone call and now I was taking an equally melodramatic and misguided approach to Gina's continuing absence from home. I was just telling myself bitterly that it would have been more sensible to have remained in New York instead of rushing across the Atlantic Ocean like a lunatic, when the phone rang.

We both jumped.

'It's Gina,' I said at once. 'It must be. She's back.'

Candy-Anna grabbed the receiver. 'Hello?'

I leaned forward on the edge of the couch, my limbs aching, and saw her eyes widen with surprise. 'Why Warren! How are you? What? No, she's not here right now – she's not back yet. Yes, that's right . . . No, I haven't heard from her—'

I interrupted sharply. 'Is that Warren Mayne, Gina's ex-fiancé?' I was remembering Gina's letter which had reached my apartment shortly before the phone call.

'Just a moment, honey,' she said into the receiver, and then to me: 'Yes, it is – do you know him?'

'Can I speak to him, please?'

'Sure.' She was surprised. She turned her attention back to the receiver. 'Honey, just guess who's here wanting a word with you! Someone out of your past!' And having fulfilled her obligation to be mysterious and tantalizing she handed the phone over to me with a dazzling smile and reached out for another cigarette.

'Warren?' I said quickly. 'This is Claire Sullivan, Gina's—'

'Claire!' He was amazed. And suddenly I could see him, very young and clean cut, his fair hair too short, his serious face pleasantly ugly, his brown eyes shining with affection like those of a well-trained spaniel. Gina had led him a terrible dance the previous year in New York; I had spent most of our meetings feeling sorry for him.

'Yes!' I said, smiling in spite of my anxiety. 'Yes, it really is me! How are you, Warren? I had heard from Gina that you were in Paris now.'

'She mentioned me?' He was touchingly gratified. 'Yes, I'm working for an American company with offices here. It's—' He stopped, as if halted by the realization that I should be in Manhattan and not in Europe at all. 'Well, I'll be darned!' he exclaimed. 'Gina didn't mention you were vacationing here! I didn't know you were in Paris!'

'Neither does Gina. It's all an involved story and I seem to have got into a muddle, to say the least. I'm told Gina's in London with someone called Garth Cooper.'

Candy-Anna clapped her hand over her mouth and shook her head frantically, but she was too late. There was a sharp gasp from the other end of the wire, and as I blushed scarlet in my confusion Warren shouted: 'What!

Cooper? Gina went to London with Garth Cooper? Why, she told me—'

I inwardly cursed myself for not having had the presence of mind to foresee the situation. 'They weren't together,' I said helplessly, making things worse. 'They just took the same plane.'

'Well, where is she now, for Pete's sake? Why isn't she back? My God, if I'd known that Cooper was going to London with her—'

'Warren, you must excuse me, but I don't really understand any of this myself. I've only just arrived and I'm not at all sure what's been happening as far as Gina's concerned. Could we meet tomorrow and talk about all this? I'm a little confused.'

'Well, I'm not.' He was obviously still beside himself with rage. 'It's all as clear as daylight to me. That damned Englishman flashed his money around and invited her to come with him on a guided tour of London! My God, if I ever see him again—'

'Perhaps if we could talk about it tomorrow, Warren, I—'

'Breakfast? Lunch?' he asked quickly.

'How about lunch?' I suggested, hoping I'd hear from Gina before then.

'Fine. I'll stop by your place at noon,' he said furiously and slammed down the receiver.

'Oh dear,' I said ineffectually. 'Why on earth did I have to be so stupid? Now I've made the situation worse for Gina than it was already.'

Candy-Anna was reassuring. 'Gina doesn't care about Warren anyway. She'd be glad of the excuse to get rid of him for ever.' Her eyes held a hint of speculation. I guessed she would be glad too, but for different reasons.

'I must go to bed,' I said exhausted. 'I feel worn out. I apologize for descending on you like this, Candy-Anna, and putting you to such inconvenience . . .'

I was assured that I was very welcome and that there was no need to apologize.

In the end I slept in Gina's bed with Gina's familiar

belongings strewn around me. Candy-Anna breathed peacefully across the room, but I slept lightly, half-expecting the phone to ring again with news, good or bad, from London. But there was no news and no phone call and when I opened my eyes at last it was eight o'clock and the sun was streaming through the slanting slats of the Venetian blinds.

Warren arrived punctually at noon. Candy-Anna had left earlier for a business appointment ('Modelling engines, honey – would you believe? I have to pose with a truck and a baby elephant.') and I was on my own when the bell rang. I went across to the door to open it.

Warren looked exactly the same as when I had last seen him. He was, I suppose, nearer my age than Gina's but I always thought of him as being at least five years my junior. When Gina had come to New York after our parents' deaths she had studied art for a while in Manhattan and had met Warren while they were both going through the long-haired Greenwich Village stage. Unfortunately for Warren, Gina had outgrown the phase more quickly than he had, and after finding success as a model in New York she had moved away first to Hollywood and then to Paris, and there had been copious stormy scenes with the diamond engagement ring being pushed back and forth and finally discarded altogether. I could not help feeling Warren had been unlucky, since he was in his own way extremely eligible and plenty of girls would have been very anxious to catch him. He came from a good family; his father was in the diplomatic service in Washington. He was not particularly cultured or intellectual, but then neither was Gina; I thought it would have been a good match, but Gina had thought otherwise, and had gone off to fresh fields and new pastures in pursuit of what she had considered to be a more glamorous existence.

'It's good to see you again,' he said, offering me his hand and smiling his bright naïve smile. 'I'm sorry I was so rude on the phone last night, but I was upset.'

'It was nice of you to come around,' I said politely, 'I was hoping that perhaps you'd be able to tell me what's been going on.'

'I was hoping you were going to tell *me*,' said Warren. He glanced at his watch. 'Look, there's a small restaurant just down the road – why don't we go out and get something to eat there? I'll bet there's nothing in the ice-box here except yogurt. Models never eat anything.'

I had naturally assumed that we would go out to lunch, so his bland assumption that I might have been prepared to cook him a meal rather took me aback. I said hastily that I would be very interested in trying a French restaurant, and together we left the apartment and went into the cool fresh air of the street outside.

I caught my breath. Looking down the road I could see the Seine and beyond that, farther up the river, the shining splendour of the Eiffel Tower. The sky was blue, the sun warm, but there was little humidity. New York seemed a million light-years away.

'How wonderful it is to be in Paris!' I exclaimed spontaneously. 'I can't think why I never made the effort to come before.'

Warren smiled condescendingly. 'It does seem exciting at first, doesn't it?' he said in the indulgent tone of a father talking to a child. 'I felt the same too, when I arrived.'

I could have murdered him.

However, my irritation ebbed when we reached the little restaurant and sat outside on the pavement under a striped umbrella. We ordered steaks and wine and then relaxed in our chairs to wait.

'They'll take hours,' said Warren. 'French service is the slowest in the world.'

'That doesn't matter,' I said firmly, putting him in his place, and to change the subject I began: 'Now about Gina—'

'Exactly,' said Warren with alacrity. 'Look, what's going on? How did you know she was in London with Cooper? What did she tell you? Did she say she'd be back in Paris to meet you? Why isn't she here? Where is she?'

I began the weary task of explanations. I told him everything, partly because I knew him well, partly because he
was obviously as worried about Gina as I was, and partly
because I felt I had to discuss the situation with someone.
He listened intelligently enough to begin with, but after
a while I sensed he was rapidly becoming too jealous to
concentrate on what I was saying.

'So there it is,' I concluded at last, ignoring the sulky
drop of his mouth and the introspective look in his eyes.
'I don't know where she is or what's happened to her,
and I'm worried – perhaps unreasonably.' I hesitated
and then asked the question I had put to Candy-Anna
the previous evening: 'What kind of person is this man
Garth Cooper?'

The waiter arrived with our order and interrupted us,
but I did not have to repeat my question. As soon as the
waiter had left us Warren said angrily: 'Well, he's English
to start with. I never trust the English. The biggest fallacy
in the world is to think they're just like us because they
speak the same language – they're not like us at all.'

I made an effort to avoid an argument on the subject of
racial prejudice. 'You mean you don't trust Cooper?'

'I never trust the English,' said Warren obstinately.
'You can never tell what they're thinking. They're always
so polite, so cool and so damned charming, and then
suddenly you find they're all set to stab you in the back.
Cooper tried to give me the impression that he wasn't
really interested in Gina at all and that he wished me
well – and then what happens? I find he's taken her off
to London for the weekend! Well, if that isn't two-faced
double-dealing, damn it, I don't know what is—'

'But as far as I can gather they were merely travelling
together—'

'Look,' said Warren. 'You don't seriously think they're
going to shake hands at London airport and go their
separate ways, do you? Why do you think she went to
London?'

'It's an interesting city,' I said, annoyed by his eagerness
to read guilt into what might well have been an innocent

situation. 'Why shouldn't she have wanted to see it with or without Garth Cooper?'

'Because Gina's all tied up emotionally with this damned man Cooper. He's a rich, successful business man of about thirty-five. He's sophisticated – he knows his way around Paris and I'll bet he knows his way around London too. He's the sort of man women drool over as soon as he enters a room, while men ask each other what the hell he has that they don't have. Gina, as usual, has gone into the whole business with her eyes tight shut – she never even stopped to ask herself if he was married or what kind of background he had—'

'You mean he's the playboy type?'

'I mean he's a womanizer. He knows I came to France to be with Gina and yet that didn't stop him from taking her out on the town and spending all that money—'

I was becoming a little tired of Mr Cooper's money. 'But Warren,' I said reasonably. 'Gina chose to go out with him, didn't she? And you're not her fiancé any more, if you'll forgive me saying so. If she chose to go out with him it's bad luck for you, but in Cooper's eyes she doesn't belong to you any more than she belongs to him.'

'She's infatuated with him,' said Warren obstinately. 'It's me she really loves.'

I was silent. It was impossible for me to say that this was highly unlikely.

'If I can only get her away from Cooper – if I could only persuade her to notice me again . . .' He refilled his glass of wine; he was drinking much too quickly '. . . she'd come back to me,' he said. 'I know it. That's why I am here. I got my father to pull some strings and fix me this job for a year. It's not well paid but at least I'm in Paris near Gina – if only Cooper would stay in England and leave me alone with her, I know, I just know, that everything would work out all right.'

I almost said: 'If it wasn't Cooper it would be some other man,' but I checked myself. I had learned long ago that it's no good arguing with someone in love. 'What *is*

Garth Cooper's business?' I said after a moment. 'Do you know what he does?'

'Sure, he deals in china and glass, some of it antique, some of it modern, but all of it valuable. He's involved with the importing and exporting of special lines of china and glass between England and France.'

'His main office is in London, I suppose?'

'Yes, but he has a small base here in Paris. He told me it's an office-cum-apartment, where he stays as well as works when he's here. It's not a big firm – he's his own boss.'

'Does he have any partners?'

He looked at me in surprise. 'But I thought you knew? You mentioned the name when you told me where Gina's call come from. You mean to say you didn't realize all along who Cooper's partner is?'

'Not Eric Jantzen!'

'No,' said Warren, 'his wife. Cooper's partner is Eric Jantzen's wife Lilian.'

It transpired that Warren had never met either of the Jantzens and that his knowledge of their existence was derived solely from his meeting with Cooper and Gina during the previous week.

'I arrived in Paris a month ago,' he said. 'It took me some time to trace Gina, and then just as I had managed to discover her address I met her by chance in one of the restaurants on the Champs Elysées. That was last Tuesday. She was with Cooper but I went up to her just the same – Cooper was very pleasant, or seemed to be, and asked me to join them for a drink, so I accepted and sat talking with them both for about twenty minutes. Or at least Gina didn't talk much; it was Cooper who carried the conversation – he went all out to give the impression that his relationship with Gina was a very casual one, but I'm not a fool and I wasn't taken in by what he said. And when I called up Gina later—' He winced. 'We had several rows over the phone. I soon realized that Cooper had misled me, and that in fact she was heavily involved with him. On Thursday I asked her if I could see her over the weekend and she said she was going to Brittany sightseeing with Candy-Anna. So I call Monday night to ask her how she made out and you tell me she went to London with Cooper.'

I was silent, thinking of Gina, wondering for the hundredth time what I should do. We had finished our meal and were drinking the last of the wine.

'Maybe I should go to London,' I said uncertainly. 'I'm so worried about her.'

'Because of the phone call?'

'Yes – yes, I suppose mainly because of the phone call. If I thought she was merely busy carrying on with Cooper I would be reluctant to interfere, but I just can't believe that phone call has a completely innocuous explanation. I keep thinking about it.'

'If you go to London,' said Warren, 'I'll come with you. If Gina's in any sort of trouble I want to be there helping her get out of it.'

'Mmmm . . .' I was hesitant, not anxious to have him constantly at my elbow but willing to admit it would be pleasant not to face another foreign country alone. 'Let me think it over. Can I call you later on this afternoon?'

'Sure.' He found a pen and a scrap of paper and wrote down both his office and his apartment numbers. 'I'll be home from work at six,' he added, and then, glancing at his watch: 'Talking of work I guess I'd better get back to the office. I've taken a long lunch hour.'

Since he did not offer to pay for me we split the bill and then shook hands again as we parted in a stilted expression of comradeship. 'Phone me as soon as you've made up your mind about London!' he called after me, as I made my escape. 'I'll be all set to go, if necessary.'

I seemed to be totally incapable of making up my mind on anything by that time. I could not decide whether I should go to London, and if I did go, whether I should go with Warren. I was afraid that after a few hours I would find him excessively annoying, but there are times when any companion is better than none at all, and this might easily be one of those occasions. On reaching the apartment again, I absentmindedly made myself some coffee and sat down on the window-seat to gaze out on the Parisian afternoon.

After some concentrated thought I came to the conclusion that the situation was less complex than anxiety made it appear. I would simply go to London. If I found Gina was merely indulging in an affair with Garth Cooper I would look like a fool, but that was the worst that could happen; at least I would be on hand to help her. But if I stayed in Paris . . . I shrugged. In that case I might as well have stayed in New York. The best thing I could do was to go to London, and if Warren was willing to help I should accept his offer. I might need all the help I could get. If he got on my nerves too badly I could always manage to escape from him.

I smiled wryly. Poor Warren! I really rather liked him. I finished my coffee and went to my handbag to find the paper with Warren's phone number on it. I was just looking at it a moment later when I had an idea.

Two minutes' searching around the living room produced the telephone directory, and sitting down on the floor, I opened it at the C section and began to turn the pages to Cooper. If he had an office in Paris which also served as a *pied-à-terre* for himself, it was possible it was listed under his name as well as under the name of the company.

It was. I saw the entry COOPER, GARTH, and the address in the Rue Piedmont, and on an impulse I reached for the phone and began to dial. It was logical to assume there would be a secretary there, or at least an answering service, and I could find out from them how long he was expected to be away from Paris and perhaps also the address of his office in London.

The number started to ring. I was just wondering in panic if the secretary or the answering service would speak English, when someone picked up the receiver.

A male voice said casually: '*Allo?*'

I fumbled for the remnants of my schoolgirl French

vocabulary, but my mind, as so often happens in such a situation, went blank. '*Monsieur Cooper, s'il vous plaît,*' I said haltingly, and then added with an American accent which even I could hear: '*Est-il là?*'

There was a slight pause. Then:

'Yes, he's here,' said the stranger in the perfect accentless English which only the British can produce. 'You're speaking to him. May I ask who this is please?'

## chapter 4

I was so transfixed with embarrassment and surprise that I was dumbfounded. My fingers clasped the telephone receiver with a tight, hot, painful grip. My mind was blank, my tongue utterly paralysed.

'Hello?' said Garth Cooper sharply. 'Hello? Are you still there?'

I said very slowly: 'Yes, I'm sorry. I wasn't aware that you were in Paris, Mr Cooper. Please excuse me if I sound surprised.' And remembering that he did not know who I was I added: 'This is Gina's sister, Claire Sullivan.'

Now it was his turn to be silent in astonishment. I tried to picture him, imagine his expression, but I could not.

'I've just arrived from New York for a vacation,' I said, 'but Gina doesn't seem to be here. I – I suppose you don't know where she is, by any chance?'

There was another slight pause. Then:

'She didn't know you were coming, did she?' he said unexpectedly. 'She didn't mention it.'

'No, it was a spur of the moment decision.' I felt weak suddenly, dangerously close to tears. All my reassuring thoughts about Gina had sprung from the supposition that she was with Garth Cooper. To find out that he was back in Paris while she apparently was still in London was somehow horribly unnerving. 'Mr Cooper, if you know where she is—' I broke off, not knowing which words to choose.

'I last saw her in London,' he said. 'We flew over together last Friday evening, and on Saturday I introduced her to someone she wanted to meet, someone with show business connexions. You know, no doubt, that she was hoping to break into films.'

'Then you last saw her—'

'—On Saturday for lunch. I've been in Paris since Sunday night, but I'm returning to London again tomorrow morning. Perhaps I could make a few enquiries for you.'

I did not know what to say. I was still so appalled by the realization that my worst fears had been proved valid that all I was conscious of was complete confusion.

'Perhaps we ought to discuss this in detail,' said Garth Cooper after a moment. 'Are you doing anything this evening?'

'No,' I said numbly.

'Would you care to have dinner with me?'

'Well . . . if you're not too busy . . .'

'Not in the least,' he said briskly. 'Are you staying at Gina's flat?'

'Yes.'

'Would it be convenient if I called for you at eight-thirty?'

'Yes . . . yes, it would. Thank you, Mr Cooper.'

'Not at all, Miss Sullivan,' he said, very smooth, scrupulously courteous. 'I look forward to meeting you.'

And the line clicked with an air of finality as he replaced the receiver.

I had time on my hands, but did not know how to spend it. I should have passed the afternoon sightseeing, visiting the Louvre perhaps, or Notre Dame, or Sacré-Coeur perched on the heights above Montmartre, but I had no heart for playing the rôle of tourist. I was too worried. For a while I considered cancelling the date with Garth Cooper and going at once to London, but when I called the airlines I found that there were no seats available on the night flights across the Channel. On an impulse I made a reservation on the Air France morning flight, and then dithered for a while about whether or not I should contact my friend at Scotland Yard again. In the end I did put through a call to Detective-Inspector Fowles, more to ease my mind than in any hope that the action would have startling results. But I was out of luck; he was away from the office. I left my name and phone number and wondered if I should have spoken to anyone else, but then decided that if I were to be in London tomorrow anyway I might as well spare myself making explanations to a stranger on the phone. Having settled that issue, I began to wonder if I might have been too ready to believe Garth Cooper when I had spoken to him earlier. It was not improbable that he had lied to me, and that he was after all connected with Gina's disappearance. I told myself I must guard against being too credulous when I met him that evening.

At length, unable to endure the confining walls of the apartment any longer, I went out and walked down to the river, but it began to rain and I was obliged to turn back again to the Rue St Thomasine. Time passed; Candy-Anna returned from work and rushed out again at six-thirty on a date. Left alone once more I had a bath, changed slowly and by quarter past eight was sitting on the window-seat and nervously watching the street below.

I began to wonder what he would look like. What, in general, did Englishmen look like? One had a stereotyped impression of Spaniards, Italians and Frenchmen being dark, slim and excitable, of Swedes, Danes and Norwegians being tall, blond and bland. Germans were fair and jolly with overweight tendencies. Slavs fair and sad with a fondness for melodrama. But the English? Would he be dark or fair? Fat or thin? Withdrawn or volatile? Perhaps, I thought, resorting to a familiar image, he would be like a typical New Englander, a reminder of the countryside where I had been born and brought up. Logic rather than instinct told me this was unlikely. This man would be

European, not American. He would think, act and speak like a European.

I was too inexperienced then to know that the English no more consider themselves part of Europe than they consider themselves part of America.

Below me in the street a taxi pulled up and my heart thudded in anticipation, but two very obvious Frenchmen got out and my nervousness receded. I glanced up and down the street. There was a woman, two children . . . and behind her a small man with middle European features. In the other direction walking up from the river were two more men, not together, of uncertain nationality. I was just wondering if either of these could be Garth Cooper when he came along.

To this day I have no idea why I should have been so positive of his identity as soon as I saw him, for he did not obviously stand out as a foreigner on French soil, but there was certainly no doubt in my mind. Perhaps the clue to his nationality was in his casual easy walk; Frenchmen are almost always either in a hurry or else idly stationary. His clothes were casual too, but not casual in the sense of being informal. On the contrary his suit was perfectly cut and his whole appearance immaculate, but he wore his clothes with an air of carelessness as if he knew he did not need to take trouble in order to look presentable. He had no hat, no umbrella and appeared to be unaware of the slight drizzle. Here was someone who expected it to rain a little during the course of each day and would have been surprised if it hadn't. His hands were in his pockets; as I watched, his right hand went to his head absentmindedly to smooth his hair, and then with a quick glance up and down the street he crossed over to the pavement beneath my window and disappeared into the building.

I experienced a stab of nervousness followed by a wave of panic. I'm never very good at first meetings. With an abrupt, awkward series of movements I stood up, smoothed my dress over my hips, fidgeted with my collar and glanced in the mirror to check my appearance. I was just wishing I were three thousand miles away when the bell rang.

Moving very slowly I crossed the room and opened the door.

He smiled, polite, charming, unconcerned. 'Miss Sullivan?'

'Mr Cooper?' I said too efficiently, and opened the door a little wider. 'Please come in.'

'Thank you.' He moved indolently across the threshold. His hair, which had looked dark at a distance, was in fact a light brown; I noticed again the trick he had of smoothing it with his hand as if he expected it to be perpetually untidy. He was tall, but not strikingly so, and without being solidly built he still managed to give an impression of durability. One felt he would wear well under adverse circumstances. He had a straight nose, a humorous mouth and wide-set, unreadable light eyes.

'Can I offer you a drink?' I said uneasily.

'No thanks,' he said. 'They have the most terrible bottle of whisky locked away in the bedroom somewhere, but since they always produce it with such enormous pride I haven't the heart to tell them it's undrinkable. Let's go straight out and have dinner. Incidentally, I must apologize for suggesting half-past eight instead of half-past seven. I forgot that Americans always eat early.'

'When in Rome,' I murmured, unable to think of anything else to say.

'Do as the Romans do?' he said. 'Or do as your sister does and treat it like a little old-fashioned corner of Manhattan?'

I was unsure whether he was amused or not. 'That's only a defence,' I said. 'One feels so foreign here.'

'Depressing, isn't it?' he agreed, taking me aback. 'The French look down their noses at anyone not born in France, but don't let it upset you. There's one race they hate even more than the Americans, and that's the

British. They haven't yet got over Waterloo.' He strolled over to the door again and held it open for me with a smile. 'It'll be pleasant to dine out with a fellow-foreigner, for a change.'

Since he had spent most of the previous week dining out with Gina I could not see why he should consider the prospect of dining with me a change but I made no attempt to argue with him. I opened my pocketbook, checked to see if I had my keys and glanced round the apartment automatically to see that all was in order. He waited by the doorway. The light from the corridor beyond seemed to slant oddly across his face, and as I passed him I looked up for no reason and found he was watching me with a closed, impassive expression which betrayed nothing.

I moved on, my face tingling, and felt his presence behind me as we moved down the corridor to the elevator. There was a curious, awkward silence. I was just racking my brains to think of some way of breaking it when he said lightly: 'So this is what Gina would look like if she wasn't underweight and over-made-up!'

He meant it, I knew, to be a compliment, but I thought the remark disloyal and unfair to Gina.

'Gina's very attractive,' I said glibly, not thinking.

'I didn't say she wasn't,' he said in reply, and opened the doors of the elevator as it reached our level of the shaft.

I really couldn't let the topic lapse on that dubious note so I said as we stepped into the elevator and he closed the doors after us: 'I only wish I were as slim and as clever with my appearance as Gina is.'

He pressed the button to the ground floor and the cage began to sink downwards. 'Well, I shouldn't worry about it too much if I were you,' he said. 'You really don't need to.'

I had taken him too seriously. My face began to tingle again and I turned aside to hide my embarrassment. Fortunately before any further conversation was necessary we reached the lobby and went outside into the wet street. He hailed a cab, and as I scrambled into the car I heard him say in perfect French to the driver: '*Le Cicéro, s'il vous plaît.*'

'Have you been to Paris before?' he asked neutrally, as the cab shot off over the cobbles.

'No,' I said. 'This is my first visit to Europe.' A thought occurred to me. 'Have you been to America?'

'I've been to New York,' he said, 'but I'm told that that's no more America than London is England.'

'Did you like it?'

'Well, yes,' he said frankly. 'As a matter of fact, I did. One is supposed to shudder, I know, and say it was terrible, but I rather enjoyed it. I took a fancy to the Pan-Am building.'

'That's near where I live!' I told him how I could see the building from the window of my apartment.

'You have one of those large modern apartments with every imaginable convenience?' he hazarded.

'Well, it's not considered modern,' I said, 'since it's at least ten years old, but I suppose it might seem large to anyone who had previously lived in a cell. And the conveniences, though numerous, are imaginary, not imaginable. But it has a good view and it suits me and it's home, so I shouldn't complain.'

He laughed. 'It sounds like my apartment here in Paris!'

'But you have a bigger one in London?'

'Slightly bigger. But I don't like living in flats. My favourite place is a cottage I own in the country, in a village called Holmbury St Mary in Surrey.'

'You mean English villages really do have names like Holmbury St Mary!'

He was amused. 'That's a very modest example of a typical English village name! They come in much more exotic forms than that. My favourite name belongs to a village in the West Country called – if you can believe it – Compton Pauncefoot . . . hey, this driver's taking a very direct but unscenic route! We can do better than this.' He leant forward and began to speak in French. I caught the names '*Champs Elysées*' and '*Place de la Concorde*' and

'*La Madeleine*'. The driver nodded wisely and turned the car into a side-street. 'Since this is your first night out in Paris,' said Garth Cooper, 'you should be allowed at least a passing glance at a few landmarks.'

And as he spoke the car swung into the Avenue Victor Hugo, and at the end of the wide boulevard I could see the floodlit splendour of L'Etoile and the Arc de Triomphe. Traffic roared past us, roared around us, roared behind us. Everyone seemed to be driving with a most reckless audacity. 'Is traffic in Paris always like this?' I said doubtfully, remembering the stately pace of the New York Avenues with the countless intervals of traffic lights and intersections.

'Always,' came the wry reply.

We reached the Arc de Triomphe, circled it and hurtled into the Champs Elysées. There were lights among the trees, crowds strolling on the sidewalks and far away, at the end of the seemingly endless boulevard, more lights, a glimpse of greater brilliance to come.

I sighed.

'It's nice, isn't it?' said the man beside me. 'I never get tired of it.'

'Nice!' I said reproachfully, my eyes drinking in everything I could see and still thirsting for more. 'What an understatement!'

'Where I come from everything is an understatement,' he said. 'It's good to hear someone who's not afraid to sound enthusiastic.'

We traversed a smaller version of L'Etoile and went on down the Champs Elysées. There were buildings on either side of us now, enormous restaurant-cafés with tables on the pavement, hordes of people.

'Paris comes alive at night. When we come back this way later on there'll still be crowds everywhere.'

'Is London like this too?'

'No, Londoners enjoy themselves secretively indoors in private clubs. Or else they cram themselves into a smoky little pub and see how much beer they can drink before closing time.'

'*Are* the English really so odd?'

'We have to do something to preserve the illusion that we're different from any other race.'

We reached the enormous width and breadth of the Place de la Concorde; with a dexterity born of sublime confidence our taxi skipped nimbly in and out of other cars which were weaving diagonal and horizontal lines in front of us. We turned north to La Madeleine then east along the Rue St Honoré and into the Rue de Rivoli which led past the Louvre.

'I'd like to go there and look around,' I said wistfully, remembering that I was due to leave the following morning for London, and thought: I'll come back. As soon as I find out what's happened to Gina I'll come back here.

'You're interested in art, then?'

'In an amateur sort of way.'

'Music?'

'Again – in an amateur sort of way.'

'That means you must be highly professional at something!'

I laughed. 'I teach English literature – I suppose you could say that I was professional at that!'

'How interesting. Incidentally, what do the Americans really think of Shakespeare?'

'I suppose most of them are aware that he was born at Stratford-on-Avon, not Stratford, Connecticut.'

'You surprise me. During August at Stratford-on-Avon one can almost imagine one is in Stratford, Connecticut. There's such a predominance of American accents in the High Street that I naturally assumed he was somewhat of a national figure in America.'

I smiled. 'The people who can afford to vacation in Stratford-on-Avon are usually people who have received a reasonable education.'

'Do you like Shakespeare?'

'Yes – very much.'

I thought he would make some comment at this point to reveal his own tastes, but he did not. Instead he leaned forward to say something else to the driver, and as he moved the glare from a street lamp momentarily threw a harsh light across his face and emphasized the fine line of his nose and jaw.

Somewhere, far away, in the further recesses of my body, my heart skipped a beat and then went on as if nothing had happened.

He turned to face me again with his casual charming smile. 'We're almost there. I hope you didn't mind the slight detour before dinner.'

'On the contrary, I enjoyed it very much,' I said. My mouth felt dry. My hands were clenched in tension and I consciously had to relax each finger. 'Thank you.' A mute voice was saying in my dulled brain: *Not that. Please not that.*

Ever since I was old enough to distinguish between boys and girls, I seemed to have an unhappy knack of falling for men who were not only totally unsuitable but also totally uninterested in me. For a long time now I thought I had outgrown it, but now I began to wonder. It seemed as if my weakness had merely been in abeyance and was now showing unmistakable signs of awaking and returning to disrupt my life.

My hands clenched themselves again. I stared unseeingly out of the window as the car drew to a halt.

Outside the taxi I found myself in a narrow street leading off a wide boulevard, and presently we were making our way into a very plush, very intimate little restaurant where waiters fluttered like black and white moths and an imposing *maître d'hôtel* cruised across the thick carpet to greet us.

'Bonsoir, Monsieur Cooper, bonsoir, mademoiselle . . .' He bowed gracefully, flourished an elegant hand, summoned a minion to escort us to a secluded alcove. I forgot my fears of a moment ago; feeling immensely important and supremely élite I allowed the waiter to pull out my chair and help to seat me as carefully as if my solid frame were as delicate as the most fragile china. A menu was put into my hands; I stared dizzily at all the French names and did not know where to begin.

'Do you want to try some French snails to start with?'

'I – don't feel brave enough for that,' I said, overcome with cowardice. 'After all, this is only my first evening in Paris. Is there something still French but not quite so exotic?'

'Vichyssoise?'

'Yes, that would be lovely.'

We considered the menu for several minutes and made our decisions. A waiter took our order; Garth selected a wine. Finally when there was nothing more to do except to wait for our meal to be served, we sat back in our chairs and relaxed. Or at least, he did. I was too tense, too anxious to introduce the subject of Gina yet, not knowing how to begin, and in the end it was he who spoke first.

'I hope I'm not being too dense about this,' he said casually, 'but I'm still not really clear as to why you decided to come here on the spur of the moment without telling Gina. You don't strike me as being a scatterbrained little girl like Candy-Anna, so I find your actions all the more striking because they're so obviously out of character. Why did you decide to come?'

I hesitated for a moment, toyed with my snow-white napkin and smoothed it over my lap very carefully before I answered: 'Your partner said nothing to you?'

'My partner?' he said astonished. 'Lilian Jantzen? What does she have to do with your decision to come to Paris?'

'Gina called me from the Jantzens' apartment on Saturday to urge me to come over.' I decided against telling him the truth. 'She sounded so carried away with Europe – so insistent that she was having such an extraordinary time – that my imagination was fired and I made this ridiculous spur-of-the-moment decision. I knew Gina was planning to return to Paris by Monday so I thought I would surprise her by arriving Monday night – however, I did send a cable forewarning her so that my arrival wouldn't be too much of a shock. But when I got here I found she wasn't back from England

and Candy-Anna had no idea where she was. That's why I called you this afternoon – I figured that as you'd been in London with her you might have some idea of how I could get in touch with her.'

'I'm afraid I know little more than you do.' His eyes, steady, quizzical, interested, met mine. It was quite impossible to read his thoughts or guess if he were as honest as he seemed to be. 'As I said to you on the phone this afternoon,' he went on, 'Gina was very eager to break into films – just as many successful young models are, I suppose. It so happens that my partner's husband, Eric Jantzen, who is an artist of some standing in London, has show-business friends, and I thought there was a possibility that he might be able to provide Gina with some valuable contacts. I'd discussed the matter with him previously and he'd said that he'd be happy to meet her, so when we were both in London last Saturday I managed to introduce them to one another. I believe he invited her to his home for a drink that evening, so that would explain her presence in the Jantzen flat, even if it doesn't explain anything else. I can't see why on earth she put through a call to America from the flat of a more or less complete stranger. That simply doesn't make sense at all. What did she say?'

The arrival of the Vichyssoise gave me time to consider my reply. 'She had been trying to persuade me for some time to take my vacation in Europe,' I said carefully, after the waiter had retreated. 'I think her call was more of an impulsive, reckless gesture than anything else. A sort of gay, with-it, "fun" gesture, if you can imagine what I mean. I know that sounds peculiar, but you knew Gina a little, didn't you.' I sipped my Vichyssoise, thankful for the opportunity to avoid looking at him as I spoke. 'Gina is the sort of person who's quite capable of calling New York collect from the apartment of a stranger in London just to say "Why on earth don't you come over and join me?" It's just the sort of thing she would do.'

He smiled. For some reason his smile made me feel uneasy, although I had no idea why it should. It was a friendly smile, frank, open and natural. There was nothing sinister about it at all, yet the sense of uneasiness persisted. 'I don't actually know Gina very well, you know,' he said after a moment. 'In fact, although I met her about six weeks previously, I saw little of her until I returned to Paris from London about two weeks ago. Even then I only took her out a couple of times. She was having trouble with a difficult ex-fiancé.'

'Yes,' I said. 'She wrote and told me that she had met Warren again in Paris.'

'You know him? I thought he was a nice young chap, if a little stupid. If he had had an ounce of common sense he would have realized that the last way to win Gina back was to chase after her like an infuriated terrier who enjoys a good bark. He met Gina by chance when I was with her, and although he joined us for a drink and the meeting began pleasantly enough, there was a rather unnecessary scene before he could be persuaded to retreat.'

'It must have been embarrassing for you.'

'Well, actually I was sorry for both of them – sorry for him because he was carefully destroying the impression he was trying to create in Gina's eyes, and sorry for Gina because I'm sorry for anyone with a difficult ex-fiancé. She was much more embarrassed than I was. I was really hardly involved – I didn't know her well enough for the scene to make any emotional impact on me.'

I said lightly: 'Candy-Anna spoke of you as if you were the big romance of Gina's life!'

'Candy-Anna reads too many romantic magazines.' He spoke lightly too. His eyes were clear and unconcerned. 'There had hardly been time for such melodrama.'

Now I was certain that he was deviating a little from the truth. 'She probably read some tremendous meaning into the fact that you and Gina travelled to London together,' I said placidly. 'She's just the sort of person who would fasten on something like that and exaggerate it out of all proportion.'

He sipped his Vichyssoise, effortlessly matching my

attempt to appear nonchalant and unconcerned. 'Probably.'

I blushed, not knowing why, only feeling obscurely that his terse comment had been a rebuff. I made a great business of dabbing my mouth with my napkin and cast around in my mind feverishly for some way of changing the subject.

'Didn't the Jantzens mention to you that Gina had made the phone call from their apartment?' I said at last, remembering that my friend at Scotland Yard had contacted the Jantzens during his routine enquiry into the situation. 'Didn't they mention it at all?'

'I haven't seen either of the Jantzens since early on Saturday,' he said. 'We all had lunch together with Gina. After that I was tied up for the remainder of the weekend on personal matters and then on Sunday night I returned to Paris.'

'But haven't you spoken to them – to your partner – on the phone since then?'

'Yes,' he said, 'I spoke to Lilian this morning, but we never discuss by phone anything which isn't strictly business. Too expensive.' He smiled. 'We Europeans don't possess your American passion for the long-distance call!'

'I hardly regard it as one of my ruling passions,' I said drily, remembering ruinous little bills arriving in the telephone company's discreet buff envelopes.

'Ah yes,' he said, 'I was forgetting. You have other, much more interesting ruling passions. How did you first become interested in Shakespeare?'

He was, I discovered during the course of the evening, extremely clever at manipulating the conversation into the precise channels which interested him. Throughout our long, elaborate and delicious meal I found myself talking far more than I normally did with a stranger; the wine was heady, powerful; my tongue seemed encouraged to give voice to a surprising amount of detail. I spoke of New England and New York, of a new life and a new world, of my parents, my work and my interests. We talked of the theatre, films, the written word, the spoken word, and I found myself to my amazement giving bold, outspoken opinions in situations where reticence would normally have made me retreat or waver. Finally as we sat facing each other over the black coffee and Grand Marnier, I realized that he now knew a great deal about me whereas I still knew absolutely nothing about him.

'Which college did you go to?' I said, knowing that the English educational system was very different from the American but assuming he would have received some form of advanced education. 'University, I mean, not college.'

'I didn't go to a University,' he said unperturbed. 'My father went bankrupt so I was put out to work at an early age, like David Copperfield.'

'Oh,' I said, not knowing quite what to say. 'But you graduated from high school – you obtained the usual diplomas?'

'By a fortunate chance I did, since my father thoughtfully staved off bankruptcy till I was seventeen, but it wouldn't have mattered if I'd been forced to leave school earlier. It was one of those schools where merely to attend it is supposed to open all doors later on, regardless of academic merit. I say "supposed to" because things are changing and now one is expected to learn something while attending school – a revolutionary idea, if ever there was one! My father would have been shocked.'

'Is he dead?'

'Yes – perhaps fortunately for him. The world where he belonged died with the second world war. Afterwards in the late forties and early fifties there were too many changes for him.' He spoke simply, with pity but without regret. 'My mother died soon afterwards. I have a sister in New Zealand and three spinster aunts in Norfolk, but apart from them I'm as devoid of relations as you are . . . I've never made up my mind whether that's a situation which calls for relief or regret. I suppose one is less restricted without relations, but—'

'—more lonely,' I said. I was wondering how he had

managed to make his money since he had clearly inherited nothing from his father. 'When did you meet you partner? Have you known her for a long time?'

'Yes, I met Lilian ten years ago when I was working in the china and glass department of a London store. I was a salesman and she was one of my best customers. One day, about six months after we first met, she asked me if I would like to try selling for her instead of for the department store. She was interested in the possibility of importing French china and glass and selling it in London – she knew people in the business, she'd worked in it herself, she thought she could create a market in certain glass which hadn't been imported since before the war . . . Well, to cut a long story short, she had the money and the flair and she knew what she was doing. All I did was to sell a saleable product. Before we knew where we were, we found ourselves joint partners in a small but flourishing export–import business between England and France.'

'I see.' I could not quite believe he had ever been a mere salesman. He was so totally removed from my conventional picture of what a salesman should be like. 'But do you – did you enjoy selling?'

'I enjoyed dealing with china and glass. Especially glass. Glass can be so beautiful, so exquisite. I always thought of selling as being nothing more than telling people who could afford to buy that they couldn't possibly spend their money in a more aesthetically pleasing manner. Do you know anything about glass?'

'Nothing at all.'

He began to talk about it, interrupting himself only to order some more coffee and liqueurs. Time, meaningless and unimportant, floated hazily away.

'Of course Lilian knows more than I do,' he said at last after speaking with the authority and enthusiasm of an expert for some time. 'She's taught me all I know.' The phrase somehow struck a discordant note; he made an amused, impatient gesture with his hand as if to brush any possible *double-entendre* aside, and added frankly: 'She's a remarkable woman.'

414

'Yes,' I said. 'She must be. But what about her husband? Doesn't he have any part in the business at all?'

'Good God, no – Lilian wouldn't have that! Anyway, Eric's an artist, with a career of his own – the last thing he would want is to be involved in an office routine.'

'I see.'

'Of course, it was somewhat tricky when Lilian and I began our venture together. Eric was a little suspicious, I think, but he had no need to worry. I'm not interested from the romantic point of view, in a woman ten years older than myself, and Lilian simply isn't interested in the romantic point of view. She's in love with her china and her glass.'

I wondered why he felt it necessary to point this out to me; it was as if he were being automatically defensive on a subject which had caused him great difficulty in the past. I said impulsively, my mind veering back to Gina: 'Do you think either of the Jantzens would know where Gina is? I'm really very worried about her.'

He looked surprised. 'Really? Why's that? I should think she enjoyed London so much over the weekend that she decided to stay on for a few days. After all she's a freelance model and can do as she pleases. And if Eric offered to introduce her to some show-business contacts it's obvious she would stay on until she met them.'

I nodded. Since I had misled him about Gina's hysterical phone call to me, I could not expect him to understand my anxiety.

'Have you contacted the agency she works for? Maybe they've heard from her.'

'Candy-Anna spoke to them today but they've heard nothing. In fact, they were very annoyed because she hadn't reported for work today. They had a special job lined up for her.'

'Hm.' He was silent. 'I'll ask the Jantzens tomorrow if they know what's happened to her.'

I nearly told him that I had resolved to go to London myself, but then held back at the last moment. It would be foolish to trust him too much. I had only his word that he had not seen Gina since Saturday afternoon, and I had already had the suspicion that he was minimizing the importance of his association with her. I felt depressed suddenly, tired; the glow of the wine had dulled and the sparkle of the evening seemed to have effervesced into nothingness. And then all at once his hand slid across the table to cover my own in a gesture I would never have expected from him, and his voice, concerned yet still casual, said quietly: 'You really shouldn't worry, you know. I'm sure she's quite all right.' I felt the tears blur my eyes and the sudden tightness hurt my throat because I knew that he was trying to be kind.

'Some more coffee?'

'No,' I said, making an effort to overcome my distress. 'No, thank you. I feel completely satiated! It was the most wonderful meal and I enjoyed it very much.'

'Would you like to go on somewhere else for a few more drinks?'

'No – no, really, I couldn't, thank you very much.' The depression about Gina was enveloping me again and I had a sudden absurd fear of bursting into tears in front of him and telling him more than I should about my predicament.

He glanced at his watch. 'Well, the night's still young,' he said lightly. 'It's not even midnight yet. Would you like to drive into Montmartre and go up to Sacré-Coeur to see the city lights? Or would you like to stroll down the Champs Elysées for a little way? Or are you too tired and want to go back to the apartment?'

I nearly said: 'Yes, perhaps if you'll excuse me . . .' but I did not. I looked up into his face and suddenly I forgot about my depression and my dread of losing my self-control. It didn't matter any more. Nothing mattered except that I was with him and that we were in Paris. I wanted to remember the evening as long as I lived and not mar a future memory by ending the evening too abruptly.

I said spontaneously: 'Oh, I'd love to sit in one of those open sidewalk cafés on the Champs Elysées and watch the world go by!' And he laughed and said: 'Why not? That's a splendid suggestion!' He paid the bill, leaving the notes carelessly on the bill and not pausing to wait for change, and we left amidst the bows of the waiters and the good wishes of the *maître d'hôtel*. Outside it was warm and the night sky glowed in a reflection of a million lights and the cobbles of the street nibbled at my high-heeled shoes.

The next three hours are hazy in my memory, not because I was too tired to remember them but because they passed so quickly that afterwards my memory was only able to recall assorted moments. I can remember the smoke of Garth's cigarette curling upwards into the night air as we sat in the café on the Champs Elysées, the flame of the match reflected in his light eyes, the shadows his hands cast on the table. I can remember hearing the roar of the traffic yards away across the wide sidewalk, the murmur of the strolling passers-by, the incessant intensity of a strange language being spoken on all sides of me, but when I try to remember now I cannot hear our own voices or recall what we said. Later we took a cab to a place in Montmartre, danced a little, drank a little more, but I have no memory of being tired or even a clear recollection of the places we visited, until finally in the early hours of the morning we were on the steps of Sacré-Coeur and all Paris lay spread out before us beneath a summer moon.

'Oh!' I said, and the meaningless syllable expressed all that I felt at that moment, joy that the evening had exceeded my expectations, sadness that it was over and would almost certainly never be repeated, guilt that I could have forgotten Gina so completely when she had dominated my mind for so long. And as I sighed and went on gazing out over the city, he said casually from close at hand:

'How long do you intend to stay in Paris?'

The magic was broken. I don't know whether he was asking the question because he wanted to see me again or because he wanted to know what I planned to do next to find Gina. I moved a little, turning slightly away from him. 'I don't know,' I said. 'My plans are uncertain.'

After a moment he said: 'What's the matter?'

'Nothing!' I was startled. 'Why?'

'I thought perhaps something had disturbed you.'

'No. I was only wishing that there could be more evenings as enjoyable as this one.'

'I see no reason why there shouldn't be.'

I did not answer.

'Unfortunately I can't cancel this trip to London tomorrow, or I'd most certainly do so. I'll be in London at least five days, possibly a week. If you were planning to go to England—'

'I have no plans at the moment,' I said too abruptly, and moved back toward the white ghostly walls of Sacré-Coeur. 'I'll have to think about that in the morning.'

'Couldn't you think about it a little now?' I could hear his quiet footsteps behind me. 'I'd like to see you again, and it seems pointless that we should have to spend the next week in different cities.'

'Well,' I said, trying to speak lightly and only succeeding in sounding hard and unnatural, 'no doubt we'll both survive somehow.'

I thought he would make some quick clever reply, but he was silent. Surprised by this unexpected reaction I turned to look at him. His face was still, his mouth shadowed, his light eyes as unreadable as ever.

'I'm sorry,' I said wretchedly, knowing that he was upset even more though there was no indication of it in his expression. 'That was a stupid thing to say. Please forgive me.'

He smiled at once. 'It was no more than I deserved,' he said pleasantly. 'It was no business of mine to tell you how to spend your holiday. I'm the one who should apologize.'

'No, I—'

'Ah, to hell with apologies and everything else!' he

exclaimed in a sudden uncharacteristic burst of impatience, and the next moment without any warning at all I felt his arms slip around my waist and his lips, cool and hard, against my own. 'And I'm sorry for that too,' he said as he released me a second later, 'if you think it requires an apology. Since we're on the subject of apologies it seems appropriate that I should conduct all my apologizing at once . . . Are you cold?'

'A little,' I said, seizing on any excuse which would explain why the colour had drained from my face and my body was trembling, 'but not much.'

'Let's go back into the square and find a taxi.'

Twenty minutes later the cab was drawing up outside Gina's apartment house and Garth was telling the driver to wait. He escorted me to the front door, but when I started to thank him for the evening he took out his wallet and extracted a card.

'I enjoyed it as much as you did. Look, here's my address and number – if you change your mind about coming to London call me as soon as you arrive and I'll come to meet you. And if you stay on in Paris, I'll call you as soon as I get the chance to fly back here from London.'

The card felt smooth and cool beneath my hot fingers as I stared dizzily down at the address and phone number. I tried to say 'thank you' again, but I could not speak.

'Goodnight, then, Claire.'

'Goodnight, Garth.'

He kissed me again very briefly and was gone. I went into the building, shut the door, leaned against it. I heard the elevator arrive at the floor, the doors opening and closing around me, the ascent to my floor, and then I stood unmoving in the darkness of the apartment, as I recalled all that had been left unsaid between us. At last, after a long time, I reached out and switched on the light.

I saw the note almost at once. It was propped against the telephone and Candy-Anna had printed on it the words: CALL WARREN MAYNE WHEN YOU GET IN. URGENT.

I gave a small exclamation. Delving into my purse I

found the right scrap of paper and began to dial the numbers with an uncertain, trembling hand.

'My God, Claire,' said Warren plaintively. 'It's nearly three o'clock in the morning! What's the big idea of calling me up at this hour? I'm not a night owl.'

I instantly felt guilty at my thoughtlessness. I had lost all track of time and had never even glanced at my watch. 'I'm terribly sorry,' I said, stricken. 'But I've just got in and I saw Candy-Anna's note to say that I was to call at once as you had an urgent message—'

'For Pete's sake, doesn't that featherbrain ever get a message right? No, I've been calling you to find out whether you've decided to go to England tomorrow. If you remember,' he paused reproachfully, 'you said you'd call me this afternoon at the office to let me know one way or the other.'

'Oh, my goodness, I quite forgot!' I was stricken anew by my carelessness.

'Yes,' said Warren politely. 'Am I to take it that you've decided against going?'

'Well . . . no,' I said confused. 'I decided I would go. I've got a reservation on an Air France flight tomorrow morning. I – I'm so sorry, Warren – I should have let you know—'

He sighed. 'I'll call Air France first thing tomorrow morning to see if they have a spare seat – what's your flight number? No, on second thoughts, it doesn't matter – I'll never be able to get the morning flight. I couldn't leave my office at such short notice. Tell you what I'll do – I'll try and get an evening flight tomorrow. Which hotel did you plan on checking in to?'

'I haven't the remotest idea,' I said weakly, realizing that Warren's companionship in London was now the last thing I wanted but not knowing how to deflect him from his inexorable course.

'Go to the Regent Palace. Or the Strand Palace. They're very good, very central, inexpensive and they cater for Americans, so you'll feel at home.' And before I could even begin to explain to him that I would rather be in an

English hotel among English people he added: 'I'll try the Regent Palace first and if I find you haven't checked in there I'll try the Strand Palace. If you're not at either I'll meet you in the lobby of the Regent Palace at nine on Thursday morning.'

'Yes,' I agreed meekly, too exhausted to argue.

'Incidentally where the hell were you this evening? I called and called and finally at midnight I got hold of Candy-Anna. I was beginning to think you'd disappeared too. I was getting worried.'

There was something vaguely touching about his earnest concern for me.

'I was just out seeing Paris,' I said.

'Not alone!' He sounded shocked.

'Of course not,' I said drily. 'Well, Warren, I apologize for not calling you back as we'd arranged—'

'But—' he interrupted and then remembered his manners. I could feel his curiosity permeating the wire which linked us, but he had neither the courage nor the effrontery to ask me outright who my escort had been.

'Yes?' I said mildly.

'Nothing. I'll see you tomorrow night, then. OK?'

'Yes – many thanks, Warren.'

'You're welcome,' he said classically. 'So long now, Claire.'

'Bye.'

I replaced the receiver with a sigh of relief and went to bed as quickly as possible. My last thought before I slid into unconsciousness was to wonder what Warren would have said if he had known I had spent the evening with Garth Cooper.

My flight left at ten, but I saw him as soon as I entered the departure lounge. He was standing by the window and reading *Le Figaro*. The morning sun slanted across the fine bones of his face, and I saw that his expression was still and withdrawn with the effort of concentration. I stopped dead. I was just wondering why on earth it had never occurred to me that we would be on the same flight, when he looked up from his paper as if he knew he was being watched and our eyes met. I saw him raise his eyebrows in quizzical astonishment, and as I blushed in confusion he smiled his easy charming smile, tossed his newspaper aside as if it no longer had any significance for him, and came casually across the room towards me.

## chapter 5

'So you decided to come to London after all!' The last traces of his astonishment had merged into an expression of satisfaction. 'I was hoping you'd come. When did you make up your mind?'

'Oh . . . not long ago,' I said uncertainly, and felt myself begin to blush at the evasiveness of my answer.

'Did you have any trouble making your reservation?'

'No.'

Fortunately at that moment our flight was called and his attention was diverted from me. We filtered out of the departure lounge, and five minutes later we were seated in the plane and waiting for the moment when it would taxi away towards the runway for take-off.

'You're a rather unpredictable person, aren't you?' murmured Garth mildly. 'I thought you had quite decided to stay in Paris.'

I smiled uncomfortably. 'I had second thoughts.'

'Really? Or had you planned to come to London all along?'

'I don't know why you should think that.'

'It's not important.' He smiled at me. 'The point is that you're here. Do you like flying?'

'Sometimes I hate it a little less than others.'

'This should be a good flight – we've got perfect weather for it.'

I tried to look enthusiastic, but I suppose I was not very successful.

He laughed. 'Wait and see!'

As it happened he was right and the flight was perfect, so perfect that I even forgot to feel nervous at the thought of so many thousands of feet of nothingness between me and the ground. We took off smoothly, soaring effortlessly away from Paris towards the west, and the sun shone with a dazzling brightness on the distant land below.

The stewardess was at Garth's elbow. 'Something to drink, monsieur?'

'Yes,' said Garth, and to me: 'This should be a celebration to mark your first visit to England. How about some champagne?'

'Oh!' I said, flabbergasted at the idea of champagne before noon, and thought fleetingly how shocked my parents would have been at anything like this. 'Well, it would be nice,' I said guiltily. 'Delightful, in fact.'

Garth turned to the stewardess. 'Champagne for two, please.'

The plane soared on, and suddenly I could look out of the window and see the coast, the flicker of white as the waves broke against the rugged cliffs of the French coast far below. I was just giving an exclamation of pleasure when the champagne arrived.

'Drink up,' said Garth. 'We're nearly there.'

'But we haven't even crossed the Channel yet!'

'That'll only take five minutes.'

It seemed to take even less than that. We had no sooner left the French coast behind when I saw the coast of England approaching.

'Where are the white cliffs?'

'We're farther nòrth than that, I think.'

We left the Channel behind. There was a river below us, an enormous estuary. Little patchwork squares of fields surrounded each of the towns we passed, until gradually the area became densely populated and I guessed we were approaching London.

'You see that winding river over there?'

I nodded. 'Is that—'

'The Thames. It looks as if we're going to fly over central London.'

And then came the most perfect part of all. The plane took a westward course parallel to the line of the river and I saw Tower Bridge, the Tower of London, the dome of St Paul's, the spires of a thousand churches, the Houses of Parliament, Westminster Abbey . . .

'Exactly like the photographs,' I said amazed, as if I had always secretly suspected the camera of lying.

There seemed to be an endless number of bridges over the river, some plain solid structures, some elaborately gothic and fanciful. I gazed down at them all with fascination and hardly even noticed the plane losing height as we flew on over the west London suburbs towards the airport. When our wheels touched the ground ten minutes later I was conscious, for the first time after a flight, of regret that the journey was over.

'That was wonderful!' I said frankly to Garth as we unfastened our safety belts. 'If all flights were like that I'd look forward to them more often. And thank you so much for the champagne.'

We had the usual tedious wait at Customs and Immigration, except that he, with his British passport, was processed through the official machine more quickly than I was.

'Where do I get a bus to the terminal?' I asked, confused by the airport mêlée and looking around for an information sign.

'You don't want to bother with a bus,' said Garth. 'I never do. We'll take a taxi. Incidentally, where were you planning to stay?'

'Warren Mayne suggested the Regent Palace. Or the Strand Palace. Do you know them?'

'Yes,' he said noncommittally. 'They're both very central. The Regent Palace is just off Piccadilly Circus.'

'That sounds fine.'

We found a cab and set off east again. The road was wide and modern, the countryside around the airport extraordinarily green and lush to my eyes, but presently the countryside ended and the suburbs began. As we approached the city there were more towering modern buildings and a massive elevated road which reminded me of the Pulaski Skyway outside New York City.

'It's not how I imagined London to be,' I said doubtfully. 'Everything's so modern.'

'Did you expect the roads to be full of horse-drawn carriages?'

I laughed, glanced around me at the traffic. 'So many tiny cars,' I said, 'and all driving along on the wrong side of the road. There are hardly any big cars at all.'

'There's no room for them.'

We drew nearer to Central London. There was a wide main street called Cromwell Road bordered with trees and stately houses.

'Are those houses old?'

'No, fairly new. I don't suppose any of them are more than a hundred years old.'

London flashed on past the windows of the taxi. Garth was mentioning English names to me, names familiar yet strange. 'This is Kensington . . . Knightsbridge . . . The park on the left is Hyde Park . . . this is Hyde Park Corner . . . Piccadilly . . . Green Park on the right . . .'

'So many parks,' I said astonished. 'And how gracious the houses are here.'

We reached the tiny Piccadilly Circus and almost at the same time the Regent Palace Hotel. Garth helped the driver with my luggage.

'How about dinner this evening? I can call for you at about six-thirty and we can go somewhere for a drink first . . . and I'll talk to the Jantzens about Gina. All right?'

'Yes . . . thank you . . .' I was dazed, overcome by the strangeness of the new country.

'You have my office number if you should want to contact me, haven't you? Till tonight, then.' He touched my shoulder lightly but did not kiss me. 'Au revoir.'

'Goodbye – and thank you.'

He got into the cab again. I heard him say abruptly to the driver: 'Sixty-two Half Moon Street,' and he turned and raised his hand briefly to me as the car drew away from the pavement.

I stood watching the car turn towards Piccadilly Circus, and then, still feeling dazed, I left the street and went very slowly into the hotel.

Fortunately they had a room available on the fifth floor, and after I had unpacked my luggage and redone my make-up I sat down on the bed and placed a call to the apartment in Paris. I had the nagging suspicion that as soon as I had left Paris Gina had returned to it, but my suspicions proved groundless, for no one answered the phone. Candy-Anna was evidently out working and there was no one else there. Having satisfied myself that Gina was still missing I wondered whether to call Scotland Yard again. I remembered that I had phoned from Paris and asked my friend to call me back, but he had probably returned the call while I had been out with Garth the previous evening. I hesitated. Perhaps I should wait till Garth had talked to the Jantzens. I had little enough information to give to Scotland Yard at present, beyond the fact that she had not after all been with Garth when she had phoned me the previous Saturday. But whose word did I have for that? Only Garth's. If I called Scotland Yard again they would begin questioning Garth, prying into his movements . . .

I would wait, I thought. I would wait until he had talked to the Jantzens. I instinctively shied away from making a move which would involve him in consider-able embarrassment and perhaps estrange him from me. Besides, I believed him. I was quite convinced that he was speaking the truth.

Or was I?

I went restlessly over to the window and stared out over Soho. I was still thinking of Garth a moment later when the phone rang and I went back to the bedside to answer it.

'Miss Claire Sullivan?' said the operator in the building. 'One moment, please. I have a call from Paris.'

For a long moment my heart thudded in relief, and then the next instant I was listening not to Gina, as I had hoped, but to Warren Mayne.

'Claire? Hi, I thought I'd just call and find out if you arrived safely and managed to check in all right. How was the flight?'

'Fine, thanks.' It was thoughtful of him to have phoned and I tried to sound cheerful. 'I enjoyed it.'

'Good. Look, I managed to get a seat on the flight leaving at six this evening so I should be with you around eight-thirty or so.'

'I—'

'I checked with the reservation people at your hotel and they have a room for me for tonight. I'll give you a call when I get in.'

'Yes, but—'

'Hey, I'll tell you something odd. I called up Garth Cooper's Paris office this morning to find out when he was expected back in Paris, and they told me he'd just left for London! So he was in Paris yesterday and possibly the day before as well.'

'Yes.'

'You mean you knew?'

'He was on my flight this morning.'

'He was?' He sounded blank with astonishment.

'Yes, we travelled over together. He—'

'But how did you know him?'

'What?'

'How did you know him from Adam? How did you get talking to one another?'

'Oh . . . I met him last night, as it happens. I called him to ask about Gina and he stopped by at the apartment.'

'He did?' Warren was frankly incredulous. 'Why didn't you tell me, for God's sake?'

'When I last spoke to you it was three o'clock in the morning and you weren't in a receptive mood for a long story. Besides, there was no news. Garth said he hadn't seen Gina since lunch on Saturday.'

Warren sounded as if he was just about to voice a

very rude word indeed, but fortunately he stopped in mid-syllable.

'It might be true,' I said impassively. 'I'm having dinner with him tonight so I hope to find out more details from him then.'

'You're having dinner?' Warren said, amazed. 'With him? Tonight?'

'Yes, so I won't be in when you arrive. If I find out anything I'll call your room as soon as I get in.'

'But—' He was speechless. Then: 'Do you think that's wise? Hell, I don't want you disappearing too! Can't you change it to drinks at nine? Then I'll be able to join you and see that you're all right—'

I was beginning to believe Warren had been born in the wrong century. He should have been a knight rescuing damsels in distress.

'Please don't worry,' I said politely. 'I'm quite capable of looking after myself and I don't really believe Mr Cooper is involved in the white slave traffic. I'll talk to you tonight, Warren – hope you have a good flight. Thanks for calling.'

I managed to get rid of him without sounding too rude, but I sensed that his faith in my level-headedness had suffered a mortal blow. I paused for a moment and felt my own faith waver. Was it possible that sanity had temporarily deserted me and that I had made an appalling mistake by trusting Garth? A shiver edged its way down my spine suddenly. Fumbling in my bag I drew out his card, picked up the receiver and asked the operator to try his office number for me.

I could hear the bell ringing at the other end of the wire. Then 'Cooper–Jantzen – good afternoon,' said a girl's voice. 'May I help you?'

'Good afternoon,' I said. 'Could you tell me the nature of your firm's business, please? I'm conducting a survey for purposes of market research.'

'We deal in the importing and exporting of china and glass between England and France.'

'I see. Thank you.'

'Do you wish to speak to Mrs Jantzen?'

'No, thank you. Is Mr Cooper there?'

'No, I'm afraid Mr Cooper's out of the country at present.'

'Oh . . . I see. Thank you. Goodbye.' I replaced the receiver slowly. Garth had told me the previous evening that urgent business in London prevented him from staying on in Paris, but apparently the business had not been urgent enough to necessitate him calling his office. I wished with annoyance that I had asked the girl when she expected him to return to London, and then wondered if there had been any reason on his part to return without telling his partner. Perhaps, after all, he was not as honest as I had supposed him to be.

Uneasiness, faint and nebulous, shadowed my mind for a moment. I pushed it aside, determined not to let my imagination lead me astray, and, seizing my handbag, I went briskly downstairs and stepped out of the hotel to explore Piccadilly.

I did not walk far since all the strain and exhaustion of the last few days seemed to choose that afternoon to catch up with me, and when I returned to the hotel I spent the remainder of the afternoon resting. At five I got up, bathed and changed; at six-thirty I was just putting the finishing touches to my appearance when the house phone rang. It was Garth, in the lobby. My heart began to beat a fraction quicker. With my mouth dry and my hands unsteady, I left the room a second later and went downstairs to meet him.

'How nice you look!' he said as he came forward towards me. 'Not in the least tired. No one would ever have thought you'd spent the morning drinking champagne thirty thousand feet above the English Channel. Did you do anything special this afternoon?'

'No, I just spent the time recovering from the champagne above the Channel! What about you? Did you go to your office?'

'Actually, I didn't let Lilian know I was back until five o'clock this afternoon. I have to admit I wanted some sleep as much as you did so I went straight to my flat. Incidentally, talking of Lilian, I thought you might be interested in meeting both the Jantzens, so I've invited them to have drinks with us at my club before dinner. I hope that's all right with you?'

'Yes – yes, of course. I'd like to meet them. Did you ask Mrs Jantzen about Gina when you spoke to her?'

'Yes.' He opened the door for me and we walked out into the street. Then: 'Why didn't you tell me you'd phoned Scotland Yard to investigate Gina's call?'

I caught my breath. I felt my checks slowly begin to burn as I wondered how I could have been so stupid not to have foreseen this happening.

'Lilian said they'd had a man round from the Yard as the result of Gina's phone call to you. I presume it was you who suggested that the Yard should investigate.'

'Yes,' I said reluctantly, too embarrassed to look at him. 'It was me.'

A cab drew up beside us in response to his raised arm, and as we got inside Garth gave the driver the name of his club.

'What made you think it was a matter for Scotland Yard?' Garth asked pleasantly, as we drove into the vortex of Piccadilly Circus and crowded our way through the traffic around Eros. 'What made you get in touch with them?'

After a while I said: 'I was worried.'

'I should imagine you were,' said Garth with amused irony, 'if you troubled to phone Scotland Yard from New York.'

I was unable to reply.

'What exactly did Gina say during the call?' he said presently. 'There must have been rather more to the conversation than you implied.'

'It was just that we were cut off,' I said in a rush. 'And when I traced the call and phoned back there was no reply. I suppose I panicked.'

He looked at me oddly as if he suspected I was still

keeping part of the truth from him, but made no comment.

'What did the Jantzens say?' I said clumsily, stammering a little. 'Did they know anything that would explain the situation?'

'Not really. Lilian was the one who let Gina into the flat but then she had to dash out to meet some friends so she wasn't with her for more than a few minutes. Eric, whom Gina wanted to talk to about show-business contacts, was delayed and apparently when he got home Gina had gone. He assumed she hadn't bothered to wait for him and thought no more of it till the police turned up later to investigate. Before they arrived he tried phoning her hotel to apologize for letting her down, but was told she had left that evening.'

'Before or after she had been at the Jantzen apartment?' I asked quickly.

'I don't think he bothered to establish that. He called the hotel before the police arrived – before he knew anything was wrong. At that stage he didn't even know Lilian had let Gina into the apartment. When the police told him she must have been there he assumed for some reason that I had let Gina in, although why he should have thought that I would be with her I can't imagine. I wasn't interested in hearing about his show-business contacts.'

'But you have a key to the Jantzen apartment?'

'Yes, I stayed there once and had a key made. I still use it occasionally to entertain clients. We always do, since it's so much more spacious than mine. For that matter, Lilian has a key to my cottage in Surrey as well, since very occasionally we have clients up for a weekend in the country.'

But I was thinking of Gina again. 'Which hotel was she staying at?'

'The Westbury, off Bond Street.'

'Then if we could prove she checked out from there after making the phone call to me it would prove that at least she was safe after leaving the Jantzen apartment!'

'I'm sure she's safe anyway,' said Garth frankly. 'To

be honest I think she's gone chasing off after one of the contacts Eric mentioned at lunch on Saturday. When he appeared to forget about her on Saturday night I expect she lost patience with him and decided not to wait around any longer. It would be just like Gina to race off impulsively with the idea that she could conquer show business single-handed.'

'I thought,' I said, 'you didn't know Gina very well.'

He smiled slightly. 'You don't trust me, do you?' He glanced out of the window. 'This is Pall Mall,' he said absently. 'At the end here is St James's Palace. Then we swing up St James's Street into Piccadilly again.'

I stared out of the window with unseeing eyes.

'You think something happened to her in the Jantzen flat?' he asked quite suddenly.

I nodded, not looking at him.

'Did she sound frightened?'

'Yes.'

'Did she scream? Gasp? Call out?'

'No . . . no, she just hung up in the middle of the call without a word of warning.'

'That's odd . . . It seems to me that if, for example, a burglar had entered the flat and accosted her she would have screamed when he arrived on the scene. But if she hung up of her own accord the burglar explanation seems unlikely.'

'Yes,' I said unsteadily. 'I guess so.'

'Actually there's not much that could have happened to her. Why should the Jantzens wish her any harm? They barely knew her. There was no reason why she should have been frightened of them.'

'No . . .'

'Presumably the police will have already established what time she left the Westbury, so we can get in touch with them this evening, if you like, to find out exact details and report that she's still missing.'

'And if she checked out after she made the phone call and not before—'

'We'll know nothing happened to her at the Jantzen

flat.' He hesitated slightly. 'You're sure,' he said, 'you're quite sure she hadn't had too much to drink? I hardly like to ask such a question but it's the only simple explanation I can think of.'

'No, I'm sure she hadn't,' I said at once. 'And if that was all that was wrong, she'd be back in Paris by now.'

'That's true.'

We turned off Piccadilly into a complicated network of short streets.

'This is Mayfair,' said Garth as we passed rows of elegant houses and a few exclusive-looking shops. 'We're almost at my club.'

The taxi made a right turn and drew up outside a stately townhouse with marble pillars flanking the front door.

'Here we are.' He got out first and helped me to the pavement beside him before he paid the driver. As the cab drove off again we went into the house and moved through a series of lobbies, past a magnificent staircase with wrought-iron banisters, and eventually into a small intimate bar which faced on to a patio.

'They don't seem to be here yet,' said Garth, glancing around at the occupants of the room. 'Shall we sit outside or will it be too cool for you?'

'No, I'd prefer to be outside.'

He escorted me to a table shaded with a multicoloured umbrella and as we sat down a waiter came over to take our order.

'A Tom Collins?' I said doubtfully.

The waiter gave a supercilious smile.

'Try a gin and tonic,' said Garth, and as I acquiesced gratefully he added to the waiter: 'And a dry martini, please.'

As the waiter disappeared into the bar a man and woman passed him on their way out to the patio. Garth saw them a second after I did, and raised his hand in greeting.

'We couldn't find you!' the woman called. 'What are you doing hiding under that ridiculous umbrella?'

'Didn't you read in the paper that it's been the hottest July afternoon for thirty years?'

They laughed, and as they came over towards us I was conscious of a stab of surprise, for they were not as I had expected them to be. I think I had anticipated a sophisticated, polished couple, the wife glamorously efficient, the husband glamorously artistic. But there was little glamour. Lilian Jantzen was plump and blonde and plainly but not outstandingly well dressed; she wore a navy-blue linen suit with conventional but unflattering white accessories. She reminded me of a housewife who, having received an unexpected invitation out, snatched the first available outfit from her wardrobe and dressed absentmindedly while planning the next day's shopping list. The result was passable but lacking in impact. Eric Jantzen was also fair and plump, and had a jovial smile which instantly reminded me of the more obvious breed of American salesman. I reflected with amusement how ironic it was that Garth, who at least looked as if he *could* have artistic talent, was the salesman while Jantzen, who looked like a salesman, was in fact the artist.

Garth introduced us. There was much smiling and shaking hands and then we all sat down again. The waiter returned with our drinks and took the Jantzens' order; I noticed that it was Lilian Jantzen, not Eric, who did the ordering, and that she ordered without consulting her husband.

'How nice,' said Lilian absently, glancing around the patio. 'This place has improved, Garth.' She began to peel off her gloves. 'Well, welcome to England, Miss Sullivan! I'm sorry to hear that you've had all this worry about your sister.'

'We were both sorry,' said her husband. He made it sound like a correction. 'Both of us. We don't understand what could have happened. We thought—'

'Have you spoken to Scotland Yard again?' said Lilian to me without waiting for him to finish. 'Have they any more news?'

'No,' I said. 'I thought I would check with them later.'

'I'm quite sure nothing serious can have happened to

her,' she said reassuringly. 'She struck me as being a very capable sort of girl who knew exactly where she was going.'

'Yes,' I said doubtfully, not certain whether I could recognize Gina from this description. 'I mean, do you think so?'

'Oh yes!' She was placid, confident. She smiled at me warmly and her eyes lost their vague, abstracted expression, as if she were perpetually thinking of something else more important, and mellowed to a softer, kinder shade of blue. It occurred to me that twenty years ago she would have been a pretty woman. 'Gina was alert – intelligent – ambitious. How can one be a successful model otherwise? I personally think she must have flown off to Rome to meet Dino di Lasci, that film producer Eric knows. Eric mentioned him to her at lunch last Saturday and Gina probably got it into her head then and there to go to Rome as soon as possible.'

'Then why did she go to your apartment at all on Saturday evening?' I asked hesitantly. 'If there was no need for her to go—'

'Eric was going to discuss the situation with her in detail, but unfortunately he got delayed and I suppose she lost patience and left. She would still have been in time to catch the night flight to Rome, I should imagine.'

Garth said, toying idly with the stem of his glass: 'But why the long-distance phone call, Lilian? Why call America?'

Eric Jantzen shrugged. 'She was young and excited – why not?' I noticed for the first time that he spoke with a faint foreign accent which I could not identify. 'She wanted her sister to come to Europe to share in the good times she was having.'

'My dear Eric,' said Garth, 'Claire didn't call in Scotland Yard because Gina was bubbling over with *joie de vivre*.'

Jantzen succeeded in looking perplexed. His round, rather comical face puckered between the eyebrows. 'Perhaps a burglar tried to break and enter – she became frightened—'

'A burglar?' Garth interrupted. 'Don't you mean a kidnapper? It seems that the only item which is missing since the phone call is Gina herself.'

'You're full of destructive criticism, Garth,' said Lilian lightly, but she did not sound annoyed. She looked at him with those mild warm blue eyes and smiled a mild warm smile, but he did not see her. He was still fingering the stem of his glass and watching the liquid nudge the sliver of lemon peel towards the rim.

'Cigarette, Miss Sullivan?' said Eric Jantzen to me suddenly.

'I don't smoke, thank you.'

'Lilian?'

'No, thank you, dear.' She gave an identical smile but spoke more absentmindedly as if to reproach him for distracting her. She glanced back at Garth: 'Have you any constructive suggestions instead of destructive criticisms?'

'None that I can readily believe in.' He accepted a cigarette from Eric Jantzen and fumbled in his pocket for a light.

'Ah, that's just it!' said Jantzen, laughing jovially as if Garth had made a witty remark. 'One resorts to the preposterous – visitors from space, perhaps. Or ghosts. Or—'

'Please, dear.' Lilian's voice was so extraordinarily placid that I had to look at her to see how annoyed she was. 'It's hardly a joking matter.'

Jantzen subsided like a pricked balloon.

The waiter chose that moment to arrive with their drinks and presently we had drunk a perfunctory toast and were sipping sociably at our glasses.

'She didn't give you any hint of what she might be planning, I suppose, Garth?' said Eric Jantzen presently as if eager to prove he could discuss the situation with complete seriousness. 'She didn't confide in you?'

Lilian was unimpressed. She was just turning to me and opening her mouth to make some remark when Garth said: 'Should she have done?'

'I thought you and she were—' He stopped, glanced sunnily around the table and then began to look dismayed as he realized the observation was going to be hard to finish. 'She seemed to – admire you?' he suggested tentatively. 'Hadn't you been seeing her in Paris? I thought—'

'Really, dear,' said Lilian, 'there's no need to make Bohemian observations to remind us you're an artist.' She stifled a yawn. 'It was perfectly obvious that Gina was in love with her career, not Garth.'

Jantzen's silence was a more eloquent denial than any words would have been. There was a pause. Then:

'I rather agree with you, Lilian,' said Garth idly. 'But I suppose we did get on well together on the few occasions when we met. She was bright and amusing and entertaining in her own way.' His eyes met mine across the table; the wink he gave me was so quick that afterwards I almost wondered if I had imagined it. 'But I prefer a different kind of entertainment.'

The muted loudspeaker system which the club used for announcements murmured in the rooms around us and we all started slightly as we heard Garth's name.

'Telephone call for Mr Garth Cooper . . . Mr Garth Cooper . . . telephone.'

Lilian shed her abstractedness as if it were a redundant article of clothing and was instantly on the alert. 'A business call, do you suppose? But no one knows you're back!'

'I phoned Briggs and Douglas from my flat this afternoon over the Rémy contract. Excuse me, please, everyone.' He stood up and disappeared quickly indoors just as I remembered that he had told me earlier how he had spent the afternoon sleeping and had not even phoned Lilian until five to announce his arrival.

The Jantzens were looking at one another. Presently Eric Jantzen said speculatively: 'Thérèse, perhaps?'

'Probably.'

They were silent. About five seconds drifted away, floated upwards into nothingness with the steadiness of the smoke from Eric's cigarette. Then:

'Who is Thérèse?' I said hesitantly at last.

'Thérèse?' said Lilian, vaguely surprised. 'He didn't tell you? She is – was – his fiancée. Such a tiresome woman! I was so glad when he finally extricated himself from the engagement a month ago.'


## chapter 6


For a moment I forgot my surroundings, forgot the patio with the gay umbrellas, forgot the Jantzens who were so pleasantly relaxed yet so subtly on edge with each other. I was back in Paris again, talking to Garth of Warren and Gina, and Garth was saying: 'I always feel sorry for anyone with a difficult ex-fiancé.' Possibilities and answers began to flash confusingly through my mind; if Gina had somehow met Thérèse, if Thérèse had thrown a scene or threatened trouble, it was conceivable that Gina might have become distraught and run away. I said quickly, not even waiting to allow the ideas to crystallize into theories in my mind: 'If they're no longer engaged then why is Thérèse calling him? Are they still on friendly terms?'

'My dear,' said Lilian in a voice fraught with implications, 'friendly is hardly the word to describe the curious attitude Thérèse has towards Garth. She still hasn't accepted the broken engagement and simply refuses to be reasonable – or even dignified – about the situation. She seems to think that by storming around creating passionate scenes and being frantically jealous, he'll finally give in and agree to go through with the wedding.' She made a neat fastidious gesture of distaste. 'So unnecessary! But then what can you expect of the French? With them nothing is ordinary or restrained; everything is *La Grande Passion*.'

'Does she live in Paris?'

'No, she lives in London and works for the French

Embassy. I must say, I'm disappointed in her behaviour – even the French could surely be expected to be more sensible about a broken love affair! Goodness me, it happens every day!'

Eric Jantzen said to his scotch on the rocks: 'She was *in love* with the man.'

'Heavens, dear, I hardly think *love* gives one the excuse to act in such an uncivilized manner!' She spoke with a detached incredulity as if love were a trivial illness to be dispelled by two aspirin and a ten-minute nap. 'No, I was disappointed in Thérèse. She was a mature, attractive woman – very *soignée*. In some ways she would have been exactly right for Garth, although, mark you, I suspected from the beginning that she would be too possessive to tolerate the little light-headed flirtations he indulges in from time to time—'

There was a chill in the air suddenly. I felt cold, desolate.

'When one's engaged,' said Eric Jantzen, 'one is expected to flirt with one's fiancée, not with other women.'

'Good gracious, dear, you talk as if Garth were an absolute Casanova! You know as well as I do that he's equally charming to every woman he meets – why, I'm certain Miss Sullivan will bear me out on that! – but he seldom really *intends* to be flirtatious. It's the women who read flirtatiousness into his attentions! And since Thérèse is pathologically jealous she would be bound to consider every small attention as a sign that he was conducting or trying to conduct an illicit affair.'

'I don't suppose Thérèse was any more jealous than another woman would have been in the same circumstances.'

'I disagree,' said Lilian shortly. 'She was totally unreasonable. It was a good thing they called off the engagement. If they'd married I'm sure Garth would have found her quite impossible to live with.'

Eric Jantzen was eloquently silent again. Driven by a compulsion to shatter that silence, I said hurriedly: 'Did Gina meet Thérèse?'

The question seemed to surprise them; they both looked at me sharply before looking at one another.

'She didn't mention it,' said Lilian doubtfully. 'I wouldn't have thought it was very likely. No, she couldn't have. If Thérèse had met Gina with Garth there would have been a big scene and Garth would have mentioned it to us later. But he said nothing.'

'I – I was thinking that if there had been some sort of scene – in your apartment – if Thérèse had found Gina there with Garth—'

'But why should Thérèse go to our apartment?' said Eric Jantzen, brow puckered again. 'There was no reason why she should.'

'She might have followed Garth there,' said Lilian. 'Garth might have arrived after I left Gina alone in the flat.'

'But Garth said he wasn't there!'

'Perhaps there *was* a scene and he didn't mention it.' She looked thoughtfully at her glass of sherry. 'Perhaps there was an unpleasant scene, so unpleasant that he had to take Thérèse away. Then Gina, who was distraught and shocked, made the phone call. And replaced the receiver when Garth returned.' She looked across at me, ignoring her husband. 'Do you think that makes sense?'

'It makes better sense than any other theory I've heard so far,' I said hesitantly. 'But why didn't Garth mention any of this to us? And why didn't Gina call me back later to explain what had happened? And where's Gina now?'

Lilian shrugged. 'Perhaps we're wrong.' She glanced towards the french windows which led from the bar to the patio. 'Here he comes . . . Garth, did Gina meet Thérèse last weekend?'

Garth stopped so abruptly that he might have been jerked to a halt by an unseen hand. His face became closed, remote, his expression betraying nothing.

'Do we have to talk about Thérèse, Lilian?' It was the first time I had ever heard him angry. 'Is it really necessary?'

'No, dear,' said Lilian vaguely in exactly the same tone

of voice as she used to her husband. 'Not really. I was merely being rude and inquisitive. Was that Douglas on the phone about the Rémy contract? What did he say?'

'No, it wasn't Douglas. It was a personal call from a friend of mine.' He sat down quickly at the table and took several swallows of his drink before glancing at his watch. 'We must be going, Claire. It's later than I thought it was.'

'Oh Garth!' said Lilian, half reproachful, half annoyed. 'After only one drink? I haven't even had the chance to ask Miss Sullivan about herself yet!' She smiled at me encouragingly. 'You'd like another drink, wouldn't you, Miss Sullivan?'

'Well, as it happens . . .' I searched for an excuse and then decided to tell the truth. 'I've had a lot to drink already today, and I'm not really accustomed to liquor, so perhaps I'll just settle for the one drink this time. But don't please let me stop you from having another—'

'Maybe some other time, Lilian,' said Garth. 'Perhaps we can all have dinner together before Claire leaves London. Meanwhile I'm afraid you'll have to excuse us.'

Lilian sighed resignedly and made a gesture of disappointment with her plump, neatly manicured hands. 'As you wish.'

We finished our drinks and went back indoors and through the house to the lobby.

'Well, I'm glad we had a chance to meet, Miss Sullivan,' said Eric Jantzen pleasantly as we parted. 'Sorry it was so brief. You must be sure and see us again before you leave.'

'Thank you – yes, I should like to,' I replied.

Lilian said: 'How long do you intend to stay?'

'I – I'm not sure. Another few days, perhaps.'

'Well, I do hope you have good news soon about your sister.' She took my hand in hers and squeezed it sympathetically. 'Garth, you'll let us know, won't you, if there's any news? I really feel quite concerned, especially as she apparently chose our flat to disappear from. However, I'm sure nothing serious can have happened. Perhaps Eric's right after all, and she flew off to Rome to see di Lasci.' But she sounded doubtful, as if Eric was so seldom right that this possibility was most unlikely.

The doorman flagged two cabs; Garth and I got into the first, and looking back over my shoulder, I saw the Jantzens about to get into the second. Eric Jantzen paused to wave a brief farewell in our direction.

'He seems pleasant enough,' I said, raising my hand automatically in response. 'But doesn't Lilian give him rather a hard time?'

'They've always been like that, ever since I've known them,' said Garth. 'I suppose they're both used to it by now.' He turned to face me, and his nearness suddenly seemed overwhelming. 'I'm sorry,' he said, 'for rushing you away like that. It was simply that—' He stopped.

There was a silence.

'Yes?' I said nervously.

His light eyes were hard and angry. 'I wanted to be alone with you,' he said abruptly. 'I wanted you to hear about Thérèse from me, not from the Jantzens.'

After a moment I said: 'Lilian didn't mean to be indiscreet. She was just wondering if—'

'If Gina and Thérèse had ever met. I didn't answer her question, did I? Well, I'll answer it now. Yes, they did meet. They met last weekend when Gina came to London and there was the most appalling and distasteful scene you could conceivably imagine.'

'Gina and I travelled from Paris to London together last Friday evening, as you know,' he said as the taxi moved into Berkeley Square. 'Lilian knew our arrival time, and – I suppose in the course of casual conversation, mentioned it to Eric, who for reasons best known to himself told Thérèse when she called to ask if he knew when I was returning to London. Thérèse went to the airport to meet me in her car, and found me with Gina. Naturally she thought the worst. She wanted to believe there was some other woman. It would have given her a concrete reason to explain why our engagement collapsed – she couldn't bring herself to believe that the fault was hers, not mine. Or perhaps it would be more accurate to say that she couldn't believe that the fault was ours – that we were incompatible. If she could have believed I had found someone else, she could have blamed me for everything and exonerated herself. So, you see, she wanted to believe the worst of Gina.

'I needn't trouble you with the sordid details of the scene at the airport. It's enough to say that merely to end the scene I put Gina in a taxi to her hotel and took a separate taxi to my flat. I half expected Thérèse to follow me to resume the quarrel but I was expecting too much even of Thérèse. She called me up instead. I told her the truth – that there was nothing between Gina and me, and even if there was it was certainly no longer her business – and hung up without waiting for her to finish.'

We crossed New Bond Street and raced eastwards to the perimeter of Mayfair.

'And you saw Thérèse on Saturday?' I said tentatively at last. 'With Gina?'

'No,' he said. 'Gina never saw Thérèse on Saturday and I haven't heard a word from Thérèse since then. She hasn't even called me. Perhaps she's at last beginning to see reason.' He took out his cigarette case and then changed his mind and replaced it in his pocket. We reached Regent Street and crossed it into Soho. 'On Saturday,' he said, 'before I took Gina to lunch with the Jantzens, I apologized for the scene, but Gina was very good about it and we agreed to consider it forgotten. Then we had lunch with the Jantzens and went our separate ways.'

'I see.'

He said wryly to me as an afterthought: 'Now you can understand why I sympathized with Gina when her ex-fiancé made such a clumsy attempt to win her back in Paris last week.'

'Yes – yes, of course.'

'Thérèse and I had been engaged three months, but I soon realized we had made a mistake. We just weren't suited. It became extremely awkward.'

I was not sure of what to say. In the end I said nothing, and as the silence lengthened he asked: 'Did Lilian mention what happened?'

'About Thérèse? Yes, she said Thérèse was rather unreasonable – and a little jealous—'

'So she did tell you.' He seemed more irritated than angry now; his eyes had an opaque, introspective expression. 'Yes. Thérèse became convinced that there was something between Lilian and me. It was quite absurd because Lilian and I are business friends only and it's been that way ever since we first met. But Thérèse saw it differently. It so happened that after Thérèse and I became engaged Lilian and I had to be in Paris together for an exhibition and conference. It never even occurred to me that Thérèse would begin to be jealous of Lilian – of all people – but she worked herself into such a state of jealousy that she flew to Paris after us and found that we were both staying at my Paris *pied-à-terre*.

'I suppose that was rather foolish of us, since such a situation is open to misconstruction, but we had done it so often before that we thought nothing of it. I put up a folding cot in the office and Lilian had the sofa bed in the living room; it was economical and convenient, especially in the early days, when every penny counted with us. However, Thérèse immediately thought the situation could have only one possible meaning. I explained a dozen times that Lilian is a dedicated career woman and simply not interested in anything except her work, but I don't think Thérèse ever really believed me. After that things became steadily more impossible between us, until in the end I decided that there was nothing to do except call the whole thing off. Unfortunately I then discovered that Thérèse was so obviously enjoying her jealousy that she couldn't bear the idea of breaking up. It was all a little difficult.'

The understatement might have made me smile in

other circumstances but at that point I was too busy feeling guilty; I debated whether to tell him that he had misunderstood me and that the Jantzens had not mentioned Thérèse's suspicions of Lilian. Before I could make up my mind we arrived at the restaurant and the opportunity to speak was gone.

The restaurant was large and dignified and, despite the numbers dining, extremely quiet. After we had ordered I said impulsively: 'It's very kind of you to keep taking me out to dinner like this, especially when you must have such a lot on your mind.'

He looked surprised. 'Do I seem to have so much on my mind?'

'Well, Thérèse—'

'She may be on the Jantzens' minds, but she's certainly not on mine.' He smiled. 'You're the one who has all the worries, not me, although I must confess I'm beginning to share your concern about Gina.'

'I'm surprised you're not more worried about her than you are,' I couldn't help saying. 'I would have thought—'

'Listen,' he said, interrupting, 'I don't know what Gina told you in her letters but as far as I was concerned she was a delightful relief after Thérèse's melodramatics, a pleasant interlude to take away the bitterness Thérèse had left behind. I wasn't seriously interested in Gina and I'd be surprised if she was seriously interested in me.'

'Why take such trouble to persuade me?'

'Because I can recognize scepticism a mile off.' Our glances met for a split second of tension across the table and then he laughed carelessly, picked up his napkin and shook it out into a wide square. 'And besides,' he said, amused, 'I'm anxious to prove to you that I'm not a mere philanderer to be regarded with extreme distrust.'

My cheeks burned. 'Have I given you the impression that that's what I think?'

But he refused to be serious. 'Don't sound as if you have a guilty conscience!' He turned and signalled the wine waiter. Then, to me: 'Will you have some wine with your roast beef?'

'No, thank you.'

'No? Are you sure? Not even a glass?'

But I was adamant. The meal continued but the atmosphere was less relaxed than it had been the previous evening, and after the meal we did not linger over our coffee.

'Why don't we go to Scotland Yard?' said Garth suddenly. 'I can see you're too worried about Gina to enjoy yourself. We'll go and see your friend – what was his name? – and report that she's still missing. And at the same time we can find out when she checked out of the hotel on Saturday.'

Relief crept over me; I looked across at him thankfully, grateful for his understanding. 'Would you mind? I'm sorry to be such bad company this evening, but—'

'Nonsense! And don't bother to apologize for anything – I can see now that I've been inconsiderate. We'll take a taxi to the Yard and get this straightened out without any more delay. Are you ready?'

I was. We left the restaurant and went out once more into the long, light, summer evening as dusk was beginning to fall. Presently we were in a taxi sweeping along the Embankment beside the river to Big Ben, Westminster and Scotland Yard.

Afterwards I felt better, even though Detective-Inspector Fowles had been unable to help much except to go over the details of Gina's disappearance and to promise that further enquiries would be made. We also found out that Gina had checked out of her hotel *after* making the phone call to New York, and that she had checked out alone, unescorted, and apparently of her own free will.

'So she was all right when she left the Jantzen apartment,' I said with relief. 'But then why did she make the phone call? And why did she hang up as if she was interrupted?'

But there were no answers to these questions, only theories and suppositions. After thanking Fowles we left the Yard and made our way by taxi down Whitehall back to my hotel.

'I don't understand it,' I said to Garth. 'I just don't understand. Can she really have gone on to Rome, as the Jantzens suggested, to meet this Italian film producer? Why didn't she call me back to say everything was all right? Unless she had a memory lapse I can't believe she'd carry on exactly as if nothing had happened.'

'Well, it's in the hands of the police now,' Garth said. 'If they can't trace her no one can. They'll find her.'

He asked me if I wanted some coffee before returning to the hotel, and partly because I was dreading the moment when I would be on my own again without him, partly because I wanted to make amends for my preoccupied behaviour at dinner, I agreed. We went to the London Hilton on Park Lane and had coffee on the second floor in the large, spacious lounge. The coffee, which was served American style, was reassuring and delicious. I began to feel better.

'I can't thank you enough for coming with me to the police tonight,' I said to Garth. 'I was dreading that visit but it all went off very well. I feel much happier now.'

He smiled, shrugged his help away as if it were nothing. We began to talk of other things, and soon the time slipped away again until it was after midnight. I think he realized before I did that I was tired; we left the Hilton, found a cab and were driven off around the edge of Hyde Park Corner into Piccadilly just as my eyelids began to feel heavy and my head was starting to ache from weariness.

But I was happy.

He smiled at me in the darkness. 'One day,' he said, 'when that tiresome girl Gina has stopped appearing and disappearing like the Cheshire Cat, you and I are going to go out again in London and have an evening like the one we had last night in Paris.'

Everything blurred, tilted, melted into darkness as I closed my eyes. I could feel the material of his jacket straining across his back as he tightened his grip on me; his cheek grazed my own, his mouth was hard, the kiss smoothly painful in its intensity. I pushed him away dizzily, overcome by emotions which I could not even begin to cope with, but he was already relaxing his grip and withdrawing of his own accord.

We were silent. There was nothing to say. It was not as if this had been yet another casual kiss in the moonlight on the steps of Sacré-Coeur. Now we were no longer casual. I felt committed, involved. Defensive barriers had become impotent, useless structures, shells behind which it was impossible to shelter any longer. There were no barriers any more and yet we were still apart, separate from one another, he with his thoughts, I with mine. And my thoughts said to me: is he really honest? Is he really telling the truth? And instinct, untrammelled by the logic of the defensive barriers, in spite of everything persistently told me he was not.

I looked at him. His face was shadowed, silent, remote from me.

'What are you thinking?' I said suddenly and on an impulse reached out to take his hand in mine as if I could dispel any suspicions by touching him. His fingers, long and strong, interlocked themselves with mine. His mouth smiled at me faintly but left his eyes withdrawn, their expression unreadable.

'Why,' he said, 'I was thinking how odd it is that we've known each other less than forty-eight hours. I feel as if I've known you a very long time.'

The taxi halted outside the hotel and he got out to escort me into the lobby. 'I'll be in touch with you tomorrow,' he said. 'I can't manage lunch, I'm afraid, but perhaps I could see you later.'

We kissed, parted; when I looked back at him I saw he was looking back at me too. And suddenly I forgot all my doubts and all my worries and remembered only that soon I would see him again.

\*

I was awakened shrilly at eight by the ring of the telephone bell at my bedside. Half asleep I scooped off the receiver and pulled it on to the pillow beside me.

'Claire?' said Warren Mayne, sounding impossibly brisk and bright. 'Hi, it's me. What's new? I tried to get you last night but didn't have any luck.'

I made an enormous effort. 'Maybe we could talk things over at breakfast? I can't think clearly at the moment.'

'Breakfast? Sure. I'll meet you downstairs at nine.'

When we met an hour later he was still bright and brisk and so obviously full of energy that I felt tired merely to look at him. 'So what happened?' he demanded, starting to fire questions at me as we sat down to breakfast and I glanced at the menu. 'Did you get anything more out of Cooper? Is there any other news?'

Over orange juice, cereal, toast and marmalade I told him about the Jantzens, my visit to Scotland Yard with Garth, and the news that Gina was alive and well after leaving the Jantzen apartment last Saturday. I also mentioned the Jantzens' suggestion that she might have flown to Rome to see an Italian film producer.

'Well, we can check that easily enough,' said Warren at once. 'What's his name?'

'Dino di Lasci.'

'Well call him up and ask him if he's seen Gina.'

His energy must have rubbed off on me; by the time we left the dining room I had recovered myself and was willing to share his determination to follow every possible lead. We spent the next hour in his room while he put through a call to Italy and finally succeeded in speaking to di Lasci's secretary. She said she had never heard of a Miss Gina Sullivan, an American model from Paris.

'Could you check with your boss?'

She apparently gave an unsatisfactory reply.

'It's serious,' said Warren. 'This is the CIA. We have reason to believe Miss Sullivan was murdered.'

I was disturbed by this gross distortion but Warren never turned a hair. 'She's going to ask di Lasci right now,' he said, pleased, to me. 'I *thought* that would get results.'

But it was all for nothing. Di Lasci came on the wire and said he had neither heard of nor seen Gina and that he was unable to help us.

Warren then called London airport and checked the flight lists to Rome the previous Saturday evening. There was no indication that Gina had ever made a reservation.

'I should have done that first,' he said disgusted, 'instead of wasting money on a call to Rome. Still, there's no harm in being thorough, I guess. Who shall we call up now? Who should we talk to? I'd like to speak to the Jantzens, but maybe I wouldn't learn any more from them than you learned yesterday.'

'Probably not.'

He thought for a moment. Then, suddenly: 'You know who I'd like to talk to? Cooper's ex-fiancée Thérèse. It strikes me she's the only possibility we've got to explain Gina's behaviour. If Thérèse came to the Jantzen apartment and created a scene—'

We argued about it for some time. I was extremely reluctant to meddle with Thérèse, but I had to admit that Warren's idea was reasonable enough.

'I can't see that it would do any harm to talk to her,' Warren insisted. 'She should be glad to meet me and find out that I want to get Gina away from Cooper as much as she does. You needn't come if you'd prefer not to, but—'

'Oh, I'll come with you,' I said hastily. 'But where does she live? I don't even know her last name.'

'Call Eric Jantzen – he was pretty friendly, wasn't he? Call him and ask him for Thérèse's second name. Then we can find her address in the directory.'

'But what excuse am I to give?'

'Just tell him the truth – that you want to check with Thérèse to make sure she hasn't seen Gina since Gina disappeared.'

Feeling nervous and ill at ease I dialled the number of the Jantzen apartment and found Eric at home. He was co-operative, appearing perfectly satisfied with my explanation. Thérèse's surname, he told me, was Mariôt. Carried away by his helpfulness he also gave me her address and phone number.

'Great,' said Warren, as I replaced the receiver. 'Let's go.'

'Without calling her?'

'She might put us off with some excuse. Let's take a cab and go over and see her in person.'

I followed reluctantly in his wake.

It was about eleven o'clock by that time. The day was grey and overcast but there was no rain and it was comfortably warm. Piccadilly Circus looked sad in the morning light, after its multicoloured splendours of the previous evening, and a crowd of tourists mingled with the down-and-outs who sat on the steps beneath Eros. We found a cab, and Warren, treating the cockney driver as if he spoke a foreign language, showed him the piece of paper on which he had written Thérèse's address.

We set off westwards again, our taxi nudging its way through the heavy traffic, and within twenty minutes were in Knightsbridge. At South Kensington Underground the taxi turned down the Old Brompton Road and finally made a left turn into a gracious square flanked by large white houses.

'Thirty-seven,' yelled the driver through the glass partition and halted the cab abruptly.

We got out; Warren paid him slowly as if he were translating shillings and pence into dollars each time he pulled a coin from his pocket.

'Well, come on,' said Warren, as the cab drove off again. 'Let's see if she's here.' He mounted the steps to the front door and examined the three bells on one side of the porch. Thérèse's name was printed on the top one. Warren pressed the knob, held it in position for a second and waited.

There was no reply.

'We should have called first,' I said.

Warren didn't answer. He was busy rattling the door

handle, but without success. I was just about to suggest that we go away and make no further attempt to break into the building, when a voice behind us said: 'Want any 'elp, dears?'

We spun around guiltily. Facing us was an exceedingly fat woman with very false teeth which she now displayed generously in a smile. "Oo are you wanting? If it's the French lady, she's gorn. Ain't seen 'er all week.'

We were too taken aback to ask her who she was. She did not look as if she were the type of person who would live at that address but obviously she seemed well acquainted with the house.

'Is that right?' said Warren, stalling, and adding clumsily: 'Would you be the maid?'

'Maid!' She looked at him as if he were an anachronism from the last century. 'Gawd 'strufe, no, dear. I come in and does for Mrs Cheese in flat B three times a week and cooks the evening meal on alternate Sats.' She pointed to the three doorbells. 'Mrs Cheese lives below the French lady.'

I realized the language barrier had put out invisible fingers to confuse us. Warren had correctly guessed her rôle but had called it by the wrong name; this was one of the famous London charwomen, not an American maid.

'As it happens we did want to see Miss Mariôt,' I said to her with a smile. 'Do you know how long she'll be away?'

'Couldn't say, dear, I'm sure. 'Ere, are you American? I thought you was. I know all about America. We watch telly and see it on the films. Skyscrapers and big cars and men with guns. My old man says it'll be like that 'ere before long.'

Warren was evidently torn between correcting her innocent impression of American life and finding out more about Thérèse. As he hesitated I said: 'When did you last see Miss Mariôt? I mean, was it a long time ago, or—'

'No, last Saturday.' She leaned her massive figure against the railing and settled down to enjoy herself. 'It was one of my alternate Sats for Mrs Cheese so there I was getting the dinner, all 'appy as a lark and singin' under my breath, and the sun was shining (makes a change, that does!) so I flings open the window and leans out to sniff the fresh air.' She paused meaningfully. Feeling something was required of us, we both nodded. 'And suddenly, my Gawd, there she was – shouting and screaming something awful—'

'Miss Mariôt?' Warren asked.

'Course it was! 'Oo do you think I mean – my Mrs Cheese? Mrs Cheese don't carry on like that. Such a carry-on it was, I could 'ardly believe me ears. Well, there she was a-ranting and a-raving and making a to-do and she shouts out: "I'll ruin you both!" she says all nasty-like, "you and Lily both of you." No, I'm telling a fib. It wasn't Lily she said. It was something else like it.'

'Lilian.'

'That's it! You know 'er? Lilian. Anyway, Miss Whatsit, the French lady, went on ranting about Lilian, and then 'er fiancé, a very nice gentleman called Mr Cooper, said—'

'It was Mr Cooper who was with her?'

'Course it was! I knows Mr Cooper. Poor man, I felt sorry for 'im all tied up with that foreigner. I used to meet 'im on the stairs sometimes and twice 'e gives me a lift to the tube in 'is car. A very nice gentleman Mr Cooper is . . . So where was I? Oh yes. So there was I breathing in the fresh air, so to speak, and all this to-do going on over my 'ead, and Mr Cooper says: "Don't be a fool, Terezz," 'e says, proper narked 'e was, and she shouts out something else and slams the door and I 'ears 'er footsteps pounding downstairs past my Mrs Cheese's door and then the front door slams and she's gorn. And I ain't seen 'er since. Nor 'as Mrs Cheese. Mrs Cheese was saying to me only yesterday that she wished Miss Whatsit had cancelled 'er order of the French newspaper while she was away as it keeps being delivered and cluttering up the 'all downstairs. But it's plain to see what 'appened. She broke it off with 'er fiancé over this Lilian – whoever *she* is (and mark you I wouldn't blame that Mr Cooper for taking up with someone else) – and then she went away to recover. No one thinks at times like those to cancel the morning paper. I told Mrs Cheese so and Mrs Cheese agreed.'

We nodded, mesmerized into agreeing with Mrs Cheese. I was trying to remember whether Garth had said he had not seen Thérèse since Friday night at the airport, but as far as I could recall he had merely said that Gina had not seen Thérèse since then. He hadn't mentioned himself.

'When was this?' I said unsteadily. 'Saturday?'

'Saturday, it was. That's right. About six o'clock in the evening. I was all set to peel the potatoes.'

And Gina had called me at nine-thirty, London time, that same night.

'Well, thank you very much, ma'am,' said Warren politely. 'You've been most helpful, and we're grateful to you. I guess we'll have to get in touch with Miss Mariôt in some other way.'

'Good luck to you, I'm sure,' said our informant agreeably and heaved herself up the steps to the front door. 'I must be on my way to Mrs Cheese. I 'opes you enjoy the rest of your 'oliday in England.'

We chorused our thanks and began to walk away along one side of the square towards the Old Brompton Road.

'Should I have tipped her?' Warren asked, worried.

'Absolutely not.'

'You think so? Maybe you're right. I wouldn't have known how much to tip anyway.' He sighed, ran his fingers through his hair. 'Boy, what a break! We sure were lucky meeting her like that. What did you make of it all? It certainly looks as if Gina wasn't the only one to disappear that evening, doesn't it? I'm convinced that Cooper's at the bottom of all this – hell, he was involved with both women and – if we can believe the maid – with his partner as well. Looks as if he was two-timing everyone on a grand scale.'

I said levelly: 'I'm quite certain he isn't having an affair with Lilian.'

'Why?'

'Well, for one thing because he's on good terms with Eric.'

'Maybe Eric doesn't know.'

'After ten years?'

We walked on for a few moments. Then: 'According to Garth,' I said with studied indifference, 'he was trying to avoid any romance with all three women, not to involve himself with them. He had broken his engagement to Thérèse. He was apparently unconcerned by the idea of Gina flying off to Rome to see a film producer. And there's no proof that he's ever had more than a business relationship with Lilian. He was trying to get away from Thérèse and Gina, not closer to them.'

'Let's face it,' said Warren ironically, 'he succeeded. He got away from them so successfully that now no one can find them.'

I didn't answer. I was feeling chilled, frozen with an ice cold pang of dread.

Presently Warren said: 'Don't tell me you're hooked on him as well.'

I still didn't answer.

'Wow!' Warren hooted. 'He sure must have a way with women! I must study his technique the next time I see him.'

'Oh, for God's sake, Warren!'

We reached the Old Brompton Road. 'OK,' said Warren not unkindly. 'You think Cooper's innocent and I think he's guilty. So what's the next step? Let's go back to the hotel and see if you have any message from Scotland Yard.'

Back at the hotel I found not a message from Scotland Yard, but a note to say that Eric Jantzen had called and could I call him back at his apartment.

I did not want to make the call with Warren breathing down my neck so I went to my room and said I would speak to him as soon as I had talked to Eric. Then, sitting on my bed, I dialled the Jantzen number and waited for Eric to answer the phone.

He sounded pleased that I had returned his call so

promptly. 'Have you heard any news of Gina?' he said. 'Did you contact the police again?'

I told him how Garth and I had visited Scotland Yard the previous evening and he listened with interest. Then: 'Look,' he said. 'Are you doing anything for lunch? Our flat is only a short bus ride from your hotel – could I come over and meet you?'

I managed to conceal my surprise. 'Thank you very much,' I said. 'That would be very nice.'

'Good! I'll be over in about twenty minutes, then.'

I hung up and then spoke to Warren on the house phone to tell him what had happened. He was as surprised as I was but agreed that it was possible I might discover something new. We arranged that I should give him a call later, on my return, and afterwards I had a few minutes in which to relax before I went downstairs to the lobby to meet Eric Jantzen.

He was already waiting for me. 'There's a good little restaurant just off the Haymarket,' he said. 'It's not far. Hardly worth a cab. Would you mind walking, or—'

I said I wouldn't mind so we set off. He talked fluently enough as we traversed Piccadilly Circus and turned into the Haymarket amidst the lunch-hour crowds, but I had the feeling he was making an effort. After we had exhausted the subject of the weather and the traffic problem in big cities we reached the restaurant, which was small and neat and obviously inexpensive, and went inside.

By this time I had formed the impression that he did not like to spend money. It occurred to me vaguely to wonder what his financial position was. Artists were notoriously poverty-stricken. I thought of his rich, clever wife and wondered why he tolerated her thinly disguised apathy towards him.

'Where did you first meet your wife?' I enquired over the minestrone. 'Was it in England?'

'Ah, so you can tell I'm not English! I shall never lose the accent, it seems. No, Lilian and I met in Switzerland. I come from Altdorf, which is the little village near Lake

Lucerne where our national hero William Tell was born. I was a young struggling artist who earned a living painting pretty empty little commercial pictures of the beautiful scenery. Lilian was a sympathetic tourist.'

It seemed that Lilian felt compelled to help men less fortunately placed than herself. 'I see,' I said tentatively, not really understanding.

'We had a lightning romance and married two weeks later in Geneva.' He smiled, shrugged his shoulders. 'Lilian's family didn't approve, but we didn't care.' His large, sad face lit up unexpectedly. 'We were young – in love. Those were happy times. I liked London and settled down quickly. Soon I was painting as I had always wanted to paint, and not painting what other people wanted. Lilian was most—' he paused for the right word '—inspiring.'

And rich even then, I thought. She must have supported them both from the beginning.

'Lilian,' said Eric Jantzen, 'is a very wonderful, very talented woman. She believed in me. She had faith. In the end when I had my small share of success, I always said it was due to her because she gave me encouragement and help when I most needed it.'

I tried to picture Lilian in the rôle of the devoted, inspiring wife, absorbed in her husband's work. The effort strained my imagination. I couldn't really see Lilian absorbed in any work except her own.

'She must know a great deal about china and glass,' I said presently.

'Yes, she knows much more than Garth. Garth's a mere business man.' He dabbed his mouth delicately with his napkin and reached for his glass of water. 'But he likes to think himself an authority on glass.'

'Tell me, Eric,' I said, looking at him with what I hoped was an honest appealing expression. 'What is *your* opinion of Garth Cooper? You probably realize that I barely know him, but my sister evidently thought highly of him so I'm anxious to discover what kind of man he really is. I hesitate to ask you, but you've known him some time and you're obviously a person of mature judgement, so I know I can believe what you say.'

As I had intended him to be, he was flattered although he tried to disguise his gratification. His face puckered between the eyebrows as he prepared to give his mature judgement.

'Of course,' he said at last, 'he's always been more Lilian's friend than mine.'

I waited. Presently he added good-humouredly, as if it were all a joke: 'Why, he's a salesman! And a good salesman: an excellent, successful salesman! He has a saleable product and he sells it in the cleverest possible way.'

'China and glass?'

'A mere sideline!' He was still amused, still speaking lightly to mask his seriousness. 'Garth's talent is in selling himself — not literally, of course! But he knows how to appeal to people, how to charm them, how to make them like him. He has a talent for playing the rôle which the English would describe as "the nice chap". But beneath the nice-chap façade he's a hard, tough, able business man. He doesn't deceive me. He may deceive others but he doesn't deceive me.'

'He doesn't sound like the right man for Gina,' I said with a worried expression. 'I hope she's not in love with him.'

'She was attracted to him,' said Eric. 'That's undeniable. But she was too young for Garth. I know the kind of woman he likes.' He toyed with his soup spoon as if it suddenly held an irresistible fascination for him. 'He likes mature, clever women, not empty-headed young girls barely out of their teens.' He looked up guiltily. 'I'm sorry, I don't mean to slight your sister, who was charming, but—'

'I understand.' I broke a piece off my roll and buttered it. 'You mean Garth preferred women like Thérèse.'

'Precisely.' He began to eat again. 'I like Thérèse,' he said unexpectedly. 'Lilian didn't, but then I hardly expected her to. Thérèse was quick, intelligent and striking – a passionate, intense, exciting woman. If I painted portraits—' He broke off with a smile. 'But I don't! However, if I did, I would have wanted to paint Thérèse.'

My jealousy, ridiculous but unmistakable, made it hard for me to listen to him saying how attractive Thérèse was. To change the subject I said with interest: 'What sort of pictures do you paint, Eric? I'm sorry I'm so ignorant of your work – I believe you're famous here in London.'

'Hardly famous!' he said brightening, and began to talk about himself with a shy, modest enthusiasm which, for some reason, I found touching. It turned out that he painted abstracts and had dabbled briefly with surrealism. I said I had seen an exhibition of Salvador Dali's work at the Huntington Hartford Museum in New York. We talked of art for a while, and as we talked he lost his air of bogus joviality so that I caught a glimpse of the person he must have been long ago, when he first met Lilian – a sensitive, vulnerable young artist dedicated to his work. I found it impossible to imagine how the prosaic, businesslike Lilian could ever have understood him.

But perhaps she never had.

'You will tell me if you have any news of Gina, won't you?' he repeated as we parted in the lobby of my hotel some time later. 'Lilian and I are both anxious to know where she is and if she's all right. You will phone us, won't you?'

'Of course!' I assured him, and thanked him warmly for the lunch before going up to my room. I knew I should call Warren to report on the lunch, but I felt I had had my fill of Warren that morning and when I reached my room I put off the phone call and lay down on my bed instead.

Within ten seconds my mind had fastened itself stubbornly on Garth Cooper.

He had implied the previous evening that Thérèse's suspicions of Lilian had come to a head over three months ago, at the beginning of his engagement. I strained my memory to recall his actual words but was left only with the memory of what he had implied. It occurred to me that Garth was clever at implying facts without saying anything outright. Now on reflection I was certain he had given the impression that Thérèse's jealousy of Lilian was past history, whereas according to the charwoman it was very much a present episode.

And that doesn't make sense, I thought. By last Saturday Thérèse should have been quarelling with him over Gina, not over Lilian. Gina was surely the centre of his attentions by that time.

I felt depressed by the possibilities of the situation and by Garth's ambiguous behaviour. Above all I began to feel depressed about Gina again, and not merely in regard to her disappearance but in regard to her relationship with Garth. I moved restlessly to the window, stared outside, turned back towards the door once more. Finally on an impulse I picked up my handbag and went downstairs to the street, in an effort to dispel the agony of passive waiting by a burst of action. I had decided to go to Garth's office. Instead of wondering helplessly about his ambiguities I could ask him about them directly instead.

His office was in Knightsbridge. I felt incapable of coping with the Underground system or even the buses at that stage, so I took another extravagant cab and sat back in the shiny leather seat as London slipped past my eyes.

I pictured an imaginary Guide, Philosopher and Friend, the rôle which I had assumed for so long with Gina. 'Dear Claire,' my imaginary friend wrote with cold asperity, 'you are letting your innate good sense run away from you, I fear. Kindly note the following observations: (1) You should never run after a man – always wait for him to come to you. (2) Never interrupt a man at his office when he might be transacting important business. (3) Dissociate yourself from this man Garth Cooper who is almost certainly not to be trusted. What does it matter whether he implies untrue facts or whether he patently lies about them? The point is that he is probably not presenting an honest picture to you and may have been dishonest about other matters of which you are unaware. (4) Why should you, who seldom have a date at home, believe for one moment that Mr Cooper is as infatuated with you as you (apparently) are with him? He has clearly been taking a romantic interest in you to blunt the edge of your enquiries into Gina's disappearance. (5) Should you wish to dissociate yourself from Mr Cooper yet not know how to begin, there is one very simple remedy: don't see him again. (6) Pull yourself together and stop behaving so foolishly. Yours in disappointment . . .'

The cab hurtled into the Hyde Park Underpass and soared up again a moment later into Knightsbridge.

I can't help it, I thought, I love him. I can't help it.

The taxi drew up past Harrods and the driver pointed across the road. 'That's the building, Miss. Sorry you're the wrong side but no U-turns allowed here.'

'Thank you,' I said. I got out, paid the fare and crossed the street. There were office buildings above an exclusive row of shops, most of the windows displaying antiques. Inside the building there was an old-fashioned elevator. A board nearby told me that Garth and Lilian conducted business on the first floor, and after I had realized that the English say first when they mean second I avoided the elevator and walked up the stairs which wound around the shaft. The door marked 'Cooper–Jantzen Limited, Importers–Exporters, China and Glass' was directly ahead of me. Suddenly wishing I had not come I walked up to the door and opened it before my nerve could desert me.

Inside was a light, airy, surprisingly modern outer office with thick green wall-to-wall carpeting and restful pale walls. A few feet away from me were two doors leading into rooms which I guessed were the partners' private offices; to my left I caught a glimpse of a file room and to my right was a gleaming desk, an electric typewriter and a very executive secretary with a curtain of jet-black hair, blood-red fingernails and cool competent black eyes.

'Good afternoon,' I said uneasily. 'Is Mr Cooper in, please?'

'Mr Cooper is out of the office at the moment.' She delicately adjusted a strand of hair. 'Have you an appointment?'

'No – no, I haven't.'

'I could make one for you.' She opened a red leather appointment book. 'What name is it, please?'

'Claire Sullivan, but this isn't a business matter. Could I wait for him, or is it unlikely that he'll return soon?'

'No, I expect him back at any moment.' She glanced at her watch as if to confirm what she had said, and stood up and moved past me towards the file room. 'Would you like to come this way, please?'

Beyond the file room was a tiny waiting room which looked out on Knightsbridge.

'If you'd like to wait here . . .'

'Thank you,' I said.

She walked away gracefully, and I sat down and picked up one of the magazines on the table nearby. It was *Punch*. Presently I put it down and picked up *Paris-Match*.

Ten minutes passed. The phone rang twice and I could hear the murmur of the girl's voice as she took the calls. The electric typewriter chattered intermittently, but presently I heard her get up and come through the file room towards me.

'Would you like some coffee?' she enquired from the doorway.

'If you're making some.'

'I always make some at three.' She sounded bored about it. 'Mr Cooper and Mrs Jantzen like strong black coffee after long business lunches.'

In the file room she picked up a percolator and wandered into the outer office again. The front door opened, ringing the small bell hooked to the hinge, and slowly shut itself after her.

I was alone.

Standing up in an agony of restlessness I went out into

462

the file room, examined the small photocopying machine, prowled around the file cabinets. In one corner was a closet with its door ajar. I glimpsed a man's raincoat hanging inside, and was just about to turn away when I caught sight of an envelope sticking out of one of the pockets. I wouldn't have looked at it twice if I hadn't noticed that the only word visible to me of the address was written in purple ink.

I thought of the letters then, the notes from Hollywood, the reams from Paris. And all of them written in Gina's favourite shade of purple.

Quickly, smoothly, before I had had time to think twice, I took out the envelope. It was empty. He had evidently either destroyed the letter or put it in a safe place and then stuffed the envelope hurriedly into his raincoat pocket. I studied the postmark. The letter had been mailed in Dorking, Surrey, at three o'clock on Monday afternoon, two days after the phone call to me from the Jantzens' apartment, and there was no doubt at all that the purple-inked handwriting on the envelope belonged to Gina . . .

## *chapter 7*

I went on staring at that empty envelope in the silent deserted office. Somewhere far away beyond the windows of the waiting room came the muffled roar of the Knightsbridge traffic; everything close at hand was very still. Suddenly outside the office in the corridor I heard quick footsteps and I just had time to stuff the envelope back in the raincoat pocket before the door of the outer office was pushed open and Garth and Lilian walked in.

'Catherine? Damn it, where is the girl? We employ her to answer the phone, not to spend half the time in the cloakroom making herself look glamorous.'

They could not see me. They were still in the adjacent

outer office and I was shielded from them by the half-open door of the file room.

'There's no need to be so hard on her – she's a very good secretary and the glamour is only put on for your benefit.'

'My God, the next thing I know, Thérèse will be calling to accuse me of having an affair with my secretary!'

I had been about to step forward to announce my presence but the mention of Thérèse made me freeze to a halt.

'I must say, Garth, you're in a very bad mood this afternoon! I can't think why you're so upset about Thérèse when you haven't seen her for days – it's I who should be upset. Eric seems to have argued himself into believing that my behaviour with you is suspect—'

'Oh, Lord!'

'Did you know that Thérèse saw Eric last Friday after you came back from Paris? He told me last night that there had been some sort of a scene at the airport with Gina.'

'Scene! That's a mild word to use to describe such a sordid, embarrassing episode—'

'Why didn't you mention it to me before?' Lilian asked mildly.

'Why should I? Why should I bore you with the unfortunate incidents of my private life?'

'Apparently Thérèse told Eric on Friday, after the scene at the airport, that your interest in Gina was merely a smokescreen to conceal your interest in me.'

'Look, I don't give a damn what Thérèse told Eric or what Eric thinks—' Garth's voice had risen in anger.

'Well, I do! I have to live with him!'

'I can't think why you bother! It's so patently obvious that you hold nothing but contempt for him that I don't know why you don't leave him.'

'I don't want to bore you with the details of my private life any more than you want to bore me with yours,' Lilian shot back. 'Besides Eric would be heartbroken if we separated.'

'And you're being noble and considering his feelings? That doesn't sound like you, Lilian!'

'Listen, Garth.' Lilian's voice had assumed the patience of an adult teaching a child to tell the time. 'The point is that it suits me to go on living with Eric at the moment. Never mind why. It's none of your business. Just take my word for it that I want to go on living with him, and that I was extremely annoyed to discover that Thérèse has apparently been seeing Eric and trying to make him as jealous as she is—'

'For God's sake, Lilian, why blame me? *I'm* not responsible for Thérèse! If Eric's jealous, ignore him. Let him be jealous! He can't prove anything against you because there's nothing to prove.'

'It's very easy to give advice like that, but not nearly so easy to carry it out. I don't want Eric upset. Incidentally, just as a matter of interest, what game are you playing with that girl Gina? Where is she and why are you hiding her?'

'My dear Lilian,' said Garth with what sounded like genuine astonishment, 'what in heaven's name are you talking about? I haven't the remotest idea where she is, and I'm *not* hiding her. Why should I be? I haven't seen her or heard from her since we all had lunch together on Saturday.'

My cheeks burned for him as his lies rang in my ears. Tears, unwanted and inexplicable, pricked behind my eyelids.

Lilian was saying sceptically: 'Weren't you having an affair with her?'

'Good heavens, no! Gina's for men of twenty-five and forty-five, not for men in their mid-thirties.'

'Gina struck me,' Lilian said slowly, 'as being for men of all ages. Didn't she at least tell you where she was going after we all parted after our Saturday lunch?'

'No, I excused myself from her and went home to Half Moon Street. I told her I'd phone her later, but in the end I didn't. I was tied up with other matters.'

'Thérèse?'

'No, I haven't seen Thérèse since the episode at the airport on Friday night.'

Another lie. I thought of Mrs Cheese's charwoman talking on the steps of the white house on the square. At six o'clock on Saturday evening Garth had been quarrelling with Thérèse in her apartment.

'I was dead tired,' Garth was saying. 'I'd had a busy week in Paris with very little sleep. I rested till about seven and then wandered out into Shepherd Market, where I had dinner at a small restaurant. I half wondered whether to phone Gina at her hotel, but I didn't. I didn't feel sociable and wanted to be on my own.'

'Well . . . the whole business of Gina's disappearance is certainly very odd, that's all I can say. I suppose you had no word from her on Sunday?'

'No, I spent Sunday at the office.'

'At the office? Here? On a Sunday? My goodness you're getting to be as much a slave to your work as I am! I thought you were always the one who told me I should never work on Sundays?'

'I was puzzled over the Rémy contract – last year's, not this. I couldn't quite work out why we paid so much tax on the profits.'

'Oh, I can explain all that to you – it's really very simple. Why did you take over the Rémy contract this year anyway? I can't remember why we decided that. It would have been more sensible if we had handled it just as I did last year. Besides, what does it matter about last year's tax? That's all closed now.'

'I had a tip that the Inland Revenue were on the warpath again against small businesses like ours. If we get any inspectors coming round I thought I would make quite sure that everything was in order.'

'Well, of course it's all in order! You know how careful I always am—'

'Wait, I can hear Catherine coming back. Let's go into your office.'

They opened one of the other doors leading off the outer office and moved quickly into the room beyond.

Pulling myself together I left the file room and returned to the adjacent waiting room just as the secretary opened the door of the outer office and let it swing shut behind her. The small bell attached to the hinge murmured faintly and was silent.

'Catherine?' called Lilian in the mild gentle voice she had adopted when I met her the previous evening. 'Is there any coffee?'

'I'm just going to make some, Mrs Jantzen. Mr Cooper, there's a Miss Claire Sullivan waiting to see you in the conference room.'

There was a long moment of absolute silence. I closed my eyes in an agony of embarrassment and prayed that when I opened them again. I would be somewhere else. But I wasn't.

'Shall I—' The secretary hesitated.

'That's all right, Catherine. Thank you.' He must have moved back into the outer office by that time for his voice was clearly audible. The next moment he was entering the file room and crossing the floor to the waiting room beyond.

'Good afternoon,' he said formally, and even before I could reply he had closed the door and we were alone together, just he and I and a thousand doubts in that quiet little room above Knightsbridge.

'This is a pleasant surprise,' he said fluently as I found myself incapable of speech, 'but I'm sorry you had to choose to call on us when you did. I suppose you were obliged to listen to Lilian and me indulging in some rather undignified bickering on subjects ranging from Lilian's non-existent extramarital intrigues to the machinations of the Inland Revenue authorities. I apologize if we embarrassed you, but at least I can remember saying nothing I wouldn't have wanted you to hear.'

I turned away, not answering, unable to meet his eyes, and stared out over London.

He moved towards me until I sensed he was standing behind my shoulder.

'What's happened?' he said abruptly. 'What's the

467

matter?'

My eyes were blind. 'Nothing,' I said. I did not trust myself to say any more.

'You've heard bad news about Gina?'

I shook my head. As he put a hand on my arm I turned away from him again and groped my way to the door.

'Just a moment,' he said sharply. There was a note of uncertainty in his voice. 'Just a moment. You must have come here for a reason. What was it you wanted to say?'

I remembered dimly that a long time ago, before I had found out that he must know where Gina was, I had wanted to ask him more about his quarrel with Thérèse on Saturday evening. Now I knew the answer; as far as he was concerned the quarrel was a secret, to be concealed for private reasons. There was nothing I could do, nothing more I could say. My common sense had been correct in telling me I should never have come to his office; it had been a stupid, foolish, misguided step to take.

'I'm sorry,' I said with difficulty. 'It was wrong of me to come here and bother you. It really wasn't very important anyway. Please excuse me.'

After a moment he said: 'I don't understand.'

I was incapable of speech again. I fumbled with the handle to open the door, but his hand closed on mine and stopped me.

'Please,' he said quietly. 'Please, Claire. You must tell me what this is all about. What's the matter? Was it something to do with the conversation I had just now with Lilian?'

I thought of the empty envelope in his raincoat pocket.

'No,' I said, and found myself looking up into his eyes. He looked puzzled and worried. I was conscious of an overpowering urge to confide in him but I knew I must not. He had lied, not once but several times, and it was now no longer possible to trust him. With an effort so immense that I felt drained of all strength I said: 'I think all this worry about Gina is depressing me more than I thought. I came here simply to talk to you and it wasn't until I was here waiting that I realized how selfish I was being in bothering you in your office. But before I could leave you came in with Lilian.'

He looked at me steadily. His eyes were very clear. 'Well, I'm glad you came,' he said at last. 'And I'm glad you turned to me when you were depressed. So why don't we sit down and talk about it? Never mind the office. That can wait. If you came here to see me, then why rush away again as soon as I appear?'

I shook my head helplessly. 'No – really, Garth – I'd prefer not to talk here—' I broke off, reached out to open the door again.

'Look, Claire—'

'I can't explain – I just don't want to talk—'

'The hell you don't. Well I do. No matter what you think I want to tell you that ever since we met—'

'I must go. Please—' I tried to open the door.

'— I haven't been able to stop thinking of you—'

'Oh don't, don't, DON'T—' My composure was fast fading.

'But Claire darling—'

I burst into tears.

'Oh God, I'm sorry . . . I don't know what's the matter with me. I've been so clumsy and hamfisted every time we meet – if it hadn't been for this wretched business over Gina—'

'We wouldn't have met at all,' I said shakily, raking through the contents of my purse for a handkerchief.

'Here, have mine.' He pressed a large white handkerchief between my fingers. I blew my nose, mopped ineffectually at my face, tried to gather together the shattered remnants of my self-control.

'I'm sorry,' I said distantly at last. 'I'm not myself. Please excuse me if I leave now.'

'Let me get you a drink—'

'No, I want to take two aspirin and lie down. I've got a bad headache.'

'I'll go down with you and get you a taxi.'

'No—'

'I insist.'

I was too exhausted to argue any more. We went out through the file room into the outer office where the secretary regarded us with impenetrable black eyes behind her curtain of black hair. Outside in the street Garth hailed a cab and gave the name of my hotel to the driver, together with a ten-shilling note.

'I'll phone you this evening,' he said to me. 'Perhaps if you're well enough we can have a quiet dinner somewhere.'

'I – don't know—'

'I'll phone you around six. Take care of yourself.' He kissed me; I felt his lips brush my forehead as his fingers tightened on my arm, and the tears pricked at my eyes again. 'Bye.'

My lips moved but I could not bring myself to say goodbye. He closed the door, the taxi moved forward into the heavy traffic and I was alone. Leaning back against the leather upholstery, my mind blank with a dozen conflicting emotions, I stared out of the window and felt my cheeks burn once more with bitter, silent useless tears.

When I arrived back at the hotel I found three telephone messages asking me to call Warren when I got back. I tore them up. In the privacy of my room at last I drew the curtains and lay down for about five minutes, but presently I got up again and went over to the mirror to repair my make-up. I felt calmer now. It seemed unlikely that I would cry again during the next few hours. My head ached dully and my eyes felt sore, but otherwise I was conscious of nothing except a numbed apathy. I felt defeated. It was typical, I thought with a detached incredulity, that the one man whom I really fell for would turn out to be a double-faced, plausible liar. I was convinced now that he was having an affair with Gina and that he knew where she was, and for reasons of his own was keeping her hiding-place secret while ostensibly pretending to help me with a hypocritical willingness.

There was no doubt at all that he had been playing a

double game. And because I knew he had been playing a double game with me I had found the scene at his office particularly humiliating and shameful. He had summed me up, guessed that his best way of handling me was to adopt a suitably romantic approach and had then played his adopted role with great skill. I had been flattered, deceived, clay in his hands. He must have thought me an innocent fool.

The tears were just beginning to prick my eyes again and threaten to ruin my new make-up when the phone rang. I nearly didn't answer it, but then instead seized the opportunity to take my mind off my troubles. 'Hello?' I said cautiously into the receiver.

'I was just about to call Scotland Yard to report *your* disappearance,' said Warren, aggrieved. 'Where the hell have you been? You said you would call me after your lunch with Eric Jantzen, and here it is – nearly four o'clock. I've been worrying myself sick about you.'

'I'm sorry,' I said. 'I was delayed. Do you want to come over to my room? I've got a clue about where Gina may be and I want to talk it over with you.'

'You have?' He was agog. 'I'll be right over. Hold everything.'

The line went dead. I sat on the edge of my bed and held everything, and a minute later he was knocking on the door. I let him in.

'How did you find out?' he demanded excitedly. 'What happened? Where is she?'

I suggested he sit down and have a cigarette. 'I went to Garth Cooper's office this afternoon,' I said without emphasis. 'I was suspicious of him. He wasn't there when I arrived but his raincoat was. In the pocket was an empty envelope which had a postmark dated Monday, three days ago. It was addressed to Garth, the handwriting was Gina's and the postmark said it was posted at Dorking in Surrey.'

Warren was so astounded that he dropped his cigarette. There was a great fuss as he snatched it up again and stamped at the carpet. Then: 'So Cooper was lying all

471

along! If she wrote to him on Monday—'

'He would have got it on Tuesday, or yesterday, Wednesday. He must know where she is.'

'Where did you say the postmark was?'

'Dorking, Surrey.'

'Surrey's south of here, isn't it? Dorking shouldn't be too far away. Look, I've got a road map of England in my room. Let me just go and get it and we can check and see where this place is.'

It turned out to be about twenty-five or thirty miles south of London.

'Looks as if it's a fair-sized town,' said Warren, pondering over his guidebook. 'Why don't we get a train down there tonight and see what we can find out? We must be able to get there by train. It looks as though it should be in the commuter belt.'

I hesitated, not certain what to do, my determination dulled by my apathy.

Warren was still browsing over the map. 'Dorking . . . Guildford seems to be the nearest other big town. Hey, listen to these names! Abinger Hammer, Shere, Gomshall, Holmbury St Mary—'

The pain of memory was so intense that I bit my lip.

He looked up. 'Something wrong?'

'Garth told me he owned a country cottage at Holmbury St Mary. He goes down there at weekends.'

'So that's it!' cried Warren. 'So that's where she is! She's at Cooper's place in Surrey!' He closed the guidebook with a bang and scrambled to his feet. 'OK, let's go.'

'Wait a minute,' I said. 'If Gina's staying in secret at Garth's country cottage she may not thank us for interfering. If she's capable of writing a letter and mailing it, it seems that she's there of her own free will and that apparently she's perfectly well and unharmed.

He stared at me. 'What are you suggesting?'

'I think you know what I'm suggesting – you're not stupid. Listen, this is what I think happened . . .' I took a deep breath, summoned my will power, tried to speak in a cool, level disinterested tone of voice. 'Gina travelled to London to spend the weekend with Garth, but they were met by an infuriated Thérèse at the airport. There was apparently a scene resulting in Gina and Garth travelling separately into central London, and naturally after that Garth would be afraid of Thérèse creating further scenes. So he suggested that Gina stay secretly at his cottage in Surrey.'

'I don't believe it,' said Warren at once. 'He's been in London all week – what would be the point of Gina staying down in the country if she had travelled to London specifically to be with him? And why didn't she call Candy-Anna to tell her she wouldn't be returning to Paris for a few days? And anyway, you still haven't explained her call to New York from the Jantzens' apartment on Saturday night.'

'Well then, you suggest another explanation which fits the fact that she's probably staying at his cottage in Surrey, unharmed, and of her own free will!'

He looked mutinous. His glance, roving around the room as if for inspiration, alighted on the telephone. 'Let's call information and get the number of Cooper's home in Surrey.'

'It won't have a phone.'

'How do you know?'

'Why would Gina have written if she could have called him up?'

He was silent. 'Well, let's give it a try anyway,' he said at last. 'There's no harm in trying.'

'All right,' I agreed doubtfully. After ten minutes of talking to various operators in both London and Surrey, he was told the house called Coneyhurst Cottage which belonged to Mr Garth Cooper in Holmbury St Mary was listed as having the number Holmbury 626.

'Could you try it for me, please?' said Warren at once.

More waiting followed. Then:

'No reply?' said Warren disappointed. 'Thank you. I'll try again later.'

'I suppose that's not altogether surprising,' I said,

trying to cheer him up as he replaced the receiver. 'If Gina is hiding at the cottage she wouldn't answer the phone.'

'True.' He brightened a little. 'At least I was right about the place having a phone. Well, what do you say, Claire? How about getting a train down to Dorking this evening, stopping overnight at a hotel there, and then hiring a car tomorrow morning to drive out to Cooper's house?'

I thought of Garth's promise to call later and to invite me to have dinner with him. If I were to speak to him, I thought, I would be weak and accept his invitation. And if I went out to dinner with him I would make matters even harder for myself than they were already. The best course I could possibly take would be to leave town for a day or two.

Warren was just beginning to look surprised by my hesitation when I said abruptly: 'Yes, let's leave right away. How do we get there?'

'Let me talk to the people at the desk downstairs and see what they suggest. Then as soon as I get the details straightened out we can pack our bags and check out.'

'All right.'

After he had gone and I was alone I opened my suitcases and began to put my belongings inside once more. I found it a relief to have something to do, however mundane it was. Just as I was finishing, the phone rang and Warren told me there was a train leaving Waterloo Station soon after seven o'clock.

'We could have a snack here at five-thirty,' he suggested, 'and then get a cab to Waterloo. The trip takes about forty-five minutes. They've given me the name of a car-rental agency in the town and the name of a hotel where we can stay, so now we're all set to go.'

After we had had dinner we went to the desk to pay our bills, and I found that there was a phone message for me to say Garth had called. I tore it up and threw it away. Ten minutes later, with our luggage stowed safely into our taxi, we were leaving Piccadilly Circus on our way to Waterloo.

We reached Dorking shortly before eight and took a taxi to the inn which had been recommended to Warren at the hotel desk in London. I think we were both amazed by Dorking. Even Warren, who had never seemed to me to be very aware of his surroundings, was silenced by the wide High Street with its rows of old shops and narrow winding side streets packed with little pubs and antique stores. Our taxi driver informed us that our hotel had been a coaching inn in the old days, and suddenly I remembered a scene in Dickens' *Pickwick Papers* and knew why the name Dorking had seemed familiar.

'Would you believe?' marvelled Warren as the taxi turned off the High Street under an ancient arch into the courtyard around which the inn was built. 'People *live* here. It wasn't built by Walt Disney. People really *live* here.'

And it was there at last that I felt I was in England. London with its vast modern buildings and cosmopolitan atmosphere had vaguely disappointed me, particularly after my brief visit to Paris, but here in Dorking I was no longer disappointed. As I entered my room and looked out of the window towards the large green hill which rose up above the town in the north-east, I had one of those curious inexplicable moments that made me think I had been in here before. But that was nonsense. No town I knew in New England bore any resemblance to this old market town in Surrey, and none of my ancestors had come from England; my mother's family was Scottish and my father had been an Ulsterman from Protestant Northern Ireland. I was a stranger here, and yet in spite of that I felt at home.

We were just in time for dinner; I had yet to get accustomed to the rigidity of English mealtimes and their inflexible hours. We ate an enormous English meal which seemed to my transatlantic ideas of finance to cost very little money, and afterwards we felt so replete we had to spend an hour in the lounge over our coffee before we could lever ourselves out of our chairs. Finally Warren went off to try to call the cottage again, but he was unsuccessful and in the end we decided to have an early night before driving out to Holmbury the following morning.

I spent an uneasy night. Supposing, I thought, Gina was indeed at the cottage, as it now seemed likely that she was. The scene would have to be handled with great care, and the more I thought about it the less eager I felt for Warren to be there with me. Warren would charge into the cottage like a bull in a china shop and besiege Gina with questions and demands and accusations. And supposing Gina decided not to come away with us but to remain at the cottage? Warren, who had been living on tenterhooks for longer than I had, might lose his head and do something stupid. I could almost visualize him carrying Gina off by force under the sincere conviction that he was acting for the best. I shuddered. Somehow I must contrive to arrive at the cottage before he did.

The next morning at breakfast I found he had already hired a car and intended to collect it directly after we had finished eating.

'I hate to tell you this,' I said apologetically, 'but I'm not feeling too well. Could we possibly postpone the trip until this afternoon? I've got a terrible headache.'

He looked concerned. 'Do you have any aspirin? You'd better go and lie down. Can I get you a doctor?'

'No, no,' I said hastily before he could get carried away by consideration. 'I'll take two aspirin and lie down and I'll be fine by noon. I'm sorry to postpone the trip, but—'

'That's OK, I understand. Don't worry about it – I'm just sorry you're feeling bad.' He thought for a moment. 'Maybe I'll drive out there on my own this morning and see if Gina's there.'

'Please,' I said with great restraint, 'please let's wait till this afternoon! I've come over three thousand miles to find Gina and when we do find her I want to be there, not stretched out on a hotel bed.'

He looked sheepish. 'Sure, I understand. I'm sorry.'

I silently heaved a sigh of relief. He decided to explore the town for a while and send some postcards to his friends, and after we had collected the car from the garage he prepared to set off on foot from the hotel.

'You can leave the keys with me,' I said. 'I don't want you losing them on your travels.'

'Good idea,' he agreed, completely serious although I had spoken lightly. 'I'm always losing things.'

He handed over the keys docilely and departed.

As soon as he was out of sight, I slipped out to the car, fitted the keys in the ignition and examined the controls. When I had lived at home I had driven a car every day of my adult life until all my reflexes and reactions were automatic and made without conscious effort; that was more than three years ago but I had driven rented cars occasionally since I had been living in New York, and had found that for me driving had become like swimming: once learned the skill is never forgotten. Driving a car in England would be different, I reasoned, but not difficult. Presently, after making sure I knew what I was doing, I started the engine, adjusted the shift and released the brake. The car trickled forward over the inn's cobbled courtyard. Soon I was easing my way carefully through the narrow arch and turning into the High Street. Dimly aware that I was more nervous than I had anticipated I crept along behind a green double-decker bus and found myself taking a right fork at the bottom of the High Street and driving on out of the town into the quieter residential districts. I stopped at the first gas station I came to and asked the way to Holmbury St Mary. To my surprise I learned that I was on the right road.

'Keep straight on,' said a solicitous mechanic. 'Through Westcott, past the Wotton Hatch Hotel. Keep going. Stick on the main road until you get almost to Abinger Hammer. Then as soon as you catch a glimpse of watercress beds on the left, watch out for a left turn. There's a white signboard just before the clock at Abinger which says "To Holmbury St Mary". Take that left turn and drive another couple of miles or so and you'll be right in the village.'

I thanked him and drove on. After a small village which I presumed was Westcott, the road ran deeper into the country, now and then cutting through sandy soil. I noticed the lush green of the foliage and glimpsed a range of hills beyond the fields to the north, but the traffic was much heavier than I had expected and it was impossible to look at the scenery as closely as I would have liked.

At last I found the side road past the watercress beds and turned left to Holmbury St Mary. The country road was narrow and winding; there was little traffic now and I was able to take more notice of my surroundings. After passing through a hamlet where the cottages were so old and pretty that I nearly missed my way as I stared at them, I finally came to a larger village with a green, a church on a hill and some assorted houses and shops.

I stopped beside the nearest passer-by and asked the way to Coneyhurst Cottage. She said she had never heard of it. Discouraged I drove on and stopped at a pub; the pub itself was closed but the landlord was sweeping out the bar.

'Excuse me,' I called through the open window. 'Can you tell me where Coneyhurst Cottage is?'

He was a tall solid man with a moustache. 'Coneyhurst?' He stroked the moustache absently. 'Sounds as if it should be up Holmbury Hill. Who lives there?'

'A Mr Garth Cooper.'

'Ah!' He looked pleased. 'Yes, I know Mr Cooper. He often comes here weekends. The cottage is nearly all the way up the hill, an isolated spot with a good view. Take the road to Peaslake up the hill – you'll pass several big houses including Holmbury House itself. Keep following the signs to Peaslake, and just before you get to the top of the hill you'll see the cottage on your left.'

I thanked him and returned to my car. The sun came out as I took the road uphill away from the village, and the light slanted through the tall trees with their brilliant green leaves and fell in patterns on the twisting narrow road. Presently the trees ended and the slopes of the hill rose steeply above me on my right. The view to the left was already worth pausing to look at, but I was too near my journey's end now and didn't stop. I passed occasional houses, including the gates bearing the inscription 'Holmbury House', and swung uphill even more steeply. There was a fork in the road; I took the turn to Peaslake, as the landlord had instructed me, and ground the shift into a lower gear. I was glad Warren had hired a small Austin. The road was now so narrow that any larger car would have been nerve-racking to drive.

I was just thinking that sooner or later I must surely reach the summit of the hill when I came upon the cottage. I had expected it to be old and quaint with a thatched roof, but I was disappointed. This was a small house, probably no more than thirty years old, and was perched firmly on the steep hillside looking out over a panoramic view across the valley below.

Parking the car off the road among the trees I got out and went slowly over to the house. All the windows were closed; there was no sign of life. I found the front door, and after a moment's hesitation rang the bell, but no one answered and presently I moved on around the house and tried the handle of the back door. It was locked. I stood there and wondered what to do. There was a small gardening shed a few yards from the house and for no reason other than curiosity I walked over and opened the door, but there was no one inside – only a few gardening implements and a wheelbarrow. As I turned away the sun went behind a cloud suddenly and a chill breeze swept up from the valley.

I shivered.

The blank sightless windows of the house stared at me, and suddenly, without knowing why, I was frightened. I retreated, moving quickly down the little terraced garden, and on the last terrace beside the hedge which marked the boundary of the grounds I noticed that part of an overgrown, weed-strewn flowerbed had been recently dug and hoed. The damp earth gleamed in the bright morning light.

I stared at it, refusing to recognize it for what it looked like. The patch was about six feet long and three feet wide. Suddenly, hardly aware that I was moving, I was halfway back to the shed. When I reached it I took the spade which was leaning against the wall and went back to the flowerbed at the bottom of the garden.

The spade sank softly into the wet earth and stopped.

I felt horribly cold. Presently I began to shiver again. Then, overcome with an obsession to see all my worst nightmares spring to the most appalling life, I stooped and scraped at the earth until at last I had uncovered a monstrous, distorted, gross object which I only just managed to identify.

It was a human hand.

## chapter 8

After I had finished being sick, I steeled myself to go back to the grave again. There was something I had to find out, something I had to know. When I had finally achieved a state of mind resembling detachment I knelt down on the ground again and bent over the hand, my nose and mouth pressed against my handkerchief. There was a ring on the engagement finger, a brilliant diamond ring which sparkled mockingly in the bright light. I shut my eyes very tightly and then opened them again. It was still there. For several repulsive seconds I thought I would check to see if the ring bore any inscription, but I gave up the idea and retreated from the grave. The engagement ring was proof enough; Thérèse had not wanted to break off the engagement and it was possible she might have continued to wear the ring even after Garth had tried to end matters between them.

The full meaning of my discovery suddenly hit me in

an overwhelming wave of shock. Garth's ex-fiancée was buried in the garden of Garth's weekend cottage. And Garth had been one of the last people to see her alive. After she had quarrelled with him and stormed out of her apartment, her neighbours had not seen her again.

If the police knew the facts, I thought to myself, they could not help but think Garth was guilty of murder. She was making trouble for him, he had quarrelled with her, he was the last person to see her alive . . .

There was ice on my forehead. On reaching the shed I found a tap used for the garden water hose and turned it on. Cold water sluiced out. After washing my hands with a fanatical thoroughness, I dried them on the full skirt of my dress and went outside again into the cool morning light. Back in the driver's seat of the car I sat down and started to tremble from head to toe.

I tried to accept the fact that Garth was a murderer but my mind balked at such an idea. I was prepared to accept that Garth had been playing some sort of game where I was concerned but I could not believe that the game included murder. I tried to think clearly. Where had Thérèse gone after her quarrel with him last Saturday in her apartment? If he did kill her, when had it taken place, and where? And why bury the body in the garden of his own cottage when he could have chosen a site anywhere on the surrounding hillside?

I could not believe he had killed her. No matter how absurd and how lunatic my reasoning might be, I could not believe he was a murderer.

My thoughts, jumbled and confused, went on and on and on. I wondered if Gina had been in some way involved in the murder. If Garth were shielding Gina – no, Gina wouldn't have killed Thérèse. I wondered for the hundredth time where Gina was and wished with all my heart that I could somehow get in touch with her, and as I thought of Gina, I thought with a stab of dread of Warren.

I caught my breath. If Warren came to the cottage and found the grave in the garden, he would instantly contact the police. Somehow I had to prevent Warren from following through with his plan to investigate the cottage that afternoon.

The problem of how I could succeed in deflecting Warren from an apparently unavoidable course of action filled my mind as I made my way back to Dorking, but by the time I had arrived in the courtyard of the inn I was no nearer a solution than I had been when I had left Holmbury St Mary. I glanced at my watch. It was eleven-thirty. Praying that I wouldn't meet Warren on the stairs or in any of the lounges I slipped into the hotel and hurried upstairs to my room.

With the door tightly closed and bolted behind me, I sat down on the bed, reached for the phone and asked the operator to put through a call for me to Garth's office in London.

I once read somewhere that a person in love can be considered to be temporarily unbalanced while the effects of the malaise linger in the mind. Certainly if anyone had ever told me a month previously that I would not report a dead body to the police as soon as I found it, but would instead phone the probable murderer to warn him of the danger he was in, I would have replied indignantly that I would never be so patently insane.

But I was. To make matters worse I was convinced that I was doing the only sane thing I could possibly do, since I had already persuaded myself against all the evidence that Garth was innocent. I sat waiting tensely in that still quiet bedroom as my call was connected, and then suddenly Garth's secretary Catherine had picked up the receiver and was saying in her cool, studiously polite voice: 'Cooper–Jantzen Limited – good morning, may I help you?'

'Yes,' I said rapidly. 'Is Mr Cooper there, please? This is Miss Sullivan.'

'I'm afraid neither Mr Cooper nor Mrs Jantzen will be in the office today. Is there any information I can give you?'

'Do you know where they are?'

'They've arranged to have a business weekend entertaining French clients at Mr Cooper's cottage in Surrey. Mrs Jantzen went down to the cottage last night to get everything ready and Mr Cooper was to go to the airport this afternoon to meet the clients' plane. It's possible that if you tried his flat you might just catch him before he leaves – do you have his number?'

'No – I only have the office number. Could you give it to me, please? It's very urgent.'

'One moment.' I heard her flick open an automatic telephone book. 'Yes, it's Mayfair – that's MAY – 7543.'

'Thank you very much indeed.' I replaced the receiver and instantly picked it up again to give the operator the new number. I waited while she dialled and heard the bell ring endlessly at the other end of the wire.

'Sorry,' said the operator. 'There's no reply.'

'Thank you.' But I could not believe I would be unable to contact him. Springing to my feet in a fever of activity I left my room and went downstairs to the pay phone which I had noticed earlier outside the lounges.

By a miracle I had the right coins. After skimming through the instructions, which seemed unnecessarily complicated, I dialled the series of numbers and waited. The line began to ring and I thought in a panic: did I dial correctly? And such was my state of mind that I convinced myself in the space of three seconds that I had misdialled. I got my money back, hung up and began again.

This time, by some extraordinary miracle, someone picked up the phone on the first ring.

'Hello?'

I had opened my mouth, drawn breath to speak, but now I was struck dumb before I could say a word.

For it was not Garth who had answered the phone. It was Gina . . .

'Garth?' said Gina, suddenly fearful as I did not reply and I realized dimly that I must have stumbled on a prearranged telephone signal which enabled her to know when it was safe to answer the phone. 'Garth, what is it? What's happened now?'

'What's happened now,' I said shakily, 'is that your sister has finally managed to track you down. Where the *hell* have you been?' Tears of relief were hot on my cheeks; the room swam in a dizzy mist of thankfulness.

'Claire! Oh God, where are you? What are you doing? Claire, I feel so bad about you, so terrible—'

'So you damn well should! I've been worrying myself silly about you and tying myself in the most impossible knots ever since you called!'

'I tried to call you back on Monday from Garth's apartment here but you'd already left New York – you left so *quickly*, Claire! I never, never thought you'd be on your way to Paris within two days—'

'What did you think I'd do, for heaven's sake? Dither about in New York while I wondered all the time if you'd been murdered or raped or kidnapped? Or stand rooted to the floor of my apartment like the Statue of Liberty while I waited for you to remember to call back?'

'I didn't forget you, Claire, I did actually try to call you back on Saturday night but your line was busy all the time, and after that I didn't get the chance to call till Monday, and by that time—'

'Why did you call from the Jantzen apartment?'

'I – look, I can't talk on the phone. Garth would be furious if he knew I'd even spoken to you. He said absolutely no one, not even you, must know where I was until Saturday—'

'But look, Gina – you must tell me more! Garth's in trouble. His ex-fiancée—'

'I know.'

'But—'

'Please, Claire darling, please – not on the phone. Listen, where are you? At the Regent Palace?'

'Dorking.'

'Dorking! But you mustn't stay there! You – you'll be in danger – quick, come back to London. Come back at once. Get the next train to Waterloo. Don't ask questions, darling, just *leave*. Do you understand? Leave right away and come here.'

'Yes, but just a minute! Where *is* Garth? I must talk to him. There's so much I—'

'He's on his way by car down to the cottage at Holmbury St Mary. But Claire, you must come to London at once. Please! You must come!'

'Yes,' I said to pacify her. 'Yes, I'll get the next train. Don't worry.'

'I'll be waiting for you,' she said with relief. 'And *hurry*!'

'What do you think I've been doing ever since your wretched phone call on Saturday night? All right, I'll hurry – don't worry, and take care of yourself.'

'You too, darling. Bye now.'

'Bye.' I hung up, leaned weakly against the wall and fumbled for my handkerchief. I succeeded in finding the one which Garth had given me the previous afternoon at his office. It occurred to me wryly that I had cried more in the past two days than I had cried during the preceding two years.

When I had recovered myself, I went back upstairs to my room and began to consider what I should do next. I had every intention of joining Gina as soon as possible, but first of all I had to prevent Warren from going out to the cottage to find her, and then I had to try and see Garth to settle matters between us once and for all. But my first task was Warren. Presently I went to his room and knocked on the door, but there was no answer so I assumed he was still out on his walking tour. It seemed that he was making his tour of Dorking in great detail.

I tried again a quarter of an hour later, and this time I had more success.

'How are you feeling?' he said as he let me into the room. 'You don't look too good.'

I could hardly have had a better opening. 'Well, no, I still don't feel very well,' I said listlessly. 'Such a nuisance . . . But I've got some wonderful news for you – I've been trying to find you for the past half hour. What do you think happened while you were out? I called Garth's office to see if he had any news of Gina and would you believe it, who should come to the phone but Gina herself! I was so amazed I could hardly believe it! She refused to talk much on the phone, but we arranged to meet at five in the Regent Palace lobby.'

'I don't believe it!' said Warren amazed. 'She did? But what was she doing at Cooper's office? Where has she been?'

'I told you – she wouldn't talk on the phone! But isn't that marvellous news? I'm going to go on resting here for a couple of hours to get rid of my headache and then we can get a train to London to meet her at five o'clock.'

'Why, that's wonderful!' he exclaimed. 'Great! Let me call up the station and find out the times of the trains to London—'

'You can go straight on up to London, if you like. But I just wanted to rest for a little longer—'

'Sure, I understand. I'll wait for you, though, and we can travel up together.' He moved over to the phone. 'Let me call now and find out the times of the trains.'

I thought it unwise to argue with him further for fear of arousing his suspicions. If he decided to wait for me I could always give him the slip, just as I had that morning, and drive off on my own in the car. I heaved a sigh of relief, and as he began to talk into the receiver, I wandered casually over to the dressing table and picked up one or two of the objects which he had left scattered around on the polished surface. There were several postcards of Surrey.

I began to glance at each of them.

'Four forty-five? I see . . . and the one before that?'

His passport lay beside the postcards. I glanced at his photo and saw to my surprise that unlike most passport photographs, it was flattering. He looked young, bold, quick-witted and handsome as he stared defiantly into the camera. I flicked through the pages to the visa section to see which countries he had visited. A trip to Brazil was recorded for the previous year. Then his arrival in Paris and the visit to London.

'OK . . . fine. Now what time does that reach London?

Is it an express?'

I stared. The visits to England and France appeared to be in duplicate.

'Just one stop, did you say?'

I went on staring. Presently I realized that the first stamp of the British Immigration Authorities was dated the previous Saturday and that the second stamp of the French authorities was dated a day later on the Sunday.

*Warren had been in London on the night Gina had made the phone call from the Jantzen apartment. He had been in London on the night Thérèse had disappeared.* Warren had been in London on Saturday and had slipped back to Paris quietly on Sunday, and he had never once mentioned it to me . . .

'Thank you very much,' he said suddenly from behind me. 'Goodbye.'

He dropped the receiver and I dropped the passport; the noise of the one muffled the sound of the other. Feeling nothing but an amazed, uncomprehending bewilderment I turned towards him with a blank expression. 'Is it all right?' I asked naturally. 'What train do we get?'

'There's one that leaves at three and I suggest we get that. Why don't I pick you up at two-thirty?'

'Fine. Thanks, Warren,' I said automatically, and feeling blank with shock, I left the room and went outside into the quiet corridor beyond.

When I reached my bedroom again I was still incapable of thinking clearly about my discovery but gradually as I stood by the window of my room and stared out over Dorking my initial shock began to recede. Why had Warren been in London? And why should he have concealed his visit unless he had something to hide? Could he conceivably have had any connexion with Thérèse's murder? I spent several minutes thinking of Warren and remembering how I had always dismissed him as a naïve, ingenuous, overgrown adolescent. Apparently I had severely underestimated him. It seemed as if he were not nearly so naïve and frank as he appeared to be.

Another thought occurred to me. Might I not also be mistaken about Warren's single-minded determination to find Gina? I had been amused and touched by the devotion which had made him decide to take a week's absence from his work and fly to London to find her, but supposing his determination concealed a more sinister motive? I thought of Thérèse again, and suddenly I was saying to myself: supposing Warren killed Thérèse and Gina saw him do it. He'd want to find her at all costs once he realized she had witnessed his crime. And perhaps he had not known that she had witnessed the murder until I had arrived in Paris with my tale of Gina's distraught phone call to New York on Saturday night . . .

My thoughts seemed to be racing out of control. I tried to apply a mental brake. There was, I told myself, no reason why Warren should have killed Thérèse. Why *should* he have killed her? As far as I knew, they had never even met.

I began to wander restlessly about the room, and picked up my handbag irresolutely before putting it down again and returning to the window. Perhaps I was being dramatic in assuming Warren wanted to find Gina in order to silence her. Perhaps Thérèse had threatened Gina and Warren had killed her, accidentally or otherwise, in order to protect Gina herself. Then, when I arrived in Paris and he had discovered from my information that Gina, unknown to him, had witnessed the crime, he had immediately tried to find her to explain the situation. If this theory were correct it would explain why Gina had not gone to the police, for if Warren had killed Thérèse for her sake, Gina would hardly have wanted to call in the police.

I pulled myself together. I could stay in my room and imagine all kinds of theories, but that would hardly be the most sensible thing to do. The best course I could take would be to find Garth and demand that he tell me the whole truth without half-truths or evasions; since he had been hiding Gina in his London apartment and, before that, at his cottage in Holmbury St Mary, he must presumably know why and from whom Gina wanted to hide.

My mind was made up. Moving quickly I picked up my handbag again, opened the door cautiously and slipped downstairs to the car, which was parked in the courtyard. The next moment I was in the driver's seat and edging the car out into the High Street as I began my return journey to Holmbury St Mary.

I was so nervous that at first I took the wrong road out of Dorking and wasted precious minutes crawling through side streets while I tried to get my bearings. Finally, more through luck than judgement, I found myself on the road to Westcott and Abinger Hammer, and after some minutes I was driving past the hotel at Wotton Hatch which I had noticed earlier. It was beginning to rain; by the time I reached the turn to Holmbury St Mary I had to use the windscreen wipers. But the shower passed and as I took the road at last up Holmbury Hill to Garth's cottage, the sun shone palely again and the rain was a mere dark cloud shadowing the road behind me.

I was driving too fast. I had to will myself to slow down. Normally the narrow winding road would have been enough to persuade me to reduce my speed to walking pace but I was so anxious to see Garth and learn the whole truth of the situation that I was forgetting even the most basic rules of highway safety.

Fortunately I met no cars coming down the hill as I went up so I arrived at the cottage without incident. But even before I could park the car I saw that this time I would not be alone at the house; a sleek creamy Jaguar had stolen my parking place, the spokes of the wheels glittering in the sunlight, the hood thrusting gently into the undergrowth which crept up from the ground to meet the bumpers. Someone had arrived before me. I was just assuming that it must be Garth when it occurred to me that I had never seen his car before. In London we had always taken cabs everywhere. Supposing the car belonged to someone else? I hesitated, shivering violently as I remembered the dead hand in the shallow grave, and then pulling myself together, I let the car roll back a few yards and parked it off the road below the Jaguar. It must be Garth who had arrived at the cottage. After all, Gina had said that he was on his way. I was becoming neurotic, imagining danger where none existed.

I got out of the car and slammed the door shut. Everywhere around me it was very quiet. On my right the wooded hillside was still and motionless. Not a breath of wind whispered through the branches of the trees; a bird sang briefly and darted into the silent undergrowth. I was alone, part of the stillness of the landscape as I stopped to listen, and when I moved forward again I felt the damp twigs crunch beneath my shoes and my breathing quicken in my throat.

All the windows of the house were still closed; there was no sign of life. For a long moment I hesitated by the roadside and then with an effort I stepped off the road and walked swiftly up the path to the front door. I touched the bell, waited. The bell seemed to ring far away, a small faint trill of sound piercing the pall of silence. I went on waiting. I was just about to ring again when he opened the door.

His face was empty of expression. He looked at me as if he didn't know me.

'I'm sorry,' I said stammering, 'but I must talk to you, Garth.'

He said nothing. He was very still, one hand on the latch, the other a tight fist at his side. As so often happens in moments of great stress I found myself noticing trivial things, that he was wearing casual clothes, dark slacks, blue shirt and, oddly, quiet-soled tennis shoes. His hair was untidy, and as I stood there watching him he smoothed it back with his hand in the old gesture which I had noticed when I had first seen him in Paris.

'I can't talk now,' he said abruptly. 'It'll have to be later.'

'But—'

'Go back to London and I'll get in touch with you there.'

I shook my head dumbly.

'Look, Claire, I'm sorry, but I can't talk now. I've got guests arriving any minute and I'm not ready for them. You'd better go back to London.'

I was stung by his air of polite impatience, his attitude of thinly veiled exasperation. 'To London?' I said quickly. 'And where shall I wait in London? At the hotel? Or with Gina at your apartment?'

He stared at me. It was impossible to guess what he was thinking. Then: 'Whichever you prefer,' he said, without expression, and began to close the door. 'And now if you'll excuse me – I apologize for being so abrupt but—'

'Don't bother to apologize,' I said, infuriated by the fact that he was no longer pretending to be interested in me, 'because I'm not going.' My eyes were pricking with the sickness of disillusionment, but my anger overcame my disappointment and wretchedness. I knew now that his interest in me had been assumed from the start to make it harder for me to find Gina, and some perverse, foolish streak of pride made me want to prove to him that he had meant no more to me than I had to him.

'Claire—'

'No,' I said, my eyes hot with unshed tears. 'No, you're going to listen whether you want to or not! Why did you tell me all those lies? Why did you tell me you hadn't seen Gina since Saturday when all the time you knew where she was? And why did you say you hadn't seen Thérèse since Friday at London airport when you quarrelled with her at her apartment on Saturday evening? You lied and lied—'

'Listen,' he said, white to the lips, 'listen, Claire. Thérèse is dead—'

'Yes!' I cried. 'Murdered! And buried over there in *your* garden!'

He opened the door a little wider and I thought he was going to let me into the house to talk to him but he merely moved out on the step beside me.

'I didn't kill her,' he said slowly. 'You must believe that. I didn't kill her.'

'Why should I believe you!' I stormed at him. 'You've told me nothing but lies from start to finish—'

'That's not true.'

'It *is* true!'

'Oh, for God's sake!' he exclaimed, as if I had touched him on the raw. 'Stop shouting accusations at me as if I had committed a mortal sin! The only reason I lied—'

'—was to deceive me,' I said. 'I expected you to be honest with me and instead you—'

'I omitted certain facts – just as you did when you first met me. It was a long time before you told me what Gina had actually said during her phone call to you in New York! If omitting facts makes me a liar, then you're as much of a liar as I am!'

'I—'

'Please,' he said. 'Go back to London. Go to my flat. See Gina and talk to her. I can't talk to you now.'

'I was so worried about Gina!' The unwanted tears now burned my cheeks; I tried to control them but could not. 'I was so worried about her . . . and one word from you – *one word* and I wouldn't have had to worry any more.'

'There was more involved than you realized,' he said abruptly. 'A woman was murdered. It was a matter of life and death. All I wanted to do was to keep you out of it—'

'As if you cared!' The harsh words seemed to sear the air between us. I bent my head, turned aside to hide the humiliation of tears. 'As if I mattered to you! There's no need to insult me by pretending any further—'

He said, interrupting, his voice hard and angry: 'There was no pretence. And no insult. And it mattered more than anything else in the world.'

I put my hands over my ears and shook my head as if I could shake the words away. My eyes were dim with pain. I didn't see him move until I felt his arms slip around me and his breath cool against my hot cheek.

'Claire—'

'Let me go!' I twisted away from him. The pain was so excruciating that I could no longer think clearly; my movements were instinctive. I ran from him, stumbling down the path to the road, and although I would have turned back in a flash if he had called my name he said nothing and I knew then that he was relieved to see me go.

I was so upset that I forgot the car. My eyes, blind with tears, never even saw it as I stumbled past. I went downhill, down the road without knowing or caring where I was going. All I was aware of was the blurred brilliant green of the beech trees overhead and the patterns of light made by the sun as its shafts pierced the leaves and slanted across the road.

After a while I stopped running and slowed to a walk. My breath was coming in short gasps and there was an ache in my side. I stopped, bent double to rid myself of the pain, and then because it was easier to sit down than to straighten my back and go on again, I collapsed on the bank by the road. I sat there for a long time. No one came. Nothing happened. Occasionally a bird sang and once far away I heard the faint hum of an aeroplane.

At last I thought: how absurd to be so upset over a man I met less than a week ago! How unnecessary! I had behaved like an infatuated adolescent, imagining myself in the midst of a whirlwind love affair. The excitement of travelling to strange countries combined with the strain of Gina's disappearance had made me momentarily lose touch with reality. However, now I could begin to act like a reasonable, rational adult once again. I could be critical once more, cool, dispassionate and practical. Love at first sight was for the magazines, or for people like Gina whose personalities acted as a magnet to the opposite sex. Fairy-tale romances were for those with their heads in the clouds. As for me, I had my feet firmly on the ground, and fairy-tales no longer appealed to me.

I stood up. My legs felt weak and unsteady but I set off walking again. I passed the gates of Holmbury House and presently found myself on an open stretch of hillside covered with ferns and heather. Before me, stretching mistily into the horizon was a sweeping view of fields, trees and the faint outline of hills in the distance. The sun shone. The countryside was beautiful. And because it was so beautiful I felt overwhelmingly aware of the stark ugliness of my grief. Tears sprang to my eyes again, and before I could stop myself I was crying, fumbling ineffectually for a handkerchief.

I sat down again by the roadside.

Perhaps it would be better if I admitted I was in love and stopped telling myself I was behaving like an adolescent. I found the handkerchief, blew my nose, pressed a hand to my aching forehead. I felt physically ill. Later, perhaps, I could chalk the entire episode up to experience and resume the comforting dullness of my normal life, but now I found it was impossible for me to be so detached.

The pain of loss was intolerable.

I thought of my lonely little apartment high above Manhattan, the evenings spent alone, the days exhausted trying to teach girls a subject most of them were not interested in learning. My safe, secure, peaceful life! I had never realized before how empty it had been.

I stood up desperately as the present reached out long fingers to taint the past and blur the future. It was as if I had no future, no past, as if my present were as fleeting and yet as horrifying as a nightmare from which there was no escape. I was nothing suddenly. I looked around wildly, praying that I would see someone I could speak to, someone whom I could use to regain my grip on reality and check the disintegration of my world, and as I glanced across the open hillside to the road below I saw a green convertible emerge into view and begin its toil up the road towards me.

I waited.

The car drew nearer. As it approached me I saw it lose speed and the next moment it had halted beside me and the driver was pulling down the window.

'Claire!' exclaimed Eric Jantzen in astonishment. 'Well,

this is certainly a surprise! What are you doing down here in Surrey?'

Since I had forgotten that Garth and Lilian were entertaining French clients at the cottage that weekend, I was almost as surprised to see him as he was to see me. Just as I was foggily trying to invent a reply he said anxiously: 'Is something wrong?'

'No,' I said. I couldn't think of anything else to say.

'You've still not heard from Gina?'

'I haven't seen her at all.' That much was true.

He shook his head in sympathy. 'You look tired,' he said kindly. 'Everything must be a great strain for you at present. Would you like some coffee, perhaps? Or some tea? I'm just on my way to Garth's cottage, which is very near here, and I'm sure he wouldn't mind if you dropped in for a while. My wife and Garth are entertaining French clients over the weekend, and on those occasions I usually spend the weekend at the cottage too. However, they won't be there yet – they had to go to the airport this morning to meet the plane from Paris.

'They will all drive down here after lunch.'

I stared at him blankly. I must have looked mentally deficient. 'Oh,' I said at last.

This was hardly a sparkling reply, but it seemed to encourage him to reiterate his invitation. 'Let me make you some coffee! Please – you look so tired! The cottage isn't far from here, less than a mile—'

I thought in panic: I can't see Garth again. I couldn't possibly face him a second time. And then in confusion: Garth's secretary told me Lilian came down to the cottage last night to prepare everything for the weekend. Garth must have come instead, and Lilian must have gone to the airport to meet the clients. But why doesn't Eric know this? Why does he expect them both to be at the airport?

'Thank you very much,' I heard myself say falteringly, 'but I don't think I feel like coffee just now.' I felt suddenly possessed with a desire to escape, and as soon as the notion crossed my mind I remembered that I had arrived at Garth's house in a car and that there was no escape until I went back to get it. 'I – I wonder,' I said stammering, '—if you could give me a lift to the cottage? It seems – I mean, I think I've left my car there.'

He looked at me first in bewilderment and then sharply in speculation. I sensed he wanted to know why I had been at the cottage and what had happened to reduce me to a state in which I was capable only of producing a series of curious remarks. 'Why, of course!' he said with reserve, his eyes watchful. 'Jump in!'

He leaned over and opened the door of the passenger seat for me. As the car moved on up the road he said to me with an attempt to recapture his air of joviality: 'You really should tell me what's been happening, you know! You don't seem to be yourself at all. What's been going on at the cottage?'

'Nothing,' I said. 'I thought Gina might be there but I was wrong. I walked away from my car down the road wondering what I should do next. I'm feeling more and more distressed with every hour that passes.'

'Why, yes,' he murmured, his eyes on the road. 'Yes, I can understand that. It must be most upsetting.'

The car purred on up the hill. We passed the houses, passed the sign which pointed to Peaslake and moved on along the twisting road to the cottage.

'Do you have a key?' I said suddenly.

'Oh yes,' he said. 'We all have a key. Occasionally, if Garth's abroad, he lends us the cottage for weekends. He and Lilian do a certain amount of business entertaining here as well. It's very useful to them.'

I was just opening my mouth to tell him that Garth wasn't at the airport after all when we rounded the last bend and the cottage came into sight.

I gasped. The words died on my lips.

'What's the matter?' said Eric swiftly. 'What is it?'

'I – thought my car had a flat tyre,' I said faintly. 'But that was a trick of the light. There's nothing wrong.'

But I was lying. The shock I had received was not on account of my car, which still stood beneath the trees, but because there was no longer any sign of the creamy white Jaguar.

Garth had vanished.

'Are you sure you won't stop for coffee?' said Eric again, parking his car where Garth had left the Jaguar earlier. 'It wouldn't be any trouble at all.'

I was too dazed to argue further. I found the idea of coffee more than welcome, and now that Garth had gone there was no reason for me to refuse to enter the cottage. 'Well, perhaps I'll change my mind,' I said awkwardly. 'Thank you very much.'

I began to wonder where Garth had gone. If he had returned to Holmbury village he would have passed me on the road. I decided that for some reason or other he had driven on over the hill to Peaslake – perhaps to buy extra food from the shops there. As we walked up to the front door and Eric produced a key I started to feel nervous in case Garth returned from Peaslake before I had finished my coffee and left the cottage.

'Come in,' said Eric, opening the door and standing back to allow me to cross the threshold before him.

There was no hall. The front door opened into a long, light living room with picture windows which faced the view across the valley below. There was a staircase to my right, and on the left were two other doors which I guessed led into the kitchen and dining room.

'Nice, isn't it?' said Eric genially from behind me. He spoke with the satisfaction of an owner, not a mere guest. 'It's very restful here after London.'

The room was filled with antiques. I noticed the Regency chairs and couch, the long carved oak chest along one wall, the grandfather clock by the stairs.

'It *is* nice,' I said absently. 'What a pity the house is modern and not an old-fashioned cottage to go with the old-fashioned furniture.'

'You say that because you're American,' he said. 'We Europeans have no fond illusions about little old-fashioned cottages with damp in the walls and woodworm

497

in the roof and icy draughts from ill-fitting windows in the winter.' He waved a hand vaguely towards the couch. 'Sit down – make yourself at home. I'll get the coffee.'

I sat down while he disappeared into the kitchen, but presently I stood up again and wandered over to the door next to the kitchen. As I had guessed earlier, it led into a dining room. There was a china closet full of beautiful English china, and opposite it a corner cupboard filled with the most elegant glasses I had ever seen. Unable to resist the temptation I opened the cabinet and took out a glass. The stem was so slender that I thought it would break in my hands, and the rim of the glass was as thin as paper. An engraved design ran lightly round the delicate edge. Putting the glass back hastily before such fragile beauty could splinter into fragments in my hands, I closed the cupboard door and wandered back into the living room.

'Eric, is there a bathroom on this floor?'

'No,' he called. 'It's upstairs. Second door on the left.'

I moved slowly up the stairs. I was thinking of Garth again, wondering what he was doing, when he would be back. I began to hurry automatically. I must not stay in the house more than ten minutes. Then I must leave, drive away in the car, never to see the cottage again . . .

I reached the landing and found I could no longer remember Eric's directions to the bathroom. All the doors were closed. I stared at them absently for a moment. Second door on the right? No, he had said the left. The second door? The third door on the left? I wandered down the tiny passage, opened the door, and walked straight into a closet containing a bundle of old clothes. checking an exclamation of annoyance I was just turning away when I realized that the bundle of old clothes on the floor was not quite that.

I stopped, looked again . . .

My scalp prickled. Horror made the breath freeze in my throat. For one long moment I stood stock still staring down at that dreadful heap on the floor, and then rapidly, hardly aware of what I was doing, I bent down, pulled aside the old coat on top of the pile and found myself inches from a woman's face distorted by violent death. At first I didn't recognize her, and then . . .

It was Lilian Jantzen.

## chapter 9

It seemed that I stood there motionless for a long time with my mind paralysed by fright, and then slowly, mechanically I closed the door and leaned against it. I wanted to move, but as in all the most appalling night-mares, the paralysis of shock made movement impossible. After a hiatus which may have lasted no longer than thirty seconds but which seemed to last at least thirty minutes, I managed to step across the passage and blunder into the room opposite. I found myself in the bedroom and facing a picture window much like the one in the living room directly below me. It was now raining outside. Snarls of water spat against the enormous window pane and trickled impotently down the glass to the sill.

It was very quiet.

I thought: whoever killed Lilian killed Thérèse as well, and who else could have killed them other than Garth or Eric? Warren might just conceivably have killed Thérèse but he couldn't have killed Lilian. Lilian must have been killed either last night, if she really did come down to the cottage then to prepare for the weekend, or else earlier this morning, and Warren has been with me since yesterday evening . . . or did he slip out last night after I had gone to bed? But no, that was before we hired the car, and without transportation how could he have made his way out here? So either Garth or Eric killed Lilian. And either Garth or Eric killed Thérèse.

I was so stupefied with the enormity of the realization that for a moment my mind refused to go further. I kept saying to myself either Garth or Eric killed Lilian;

either Garth or Eric killed Thérèse, and yet the simple question: which one? was something my mind refused to phrase. But suddenly I remembered something. If Gina was staying at Garth's flat she would give him an alibi for the previous evening. He could not have killed Lilian this morning since the house had been empty on my first visit and the body was too stiff to allow for the possibility that Garth had killed her on his arrival less than two hours ago . . .

I had to speak to Gina. If she could tell me that Garth had spent the previous evening with her I would know for certain that he was innocent.

There was a phone extension next to the bed. After fumbling dizzily in my purse for the number I picked up the receiver with shaking fingers and dialled O for the operator.

The line purred three times. Then: 'Operator,' said a pleasant voice into my ear.

'I wonder if you can help me,' I said in a low rapid voice. 'I'm trying to get through to a London number – Mayfair 7543. Could you try for me, please?'

'Mayfair 7543? One moment.' The line clicked and she was gone.

I waited. And waited.

'Trying to connect you,' said the voice.

I went on waiting. My heart was bumping painfully against my lungs. My palms were so damp that the receiver slipped and almost fell from my fingers.

'Trying to connect you,' said the voice again.

It was not until then that I remembered the code Gina and Garth had established with telephone calls.

'I'm sorry,' said the operator kindly, 'but there's no reply.'

'Wait,' I said unevenly. 'Please ring twice, then hang up, then ring again. Please.'

In Britain perhaps they are more accustomed to eccentrics than they are in America. I could just imagine the smart retort I would have received from a New York operator if I had made the same request.

'One moment, please,' said the voice placidly, and I heard her begin to dial again.

Maybe my request had provided her with an interesting variation in routine. I heard the bell ring twice at the other end of the wire, then a silence. Finally the bell began to ring again, but Gina hardly waited for it to ring once. There was a click as she picked up the receiver.

'Hello?'

'Go ahead, caller—'

'Gina, it's me. Listen. I can't talk. Just tell me one thing. Where was Garth last night?'

'Garth?' said Gina puzzled. 'Last night? Why, he was here! He bought some groceries and I fixed him dinner. He was tired and went to bed early. Why?'

'Get off the line,' I said rapidly. 'Call the police. Lilian Jantzen's been murdered and her body is hidden in Garth's cottage. Get the police at once.'

I heard her gasp. 'I'll call them right away,' she said and hung up.

I listened to the empty line for a second longer, too mesmerized by my knowledge even to replace the receiver in its cradle. Garth was innocent. And downstairs, alone with me in the house—

From somewhere far away on the dead line I heard a low stealthy click.

I froze.

Eric Jantzen had been listening in downstairs on the living-room phone.

The receiver fell out of my hands and clattered on to the table. I could not breathe, speak or move. And then as I stood there in a paralysis of panic I heard his soft measured footsteps coming slowly up the stairs towards me.

I managed to move. I crossed the room, my feet making no noise on the thick carpet, and opened the door. He was at the top of the stairs. When I came out into the passage he stopped. We faced each other.

I thought: If I could edge towards the bathroom, I could lock myself in . . .

But he moved forward towards me and I stepped back into the bedroom.

'Rather rash of you, wasn't it?' he said, still determined to sound jovial. His little eyes, narrow above his fleshy cheeks, were empty of expression. He moved like an automaton, steadily, with precision.

I backed away until I was against the picture window and could retreat no more.

He stopped. 'The police will arrest Garth,' he said. 'You must realize that. All the evidence points towards Garth.'

'Yes,' I said. Garth must come back soon from his expedition to Peaslake. I had an advantage in that I knew Garth was nearby while Eric thought he was still in London. If I could keep Eric talking until Garth arrived—

'But you don't believe Garth killed Lilian, do you.' He said. 'That's why you phoned your sister. She was able to give him an alibi.'

I said, playing for time, 'The alibi was for last night. He could have killed her this morning.'

'And the police will find out she wasn't killed this morning,' he said. 'I killed her last night, here at the cottage.'

There was a silence. After a while I managed to say: 'I don't understand.'

'I was justified in killing her,' he said as if this explained everything. 'It was no more than she deserved. She was a murderess.'

I stared at him. He found a handkerchief, mopped his face, and I saw for the first time that he was profoundly moved.

'She killed Thérèse,' he said. 'My wife killed another woman. My wife. Lilian. She was a cheat and a fraud and a murderess.'

He was crying openly now. As I watched him with mingled horror and pity, he twisted his handkerchief in his hands. Presently when he was able to speak again he said: 'Lilian said it was an accident that Thérèse died, but

I don't think it was. I think she meant to kill her. Thérèse knew vital – damaging facts—'

'About Lilian.'

'About Lilian. Lilian had swindled Garth out of ten thousand pounds last year by pretending the company owed more to the Inland Revenue than it actually did. Lilian did the books, filed the tax returns; two years ago she had got into debt by trying to expand the business still farther, handling contracts which were a little too big to handle. Money was lost, and the profits were low that year. But she had expected the profits to be higher and she had already spent her share . . . she needed money, and as time passed the need for money became pressing. So she cheated. She took money which should have been split between herself and Garth. She could have taken out a loan – borrowed the money somehow – but no, she had to cheat. "If I borrowed there would be so much money wasted in interest," she said. "Money that could be put into the business." She was quite ruthless where the business was concerned. She wouldn't listen to reason. "Garth will never know," she said. "He always leaves the books to me. He'll never find out." So she took the money and cheated him and laid herself open to blackmail.'

After a moment I said: 'But how did Thérèse know that Lilian had cheated Garth?'

'I told her,' he said simply.

There was a silence. Everything was very still.

'It was like this,' he said suddenly. 'Thérèse was an ally, a friend. She wanted to break up any attachment existing between Garth and Lilian as much as I did, and she was convinced that an attachment existed. Three months ago she followed them to a conference in Paris – they were both staying at Garth's *pied-à-terre* . . . well, we needn't go into that. Thérèse saw me afterwards and expected me to make some sort of scene with Lilian. She didn't know that Lilian wouldn't have cared if I had. Lilian wanted to leave me. She's had no use for me now for some time.'

Tears furrowed his face again, and the rain wept with him, hurling itself against the windowpane.

'But I loved her,' he said. 'I was prepared to do anything to prevent her from leaving. When Thérèse asked me why I would not fight with Lilian over the episode with Garth in Paris, I told her the truth – that Lilian would have welcomed the chance to be rid of me and that to make a scene would have been pointless. I told Thérèse that the only reason I managed to keep Lilian living under the same roof with me was because I knew she had cheated Garth and I threatened to tell him so unless she stayed with me as my wife.'

'What did Thérèse say?'

'Nothing – then. Oh, she probably had a row with Garth but she didn't approach Lilian. That came later.' He stopped. 'Last Saturday,' he said painfully. 'Less than a week ago. Last Saturday she stormed into our flat when I was out and Lilian was there alone, and told Lilian that she would make trouble for her unless she left Garth alone. She had had a row with Garth earlier, she said. She told Lilian that Garth was pretending to be interested in a young American girl who had arrived with him the previous evening from Paris, but that she herself wasn't deceived for a moment; Garth's interest in Gina was merely a smokescreen to conceal his interest in Lilian. Thérèse told me the same thing when I had seen her the previous evening; after she had met Garth and Gina at London airport she phoned and asked to see me, and when I met her she told me exactly what was on her mind. And I agreed with her. Gina wasn't Garth's type. I too believed that he was merely using her as a smokescreen.

'I saw Thérèse on Friday night. Early Saturday evening she had a showdown with Garth at her flat and then, still not satisfied, she came to our flat and saw Lilian herself. It was then that she told Lilian that unless she kept her hands off Garth, Thérèse would tell both Garth and the Fraud Squad that Lilian had cheated him out of a considerable sum of money. It was the worst thing she could possibly have said. Lilian lived for her business – it was husband, child, lover, everything to her. She had started it, built it up, nurtured it to success. Where the business was concerned she was fanatical – irrational. She would do anything to protect it. And then along came Thérèse talking of the Fraud Squad, criminal proceedings, the business's reputation smeared beyond repair . . .

'I don't know what happened next. Lilian said she and Thérèse came to blows and Thérèse accidentally slipped and struck her head and died. But I don't think the death was so accidental as that. I think Lilian deliberately killed her . . . But there was Thérèse – dead – killed either by accident or design – and in our flat!

'When I came in half an hour afterwards Lilian had dragged the body into the spare bedroom and locked the door. She was more distraught than I had ever seen her look before. She told me what had happened and said I must help her, and it was then suddenly that I saw what I could do; I promised to help her get rid of the body if she would agree to give our marriage a completely new start, never see Garth except at the office and allow me to come with her on all her business trips with him.

'She said she would. She promised. She swore she would do everything I said. So I went out again, to a place I knew down by the river in Pimlico where they sell secondhand trunks and suitcases. Lilian said she must establish an alibi – she rang up a friend, suggested they go to the cinema together. I left her while she was still talking on the phone . . . I had completely forgotten that a few hours before, at lunch, I had invited Gina to call at the flat for a drink that evening. The thought of Gina never even crossed my mind.

'I couldn't find a trunk at that hour – all the shops were shut, even the one I had thought of in Pimlico, and so I decided I would have to use one of Lilian's large suitcases instead. I went back to the flat, and not realizing that Lilian had already left for the cinema, I called out to tell her that I hadn't been able to find a trunk for the body and that we'd have to use a large suitcase. When there was no reply I realized she had left. I set to work at once, found the suitcase, managed to shut the lid with the body inside. Then when everything was ready I took the case out to the car and drove down to Holmbury St Mary. I thought that if I buried the body in the garden of the cottage no one would come across it, and if the grave was discovered, they would suspect Garth and not us. Garth never bothered with the garden, although sometimes he talked vaguely of hiring a gardener – I thought there was a good chance he wouldn't stroll to the bottom of the garden till the weeds had grown over the grave again.

'When everything was finished at the cottage I went back to London to the flat. Lilian had returned from the cinema and was waiting for me. She said: "How did you get rid of Gina when you got back from Pimlico?" I didn't know what she meant. And then I remembered that I had told Gina to come by for a drink. "I let her in," Lilian said. "Didn't she wait for you to come back?" And I realized that Gina might have been there when I called out to Lilian to tell her I couldn't find a trunk for the body – she might have been hiding nearby when I had put the body in the suitcase. We talked it over, Lilian and I. It was possible Gina hadn't bothered to wait for me and had left before I returned, but we had to make sure. We tried to find her – and couldn't. She had disappeared. Vanished. There was no trace of her.'

'Garth was hiding her,' I said shakily. 'I found that out today.'

'Garth's a clever actor. He had us both convinced he hadn't set eyes on the girl since last Saturday, when we all had lunch together. At least he had me convinced. Lilian . . .' He broke off, staring into nothingness, his mind abstracted and remote from me.

I hardly dared breathe for fear of interrupting his train of thought and reminding him of my existence in the room. I wanted to ask why he had killed Lilian but I let the silence linger on unbroken as the rain swept across the hillside from the valley below.

'The police came later,' he said after a while. 'We

heard then about the hysterical phone call Gina had made to you. The police found nothing at the flat, but we knew then that we had to find Gina somehow. She was dangerous to us. We wondered if she would go to the police but Lilian thought not. The police might have thought Gina and Thérèse had quarrelled over Garth and Gina would be a chief suspect if enquiries were made into Thérèse's murder.'

I waited, my body aching with tension, and as I watched him he raised his eyes slowly and looked at me. I said quickly, seizing the first subject which came to mind: 'I don't understand why Lilian died.'

'Because she broke her word,' he said. 'After all I did for her – after I had disposed of the body and managed to conceal her crime – after all that she broke the promise. She promised she would give up Garth altogether and give our marriage a fresh start, but she didn't mean it. This so-called "business weekend" here at the cottage was fictitious – there were no clients expected to arrive in London on the Friday morning plane. I had a hunch she was lying to me and I called Rémy International in France to check whether the two men were due in England this weekend. I was told that they weren't. As soon as I found this out last night I drove down here to the cottage – Lilian had arrived here earlier, supposedly to prepare everything for the visitors. When I got here she pretended to be astonished – she denied everything – said I was out of my mind . . .' He stopped. Then: 'Out of my mind,' he repeated, as if amazed by his own choice of phrase. 'She said I was out of my mind . . . I told her I knew very well she had merely planned a weekend with Garth, but she wouldn't admit it. She went on lying – on and on . . . And then suddenly there were no more lies, only silence. It was a terrible blank silence. Afterwards I was so upset that I panicked and rushed away back to London – I only stopped long enough to push the body in the cupboard and then I drove and drove all along those twisting country roads. It was all so dark and still and silent . . .

'This morning I managed to pull myself together. I knew I must drive down again to the cottage and bury the body. I must pretend to be normal, act as though nothing had happened. That was why when I stopped to talk to you I invited you here for coffee – I was so anxious to appear normal, as if nothing was wrong. But why did *you* come down here? Why were you so shaken? I seemed to sense you suspected me. When you made the excuse to go upstairs I thought: supposing she wanted the excuse to search the house? And you were gone such a long time . . . Then I heard the faint ring the phone makes whenever the extension in the bedroom is used, and I knew what must have happened.'

'I wanted to ask my sister where Garth was last night.'

'But why should she have known? Where was Garth hiding her anyway?'

'In his apartment,' I said.

He stared at me. 'She had been with him in his apartment all this week?'

In a flash I saw how I could catch him off balance. 'Why do you think Gina came to London with him from Paris?' I said. 'Gina was infatuated with him. You were wrong in suspecting your wife was involved. It was Gina, not Lilian who was infatuated.'

He went on staring at me. 'But this business weekend which proved to be non-existent—'

'Rémy International must have misinformed you. Garth's secretary confirmed the appointment when I spoke to her earlier today.'

After a long silence he whispered: 'I don't believe it.'

'Well, you didn't believe Lilian,' I said, 'so there's no reason why you should believe me. But I think Lilian was telling the truth. Besides, I don't think Garth would have been interested in an illicit weekend with her. He had other fish to fry.'

'I don't believe it,' he repeated. 'I don't believe it.' He was very white. I saw him begin to tremble as he half turned away from me, and then he was struck dumb as he began to realize what I was suggesting . . . he had killed his wife for an infidelity which had existed only in his imagination.

I moved. I darted across the room, tried to push past him into the passage beyond, but he caught me by the wrist, jerked me back into the room. I struggled wildly but he was much too strong for me, and although I screamed and screamed for help none came.

I was powerless, frantic with terror. I tried to scream again in one last desperate burst of strength but his fingers closed around my throat and the scream died on my lips. The room tilted, swirled before my eyes, and as the blood started to sing in my ears I knew dimly that all was lost and that there was nothing more I could do.

## *chapter 10*

The pressure eased very suddenly. There was a roaring in my ears but gradually that too ceased. I found I could see again. I was on the floor, the carpet grazing my knuckles, and as I struggled to my feet I saw Eric was standing a few feet away from me, his eyes staring at the doorway.

I turned my head slowly, frowning at the pain, my mind clouded with shock, my whole being numbed with incomprehension, and found myself looking at a black, ugly automatic. The automatic was held by a strong firm hand and looked as if it were comfortably at home there.

'Are you all right, Claire?' It was Garth's voice.

It was too painful to nod and my own voice seemed to have disappeared. I managed to stand up but immediately sat down again on the edge of the bed.

'Did he hurt you?'

'Well, of course he hurt me!' Shock made me unreasonably angry. 'Where the hell were you? Why did you go away? I was nearly killed!'

'Whose idea was it for you to come back here?' he asked

mildly. 'Not mine! God Almighty, you almost *were* murdered!' He swung back to Eric. 'We'll go downstairs. You can lead the way. Clasp your hands behind your head. I don't want to have any accidents in transit.'

Eric moved blindly out into the passage.

'Come on, Claire.'

'Don't you order me about!' I stormed. And then, stammering: '—I'm sorry – I'm not myself—'

'I understand.' He waited for me by the doorway, his eyes still watching the other man, but when I reached him, he took my hand in his and held it for a moment. 'All right, Eric. Move on.'

It was then I saw that the door of the adjacent room was open and what looked like a portable tape recorder playing silently just beyond the threshold.

'Switch that off, would you, Claire? Just pull the plug out of the wall but don't touch the machine.'

I mechanically did as I was told. My mind refused even to try to reconstruct what had happened, but I was dimly aware that Garth must have somehow managed to record most, if not all, of my conversation with Eric in the bedroom. We went downstairs.

'Stand right there, Eric, and don't move. You can put your hands down. Claire, I'd advise you to have a shot of brandy. There's a bottle under the sideboard over there and a glass in the dining room.'

He went to the phone, the gun still in his right hand, and removed the receiver with his left. Putting down the receiver on the table he began to dial, still using his left hand.

He dialled nine-nine-nine.

'Police, please.' He saw me still standing motionless by the dining-room door. 'Please, Claire – get the brandy and sit down! You look – hello? Police? My name is Cooper and I'm speaking from Coneyhurst Cottage on Holmbury Hill – it's the last cottage before Peaslake on the Holmbury–Peaslake road. Could you come over here at once, please? A woman's been murdered.'

I went into the dining room in a haze and tried to find

a glass which I wouldn't be afraid of breaking but all the glasses were the fragile collector's items which I had noticed earlier; my fingers were still so unsteady that I was convinced I would drop any glass I touched, so at last in despair I went to the kitchen and took a cup from the cupboard.

Garth had just hung up when I emerged into the living room once more with the cup in my hand. 'Good God, you can't drink Courvoisier out of a teacup!'

'It's a receptacle, isn't it?' I said doggedly. 'What can prevent me drinking out of it if I want to?'

It showed the measure of our shock that we were so ready to argue over trivialities.

Eric said he wanted to sit down.

'All right. Take that chair over there.'

'I'd like a drink too,' he added.

Garth motioned me to pour one for him. Then he said harshly: 'How can you be so calm, Eric? If I hadn't been in the house you would have killed Claire too.'

'No . . . no, it was just that I – I suddenly saw – realized—'

'That I wasn't and never had been interested in having an affair with your cold, clever, crooked wife? That you had killed her for nothing?'

Eric said stumbling: 'It was such a shock . . . I was overcome . . . I wanted to kill her for telling me, showing me the truth—'

'If you had had an ounce of sense you'd never have listened to Thérèse. Good God, you could have had your wife and good luck to you! Couldn't you guess I could hardly wait to get enough capital behind me to work my way out of the partnership? Did you ever really think I was the kind of man who enjoyed answering to a woman and being told by her what to do the whole damned time? Lilian was still the boss, you know, even though we were officially partners. It was she who had picked me out from the obscure ranks of all the salesmen in London and selected me to work for her – and, my God, she never let me forget it! I was grateful to her and glad of the opportunities she gave me but I got pretty damned tired of playing second fiddle day in, day out, year after year—'

'Then why did you stay with her?'

'I very nearly didn't! We had our quarrels and disagreements, but I knew I could never make so much money so quickly elsewhere and I wanted more than anything else to amass capital, be independent. But unlike you I don't expect my wife to support me while I indulge in unprofitable speculation. When I marry we'll live on my money, not on my wife's.'

'Lilian understood—'

'She understood nothing but the business! And cared for nothing but the business! And you know that as well as I do. Just because you had the misfortune to be in love with her, don't make the mistake of assuming she also knew what love meant. Maybe she did once, long ago, when you first knew her, but certainly I never once caught a glimpse of understanding in her. She wasn't interested in love! She didn't care – not for you, not for anyone. She was narrow-minded and cold and utterly selfish. If you hadn't been so unbalanced as to try to strangle Claire just now I'd feel you were justified in murdering Lilian, and I wouldn't be aiming this gun at you at all.'

'I didn't mean to harm Claire – I was overwhelmed – dazed—'

'You did mean to harm her! You put your hands deliberately round her throat and equally deliberately tried to throttle her into unconsciousness.'

'I didn't know what I was doing—'

'Tell that to the police, not to me. I might become "overwhelmed" and "dazed" too and feel an uncontrollable urge to pull the trigger.'

There was a heavy silence. At last Garth said to me: 'How are you feeling now?'

'Better.' I gripped the cup tightly but my fingers were still trembling. 'Where did you go after I left here?'

'Nowhere. I drove the car up to the top of the hill and

hid it in the bushes. Then I walked back and prepared to set up my tape recorder. I'd found Lilian dead when I arrived earlier, but since I was still expecting Eric to turn up I went ahead with my plans to tape a confession. Unfortunately I set the machine up in the living room, which was no use at all when you both moved upstairs to the bedroom. I was forced to come out of the cupboard under the stairs where I'd been hiding and follow you upstairs, tape recorder and all. Fortunately it was reasonably portable.

'I'd been working towards it all week. Eric was right in believing that the business weekend was a fiction, but wrong in assuming Lilian knew it was fictitious. She didn't know. I planned to have a showdown with both the Jantzens, since I believed they were both involved in Thérèse's murder, so I invented the visit of the representatives of Rémy International and paved the way for luring both of them here to the cottage where Thérèse was buried. I reasoned they would be more likely to be trapped into an admission out here in a remote spot, with Thérèse's grave only a few yards away at the end of the garden.'

'No wonder you were so anxious to get rid of me this morning!'

'Yes, I'd just found Lilian's body and was trying to work out what I should do next; for all I knew Eric would arrive any minute – I'm sorry if I was too abrupt but I was worried in case things went wrong. I'd taken a gamble in not going to the police. When I heard that Thérèse was dead and that Eric had taken the body out of the flat to dispose of it, I knew immediately that when the body was found I'd be the number one suspect. And if the police believed that Gina and I were involved with one another, Gina would be suspect number two. Thérèse was jealous, quite capable of initiating disastrous scenes; it was Gina and I who would immediately come under suspicion if she were killed, not the Jantzens, who had no such obvious motive for murdering her. I had a key to the Jantzen apartment and had no alibi for

Saturday night – to the police that would all add up to motive, means and opportunity for committing the crime. The same applied to Gina – she was actually there at the scene of the murder, and her presence could be proved by the phone call she made to New York and your report of the call to Scotland Yard.'

'What did Gina do after she had phoned me that evening? And why did she hang up so suddenly?'

'She thought she heard the front door opening, but it was a false alarm – a noise from the flat below. By the time she realized this she'd already replaced the receiver and cut off the call. She pulled herself together and saw she had to get out of the flat at once – she told me she'd panicked as soon as Eric left with the body, and made the call to you without even pausing to think what she was doing.'

'Yes,' I said shakily. 'That sounds like Gina.'

'However, after cutting herself off from you she left the flat, found the nearest callbox and dialled my number. I was the only other person she knew in London. I told her to come over to my flat at once, and she did. We reasoned that the Jantzens would work out that she had seen too much, so I decided she must lie low and communicate with nobody. Early the next morning I drove her down here, as I knew the Jantzens intended to be in town all week.'

Eric said unexpectedly: 'But we checked the cottage! On Monday I drove down here—'

'Gina had left by then – fortunately. Later on Sunday evening she discovered Thérèse's body, just as Claire did this morning. This so unnerved her that she immediately called a taxi and left for Dorking, where she put up at a hotel. She tried to contact me but by that time I'd left for Paris – I had to go for unavoidable business reasons, and besides I was anxious to act normally, as if nothing had happened. Gina nearly wrote to me in Paris but remembered I was returning to London on Wednesday morning and that a letter to Paris might miss me. So she wrote to my home address in London in order that, as soon as I reached home, I would know where she was and where I could contact her. When I heard what had happened I told her to come to my flat in London. I didn't think it was safe for her to stay anywhere else. On my return I began to set the scene for the showdown at the cottage; I knew by then where Thérèse's body was and I thought I could see a way to establish our innocence and prove the Jantzens' guilt.

'I was puzzled because Lilian wasn't here to meet me – we had arranged that she was to come down here last night to get the place ready, and when I arrived I intended to tell her that Rémy International had postponed the visit at the last minute, and to suggest she and Eric have lunch here with me before driving back to town. As soon as Eric arrived I was going to launch into my counsel for the prosecution act for the benefit of the tape recorder. Having planned everything so carefully it gave me a shock to find Lilian wasn't here when I arrived. On an impulse I decided to search the house, and a couple of minutes later I opened the door of the cupboard upstairs and found her.'

In the armchair by the fireplace Eric moved. I started nervously, but for nothing. He had merely leaned forward and buried his face in his hands, as if the mention of Lilian's name and the manner of her death were sufficient to remove him from us, a human being cut off and isolated by grief and despair.

I wondered how long the police would take to arrive. Surely by now they must be well on their way! My fingers fidgeted endlessly with the cup in my hands and as I glanced at Eric again I saw him start and look up abruptly.

'What's that noise?'

Garth didn't move. 'What noise?'

'I thought I heard a noise in the kitchen—'

'Stay where you are!' Garth had the gun trained on him. His back was to the kitchen door. 'You needn't think you can fool me with that kind of trick.'

But I was taut once more with nervousness, every muscle in my body ached with tension. I turned to face the kitchen door, the cup slipping in my clammy hands, and to my horror I saw the handle begin to turn.

I screamed.

Garth swung round but he wasn't quick enough. The door was already wide open.

'All right, Cooper,' said a cool, tough voice I barely recognized. 'Put down that gun.'

I stared incredulously, unable to believe what I saw, and found myself face to face with Warren Mayne.

It all happened so quickly that now as I look back I find it hard to recall the scene in any clear detail. I remember crying out something to Warren; I remember Garth, caught off-balance, lowering his gun for a moment – and then in a flash, Eric was upon him and they were fighting for the weapon.

Warren shouted something, but neither of them paid him any attention.

'Help him – separate them—' I scarcely knew what I was saying. I darted forward, but before I could reach Garth, Warren said sharply: 'Keep back, Claire. Cooper, drop that gun, or I'll—'

'No – no—' My voice rang high-pitched and terrified in my ears.

Garth slipped on the carpet, fell sideways against the table. The gun jerked out of his hand, spun in the air and thudded dully upon the carpet six inches from Eric's right hand.

For the last time that day, I heard myself scream.

'Right,' said Warren busily, moving in as Eric seized the gun. 'Now then—'

There was a deafening explosion as Eric pulled the trigger. I smelt acrid smoke, glimpsed the horrified expression on Warren's face, and then just before I fainted I saw the gun fall from Eric's hand, the blood run from his mouth as he lay dying.

## chapter 11

When I regained consciousness the room was full of policemen and Eric's body was covered with a sheet so that I could no longer see his face. Warren, white and stupefied, was saying helplessly to no one in particular: 'But I don't understand. I thought . . .' But he could not even bring himself to say what he had thought. My head ached, my mouth was dry, and someone was holding me in his arms as if I were a fragile piece of bone china. I stirred, turned fuzzily towards him. I was lying on the Regency couch and my head was propped against his chest.

'Here,' he said. 'Drink this.'

Brandy burned my throat again. My brain stirred and I felt more capable of physical movement. A police inspector, seeing that I was conscious, came over and asked me kindly how I felt.

'Almost all right, thank you,' I said with an effort.

'Good. We'll take a statement from you just as soon as possible and then someone can drive you back home. Now, who did the suicide weapon belong to? Was it yours, Mr Cooper?'

'Yes, it was.'

'May I see your licence for it, please? Just a formality, you understand.'

'Yes.' He rose to his feet, placed some cushions gently under my head and stooped to see that I was comfortable. Our glances met. I smiled shakily, and felt better.

'Now, young man,' the inspector was saying paternally to Warren. 'I noted you were carrying a gun too. Do you have a licence?'

'Well . . . no,' said Warren confused. 'It's not an English gun. I bought it in Paris. I'm an American citizen.'

'Dear me,' said the inspector mildly. 'Quite an international history. Thank you, Mr Cooper,' he added, glancing at Garth's licence and giving it back to him. 'Now I think we'll take a few statements. Supposing we start with you, Miss Sullivan – if you're well enough, of course.'

I said I was. We went into the dining room and the inspector and I sat down at the table, while a sergeant sat on a chair in the corner with a pencil and notebook. Under the inspector's direction I told my story from start to finish, beginning with Gina's phone call to me the previous Saturday. The inspector listened and nodded sympathetically, for all the world as if he were a family doctor chatting with an old friend who sought advice. In the corner, the sergeant's pencil whispered steadily across the pages of his notebook.

At last, when I had finished and there was nothing left to tell, the inspector thanked me and said he would have one of his men drive me back to the hotel in Dorking.

'I – I'd rather wait for Mr Cooper,' I said awkwardly. 'Is it all right if I stay here?'

'Mr Cooper may be rather a long time, so I wouldn't advise you to wait. If I were you I'd go back to the hotel and rest for a while. Maybe you'd like Mr Mayne to drive you back? I doubt if we need keep him long.'

I had insufficient strength for an argument so I gave in meekly.

'And you'll keep in touch with us, please, if you don't mind,' said the inspector cosily. 'We'll want you to sign your statement when it's been typed and you've had a chance to read it over.'

'Yes,' I said. 'Yes, of course.'

In the living room, someone was taking photographs of the body. More police appeared to have arrived. The house was overflowing with dark-blue uniforms. The inspector asked Warren to step into the dining room and as he obeyed uneasily, I looked around for Garth but there was no sign of him. Wandering into the kitchen I looked out of the window and saw him with three policemen at the bottom of the garden by Thérèse's grave.

I sat down on the couch again to wait. After about ten minutes Garth came back into the living room and moved swiftly across the room towards me.

'Is everything all right? Is someone going to drive you back to Dorking?' He glanced with distaste at the body still waiting for the ambulance, as if it were wrong for me to be in the same room as such a macabre object. 'I'd drive you back myself but I can't leave till I've given a statement to the police.'

'I think Warren will drive me back. The inspector offered to get one of his men to chauffeur us but I said I'd wait.' Because I wanted to talk to you, I might have added, but there was no time; Warren chose that moment to emerge from the dining room. He looked older, graver and more careworn than I had ever seen him look before.

'I want to apologize,' he said, walking right up to Garth and planting himself on the carpet before him. 'I just don't know how to say it. If Jantzen hadn't turned that gun on himself—'

'Quite,' said Garth, embarrassed by this naked display of emotion, even though the display was made with obvious sincerity. 'But he did. Forget it – it's all over now.'

'Yes, but if I hadn't been such a fool and messed everything up—'

'Could you take Claire back to Dorking, please? She's had a tough day and I don't think she should be here a moment longer.' He turned towards me; there was an expression in his eyes which made my heart turn over. 'I'll be in touch with you.'

'Yes – all right, Garth.'

'And don't dare jump on the night flight to America.'

'No, Garth.'

'If you do, I'll be following you on the morning plane.'

I could not speak, but managed to smile. There were tears in my eyes. Everything seemed to shine and glitter hazily in the dim artificial light from the ceiling above us.

'Mr Cooper?' said the inspector's voice politely from behind us. 'Perhaps we could take your statement now, sir.'

'Yes,' said Garth. 'Yes, of course.'

'Come on, Claire.' Warren's hand was on my arm. 'Let's get away from here.'

I followed him slowly out of the cottage. It was late afternoon, but still raining so hard that it was already twilight. The rain felt cool and refreshing against my cheek.

Warren led the way over to a small blue car which was unfamiliar to me.

'But this isn't the car I came in,' I said stupidly.

'No, we'll have the car agency people pick up that one later. This is the car I hired to drive out here after you.' He helped me get in, shut the door and went around to the other side to slide into the driver's seat.

'But I told you I'd spoken to Gina in Garth's office,' I said, memory returning. 'You were all set to go to London. Why didn't you go?'

'I figured you weren't being quite on the level with me.' He switched on the engine. 'You were acting too oddly and looked too shook up. After you'd left me to go to rest in your room, I called Garth's office to check to see if Gina had been there, and the secretary thought I was some kind of nut. So I went to your room and got no answer when I knocked on the door. That was when I got convinced you hadn't been on the level with me. When I went out into the courtyard and found the car gone it didn't take much brainwork to figure you'd gone off somewhere on your own, and where else would you go but to the cottage? After a bit of difficulty I managed to hire another car and come right on here after you. I couldn't think what you were playing at but I thought it wouldn't do any harm to find out.'

'I should have trusted you,' I said ashamed. 'But the evidence was all against Garth and somehow I wanted to prove to myself that he was innocent before I told you what I'd discovered.' I began to tell him how I had found Thérèse's body in its shallow grave, returned much shaken to Dorking, and tried to telephone Garth only to have my call answered by Gina herself. 'She told me to join her at once in London,' I said. 'But I was too stupid to follow her advice. I felt I had to try and see Garth at the cottage and find out what was going on.'

'I can't imagine why you were so convinced Garth was innocent,' said Warren, interested. 'Was that feminine intuition, would you say?'

'Yes,' I said wryly. 'I guess you could call it that.'

We were freewheeling gently down the narrow twisting road and had just passed the spot where I had met Eric earlier. I glanced out across the beautiful view again, but the rain made the landscape misty and the light was too obscure to enable me to see far.

'He seems to like you,' Warren ventured delicately, after a pause.

'Yes,' I admitted.

'I guess he wouldn't have said that bit about following you to America if he'd been interested in Gina.'

'I guess not.' So that was his point!

'Maybe there never was anything much between him and Gina. Maybe I just read too much into their relationship. Maybe it was all pretty casual after all.'

'Maybe.'

This seemed to cheer him up. His new, older, more careworn expression lasted until we reached the junction with the main road at Abinger Hammer, and then he hummed gently under his breath all the way to Dorking.

The mist and early darkness made the town look mysterious and ghostly and very old. Not even the twentieth-century traffic could detract from West Street's antiquity, the ancient houses, the little pub built centuries ago, the glimpse of cobbled side streets. We reached the High Street, crawled past modern shops and returned to antiquity as we drove under the arch of the inn and into the courtyard beyond.

'Let's see if we can get something to eat,' Warren said. 'We're too early for dinner but maybe they have tea.'

'I'd like some coffee.'

We entered the hotel and wandered through the lounge towards the reception desk. Someone was checking in, someone tall and willowy with familiar blonde hair straying from underneath a preposterous hat. She wore an incredibly ugly coat, macabre stockings and flat-heeled shoes, and still managed to look beautiful.

Parisian perfume wafted delicately across the lobby towards us.

Warren and I simultaneously opened our mouths, but she turned before we could speak and smiled her radiant, dazzling smile as she caught sight of us.

'Darlings!' she exclaimed tremulously. 'How utterly wonderful to see you both again! I'm so sorry you've had such trouble finding me . . .'

'You won't believe it,' said Gina, 'but none of this would have happened if I hadn't been so inquisitive. You remember Miss Stick, our old Sunday-school teacher back home? She always used to tell Mother that my curiosity would be my undoing, and she was so right. It was.'

It was an hour later. After our confused, disjointed reunion in the lobby of the hotel, and my discovery that when the inspector had been interviewing me Garth had called Gina to tell her it was safe for her to come out of hiding, we had spent some time talking in one of the lounges before I had excused myself to go upstairs to my room. Gina had followed me ten minutes later and was now reclining gracefully on the end of my bed while I, propped up against the pillow, had slipped back into my rôle of guide, philosopher and friend.

'You mean,' I said drily, 'that your curiosity was the sole reason for your so-called undoing?'

'The sole reason,' said Gina with conviction. 'Honestly. You see, there I was – in the Jantzen apartment on Saturday night and waiting for Eric to arrive to have a drink with me as he'd promised, and to tell me all about Dino di Lasci and the Italian film scene and all the rest of it, and Lilian had just excused herself and rushed off somewhere, and there I was – all alone with nothing to do except to wonder what Garth's relationship with Lilian was (and you must admit, darling, it was rather *peculiar* to think of a man like Garth working with a woman on an earnest businesslike plane, especially as Lilian was rather attractive in a cosy maternal sort of way) and—' She lost her way in the labyrinthine sentence, drew a breath and started again. 'So I thought I'd just have a tiny peep around the apartment. Not a big snoop or anything, but just a little peep—'

'What were you expecting to find?' I said with interest. 'Love letters, half burned in the grate? Compromising photographs?'

'Well, not *exactly* . . . I'm not really sure what I expected to find, but I just thought it might be interesting and I had nothing else to do—'

'So you went and looked around and while you were out of sight Eric opened the front door and called out to Lilian that he hadn't been able to get a trunk for the body.'

'So you know already,' said Gina disappointed. 'Yes, I guess you would by now. But darling, can you imagine! I was in the master bedroom, and after he said that, I couldn't even move, let alone speak. And then I thought he was going to come into the bedroom! I hid behind the door and watched through the crack, and he opened the door of the room opposite which must have been some kind of spare room and then I saw it – the body, I mean – and of course I recognized it at once because Thérèse had made an awful scene at the airport when Garth and I had arrived the night before. Well, naturally I was just stiff with fright. I couldn't do anything except watch. He got a suitcase out of the closet and – no, I can't even talk about it. It was so awful. Finally after hours and hours – minutes really, I guess – he went out with the suitcase and I was alone again. Then I kind of went mad. I wanted to scream and couldn't. I nearly ran out of the apartment and then I thought that if he came back for something he'd forgotten we'd meet in the elevator, so I forced myself to stay in the apartment for a few minutes. But I was so terrified I felt I had to talk to someone – anyone – but preferably—'

'Me,' I said.

'But Claire, you're always so marvellously cool and sane and well balanced—'

'So well balanced I shut my eyes and dived right in to share all the fun.'

'Well, of course I was horrified when I tried to call you back later and found I couldn't get through. As I told you on the phone, I called back twice later on Saturday night from Garth's apartment and the line was busy each time—'

'I was calling Scotland Yard and having your call traced.'

'I meant to call again on Sunday but Garth drove me down to the cottage to hide and I found the grave in the garden – heavens! I was in such a state after that that I couldn't even make a phone call. Finally on Monday I tried again – and got no reply—'

'I was *en route* to Paris by then.'

'Then Garth said he'd found you in Paris! Honestly, Claire, I could have wept. When I thought of all that money you must have spent – on a wild-goose chase! And all because I'd been so selfish and dragged you in without even *thinking*—'

'All's well that ends well,' I said mundanely. 'At least I had a trip to Europe.'

'I don't think all's well that ends well at all,' Gina objected. 'You won't be able to buy your little red car—'

I remembered vaguely that at one time the idea of possessing a car had seemed important.

'—I missed several important modelling dates. Warren has probably lost his job by taking off without proper permission to come and look for me . . . By the way, wasn't it sweet of him to go to all that trouble? There's something terribly *comforting* about Warren. When he says he'll move heaven and earth you know he probably will – you know he's not just saying it to sound impressive. When I saw him with you in the lobby I felt a lump

524

in my throat. After all, it's marvellous to know someone cares *that* much.'

'Hm,' I said.

'And you know, Claire, to be absolutely honest and frank with you and to tell you the complete truth—'

'Please do.'

'I was a little disappointed in Garth. He was so glamorous in Paris! Yet when I was forced to share his apartment with him I found I was bored. Isn't that terrible? But it was true. I thought it would be so romantic to have him hiding me and to be forced to live at close quarters with him for a few days, but the odd thing was that he seemed to lose all interest in romance. Of course, I realize he had a lot on his mind, but . . . well, never mind. But even when he was at home and resting he just liked to read and listen to Beethoven quartets or something. There wasn't even a television. I did my best not to be a nuisance – I fixed him meals and cleaned every room until it looked like something out of an advertisement, but . . . well, nothing happened. I'm sure if it had been Warren—'

'Yes,' I said. 'Warren's much more suitable for you.'

'You told me all along I should marry him, didn't you?'

'I do remember mentioning it now and then—'

'I think I will. I feel after all this that I just want to settle down and be an ordinary housewife and have six children.'

'Wait till that feeling's passed,' I couldn't help saying anxiously, 'and then see if you still want to marry him. After all—'

There was a knock on the door. Gina swept across the room to answer it.

'Warren!'

'Gina!'

They faced each other starry-eyed. I swung my legs off the bed and went over to study the view from the window. Outside it was dark and still raining and the town lights were blurred as I stared out into the night.

'By the way, Warren,' I said suddenly without turning to face him. 'Why didn't you tell me you'd been in England last weekend?'

'Last weekend?' echoed Gina. 'In England? Were you, Warren?'

I glanced round. He was looking sheepish. 'How did you find out?'

'I saw the stamps in your passport. Why didn't you tell me you'd been in London?'

'I—' He blushed. 'I guess I acted stupidly. I was worried about Gina . . . and I didn't trust Garth. I followed them to London and then tried to do some amateur investigation of Garth's background. When I found out he had a fiancée and that no one seemed to know if she was still engaged to him or not, I called up Thérèse and arranged to meet her on Saturday evening. She didn't show up – since she was already dead by then – and after that I figured maybe I was making a fool of myself and it would be best if I went back to Paris. I got cold feet, I guess. I didn't mention it to you because – well, I'd behaved stupidly, and—'

'I don't think it was stupid at all!' said Gina indignantly. 'I think it was just wonderful of you to be concerned over me! When I think of all that trouble you went to—'

They gazed at each other in dizzy admiration, as if neither could believe the fairy-tale slice of good fortune which had befallen them. I began to feel distinctly *de trop*.

'Well,' I began. 'Now that that's all explained—'

The telephone rang. Gina, being nearest, picked up the receiver. 'Hello? Oh, he*llo*! Is everything – yes, thank you. Yes, who? *Claire*? Yes, she's right here. Just a moment.' She turned to me in surprise. 'It's Garth,' she said, and added mystified: 'He says he wants to speak to you. Do you suppose it's about some new development?'

'No,' I said. 'This development has been going on for at least four days.' And I crossed the room towards the waiting telephone.

*

'I should have let Gina speak to you on the phone when you arrived in London,' Garth said to me. 'You had every right to be angry with me for not being honest with you and admitting I knew where she was, but the situation was so extraordinary and so dangerous that I was reluctant to involve you. It seemed to me that the less you knew the better. If you knew nothing I reasoned that you couldn't be a danger either to yourself or to us. But I was wrong.'

It was Saturday night, exactly a week since I had been sitting in my Manhattan apartment and trying to trace Gina's call from Europe. Garth had taken me to dine at a penthouse restaurant, and far below us, spread out in a panorama which seemed to stretch into infinity, lay the lights of London, the complex arteries of an enormous city pulsing with a life-force two thousand years old.

'Have you forgiven me yet for not being quite honest with you?'

'You were honest about the things that mattered. That's all that counts.' I was feeling too starry-eyed to take issue.

'But you didn't believe me! Why were you so convinced I preferred Gina to you?'

'Was I?' How could I explain that I assumed every attractive man preferred Gina to me?

'Yes, you were! Now you're the one who's not being quite honest! You thought all along that my feeling for you was assumed and couldn't possibly be genuine—'

'Well, it all happened so suddenly! And you *had* been dating Gina!'

'A few casual evenings out in Paris to take my mind off Thérèse—'

'And you did travel to London with her!' Once I got started it was hard to let up -- my schoolteacher logic, I guess.

'Thanks to careful engineering on her part—'

'And she ended up by living in your apartment, cooking your meals—'

'Let's say she tried to cook. I hope Warren's handy in

the kitchen, otherwise they'll both starve. Incidentally, how's your cooking?'

Far below us the lights of London pricked the darkness with dazzling brilliance. A passing waiter paused long enough to refill our champagne glasses from the bottle in the ice-bucket.

'Well,' I said, 'I do a very, very classic soft-boiled egg.'

'Really? Just right for breakfast.' He raised his glass to me with a smile and his light eyes were no longer unreadable. 'To your classic boiled eggs!' he said lightly. 'And to the first opportunity I have to sample one!'

We were married three months later.